THE GARBAGE MAN

A THRILLER

TESSA PACELLI

Zero Day Books, LLC New York, NY

Library of Congress Control Number 2025940473
ISBN 979-8-9990939-0-5 (ebook)
ISBN 979-8-9990939-1-2 (paperback)
ISBN 979-8-9990939-2-9 (hardcover)
This is a work of fiction. Names, characters,
places, and incidents either are the
product of the author's imagination or are used
fictitiously. Any resemblance to actual
persons, living or dead, events, or locales is entirely coincidental.

Printed in The United States of America.
First Edition 2025
https://tessapacelli.com

Big Data [big dey-tuh]

Noun

A vast quantity of diverse information that arrives in ever-increasing volumes and ever-increasing velocity.

"The great danger of Big Data occurs when it is fed into algorithms to track and manipulate you without your consent or knowledge."

"War is 90 percent information."

—*Napoleon Bonaparte*

CHAPTER ONE

IT WAS THE kind of place where perfection was impossible to avoid. The chef had examined, prodded, cooked, and discarded four separate racks of lamb before approving the one in front of her. The vegetables nearby might have been smuggled from a fairy tale: an infant squash, tiny and brilliantly yellow, nestled next to an extremely petite zucchini, the stem delicately edible. Nearby, a thumb-sized eggplant reclined upon a whipped exhale of exotic tuber, flanked by long strands of a rich red super negin saffron priced at $9,000 per pound. The plating was a feat of color and geometry; the lighting, decor, and music designed to calm, delight, harmonize. One look around and the message was unmistakable. Either by nurture, force, or some unspeakable hoodoo magic, everything here was not just special, but extraordinary.

This table was no different. Four second-year MBA candidates from *The* Harvard Business School, three high-level executives at one of the most desirable employers in the world, two bottles (so far) of four-figure Bordeaux, one final-round recruiting dinner. These men and women dressed the part, acted the part, lived the part. Some were outright to the manor born, the finished products of breathtaking privilege, access, and sometimes, hard work. The rest? To the *manner* born, self-sculpted from mediocre privilege, middling access, and always, hard work. Both groups had in common the fact that their lives were going exactly according to plan.

In this crowd, Kayla Masouvi should fit in perfectly. The Masouvis were the American dream. Her father, Kayvan, had come to the United States from Iran with twenty-five dollars in his pocket, barely speaking English, rising to be a top sales executive. Rags to riches through luck and pluck, just like the story. In the Masouvi home, the highest achievement was expected. Was respected. But now her family was destroyed, the doors shut, and the privilege revoked, replaced with pity, contempt, guilt by association. The past few years had shattered her life, shattered her identity, shattered her dreams. Dreams that did not involve this company or any company, dreams that were the *opposite* of being here.

But that is a story for later.

"Some people just don't get it," said the recruit to her left. "But I love it." What was his name again? Giles? Mick? She frowned because she couldn't remember, and the vague unease from that compelled her to tune in to his conversation. Palm Beach. Golf courses. Then: Wall Street, St. Bart's, *yachts*. She almost had to laugh. She almost rolled her eyes.

Stop being such a spoiled brat. The voice in her head. Pretty mean. Usually spot-on.

His name. It came to her. Miles. Miles was in the running to work for the chief financial officer, who sat at the end of the table, grumbling into a wireless headset while awkwardly turning his phone sideways to peer at spreadsheets. Snatches of his conversation wafted over, mostly related to *how difficult these godforsaken documents were to view on a phone*. Kayla groaned internally and speared a midget zucchini, resolving to make her square little self fit into whatever round hole provided the best salary. She needed a steady job. A lucrative, steady job.

"What about you, Kayla?"

"Me?" Six sets of eyes swiveled in her direction. The man asking was Rick Monahan, CEO of General Recycling. His smiling, handsome face radiated pleasant professionalism. She ignored it, zeroing in on a small twitch in his right eye. She'd taught herself to observe behaviors just like this. Years of painstaking training to spot tells. The media portrayed tells as dark magic. Mind reading. Soul reading, even. Reality proved far more tedious. Tells merely represented careful observation, because humans give away everything in how they look, act, and react.

Frederick Douglass Monahan. The origin story of this titan of American business is long. Nail-biting. Heart-wrenching. Heart-warming. We'll save it for later. Back to that small twitch. Kayla read it in an instant.

Whatever you say, don't bullshit me.

A blink.

I see you.

"Hobbies," he said, showing some mercy. "We're talking about hobbies."

"Well"—Kayla swallowed the mini zucchini whole—"I play poker." Poker was not a hobby, exactly. It was, among other things, how she was paying for her education. But this was not the right answer, and the faces at the table confirmed it. Poker was too *lone wolf* (not a team player), maybe too analytical (bad with people), maybe too superstitious (bad with numbers), maybe seedy and distasteful. All these associations reflected on the surrounding faces—except for Monahan's. He seemed to think they had some kind of inside joke going.

"A card shark," he finally said. "Remarkable."

She laughed and shook her head. "Not exactly. It's mostly numbers. Odds, educated guesses, statistics."

Monahan dug into his food. Everyone followed his lead. He savored his lamb for a moment, then slid his fork down. "But it's more than just statistics, right?"

Kayla's bite turned out to be an unexpected bit of gristle. She longed to spit it out, but everyone was watching. She gave up and swallowed. "Ah, long-tailed relational probabilities, to be exact."

He tilted his head and gave her that look again.

Kayla decided, as suggested, not to bullshit him. "Okay, well. Exploitation."

"Of addicts?" Monahan raised one discerning eyebrow. "People who belong at Gamblers Anonymous?"

Well, there it was. Uncomfortable silence fell on the table again.

Kayla cleared her throat. "Of anyone who sits down at the table. Everyone has a weakness. Poker finds it."

"Your fatal flaw."

"Right," she said nervously. "Like your Achilles' heel."

He took a sip that probably cost a hundred dollars and considered his hands. "So, what's yours?"

She almost choked on her food. "Excuse me?"

"We'll all share." He waved his hand around. "You can go first."

Kayla thought fast. "Napoleon once said that war was ninety percent information." She took a sip of her wine, swallowed it down, and turned her palms upward. She would say nothing more. Her dining companions froze in shocked silence. The restaurant itself seemed to still.

But Monahan laughed, and apparently, the world along with him. "Fair enough. Well, then, if you won't share yours, what about mine?"

"Yours?"

"Have at it." He leaned back. "As it relates to poker, of course."

Of course. She cleared her throat. "Well, most whales aren't hungry. No killer instinct." She instantly regretted the words, because Monahan was not a typical whale, poker parlance for a big-money player. He was born into poverty on an Indian reservation to a Native American mother and a Black father who would go to jail for murder before the boy's tenth birthday. A terrible start that only a superhero could overcome.

The Mean Voice spoke up. *Stupid girl. Why can't you shut your mouth?*

He raised an eyebrow. "But you have one? A killer instinct."

"Well, my version." She shrugged, ignoring the Mean Voice. "Remembering that I'm not as smart as I think I am."

Monahan stared. Kayla stared back, unblinking. The table expanded and contracted with restless energy.

"Can we go back to Achilles?" Miles's voice, calm and self-assured, interjected at her left ear, shifting the moment. "I always wondered why he didn't put armor on his heel. Seems like an easy fix to me." Miles. Mr. Palm Beach. Golf. Yachts. He fixed his eyes on her, and she had to control her reaction. They were an outstanding and unnerving Windex blue, startling even in the mellow restaurant light.

"Uh, well, he didn't know about his heel," Kayla responded.

Monahan turned to one of the other recruits, and Miles

turned to her. "Didn't know?" he asked, leaning forward. Kayla took a good look at him. A mop of blond hair a three-year-old might weep for. Muscles. And apparently an interest in Greek mythology.

"Yeah. The gods gave Achilles a choice—to live a long life with no glory or a short life with eternal glory. He chose eternal glory."

"And got a bum heel." He grinned. Perfect white teeth. Kayla just about rolled her eyes again.

"Exactly." She tried to sip her wine and ended up with a nervous gulp. God, how much longer was this dinner going to drag on? She couldn't take much more.

"You know your mythology. Is that what you studied in college?" Miles sipped his wine. Like a normal person, Kayla observed darkly, a normal person just chatting up a colleague at a recruiting dinner, versus a crazed, restless, insomniac nut job white-knuckling the table edge and counting the minutes.

"You didn't memorize the résumés of the competition?" HBS had the résumés of each student posted and accessible for all, and General Recycling HR had helpfully listed the names of each RSVP.

You're horrible, came the Mean Voice. *What the hell's wrong with you?*

She clenched her teeth and shook her head. "I'm sorry that was obnox—"

"Princeton undergrad, classics major, economics minor, honors thesis on the works of Ovid." He paused. "Something about dreams and female sexuality, if I remember correctly." Miles cast his eyes around the room and then back to Kayla, and for a second, something changed in his face. The golden-boy professional veneer fell off, and a quiet darkness bloomed, even though the words remained light. He eventually smiled. "Don't get any ideas. I can recite theirs, too."

Kayla stared for a second, then broke out into a laugh, mostly startled, genuinely impressed. "Show-off."

"And you have nothing to say for yourself, I take it."

"I'm above all this," she deadpanned.

"Dying to be unemployed, huh?" Maybe not deadpan enough.

The look on Kayla's face made Miles scramble. "Oh, sorry, I didn't mean—"

"Time for a toast." Monahan addressed the table, interrupting them. He waited for everyone to quiet, then went on. "I salute your weaknesses. Your fatal flaws. May your fate be that you find yours and fix them"—he aimed his Bordeaux at Kayla—"before someone else does."

The finest crystal made the most pleasing clink, and these glasses were no exception. "Here's to working together"—Miles turned to Kayla and raised his wine—"at the coolest company on the planet."

Kayla smiled, said nothing, sipped her grand cru, and launched a deep, fervent wish for exactly, specifically, the opposite.

CHAPTER TWO

DINNER ENDED, THRUSTING a metallic, nauseating despair upon her. Recruiting events had that effect, because they were all about the F word.

The Future.

Her dream wasn't any of the following: to be a private-equity wizard or a management consultant, to work in marketing, finance, or procurement. She had no special interest in next-generation garbage collecting, the business of General Recycling. Kayla only dreamed of running her own little investment fund, supported by her own little wits, at a poker table. She longed to play poker professionally, but that was out of the question. She needed one of "those" jobs: high paying, long hours, great benefits, all-consuming.

And you're lucky enough to maybe get one, she dutifully reminded herself.

After a string of long, professional, enthusiastic goodbyes, the night was over. Outside, a wild ice wind whipped through the urban canyons of the Midtown skyscrapers, snatching her body heat. March in New York City. The cruelest month. Her hotel was ten blocks away. It was only nine thirty. The night was young, very young. And her mood was terrible, very terrible.

There was only one cure for that combination. She whipped

out her phone and ordered a car service. Destination: the Borgata Casino in Atlantic City. Kayla's base camp. Where there was a hotel room always comped for her and a marker (a casino-provided loan) if necessary, because she played long and hard nights, wrung-out of long and hard days. This place, and others like it, were where and how she'd financed most of graduate school. She had, in fact, paid for this fancy degree that she longed to reject with all the blood, sweat, and tears she could muster. Mostly blood and tears, really. Sweating was for amateurs.

Minutes later, she leaned back into cool leather as the Hudson whizzed by.

Her phone rang. The caller ID flashed. *Mr. A.* Immediately, her blood pressure zipped, her heart rate, too, and her shoulders tensed. A call from Mr. A had that effect these days, and it made her sad. So sad. Because he was Mr. Amazing. And he deserved better than her.

But anyway.

She cleared her throat. "Hi."

"You're still alive, I see." The voice chuckled low and throaty, radiating affection and love, and maybe some scotch and a furtive cigarette or two. Even over the scratchy mobile phone lines, the posh British accent beamed through like a beacon, all Earl Grey tea and Yorkshire pudding and fog-swept moors and charmingly decaying castles. The Queen's English, indeed.

Desire stabbed her right between the legs. She ignored it. "By the skin of my teeth." She laughed. "How was your night?"

"Good." He cleared his throat suspiciously. Yes, definitely smoking again. "But I didn't have dinner with the CEO of the hottest company on Wall Street."

She picked some imaginary lint off her pant leg. "Lots of competition."

"Monahan would be lucky to have you join his shabby little start-up."

This made her laugh out loud. General Recycling was a public company with a market cap deep in the double-digit billions. BUGS on the NASDAQ. Not too shabby, not little, not exactly a start-up. She caught her breath. "That's what he's plotting right now, how to make sure I take the job he hasn't even offered me yet."

A pause. "Interviews are all day tomorrow?"

"Uh, yes." Shame blossomed now, crowding her thoughts with its black, foul-smelling sludge. *Don't ask*, she willed him. *Don't ask where I'm going.*

That way I won't have to lie. Or tell the truth.

A loud male voice shouted in the background. He was out. At a club, a bar. Harvard Square. Downtown Boston. Somewhere. "Well, call me when you get back to the hotel. You can fall asleep to me telling you how wonderful, smart, talented, and beautiful you are."

She hesitated. And she who hesitates is lost.

The line cackled. He hissed out a restless breath. "You're not going back to the hotel, are you?"

Once upon a time, Sameer Anithi—academic superstar, marathoner, second-generation British Indian, #8 on *London Magazine*'s Ten Most Eligible Bachelors, scion of The Anithi Group real estate empire—was all she needed to chase away her darkness. Sameer was a permanent refuge from shame, from the nuclear winter she was living through. If Sameer Anithi loved her, that was good enough.

Right?

"Kayla, I thought we talked about this. Cold turkey, right? That was the idea?"

That was the idea. Time to grow up. Time to stop hanging out in casinos until four in the morning. Sameer would propose soon. Something intimate, romantic, heartfelt, wonderful. He had accepted an offer at Goldman Sachs, the Anithi Group banker of record, in NYC. He did that for her, so they could be in New York. In a few years, they would move back to London. He made no secret of the fact that he hated her poker with a genuine, unfettered passion. And poker was a security risk. How many unsavory groups would love to kidnap Sameer Anithi's wife? No. No. Nope. It was Sameer or poker. She chose Sameer. Of course.

"I—I..." She trailed off into a heavy silence.

"We'll talk later," he finally said, disappointment creeping into his voice. "Drive safe." Those two words held such longing and defeat that her throat shriveled. She barely croaked out her response. She closed her eyes and pressed on them. Little circles, right on the orbital bone. A relaxation exercise from the life coach. But the moment her eyes shut, a number flashed before them.

$2,123,400.79.

The bill.

The bill came in the mail each month and announced her name at the very top. At the bottom, a seven-figure total Kayla did not incur, but did guarantee and cosign. Kayla was indebted to an esteemed law firm we shall call Blah, Blah, and Blahbedy-Blah, LLC (Blah for short), where the partners' hourly rate hovered in the low four figures. The best white-collar defense money could buy. At least that was the pitch. Blah handled her father's criminal case and would only take him if Kayla, with her Harvard MBA and her Harvard earning power, cosigned the debt. She had two choices: pledge her future income to Blah in a blood oath or throw her father to the wolves.

And the fun was far from over. Kayvan Masouvi lost his insider trading case and was awaiting sentencing at Rikers Island Prison. There was an appeal to fund and, if successful, the breathtaking expense of a new trial. So there would be no delinquency, no bankruptcy, no avoiding this bill. And there was no one else to pay it. Kayla was an only child. Her mother was dead. Her extended family was lovely but poor. The buck literally stopped with her, but she had an amazing boyfriend, who was about to propose, a man for whom this number was the wave of a few fingers. And even if he wasn't in her life, her résumé meant she could get the (high paying) job she needed. She was so amazingly lucky to have all the above. So lucky. She knew all this.

She just couldn't *feel* it.

Back in the real world, the car slipped into the Holland Tunnel. They were leaving New York City. Last chance to turn around. To go back to the hotel. Her phone chimed. Sameer? Words of love and encouragement, convincing her to go back?

No. The Borgata poker host.

Private game tonight. The Suite. You in?

Rich people did everything different, including play poker. They did not sit on the casino floor with the hoi polloi. Instead, the high-limit poker host happily organized a game around him or her (though it was always a him). Kayla was highly familiar with the drill. The whales only played with other whales or pros in a private suite, with a pristine table and a dealer of their choice. These games were the holy grail, for the reasons Kayla herself had recounted to Monahan.

Most whales aren't hungry.

The car exited the tunnel and approached the Turnpike. Her eyes hungrily tracked the signs, the arrows, the exits, her fingers drumming the handrest. The light changed. The car accelerated. The on-ramp to the great state of New Jersey loomed ahead, reaching for her with its concrete and gravel tentacles, those irresistible octopus limbs. Seconds ticked away, the next twelve hours in nominal limbo, until the highway, predictably, claimed her.

CHAPTER THREE

THERE WAS AN order to this process.

Kayla collected her chips and said her hellos. Then she plunked down on an overstuffed couch and centered her thoughts. Meditated. Poker was a mental game as much, if not more, than a pop quiz on probabilities and statistics. And private games required extra prep because of the money at stake, the lack of anonymity, the need to be an entertainer and a player. Above all, the whale must have a great time. To lose but have fun doing it. That would ensure his return to repeat the cycle.

Tonight she would play in the most deluxe accommodations in the house, a five-bedroom ode to Atlantic City opulence, what there was of it, at least. Up the private elevator she went, happy, calm, and confident, carefully balancing her rack. Seventy-five thousand dollars in Pumpkins and Barneys, Pumpkins being big, round orange $1,000 chips, and Barneys (like the dinosaur), smaller purple $500 chips. The blind bets in this game were $500/$1,000. This meant that one player seeded the pot with $1,000, and the player to her right had to bet $500, each and every round. The table rotated positions clockwise. She would need Pumpkins and Barneys.

The elevator opened to the suite, where, immediately, the sound of shuffling chips and harsh male laughter jammed out.

This was perhaps the most tiresome feature of poker. It was very *guy*. Some of it was funny; some of it was sexist and alienating. The air was full of its usual pumped-in perfume, cigarette smoke, and extra oxygen. Nothing new, and yet, tonight, something in the air jabbed her insides. A tiny wrench even gripped the back of her neck. Tightened. Somehow, tonight was different.

Tonight was wrong.

She brushed the feelings aside.

You got this.

A man in a suit appeared to her left, probably a personal assistant. She slapped on a smile and followed him, passing a living room and a terrace with a sundeck on the left, bedrooms to the right. Several large men with earpieces stood as still as statues, in the manner of all high-end security, trained to disappear into the wallpaper unless needed. At the end of the hall was a game room with large-screen TVs, a glittering wet bar, and in the middle, a brand-new poker table. Angela, a Borgata veteran dealer, shuffled cards in the dealer pit. And seated at the table was none other than Frederick Douglass Monahan, with only his chips for company. One empty seat yawned across from him.

The CEO of General Recycling. Here. Alone.

Angela shot her an uncomfortable smile. "Hi, Kayla."

If not for Angela's familiar, friendly face, Kayla would have turned on her heel and left that second, because this was just too weird. The kind of weird that would throw off her game and make playing a bad idea. But Angela was one of her favorite dealers, sweet and motherly. She'd dealt at the Borgata since Kayla was a kid playing the $1/$2 tables. So she recovered. And then remembered. Walking in, she heard voices. She was sure of it. Chips clicking. Men laughing. Playing. But the tightly shut doors and darkened rooms emitted no signs of life. Neither did the pristine, virtually unused bar.

The sound poured out again. From behind. She whirled. A screen played a poker tournament. Loudly.

Monahan aimed the remote. "Sorry. I've got a piece of one of these clowns." This was slang for a financial stake in the outcome, such as providing a tournament entry fee for a percentage of winnings. He shrugged and hit mute before extending a hand. "Welcome to the game." Monahan towered over her, and she had not noticed this before. He was tall and in great shape—no middle-aged paunch, no slumped shoulders, with a mouthful of teeth so white and perfect, they must be veneers. His handshake was firm and uncompromising—that she remembered.

She shook his hand for the second time in twenty-four hours. "You got here fast."

He twisted his index finger in a swirling motion. "Helicopter. Beat the traffic."

"Anyone else joining?" She placed her chips on the felt.

"They tapped out." Monahan's voice boomed across the cavernous space, producing a faint echo.

Out...out...out...

So this game would be heads-up. Her stomach plummeted. Heads-up was what some consider the purest poker. Just you and one opponent battling wits, its own little skill set, only moderately related to playing at a full table. Not her best format. Certainly not good enough to play high limit with an unknown opponent possessing an unlimited bankroll.

"Not enough fish here," he finished smoothly. His eyes twinkled, dark brown and warm, and yet they examined her. Poked. Picked. One of Kayla's signatures as a player was her poker face.

She even briefly had a nickname: No-Read Masouvi. But tonight it was a struggle. She had to summon up everything she'd learned over the years, from the first moment she sat with her dad in their old linoleum-paneled kitchen, cross-legged on the floor, playing penny-ante five-card stud. He'd taught her most of what she knew, and she had to thank him at this moment for every lesson—some of them so very painful—on hiding her intentions and emotions at a poker table. Because Monahan almost got through. He almost turned all her skills into hot butter.

But he didn't.

The Borgata was *her* home turf. In fact, it was almost her home. She knew the staff. She was a VIP. Heck, she'd visited this suite for poker games many times. She'd played thousands of hands right here. Would Rick Monahan intimidate her?

Like hell.

"There's at least one now." She sat down and turned to the dealer. "Angela. How are you?"

Angela palmed the cards perfectly with her long, obscenely manicured nails. "Ah, um, good," she said, blinking. She pulled a deck out of the Shuffle Master and gave it a flap. "Ready to play?" She glanced at each of them.

Kayla: "As I'll ever be."

Monahan: "Excellent. Let's go."

No-Limit Texas Hold'em is the most popular poker game spread in casinos today. It is the easiest to learn, requires the least complicated math, and has the benefit of each player getting only two cards, which makes it fast to deal. In addition, No-Limit Hold'em received unbeatable press when one Chris Moneymaker (real name) captured the most legendary hot streak of all time. Starting with a fifty-dollar "satellite" tournament—where the prizes are tickets to bigger tournaments—Moneymaker went on to win the 2003 World Series of Poker Main Event, which has always been, and probably always will be, a No-Limit Hold'em game.

Two cards, face down. Three in the middle of the table. The flop. A round of bets. Another card—the turn. Another round of bets. A final card—the river. Last chance to bet. Showdown, if everyone hasn't folded before then. Two cards in your hand, five on the board. The best five-card hand wins, "best" being a codified list that varied in probability from 649,743 to 1 (a royal flush—single suit ten, jack, queen, king, and ace), to winning with a high card.

Kayla sipped wine and took hands. She started off ahead and never gave up the lead. Her chip stack grew and the hours dissolved like drops in the ocean. Kayla routinely played ten, twelve hours straight, rarely got bored or tired. Eventually, though, the immutable, unarguable laws of recursion suggested that she should leave. Now. She did a few stretches the physical therapist had taught her and winced at her tight shoulders.

Yup, time to stop. She tossed in her cards. "I think I'll call it a night."

Monahan ignored her words. "Let's take the blinds up. And the buy-in. Two hundred K buy-in, and one thousand / five thousand blinds."

She shook her head and stifled a yawn. "I can't."

"Sure you can."

Ah, the goaded and the goader. In a lesser story, Monahan would intimidate her. Dig around in her insecurities, hit pay dirt. She would sit right back down and she would play out of her depth, and she would either (a) screw up and lose everything or (b) have a Cinderella (Moneymaker?) night and win big.

But this is not a lesser story. And Kayla was too smart for all of that.

She laughed and got up, searching for her rack, which had disappeared. "I don't play outside of my bankroll. And that is most definitely out of my bankroll." Where was it? She frowned and ducked under the table.

Monahan nodded, his face oddly serious. "I completely understand," he said. "And I don't want you to do anything that would make you uncomfortable. So I'll make you a deal."

She stopped her search and froze. "A deal?"

His stare, unblinking and truly unsettling, bore deep into her. She counted the seconds, forced herself to not look away.

"A bankroll for your bank account…and a job."

Watermelon. Caterpillar. Ketchup. The nonsense words she planted in her head to keep her reactions from materializing. She waited to reply. Studied him. But he was a pro, too. He gave her exactly nothing. Finally, she exhaled. "A what for a what?" Her voice, steady. Her face, amused. She was proud of both.

"You heard me." He glanced at his watch. "We'll play for an hour. If you're ahead at the end, or even if we're tied, you'll win four million. Well, three free and clear. Your very own bankroll. One as a stake. Give your professional poker career a jump start. Pay off any burdensome expenses you may have." He nodded gravely, like someone had quoted him the current number on the bill from Blah. "But if I win, I empty your bank account." Now his eyes danced like someone had sent him her current bank balance, which was more or less zero.

She measured her breathing. She said nothing.

He went on. "You come to work for me. Three years. A solemn commitment. No matter how badly you want to take off for Vegas. At the end, you get the money, just the same." He thought for a moment. "And I need to you start as soon as possible. No later than the first week of July."

How generous. How crazy. Months later, Kayla would think long and hard about this moment, precisely because at this moment…she hadn't thought at all. Hadn't considered Sameer and how it was wrong, wrong, *wrong* to decide this without him. Hadn't asked why. Sure, the money meant nothing to Monahan, and he probably tossed it around all the time, but why her? Any of the others at the recruiting dinner made it through a résumé cut, rounds of interviews, and a raft of ridiculous personality tests. Each of them would do a great job. Add in the dozens of equally qualified candidates who hadn't even made it that far. Why would Monahan thrust this job on someone who didn't seem to want it?

But none of that registered, because Monahan was dangling her dream *right in front of her face*.

That registered.

With a completely uncharacteristic lack of control, she blurted out those two fateful words.

"I'm in."

CHAPTER FOUR

A FEW MINUTES later, each of them sat behind exactly $200,000 in nice round plastic-covered clay. Now, of course, it was funny money. All that mattered, all she needed, was to end the next hour with $200,001. Then her dreams would come true.

Well, good luck with that. She had a serious problem. A car crash of exhaustion had slammed into her. She tried to swallow away her sandy, crusty mouth. No dice. She tried to power through a hopeless spaghetti brain, but her mental powers hung by a thread. Each blink stabbed her gritty eyes, the pain like tiny shards of glass. She was operating on muscle memory and instinct. She needed eye drops. Nourishment. Sleep.

Thirty-five minutes in.

Somehow she was winning, but just barely. Starting stack: 200,000. Current stack: 204,000. Her insides roiled from the stress. Unpleasant aches zapped her, sudden jolts of pain everywhere and anywhere.

Forty-five minutes in.

She lost one hand, and now, for the first time, she was behind. 190,000. Fifteen minutes left. Fifteen minutes was a lifetime in poker. She visualized, engaged in positive thinking.

I'll get a good run of cards. I'll have my dream job. She pictured it all. Pictured herself on the felt. Playing. Winning.

Fifty-five minutes.

198,000.

She closed her eyes for a second.

You're screwed. Done. Finished, the Mean Voice hissed in her head.

Nonsense, a more optimistic voice shot back. *There is time. Relax. Focus.*

When she finally opened her eyes, her cards were in front of her. Her opponent waited.

Fifty-six minutes.

"Don't fall asleep yet," he said. "It's always that last ski run of the day where you break your leg."

"I'm good." She exhaled and peeled her cards. Two black nines. Warmth enveloped her body. The nines had always been good to her.

Fifty-seven minutes.

Monahan had the first action. He glanced at his cards and raised to 15,000. A substantial raise—triple the big blind, aka the largest bet.

Kayla considered her options. If she folded, there was time for another hand. But the odds frowned on that idea. It would, most likely, be worse.

Realistically, this was it.

She waited. Waited. Then re-raised, big. Monahan, if he was truly playing to win, would never fold in this spot. If he did, she would have 213,000 and she would then simply run down the clock.

Fifty-eight minutes.

So, as expected, he threw some chips in. A call. They would finish the hand, but this would almost certainly be the last hand.

Angela spread the flop. Three cards. And oh…what a flop it was. The other two nines, the nine of hearts and the nine of diamonds, stared back at her, along with the ace of hearts. She had flopped quads, an exceptional hand. Not impossible to beat, but so unlikely to lose that in the poker canon of best practices, a player with quads should virtually always proceed as if she has the best hand.

Her luck just turned big. She had to finish the hand. That was it.

Fifty-nine minutes.

Monahan bet into her with all of his chips.

"I've got aces full," he announced. "All in." A full house, which was a hand with three of one card and two of another. This meant he held two aces in his hand. An exceptional hand.

But it did not beat hers.

She pretend pondered. Dithered. Ran down the clock just to be sure.

Time up.

Officially the last hand.

"Call," she said.

They both turned over cards.

Monahan showed the ace of spades and the ace of diamonds. Aces full.

"Wow," he said, squinting at her two black nines. "You got me." He grinned at Angela. "Turn and burn, my dear. Let's make her poker career official."

And yet…Kayla would have to earn this win, because Monahan could make a better hand: quad aces, four of a kind that would beat Kayla's quad nines. Of the four aces total in a deck of cards, two were in his hand and one was on the board. There was one and only one card saving him. The ace of clubs. One card out of forty-five unknowns left in the deck translated to a roughly 4 percent chance. Kayla, like any poker player, had been on the losing end of such odds before, and worse, but…right now? *No.* Right now her odds would win the day. She was sure of it.

The turn was the seven of clubs.

Yes. She breathed out. She breathed in.

And the river.

Was.

The ace of clubs.

The board shrank to a pinpoint. Her eyes glazed over.

"Damn," muttered Monahan under his breath. "I'm sorry, Kayla."

She swallowed and modulated her panic, closing her eyes and breathing out. *Control. Control. Control.* Eyes open. She was back. Unfortunately. She swallowed and stared at the felt, her lips pursed. No emotion, no tears, no reaction.

"I'll have the wire details to you in the morning," Kayla said. At least, she thought she said.

"At your leisure." He stood up, extended a hand. "Welcome to General Recycling, Kayla."

Another handshake. She stared at his hand and forced herself to comprehend, pushing against all the resistance in her head that screamed *NO*. That refused this outcome. All of it.

She just landed herself a job.

Congratulations to me. She sobbed bitter, sarcastic tears, but only in her head.

In reality, she grasped his hand. Thanked him with a calm smile.

"Enjoy the rest of your break," he said. "I'll see you in July.

Come to my office on your first day. You'll be working directly for me."

She murmured something. Not words. Maybe words. She turned. She walked out the door. Normally. Not too fast. Not too slow. Once outside the door, the façade fell away.

She fled.

CHAPTER FIVE

"YOU DID WHAT?" Sameer's pallor was as white and cold as his warm brown skin could ever get. They sat in a booth at John Harvard's, a pub in Cambridge. His face held pure astonishment, and for a second he froze, a fry halfway to his mouth, processing the information that Kayla had taken the GR offer. Or, more precisely, had the GR offer thrust upon her by the quad-ace-slinging Rick Monahan.

"There's no excuse, Sameer." Nope. None. And now she was working for the Garbage Man. In New York. For three years. In exchange for a...poker bankroll. A complete disregard of their much-discussed plans. She might as well have actually slapped his face. Now, only now, did the guilt and shame flood her body.

What the hell is wrong with you? The Mean Voice yelped. The room seemed to dim and chill.

Kayla wrapped her arms around herself and shivered.

Sameer dropped the soggy fry into a grease-splattered basket and leaned back, gazing at her, outwardly calm. Only on the outside. Kayla imagined his insides as a blue-cold flame of sadness and fury. He had that slow burn thing going on. A kind of smolder. Which she loved, usually. "We're supposed to make decisions like this together."

"I know." He was perfectly correct. Kayla had all the excuses ready. *I was tired. Overconfident. Stupid.* And all of them were true. But not the truth. Monahan offered her heart's desire on a silver platter, simple as that. She rubbed her forehead. Her hand came away with dry flakes. Gross. She brushed it off, trying not the think about the fact that her skin was peeling off in layers.

He laughed. Harshly. Not his usual laugh, smooth and slow. Which she also loved. "But it works out, right? You work for Monahan, save money, help your dad get out of his mess, and play poker." He sipped his beer and eyed her. "And you don't have to be married to anyone, because you don't actually want to be married to anyone."

Yeah, pretty much.

"I don't know what my problem is, Sameer." And she didn't. A headache stabbed her like an ice pick to the brain. She jammed fingers into her temples. Didn't help. "I wish I could be someone different. Someone who deserves you." The story of her life lately. Wishing to be the Girl Who Deserved Sameer. The Mean Voice *loooooved* this topic.

How many girls would die to trade places with you?

You'll never meet another Sameer.

How could you live after rejecting the best man in the world?

Maybe you have to kill yourself.

Oh yes, despair, misery, suicide, and/or spinsterhood awaited if she broke up with Sameer. If she rejected the once-in-a-lifetime opportunity to be the Girl. That was the Mean Voice. Nothing new. But finally admitting the truth to herself…that was new. The truth forever hanging between them like a sorcerer's dark cloud.

She wasn't.

She. Just. Wasn't. The Girl.

And wishing to be her was madness. Futile. The kind of internal agony that made characters in Greek tragedies gouge out their eyeballs.

Sameer pushed his food away and echoed her thoughts with his own. "I was just in denial. Maybe I was hoping…things would change." He crossed his arms over his chest, a defensive posture so very unlike him. "And now I guess it's obvious they won't."

Oh God. This was happening. Now. *Here*. She glanced at the other tables, chock-full of fun. Smiles and laughter. Low intimate voices, loud boisterous ones. All around her were dreams in the process of coming true. Dreams of Ivy League–approved french fries and fancy degrees and perfect boyfriends and bright, shining futures. "I love you," she said, "more than anything." Tears squeezed out of her eyes.

He exhaled and grimaced, like his chest hurt. His arms fell. He pressed white fingers to his temples. "I know, K," he said, his voice slightly muffled by his hands. "I love you. You love me. And I know you"—he searched for the word—"you *burn*. You have miles to go before you rest. You're not ready to be married. I love you, and I know all this. You can't help it. That's who you are."

She glanced up at him. "How much do you hate me?"

He shook his head, his eyes boring deep into hers. "Maybe you just caught me on a good day." His voice lowered, softened. "Or maybe that's not me."

"I need to make it on my own. Before I can be…what you want."

Her hand twitched on the table. He covered it with his. "I know," he said. He turned her palm to face his. She gulped. He entwined their fingers. Squeezed. "We have to break up."

A muffled sob jutted from her chest. And again. Sameer responded with only a clotted exhale. That was Sameer. No big emotions in public.

But after a minute he lifted her chin, smiled into her miserable, snotty, tear-stained face, and kissed her lips. A messy, gloopy proposition. "Hey. You'll get poker out of your system. All those nights that end in the sun, whatever it is you need to prove. Then you'll be ready. Or not. We'll let the gods decide."

"Yes." This was the dark mirror image of a marriage proposal. Tears. A kiss. *She said yes.* All that was missing was a ring.

And all the rest of it.

Whatever it is you need to prove.

How much would be enough? Would that day ever come—the day when being Mrs. Anithi would be enough?

I'll grow into the Girl.

I will.

That light at the end of the tunnel wouldn't be an oncoming train after all.

Right?

CHAPTER SIX

AND THEN IT came.

Graduation and the few miserable, lonely, restless months before her start date. No casinos. No poker. It hurt too much. Images from that night at the Borgata would flash in her head like a terrible omen, the turn of the screw, the moment where it all fell apart.

Good thing she had a job now.

Sameer returned to London, many time zones and life goals and mindsets away. They had agreed not to talk, only texting each other in heartbreaking, awkward conversations. Her father was in Rikers. They weren't talking. Her friends had scattered across the world. No time to talk. Her mother was dead.

Well, they talked. In Kayla's head. And her mom said it best.

It's time to leave the past behind.

And so she did. July came, and she threw herself into her new job. Into bugs. And General Recycling's garbage-eating bacteria were not just any bugs. They *saved the world.* She studied them so hard and long, she could recite the origin story of *Ideonella Schechterensis Chewinformis* (*I. Chew*) and its fellow trash-eaters like an AI algorithm on the fritz. Along with his partner Evan Schechter, Frederick Monahan, the whiz kid who enrolled in MIT at sixteen, developed highly specialized bacteria that broke down waste into usable parts. *I. Chew,* the most famous of the bugs, ate plastic. GR had taken the transformative dream of recycling and made it real. Without Schechter and Monahan, trash would poison the planet. Not long after the IPO, Monahan became CEO and Schechter retired, disappearing to a private island from where he directed his chief philanthropic effort, the Genesis Foundation, whose motto seemed to fit nicely with GR's mission:

We will heal the planet.

The company occupied a seventy-seven-story high-rise in a massive, glittering, peak-cycle NYC development called Hudson Yards. Monahan himself sat atop a vertigo-inducing, all-glass observation deck called the Needle, above every other tenant, above the clouds, depending on the day. The #grmafia called his office the Temple, and not just because Monahan had outfitted it like a Buddhist house of worship. Her desk was a stone's throw away. As for her apartment, Kayla's own coveted sliver of housing came courtesy of the most stunning corporate perk imaginable: the GR housing lottery. The winners scored upscale apartments in GR-owned buildings for dirt cheap. Kayla's was in the same building as her office, a dozen floors away. She had won the commute lottery, too.

And then there was the actual job. Executive strategy. Grueling hours and too many projects analyzing this and that. As promised, she reported only to Monahan, who traveled constantly, emailed constantly, called constantly, and had not appeared once in person. When he finally appeared, one mid-October day, it was simply to hand her a seemingly impossible project: cut the budget of the entire bacteria department by 25%. And with that assignment, it was finally time to meet the bugs.

ꟹ

"You are in for *eh* treat." The CBO (Chief Bug Officer) leaned into a retinal scan as green light crisscrossed her face and a large door beeped open. Marcella Minieri, PhD, microbiology, Oxford ("Top Bug," she quipped). They entered a narrow hallway with a locked door at the end leading to the main facility. To the left, behind a sign that read STAPH ONLY was a tiny room with four identical cluttered desks, all shoved together.

Minieri was straight out of mad scientist central casting, down to the crazy hair and the seen-it-all, pipetted-it-too, and injected-myself-with-some-of-it stare. She went to school with General Recycling's long-gone cofounder, Evan Schechter, and Minieri's office featured many pictures of them. Wielding pipettes like deadly weapons. Speaking at scientific conferences. Grinning in full cosplay at Comic Cons and Star Trek conventions. The last picture depicted a group charity run, the team sporting T-shirts with the words Time to B. Cereus About ALS.

"He retired, right?" Kayla studied the pictures. Schechter made a very compelling Mr. Spock. "Does he ever come in?"

"'Retired?'" Minieri laughed. It was quite a laugh, honking and stuttering. Kayla swallowed her reaction. "The Director? If you meet him, don't, ah, repeat such a comment."

"You call him the Director?"

She laughed, again. Kayla was ready this time and smiled serenely. Minieri explained. "He tried to get a movie made once. Pretty odd, yes, for a bug grad student? His idea was"—and at this she drew an imaginary marquee in the air—"*Jaws*, but in a petri dish."

"Wow."

"Yeah. *Wow*. So then the whole lab says, 'Who does he think he is, Steven Spielberg?'"

Kayla got it. "Ah. 'The Director.' Hollywood dreams."

"Yes, exactly. Thinks big. Big dreams." Minieri leaned into the next retinal scan and opened the door to reveal a fantastically long and tall space, with thirty-foot ceilings and rows like roads in a massive housing development. On each side sat twenty-foot-wide transparent cylindrical vats of brownish liquid that burped and tremored. Dark green and blue lights cast everything into an alien-spaceship pallor. The smell remind Kayla of her high school biology lab: preserved things, metal, and weird gloopy organic matter, maybe rotting, maybe just reproducing. The HVAC buzzed in the background, working very hard.

"It takes fifty-eight days for *I. Chew* to fully consume and metabolize the pellets. The plastic pieces rotate through the facility, each vat, more digestion." They continued down the row of vats, and in each one, as they progressed, the colorful pellets of plastic seemed to melt into a yellowish-green gel that grew ever more pale and clear until the final sets of vats, at the very end, had what seemed to be…nothing.

Minieri stopped there, and Kayla walked right up to the double-thick plexiglass and peered in. Nothing floated in or around the water. It sparkled like a swimming pool.

Minieri patted the side and gazed at the water with distaste. "After all the work, you would think that our little saviors would get some rest. They deserve it."

What? "Right. Of course."

"But. No. We kill them. Slaughter," Minieri said. "Annihilation." She closed her eyes and sighed. "Perfect, clear water."

And that actually made Kayla sad. Damn was she sleep-deprived, because she was actually feeling some serious, deep-hearted sympathy for bacteria. After all that work, what did the little guys get? Dish detergent. *Bleach*. Cell walls doused with toxic chemicals until they burst and vomited their insides out, and that was it. "When you put it like that, it seems pretty cruel."

Minieri peered at Kayla over her glasses, eyes boring into her. "You remind Rick that without these little miracle bugs, he'd be—ah, what is the expression?—S-O-L."

She nodded uncertainly. Okay, yeah, she was going to "remind" Monahan that he would be "shit out of luck" without these vats of *I. Chew*.

"People forget. People change." She hardened her stare at Kayla. "Remind him."

They made their way back to Dr. Minieri's office. When they reached their destination, Minieri laughed and patted Kayla on the shoulder. "I should warn you. Monahan gave your predecessor the same assignment, and she got nothing. She had to go back to Monahan empty-handed."

Kayla stopped short. "The other girl?" She swallowed and started again. "Somehow the interview process made me feel like this was a new job." She winced, in her head. Yeah, the "interview process" where she bet her life on a poker game and landed here, at the mercy of Rick Monahan. Sure, she had a contract. She must give best efforts, he had to pay her as agreed. But contracts with billionaires were reliant mostly on their goodwill. If he wanted to screw her over and invite her to sue him…For a moment, she low-key panicked. Was that what happened with the "other girl"?

"Did she get fired?" Kayla blurted out.

Minieri thought for a second. "I don't…ah. Olivia." She

nodded. "Olivia. Sorry. That was her name." She seemed to have misheard the question.

"So…where is Olivia now?"

"I don't know," she said. "Ask around. And not your boss."

CHAPTER SEVEN

Text message

Today 10:47 P.M.

Miles:

Fun Floor?

Miles's toast (curse?) from the recruiting dinner had come true. He now worked for the CFO, a job achingly similar to Kayla's, just triple the Excel and half as much PowerPoint. So while Kayla spent her time on Monahan's insane strategic projects, Miles spent his time on the CFO's insane finance projects. He actually made Kayla feel better about working for Monahan. The projects the CFO dumped on Miles were a hundred times worse than hers. Kayla kept a sleeping bag and pillow at her desk. Miles had a foldout cot ("Far superior to a sleeping bag," he insisted). Unlike Kayla, he hadn't won the General Recycling housing lottery and lived in Harlem.

"Knock knock." Miles rapped gently on her office door, which was open. Eleven P.M. and they were both still hard at work. No surprise.

"Hey." Kayla grinned and rolled her eyes at the massive spreadsheet broadcasting itself across her double-wide computer screen. "The chicken broth project."

Miles nodded. "Yeah. Right. How'd your visit to the underground go?"

Kayla finished typing an equation and hit enter, then sat back. "Do you remember that scene in *Office Space*? The guy with the stapler who lives in the basement?"

"That bad?"

"Mostly. But with chicken broth instead of staplers." Kayla examined one of her formulas, found an error, frowned, and typed.

Miles cast his eyes over the side table in Kayla's office, covered with papers, protein bar wrappers, and sodas. "You had dinner, I see."

"That was lunch." Kayla finished typing, but her fingers hovered over the keyboard. She had something to add but couldn't quite remember...and she was starving. Ahh, *eff it*. When had she last eaten an actual meal? Not lunch, right. How about breakfast? She thought hard and, disturbingly, came up empty.

Miles seemed to read her mind and held out his hand. "The Fun Floor?"

The GR company culture demanded massive amounts of sweat equity, and nowhere reflected that better than the Fun Floor, which featured perks galore, from the sublime to the ridiculous. A giant cafeteria with a dozen different cuisines, custom chef services for special diets, and snacks for days, all free and always open. Squash courts. A game hall. On-site doctors, psychologists, psychiatrists, performance coaches, personal trainers, and a full-size luxury gym with classes running around-the-clock. The #grmafia might crunch garbage numbers (literally) until the wee hours and then sweat all that poison out. The funniest, oddest, and maybe most chilling aspect of life at GR? The two A.M. classes were far from empty. Depending on your point of view, this was either #workhardplayhard or a #dealwiththedevil.

She stared at her computer and groaned.

"Come on." He dangled his hand out. "A few hours of shore leave before diving back into trench warfare."

He made her laugh. "You're mixing your military metaphors, I think." She met his Windex blues, still getting a little jolt of guilt at the thought of the recruiting dinner, where she had pegged him as a shallow, good-looking finance bro with no soul. That had dissolved right quick after the Red Bull–fueled evening they spent singing (badly) to Depeche Mode's "Violator" on the Fun Floor's karaoke rooms, which sat alongside Japanese-style reserve-by-the-hour "refresh" rooms (that neither one of them had ever, ever rented). These rooms had twin beds and sinks that were positively not for sex (LOL) but *were* a lawsuit waiting to happen. Like Kayla, Miles had been a "devotee" (Depeche Mode superfan) since high school, and this made her unnaturally happy, finding someone she had something in common with, even if their shared interest was eighties music normally reserved for depressed, emo teenagers.

"So I am." He wiggled his hand.

"Hell…fine. Yes." Kayla placed her hand in his. Like a rom-com cue, an actual electric shock zapped them. They both yelped, and then laughed, Kayla with some embarrassment. Over the last several weeks, her body had given off the little tells it always did when she slowly, inexorably, became attracted to someone.

And now that someone just gave her a legit electric shock.

So far she'd shrugged it off. She was lonely. Overworked. Exhausted. So was Miles, and they had bonded over all that. How could they not? They spent all hours at work, ate together most days, even worked out together, whenever that happened. Kayla had coined a term for all of this. *Violent proximity*. That's all it was. Violent proximity explained the tiny flutter in her stomach when, like tonight, Miles appeared at her door to hang out. Kayla put a hand to her forehead. She had not thought of herself as a sexual being for months. Anyone other than Sameer felt wrong. It was just the hours, the trenches. If she ended up doing something stupid, the trenches made her do it.

Back to the electric shock. "Stop rubbing up against my sleeping bag." Kayla saved her stupid self, or tried to.

"Only if you admit you want me…" Miles widened his eyes. Just for a second. She groaned and made to punch him. "… to buy you dinner," he finished, sidestepping her.

Ha. Everything was free on the GR Fun Floor. Kayla ran with it. "As long as you know I don't put out 'till the fourth date."

Kayla thought back on this comment an hour later, when they sat, in a crazy food coma, nearly slack-jawed on a way-too-comfortable table and couch situation. She could almost, kind of, accidentally, brush an arm against Miles's leg, or accidentally be close enough that, should Miles choose to brush up against her, you know, accidentally, *it* could happen. Eyes locking and all that. But nope. Because there was one thing missing from the Fun Floor. An undoubtedly smart item to omit.

Booze.

They were not drunk. They were not "drunk", just stuffed and burned out, and Kayla could not stand the idea of going back to work and to her desk and jockeying any more Excel spreadsheets. Miles's face had exactly, specifically, the same sentiment, probably down to the Excel dread.

He furrowed his brow, like he was searching for a way to procrastinate too.

He lifted a finger. "I have an idea," he said.

CHAPTER EIGHT

GOOD LUCK, KAYLA thought. *We're screwed.*

Directly ahead gleamed GR's bespoke coffee roaster. High-end, sustainable, organic, ethically sourced, fair trade, always open. She would get a black eye or whatever they called an espresso plopped into black coffee. Her favorite poker pick-me-up. Murder on the stomach, a zap to the brain. She would chug it and get back to work.

Oh, who are you kidding?

Coffee would not do. No way. She thought for a moment. There was an actual drug dealer around here somewhere, on the floor, for real. One of the maintenance guys apparently sold high-quality speed and other stuff, and at the moment speed would theoretically be the best choice. She would honestly have sought him out, but drugs did nothing for her. Plenty of experimenting had never once yielded what others seemed to get. Namely, anything resembling a high. For years she assumed it was a big joke, or a delusion. The way sociopaths talked about emotions. Something they had long concluded that other people just made up. But that changed after the many friends—including Sameer, who would not lie to her—she had the displeasure of observing high while she, no matter what, remained fully sober.

Well, okay, she never tried speed. Maybe it would at least

keep her awake. She had work—presentations and spreadsheets and documents with titles like "Input Cost Controls for Chicken Broth Operations." She had to laugh. If by some miracle speed did give her a high, said high would surely die in agony.

A group of people walked by in loud conversation, all of them surprisingly chipper for this time of the night. A few of them knew Miles and nodded hellos, and one man broke off and headed to their table.

"What's up, guys?"

Miles roused himself, with great effort, from their shared food coma. "Hey, man."

The two exchanged pleasantries. The newcomer glanced over at Kayla. "How's it going?"

Kayla blinked and dragged her brain back to attention as Miles introduced her to his friend, whose name she promptly forgot.

"Man…you guys look like shit," he pronounced in a slow drawl. "Like you need to wake up."

Thanks, ass. Kayla frowned at him and raised an eyebrow, but before she could say anything, he piped up again.

"Have you tried the VR Arena?"

Kayla laughed. "Is that in the Teen Lounge?" There was, in fact, a Teen Lounge, along with a daycare center and a massive, obscenely stocked children's playroom.

He shrugged at her. "We just came back." He hooked a thumb at his friends, who were laughing, talking, animated. And fully awake. "It's awesome. It's literally better than the best night of sleep. Better than speed, I swear."

"What?" Kayla wasn't laughing anymore.

He held up a hand. "I swear. No joke."

"No joke," Miles echoed, blinking.

A guy in the waiting group hollered over, "Hey, dude! Let's go!"

"One sec." He turned back to Miles and Kayla. Now he had their full attention. "Anyway," he said. "Gotta go. But, it is *highly*"—he leaned down on the table for emphasis—"highly recommended."

"Thanks for the tip," Kayla managed as he walked away.

A minute later, Miles heaved himself upright, brushed crumbs away, and laughed. "Come on. Get up before you melt into place and get stuck to the seat. Might as well, right? Can't be worse than that espresso-in-coffee thing you do." He started for the exit.

She stood up and stretched, then sighed and followed him. "Is it *Call of Duty* in space suits or something? I don't think I'm the target audience for that." They reached the elevators, and Kayla had a decision to make. She could either (a) head back to her desk or (b) finally, for once, go to her actual apartment and sleep in her actual bed, where she wouldn't wake up with cookie crumbs smashed into her hair and an extension cord digging into her back. But...she had work due tomorrow, and if she went to bed she would never get it done in time, not since Dr. Minieri had forwarded her an additional thousand pages of financials attached to a one-line email: *Knock yourself out.*

A thou-san-d pages. She'd analyzed about a hundred.

Her real, actual bed called out to her.

Pick me! Pick me!

That was where she wanted to go, and badly. But the idea of getting the energy to power through nine hundred pages of financials was… dreamy. To be done, email it over, go to bed, and wake up without it hanging over her head.

Wouldn't that be wonderful?

"It's literally better than the best night of sleep."

What the heck. They exchanged glances. Miles hit DOWN, which would take them to the main Fun Floor, where concierges would direct them to the VR arena. The elevator opened. They stepped in.

"I hope I don't regret this."

"You heard the ad man," he drawled. "Better than speed, I swear." Well, Kayla wouldn't know. But he mimicked his friend so perfectly that Kayla had to giggle.

The elevator opened onto a series of desks. Even at this late hour, a few concierges tapped purposefully into iPads, all of them bright-eyed and well-rested.

"Hello, Ms. Masouvi. Mr. Ballard. What can we do for you?" A tall, vaguely Hispanic-looking man with a charming accent, dazzling white teeth, and a nameplate reading SACHIN glided over to her. The security system had identified them during the elevator ride. A few flicks and he'd have the details of their dinner.

Kayla glanced at Miles, who shrugged and grinned. "We've heard about the VR Arena."

Sachin flashed a grin right back at him. "Yes. The virtual reality. An amazing new product. We're one of the first in the world to have it."

More marketing. Kayla yawned.

Sachin extended a hand. "Please. Follow me."

Into a different, hidden elevator, with no buttons. Up. The door opened to a long hall lit with running green and blue lights that would look perfect as the entrance to Space Mountain at

Disney World. So cheesy, Kayla almost rolled her eyes. A right turn. At her feet, tracking lights blinked and directed them. The walls had dark gray paneling and nothing more. At the end, one lone door, ringed in blurry white lightbulbs like the entrance to a carnival sideshow. Sachin slid his hand into a fingerprint reader and presented his eyeball for a retinal scan. It swooshed open.

"Enjoy," he chirped, disappearing behind the corner. Kayla stared after him for a second, too tired to put words or thoughts to this oddness. They stepped in. Another amenity concierge sat inside, perched on a tall chair in a small white room that held a bony-looking love seat and nothing else. Her name tag read, simply, Host. An aura of emptiness radiated from the room and oddly, from the woman. The walls somehow cancelled out all the machine noises of an office building. Total silence. Sensory deprivation. A sliding door behind her led somewhere, like a blind white eye.

"Welcome," she said. "Welcome to our newest amenity." She pressed a button on her iPad, and the door behind Kayla and Miles shivered closed. "Welcome to Resilusio."

CHAPTER NINE

A GREEN LIGHT pulsed. An electronic voice spoke.

"Ready."

The next door opened to reveal a cavernous space, five thousand square feet of all gray, punctuated by more blue and red lights, as quiet and solemn as a mausoleum. Tethered to the ceiling were the oddest contraptions: slick, formfitting bodysuits spiderwebbed entirely with twinkling luminescence. Electrical impulses fluttered through them, from the deflated top of a head, stopping at limp, empty wrists and ankles. Overlaid on the bodysuits were a helmet, goggles, and harness that encompassed the entire body, suspended over a floor that vibrated and hummed with movements that resembled an inhale and exhale. In the corner, away from the breathing floor, was a machine Kayla finally recognized: an omnidirectional treadmill and body gear, a rig used in some VR applications. But this creation was something far past that. A giant, sensing, touching, free-form VR gaming arena.

She gaped at the technology, the magic of it all.

"We're one of the first to have this." The Host echoed Sachin, beaming at the grunting, trembling behemoth with what seemed like genuine affection. "Resilusio. A brand-new virtual reality," she went on, "to open the door to a brand-new universe. The metaverse."

"What did you call it?" Kayla asked.

The Host paused and examined her. "The metaverse," she repeated.

"No, I know what that is...sort of. I meant more...you had a name for it."

"Oh yes. This is Resilusio," she repeated, complete with the starry eyes of a newly minted cult recruit. "From the Latin. The 'real illusion.'" She swept her hand out again, the Vanna White of apocalyptic technology. "One might call these 'VR rigs,' like that old junker in the corner, but they are much more than that. They immerse you in a true reality. No pixels, no block people. The Resilusio experience is as real as this world here. Now."

"How do you—" Kayla began.

The Host interrupted her. "You know that movie *The Matrix*?"

Kayla paused. "Uh, of course."

"Well, the Matrix is here, Kayla. Minus the giant machines that harvest humans." She giggled at her own joke.

Kayla stepped forward and ran her fingers over one of the complex, shimmering suits, examining the thick electrical cord snaking to the ceiling. Though it did not move (or did it?), she had a vivid vision of it leaping at her, calling to her, wrapping her body in its embrace. She recoiled, just a little.

Wait. *What?* A trick of the eye, that was all. Except now the suit did something else. It sighed, like an annoyed parent, patiently waiting for her to get with the program and strap in.

Or did it?

It's not alive. It's just metal. Plastic. Electricity. Wires.

A machine.

"That's not your imagination." The Host laughed. "It's alive."

"Well…not really," she amended a second later, in response to Kayla's alarmed stare. "It's still a machine. Metal and electronics, but the forefront of AI. It waits in eager anticipation. To share this world with you and give you both"—she exhaled theatrically—"the most amazing experience." She ran her hand over the rippling, mercurial fabric, which would envelop Kayla's entire body like some crazy S&M fever dream. It puckered to meet her, just a little.

Yes. Exactly. This was a machine. And a machine cannot be alive, no matter what this kook parroted.

"Would you like to try it?" the Host asked.

"Does it hurt?"

"You'll love it," she whispered. "It's not a game—at least, not like you'd expect. Nothing that tiresome. It will wake you up, rejuvenate you, bring you back to life, because it gets you. It will give you what you need, whatever that is."

Sounded like a crazy new drug. Or maybe an even crazier cult. *But it's not,* she reminded herself. *It's just a rec room activity at my sick grind of a job. Another "perk." Another way to keep us all here all the time.*

It's harmless.

She caught sight of herself in the mirror. There were mirrors everywhere in this room. How had she not noticed that? Her face had lines. A pasty pallor coated her skin from a prolonged lack of sunlight and fresh air. A rash had sprouted on her neck. The reflection in this mirror was tired, weary, *old.* Old! She wasn't even thirty, and here she was, the face of a woman who might easily be a decade older. She needed a pep. A lift. She had a night's worth of work to do. If this contraption woke her up enough to finish by the morning, well, bring it on.

Behind her, Miles appeared, his face a mirror to her own wonder, gaping at the madness, his eyes extra glassy in the cold blue light. "Well, if it matters, I'll be there the entire time," he piped up. "We'll be together."

Kayla thought for a moment. "Let's go," she said. "I'll try anything once."

"Splendid." The Host's eyes came alive with a vaguely creepy energy as she disappeared into the walls via a door so silent and secret she might as well have dissolved into thin air. She returned with two bodysuits made of a shiny, synthetic material that whispered light beams, shot through with a gossamer metallic fabric and punctuated by tiny pinpoints of green…somethings. Lights? Sequins?

She handed one to Kayla, who fingered the iridescence, catching it in the limited light. "Motion detection," she intoned solemnly. "Lockers on the right."

Kayla kept her eyes down in the changing room. She didn't want to see herself. She came out to see Miles looking like he was ready for a *Muscle & Fitness* photo shoot.

He ran an appreciative but respectful eye over Kayla. "It suits you."

Kayla shook her head. She still sucked at taking compliments. "I look like I belong in a bad eighties music video."

"Ha. Funny you should mention the eighties." The Host spoke from behind her, making Kayla jump and turn. She'd been standing there, silent, the whole time, like an AI-generated apparition.

The Host's eyes got dreamy for a moment. "Did you ever feel you were born in the wrong decade?"

Kayla stared at her. "Well, yeah, actually."

She nodded seriously. "Resilusio understands."

Before Kayla could ask what the hell she was talking about, the Host disappeared and an assistant materialized, clutching a handful of sticky sensors, like the kind doctors use for EKG or EEG procedures. One by one, she peeled the adhesive backing and stuck them to their bare skin, the back of their hands, the tops of their feet. An especially tiny row stuck to each finger. "Haptics," she explained. Beyond wacky.

"Will these come off?" Kayla asked, pulling ineffectually at one. The adhesive vacuum-suctioned to her body like a tiny plastic leech.

"They release automatically." The assistant pulled gloves over Kayla's hands and booties over her feet.

"Nifty," she muttered.

It took a full fifteen minutes to strap, slide, adjust, and tighten Kayla and Miles into the smooth snakeskin of the bodysuit. The assistant slid the helmet and goggles over their eyes and hooked them to the ceiling.

"You can't fall," her disembodied voice advised. "Don't worry. And you can't die, at least not for real."

"That's nice to know."

"Get ready."

An image materialized before her eyes. A chemical spill, dark liquid, oozing at first, then blossoming into a Rorschach test. Then, a bright light. It melted away to leave a blank space with a menu hovering at eye level.

"Welcome, Kayla Masouvi and Miles Ballard," a warm female

voice intoned. "For your first visit, Resilusio has created a special experience for you. Would you like to join?"

To her left, Miles materialized, wearing his clothes from earlier. Clothes that were currently hanging in a locker. She was the same. For a moment, they both just stared. Then they exchanged glances. Shrugged. Nodded.

Miles replied first. "Sure." A second later, the menus zoomed open. An invisible hand scrolled quickly, like a computer program run amok.

The Host's voice spoke directly in Kayla's ear now. "Should you need to leave the world for any reason, say 'exit.' The program will take you to the welcome screen. And Resilusio connects to the outside world. If an emergency arises, it will notify you."

"So you're saying this is safe and that I can trust you." Miles scanned the empty darkness. "That we can trust you." He met Kayla's eyes, and something in them made her pause. Maybe this was a bad idea…

"Absolutely." The woman's voice held a chilly smile. "You're in good hands."

CHAPTER TEN

FROM A PITCH-BLACK darkness, saturated almost to blue, they materialized in the middle of a…mosh pit? A mosh pit at a… concert? Klieg lights. A stage. A *crowd*. The sun had gone down… twenty minutes ago. She frowned, because that information was in her head, as clear as day. How?

Miles stared at their surroundings with his own wide eyes. "What is this? Where are we?"

She shook her head and looked down at her body. Ran her fingers over a black-and-white cropped top. Long sleeves. Striped. She gaped at the authentic feel of the fabric. Dug under. Skin. "What the fuck," she whispered.

Her legs. What about her legs? Skin, fabric. Real. *Real*. Acid-washed cutoffs, one rip patched with the same fabric as her top. Her mind rippled. She had made them herself, from an old pair of jeans, accessorized with a black faux-leather belt that sported a giant buckle. Further down she examined two layers of neon-green socks, scrunched white boots with pointy toes. She stuck her foot out, examining. Admiring.

Miles stared at…her hair. "Do you want to see it?" He gestured. And…Miles…His hair was now dark brown with some of the most aggressively frosted tips this side of a costume party, short and spiked on one side, long and floppy on the other. He wore a black porkpie hat, a white shirt with an oversized collar, reaaalllly tight black pants, and a blazer with rolled-up sleeves. Jelly bracelets hung up and down his arms in a jumble of neon colors. One lone earring, some kind of baroque-inspired silver, hung in his ear, and around his neck, a matching…

Kayla leaned forward. "Is that a…? What do you call them?" She wasn't 100 percent sure of the terminology. Two leather strings with a pasty turquoise brooch holding them together.

He looked down and fingered the item. "Ah, a bolo tie," he said. "I grew up in the Southwest. Well, Utah. Close enough. I know my bolo ties."

"You did?" They had never discussed their families. Where they were from. Not that she wanted to. Too painful. Maybe that was why. Before she could ponder this, though, he rummaged in his pocket and held out a folding mirror framed in a plastic purple.

He stared at the accessory. "I knew that was in there," he said, with shock. "I knew there was a mirror in my pocket." He flipped it open and handed it to her, still dazed.

By now she had detected the distinct eighties vibe, and the view in the mirror, of her hair, sealed it. Big, bottle-blond, curly to the moon, and enough hair spray to punch a hole in the ozone. And, no kidding, in one ear, an earring that read BOY, and the other, she turned her head—though she didn't need to—TOY. "Omigod," she breathed and tore her eyes from the compact. "What on earth is this?"

Miles dug into his pocket again and came out with a travel-sized hair gel and a tiny metal aerosol labeled Binaca. He held it out, confused. Something occurred to Kayla.

"It's a breath spray."

He turned it over in his hands. “Come again?”

She took it from him, uncapped the bottle, and sprayed some peppermint nastiness right in her mouth. “See?” She inhaled. “Fresh breath.” She handed it back and busied herself examining her face in the compact again, bringing it closer, farther, touching her skin, her hair. It all felt real and correct, like it was her actual head and face. She tugged on an earring…*Ouch.* That. Was. Her. Actual. Ear. “Wow.” Not much else to say.

“This is a virtual reality video game?” Miles said. “Where are we?”

They were in the front row. Of a concert. A time-warped 80s concert. She took a full turn around. People everywhere, screaming, all in their late teens, early twenties. Several Pat Benatar clones, men and women dressed like Robert Smith from The Cure, and many, many Madonnas. Bleachers rising for many levels. A stadium. The night sky darkened, and again, she remembered, the sun had just gone down. A blink later, lighters filled the stadium, a million little fireflies bobbing and weaving in the warm, heady California air.

California air. *Oh God,* that had just sort of…leapt into her brain.

“No place has air like Southern California, right?” Miles took a deep breath. She whirled.

“What did you say?”

He circled his finger around the space. “That desert oasis thing. And the night. Nothing matches the night. Those LA nights.” And then he looked confused. “How…?”

Kayla stared, again. Too many questions. A sound machine boomed, the noise of a cannon firing, extra loud because they were so close to the front. "Resilusio," she yelled, her voice dissolving into the roar of the crowd, "give me a hint."

Miles gestured at the stage. Banners unfurled. Two giant letters.

DM

"That's your hint." He had—somehow—heard her over the roar. Then he frowned. "I think."

Kayla's breath came in hard and fast. "No." She turned to Miles. "It's not."

Confusion scribbled over his face. "It's not what?"

On June 18, 1988, Depeche Mode played perhaps their most famous gig of all time: the 101st and final concert of their *Music for the Masses* Tour at the Rose Bowl in Pasadena, California. Two documentary filmmakers followed the band on the entire trip, sharing a bus with eight teenage Depeche Mode mega fans who won their seats in a nightclub giveaway. Kayla had listened to the album of the "101 concert" so many times, she could recite every breath in the lead singer Dave Gahan's vocals and every roar of the crowd, and had watched the documentary *Depeche Mode: 101* at least 101 times. She always thought of it as a love letter to a time that seemed easier, kinder, and...cooler. She was born well after the concert, well after Depeche Mode's heyday. So it wasn't nostalgia, exactly. Just longing. Which was different, and sometimes not as bad, and sometimes the same and sometimes worse, and sometimes unbearable. She had learned to bury these kinds of overwhelming feelings, because otherwise they might consume her. But she always believed exactly what the Host had said earlier: that she had been born in the wrong era. And here she was, in the right place, at the right time, for once. Somehow.

Maybe for the first time in her life.

And the first row! Pressed up against hordes of sweaty, real

(?) people. The band launched into one of her favorite songs, "Behind the Wheel." She took a deep breath and decided to *go with the flow.* She giggled at her own eighties-perfect turn of phrase. Next she'd be calling everything "rad." Depeche Mode's lead singer, Dave Gahan, old as the hills (to Kayla) in the real world but young and vital in this fake reality, appeared, all leather and white jeans and billowing shirts and soulful moody magnetism that brought the electronic music to life. Lights flashed like a Morse code, right behind her. And oh, Resilusio had all the scents of a real concert. Spilled beer, sticky soft-drink sweetness, smoke, the desert air, and the guy next to her, slam-dancing in a soaked tank top.

He smelled.

IRL, she was in a space suit, on her office amenity floor. She took another deep breath and regretted it. He smelled…accurate, here in the front-row mosh pit, standing room only, and no one ahead of them but burly, bored security. Each band member was perfectly, historically accurate. Gahan, owning the stage with his moody charisma. Martin Gore playing the keyboard, the guitar, the kazoo. Alan Wilder, who left the band in 1995. And Andy Fletcher, dead in the here and now. She sang along to every single song.

And when Gahan threw his shirt into the audience…

She caught it!

She and Miles danced and jumped and twirled and sang "Everything Counts" with sixty-five thousand other fans, and the experience was exactly as Kayla imagined actually being there would be. Something spiritual. A commune with humanity, but only the good ones. A reason to live, almost.

After the sing-along ended, Miles slipped his hand in hers

and held it for a few seconds, seconds that felt good, that felt like an eternity of good, the way it does when you actually are seventeen and every new experience is destined to burn a spot into your consciousness until the end of your life and every romance, real or imagined, is like a clap of thunder to your heart. It was beyond odd to have that feeling again. He leaned in and said something to her. Garbled. He had to repeat it.

"Having fun?"

"Whatever this is, it's amazing." Kayla decided not to think too hard about anything in real life right now. "You?"

"It's pretty ridiculous." He squeezed and finally let go, which made Kayla sort of sad and sort of relieved and sort of disappointed and all sorts of *sort of.* Ah, seventeen. Miles seemed to read her mind. "For once, the hype was real."

"It's a dream." She sighed and looked around, and in that moment, the world around her rippled. The colors seemed to *#ref* out, like someone hit the wrong key on a computer. The magic dimmed for a moment, then sprang back to life.

"What's happening?" She turned to Miles.

Miles seemed to think. "They're doing a special encore, for you."

"Improvising?"

"I think so. That's..." He looked alarmed for a moment. "Ah...a...thought that I had?" He said it as a question, and Kayla understood. This program got into your head somehow.

He furrowed his brow. "Wait for it," he whispered. Then he looked alarmed. "I don't know why I said that."

But before she could formulate a thought about this weirdness, the opening chords of the next song blazed across the Rose Bowl. Kayla froze.

Miles said nothing for a minute. He held her eyes, and she read in them that he had given himself over to this experience, just as she had, and a tiny stab of wanting pricked her. Desire. And then, God, the seventeen-year-old's version of it, which was pretty amazing, and definitely more than a prickle. But, fortunately, Miles looked ridiculous, and—she touched her hair—she looked ridiculous and then the band launched into a song that was not on the set list for the 101 concert. A song that the band had not yet recorded. A song that first appeared on *Violator*, an album released on March 19, 1990, a year and a half from "now."

And yet...here it was, in pretend, make-believe 1988, Kayla's all-time favorite song from her all-time favorite band. Like crazy magic, the opening notes of "Waiting for the Night" wafted through the desert air. A dark song, which fit. The last couple of years, Kayla's outlook on life had profoundly darkened, even though she covered it up. "Waiting for the Night." She got it. Always got it. Even before her mom, before her dad. Before this job. Waiting for the opportunity to hide from the world, from reality, from responsibility, from pain, and even from pleasure. She closed her eyes and fell into the music. When she opened them, Miles had those Windex eyes riveted on her.

He stepped closer, so tentative, so tiny. The revelers jostling inside the mosh pit fell away, and they had their own little magical space. For a second, a brief second, she leaned into it.

And then she stopped. Sameer flashed in her mind. His face, his hands, his eyes. And she wished for him. Sameer, hollering and dancing here, though he never really liked Depeche Mode, he never really hollered, and he wasn't one to dance at concerts or anywhere else.

For a brief second, she allowed herself to miss him. Miss

everything about him. Everything, all at once. “I’m sorry.” She shook her head and stepped back. “I should go.”

“No. I’ll go,” he said. “This concert is for you.”

God, he understood. “I’ll see you,” she managed.

“Be careful.” His eyes bore into hers. “Promise.”

Careful about what? She squeezed his hand anyway. “I will.”

“Resilusio,” he said to the summer air. The world rippled. “Exit.”

CHAPTER ELEVEN

KAYLA WOULD REMEMBER only snapshots of what happened next: that soon after, she exited Resilusio, returned to her desk and powered through her work. In another flash, she stood up from her computer—completely done. Now she was pretty confident that a significant cost cut to the bacterial production—20 percent, or even 10 percent—was impossible. Facts were facts. It was not like she controlled the price of acrylic polymers and precision thermometers. She prepped an email to Monahan and fired it off. The next moment, or so it seemed, she woke in her apartment, rain pinging her windows and a message pinging her phone. Miles.

Are you okay? That game messed me up.

That brought a memory of the concert, a hazy image without the sharp pinprick moments of a real memory. "Real" was now a shaky concept. The events blurred into a dreamlike jumble, an imagining of something that never happened. A visualization. Examined too close it dissolved like smoke in air, producing a knot of unease in the pit of her stomach, a *not right* that pressed against her spine from the inside out. Maybe her puny human brain couldn't cope with, or simply didn't like, the complex swirl of electronics. And then came the guilt. She had gone to the concert of a lifetime with Miles. Not Sameer, the love of her life.

Miles. And though Sameer was no longer her boyfriend, it felt wrong. Like cheating. But it wasn't. So that was confusing. She shrugged and decided that yes, it happened. It really happened. But it didn't need to happen again. She texted Miles:

Never again.

Then she made a black eye and chugged it with a grimace.

On the elevator ride to her office, her eyes fixated on the button to the Fun Floor. Her finger even hovered over it.

Resilusio.

An unpleasant, unfamiliar longing washed over her. She pushed it aside. The Resilusio experience was just entertainment. Short-term medicine for her overworked, strung-out brain. But all day, even as she typed presentations and pored over spreadsheets, Resilusio danced in the corners of her consciousness, cold electronic tentacles calling her back to that living, breathing machine.

She yawned. Frowned. Narrowed her eyes as an email from Monahan pinged. A reply to her note with the cost cuts. One line. Two words.

Keep looking.

Here he was, reinforcing Dr. Minieri's warning that she needed to find her cuts, or else.

Should she believe Dr. Minieri?

What happened to Olivia?

Either way, she had to review her work. And so she gritted her teeth. Focused.

And came up empty.

By six P.M., she was running on fumes. And everywhere her mind traveled, she found only despair. Hopeless situations. A felon father. A (joke of a) personal life. Her job, which was going to send her to either (a) unemployment or (b) an early grave, long before she snagged the brass ring of the poker bankroll in *three years*. Might as well be three hundred years. By then, the stress would turn her brain into mashed potatoes.

At midnight she took a good, hard look around her. Empty cubicles. A pitiful sleeping bag under her desk, lousy with crumbs and lint and food wrappers. A computer keyboard with numerous stuck keys, because she ate every damn meal typing. Monahan's tightly shut door. And, of course, the motion sensor lights. All off.

Because no one is here but me.

She checked her phone. Nothing from Miles. Even he had gone home. If she hadn't felt sorry for herself yet…well, she did now. Her hands sported crusty pale skin. She did not dare look in the mirror to see her face. Talk about Halloween.

I can't sit in this fucking Aeron chair a moment longer.

For real. That was no exaggeration. She sprang upward like the damn thing was on fire, ran to the elevator.

Maybe I'll just catch that 12:30 A.M. spin class instead of visiting the Matrix.

Oh, definitely. And England would crown her queen tomorrow.

When she got to the concierge floor, the lineup had changed. Only one person sat behind the desk. The woman with the name tag HOST. Somehow the air was…greener. The lights were dimmer. More ghostly. Or maybe her brain was just incapable of proper functioning.

"Welcome." The Host stood up, fully awake and perky. "It's lovely to see you again. Did your last Resilusio experience rejuvenate you?"

"Yes." This was not a lie but also not the truth. "It did."

She exhaled and nodded with satisfaction. "Come in. Let's get you rigged in and chilled out."

Kayla smiled weakly and followed down the elevator and into the arena, which was not, this time, empty. Another user floated nearby. A man in a pantomime of wandering, hands splayed ahead like a blind squirrel up a tree. He gave off such an air of desperation, hunger…panic even, that she gasped and stared, mesmerized. He was searching for something. What?

Come to think of it, what exactly were the boundaries in Resilusio? Maybe none, an idea that unnerved her so completely and efficiently that she nearly turned tail and ran out of there, chewed sleeping pills, and crawled under her desk.

But the Host popped in front, blocking her view of the desperate man.

"Swimming in the ocean." She nodded at him. "Somewhere in the Caribbean, maybe."

"Must be some ocean," Kayla muttered.

The Host, alone this time, hustled to strap her in, her deft hands moving fast. In under five minutes, Kayla was ready to go. An ink spill blossomed before her eyes.

"Enjoy," the Host whispered. The word was not blandly solicitous. It sent a shiver convulsing over her shoulders.

It was, in a word, sinister.

CHAPTER TWELVE

NO MATTER. SHE was an astronaut again, hovering over the earth.

"Where to?" trilled the Host.

She thought for a second and then blurted out the place that was possibly her favorite city. A city that reminded her of her father, of better times. Before Kayvan Masouvi went away, before the Feds seized all their assets, one of their father-daughter hobbies—after poker, that is—was collecting Art Nouveau, Impressionist, and Post-Impressionist art. They had owned some Toulouse-Lautrec pieces. Some dreamy Muchas. One precious, perfect sketch by Gauguin. All collected on father-daughter trips to…"Paris," she replied.

"Day or night?"

"Night."

A whoosh and a drop and she was hovering over the city, the Eiffel Tower soaring ahead and the lights twinkling in picturesque, travel-website unison, pretty little blues and whites and reds. As requested, it was evening. A clear, cloudless, bright-dark summer sky with a blue-cheese moon. But this time, the Resilusio brain didn't automatically plop her down in the middle of a story.

It waited.

For what? The metaverse was behaving differently this time.

She wasn't sure why, but she was glad, because she was not in the mood for a time-warped Depeche Mode concert. She needed to unwind, but not like that.

Well, not exactly like that. "Take me to the hottest nightclub in Paris." Maybe she said it out loud, but her mouth was not open. No vocal cords vibrating. And yet Resilusio obliged. She zoomed past the pretty lights and the pretty trees and the pretty shops and the pyramid of the Louvre, all the beauty of the storied city, and hurled through to a business district, not beautiful anymore. Office parks spread out below her, short squat buildings and skyscrapers and empty parking lots and bland, tight, depressing landscaping. Next came grit—factories and smokestacks and inner-city tenements with poor lighting. Drug dealers on corners, prostitutes, garbage everywhere, and clothes lashed across fire escapes. She landed on cracked concrete like Superman. This time, with no Depeche Mode to distract her, she examined her body more closely. And the accuracy terrified and stunned her: the scar on her right thumb from when she slammed it in a car door at seven, the ill-advised tattoo on her hip, all the moles and freckles, even her currently chipped nail polish. She stared at her hands, mesmerized, horrified, marveling at how perfectly it was all her and yet not her. *IRL*, of course, her hands sat inside gloves, with electrodes and sensors worming out.

But not here.

"The real you." A voice laughed to her left. Kayla whirled. The Host. Kayla reached out a hand. The Host met it with her own, and her fingers closed around Kayla's, soft and implacable. The woman nodded. "Now you'll surely understand our motto."

"Which is?"

"Believe your eyes." She laughed. "And you'll see it fits. This

world is you. As good or as bad as you wish, yet always you. You don't have to be anyone"—her body darkened, fading until she was wisps of smoke and a flickering movie reel—"but you."

Kayla turned her attention to the world. A street with almost every building darkened, shuttered, abandoned. All but one warehouse, directly ahead, which pulsed with flashing green lights, cavernous echoes and industrial music. Not exactly Kayla's style, but she'd given Ms. Resilusio rather vague directions.

A bouncer stood in front, legs spread. He was a large man, dressed as a biker, leather vest, jackboots, frightening tattoos, tree trunk arms. He nodded at her. "Your table is in the back, stocked with the usual."

Kayla didn't miss a beat. "Thank you." Tonight, at this club, she had VIP status.

"Enjoy your night, madame." The bouncer heaved open a massive battered door. Industrial music poured out—deep, body-shaking thumps, the occasional screechy hiss, zoned-out vocals. Smoke hung in the air like a bad omen, frozen in the strobe lights that flashed with shattered-glass bits of color.

She stepped in.

The smell, as before, was marvelously authentic. Heady, animal, and mildly dangerous. Rust and iron. Spilled booze and sweat. The patrons of this establishment dressed like they teleported from a goth convention. Sharpie lipstick and Wite-Out nail polish and glue-stiff hair spiked high and immobile. Slick skin and dominatrix heels. The clank of metal and chains. Clothes styled like leftovers from a bear attack, with mottled fur that resembled roadkill. A woman bumped into her, splashing a few glugs of her drink. She mouthed *Sorry*, then examined Kayla's outfit and…laughed. Actually pointed at her and laughed.

Kayla wore—what else?—her ratty after-hours sweats. Marvelously authentic, indeed. Time to fix that. "Resilusio, I need to look the part," she said.

Her bottom half morphed into Doc Martens and ripped fishnets. Cheap lipstick, chemical and waxy, coated her mouth. Something crusted over her eyes. Too much eyeliner, probably. Metal clanged on her torso, cold and unyielding. She caught sight of herself in a huge, dirty mirror. A ripped Kiss concert tank with a chain mail vest draped over it. A leather skirt, pleated and metallic, heavy but—she moved her hips—swishy. Now, in full costume, she stood on the edge of the dance floor. The endless space yawned on and on, writhing and pulsating with people and their moshing clangs like a giant chained monster. She stepped in, tentative at first, and then with more confidence. Freed from her normal inhibitions in a real nightclub, she completely cut loose, dancing wild and crazy. She was not much of a dancer, but that was the beauty of this place, of this world, and the appeal was hard to miss. It didn't matter. It was *her* world. She was herself, only herself, and yet completely anonymous. Dancing like a punk rock maniac. Dressing like one, too. No judgment.

A man grabbed her and swung her around, grinding into her. Normally, she would never let this happen—a strange man pressed against her, touching her, panting on her neck. But here it was, of course, completely safe. The basic premise of Resilusio was inarguable. Freedom. Fantasies. No filter. From deep in her gut erupted a desire to drink it all up, a craving for more. All her boundaries flung to the wind. The pleasure was a palpable thing, a warm buzz radiating out. Fingers, toes, head. Everywhere.

She wandered over to the bar, ordered shots of vodka, downed them, and raced back to the dance floor. But she moved too fast.

A passing, metal-spiked shoulder drew blood from her hand. And, as before, it *hurt*.

"Ow." She said it out loud, startled. She had to remind herself that Resilusio inflicted pain.

"If you need a bigger pain tolerance, Resilusio can help with that," came a husky voice. A laugh like burnt sugar filled her ear. "Then again, some people like when it hurts."

Kayla turned. A shadow moved into the light, revealing a woman. Tall, punk pretty, dark hair sticking up everywhere, dyed on the ends, a pastel color that glowed in the lights. Leather pants, animal-clawed T-shirt, and no bra. She gazed at Kayla with analytical intensity, clashing with the fantasy-come-to-life setting. Kayla looked away quickly, embarrassed.

The music rattled her eardrums. She winced. God, was she now too old for loud music? Depressing. In the meantime, the girl came closer, leaning in, gifting Kayla with a dark musk, her lips to Kayla's ear. "I'm glad you picked this place, Kayla. We can talk here." She searched Kayla's face with reptilian-pale eyes—Kayla could not have named the color if her life depended on it—that morphed to a glassy black as she scanned the room, scrutinizing anyone glancing their way. "For the moment, at least."

It was a strange feeling, to not fear the unknown, because it wasn't real. To be just…curious. How did this woman know her name? Why was she so…paranoid? Was this part of the fun?

Part of the game?

Two men grinded against each other to Kayla's left, building their union to a crescendo that culminated in nearly knocking the girls to the ground. Her friend scurried away just in time, pulling Kayla closer. To safety. To their faces being so close they were almost touching.

This girl smelled good. Like she'd found the perfect perfume, made just for her. "Who are you?" Kayla asked, not moving.

An avatar? Is that even allowed? Is she a she, *even? Is this Milo from finance? Jennifer from the mail room? Or is everyone always their real self here?*

Who the hell knows?

She shrugged and laughed to herself. When she lifted her eyes to the girl's, a frown had deepened there.

"You need to focus, Kayla."

"How do you know my name?"

"That's not important. We don't have much time." Her breath tickled Kayla's cheek. "Promise me that as soon as we're done talking, you'll end your session. You'll get out of here."

"I'm not 'here,'" she said, stupidly. "I'm in a *rec center*. In an office building."

"Very funny. As soon as we're done, take your helmet off. End it."

"Why? None of this is real."

"Please. Trust me." Her eyes widened, the pale orbs capturing and reflecting the most mesmerizing kaleidoscopes as footsteps approached.

Kayla stepped back. "No. Really. How do you know who I am?" An odd, unexpected shiver coursed through her. The room rippled, bodies melting into thin, yielding flesh and hard, gleaming metal. Blood, nails, spikes, broken glass, moans, writhing—

"Listen to me, Kayla. I have a minute, maybe. That's it." She leaned in again, her cheek touching Kayla's. It sent more shivers through her, different ones though.

She repressed them.

"Your boss will ask you to cross lines. They will be minor—at first. Don't fall for it. That's how he traps. You'll never get out, and when the time comes, he will dispose of you, throw you away like...garbage."

"Who the hell are you?" Kayla fixed her eyes on the girl, lingering on each word. "Why are you here?"

"I told you," she replied. "To warn you."

Kayla considered this and found it unconvincing. "Rick hasn't asked me to do anything wrong. If he did, I don't need your help to do the right thing."

The girl ignored Kayla's words. "I was hoping you wouldn't be here. So soon. So fucking soon," she muttered and pressed her fingers to her lips, thinking. "The protocol is six months of baseline."

"What protocol? What are you talking about?"

A bouncer opened the massive front door. A crowd stomped in. "I have to go," she said abruptly. "Share nothing with anyone. When the time is right, I'll find you. In the real world."

Was this still a game? Harmless fun? "And how will I know you? When the, uh, *time is right*?"

She glanced at the door and then at Kayla. "Easy. I'll know things about you that you've never told anyone."

Kayla backed up. "What the—"

"There's a way out for you," she interrupted. "I promise. But never come into Resilusio again. I can't protect you after tonight. No Depeche Mode concerts, no nothing."

Kayla opened her mouth to speak, but the door opened

again, distracting the girl. She scanned the new patrons. Her back stiffened. A moment later she fled, melting into mohawks and white talc faces and the jeer of metal and a thousand body piercings, stomping boots, and scraping heels. The crowd closed in on her like so many doors. One bump and grind later, she disappeared.

CHAPTER THIRTEEN

OLIVIA.

Olivia Olivia Olivia OLIVIA.

Kayla woke the next day with one word in her head. No explanation necessary. She must find her predecessor. Like yesterday. But she refused to search for Olivia at work. So, of course, the day dragged. She finally met with Monahan, who now tasked her with selling twelve enormous data centers "quietly" and asked her for an update on the cost cuts. Awesome. What did a garbage company need with a Google-gaggle of data centers? GR hauled garbage. It wasn't, ah, Google.

Olivia, Olivia...did you have to sell secret data centers too?

Finally the day ended. She rode the elevator to her apartment, got into her sweats, ordered sushi, then hauled herself to her "home office": her personal laptop and bed. She slapped on a VPN, cleared cookies, bought new antivirus software, and got to work.

And nearly choked to death on her spicy tuna roll.

Olivia Justine Chen, the predecessor she hadn't known existed, had disappeared without a trace:

NO CLUES IN CASE OF GARBAGE EXECUTIVE

OLIVIA CHEN: VANISHED BUT NOT FORGOTTEN

Kayla searched hungrily for pictures and found a girl with

bright eyes and a cheerful smile. Tasteful jewelry. Thick shiny hair. A face that telegraphed nice, reliable, hardworking, sweet. The police found untouched bank accounts, no evidence of drug use or gambling debts. No boyfriend, no love child, no sordid affairs, her car parked at JFK airport's long-term lot. But most chilling of all was the information in the final article:

MYSTERIOUS DISAPPEARANCE OF WEST VILLAGE RESIDENT

Olivia didn't live in GR housing. That really didn't make sense, for both work and sleep maximization. Monahan would have arranged a place for her, for sure. For some reason, she must have declined.

"Olivia would never leave us. Never in a million years," her sister Francine sobbed in the *New York Post*. In the accompanying picture, Francine stood with assorted family members, all miserable and terrified, holding up signs:

#BRINGOLIVIAHOME

#OLIVIACHENMISSING

They stood in front of a computer repair store that seemed to be somewhere in NYC, or a city at least. Kayla squinted. *Byte* something.

The internet yielded nothing else on Olivia's whereabouts. She drummed her fingers on her arm. She had to figure this out. Soon a plan materialized. *Maybe good,* she thought. *Maybe bad.* She got dressed, slipped on a hoodie and sunglasses, disappeared into the subway, and reappeared in the Bronx, found an off-brand telecom store, and bought a burner phone and an old, creaky laptop. She did a few searches and came up with potential phone numbers for her next move, texting them one at a time. Number three worked. One conversation later, she disappeared into the subway again, this time with a destination.

Bark and Byte, Park Slope. *Groom your dog AND fix your computer!*

While u Wait!

She arrived and peered in. Two spaces, separated by a glass partition. Computer repair on the left, pups on the right. The dog side had a line. The computer side had no customers. A bored guy in a purple and yellow polo shirt perched behind a cluttered counter, fiddling with a phone.

Inside, she breathed the oddest combination of disinfectant, shampoo, wet dog, and the high, nose-zapping metal/plastic jumble of electronics. She approached the computer side, where the technician, with a name tag that read HERB, eyed her like a dog that might pee on his floor.

"Hi," Kayla ventured. "I need to get a quote on a repair."

He gestured for her to hand over the laptop, which was hilarious, since this was the oldest, most decrepit specimen Kayla could find. Herb the computer repair guy examined it, raised an eyebrow at her, and then closed it gently.

"Well?" she asked. "Do you think you can help?"

After all the time in the world, he nodded. "Come with me."

He led her through a sterile white and blue corridor. On the left, technicians bent over electronics. On the right, groomers clipped and shampooed dogs. They reached a tightly shut door at the back. OFFICE. Herb twisted a key in the lock and disappeared, shutting the door tightly behind him.

Inside she found an aging clutter of desks, chairs, tables, cabinets, and a closed door that might lead to a closet. It opened, and a woman stepped into the light. Kayla nearly let out a scream.

"Didn't mean to startle you," she whispered. "Can't be too careful." The woman matched her picture exactly: Olivia Chen's sister Francine. Petite and thin, with her thick straight hair pulled into a baseball cap. Her face had the tightness of permanent worry. She gave Kayla a weary nod. "I bet you know that by now."

Well, *now* she did. Her suspicions got confirmed right about...now.

"Um." Kayla put a hand to her head, willing her brain to *think*. She stepped back and took a deep breath. "Thank you for meeting me."

A brief nod. Francine sipped from a travel flask and gestured at a pot of weak tea sitting on a hot plate. "Want some?"

Kayla agreed to a glass, just to have something to hold. "Olivia didn't get fired," she said sickly.

"Is that the story now? No." Francine poured her some tea, gazing at Kayla steadily. "She disappeared. Without a trace. If I were you, I'd be worried for my life. Or at the very least, my sanity."

A cold ice cube of fear dropped to Kayla's chest. "What are you talking about?" The second time in twenty-four hours she'd asked a complete stranger this type of question.

Francine shook her head and closed her eyes, rubbing her temples. "Livvie might be alive. She could still be out there... somewhere. But what I have to face is that before she disappeared, she went crazy."

Kayla's eyes nearly bugged out of her head. "What?"

Francine pulled out a phone and showed her a video. Surveillance footage, shot from the corner of an exam room. Olivia, yelling and screaming and pulling out her beautiful thick hair. Not an expression. Actually *pulling it out.* In clumps. Kayla stared, unable to look away. Her face had deep scratches and—

she peered closer—an actual gaping tear in her cheek opened and closed like a second mouth. After a few minutes of mania, a white-coated doctor entered the room and gave her a shot of something. She collapsed onto two waiting orderlies, who led her away.

Francine watched Kayla closely as she put the phone down. "Soon after she recorded this, Olivia disappeared."

"How—" Kayla swallowed. "How did Olivia get to be like that?"

Francine threw her hands up wearily, tears in her eyes. "Livvie had no history of mental illness. Worked long hours, but that's normal at GR, from what I hear. No drugs. I can promise you that." She paused. "The best idea we have so far? She was spending a lot of time in a virtual reality world. Something on the perk floor called Resilusio."

Kayla's throat went dry. "Resilusio," she echoed.

Francine nodded and opened her phone again. Another video. Olivia, sane, or so it seemed, speaking into the camera. Messy hair, bloodshot eyes, pasty skin…telltale signs of sleep deprivation. Kayla noticed a queasy familiarity with her own life. "If you are watching this, please know I was not crazy before. No doctor has ever diagnosed me with mental illness. Resilusio made me crazy." Her eyes flashed wildly for a second, and her voice broke. "I swear to God. I cannot stop myself from going b-back. And it's making me insane."

Olivia started like a frightened deer as a loud noise, like a glass breaking, erupted somewhere off camera. She sighed heavily. "I want everyone to know, but most of all my family, that I am so sorry. For everything. For all the sorrow I've caused. I also want to beg anyone watching this to take action. Because someone needs to stop—" Abruptly, the video cut off.

Francine sat frozen for a moment, gazing at the black screen. "I'm glad our parents aren't alive to see this." She snapped out of it and glanced at her phone. "We can't stay here much longer, so I'll tell you everything I know. Olivia said that Monahan was cataloging people's garbage. Collecting details of literally everything they threw away."

Francine knelt down and rummaged through boxes, finally opening one. She shuddered, her mouth set in a grim line as she continued to search. "Then he funneled all that data into the VR game to create user profiles. To 'teach' the AI about the user. Train it. To get him or her obsessed. Addicted."

"So it's not just some new perk."

"No, Monahan came up with the idea. Had it developed. In secret." Francine stopped searching and straightened, fingering something. A flash key. It glimmered dully in the unforgiving office light. "This was Olivia's research. I don't even know what she went through to get it out. She said if anything happened to her, to give it to someone I trust completely. Someone not working for GR." Francine looked down, her face straining as if she was about to cry.

"You're breaking that rule," Kayla said gently. "But I think Olivia would understand."

"What's in here destroyed my sister." Francine thrust it at Kayla. "Maybe you can find some answers. Maybe you can get justice."

CHAPTER FOURTEEN

SHE ENDED UP using that decrepit laptop after all.

The flash key held a trove of documents. The first few were financial projections. Estimates. Years one to five. An unnamed, unidentified business that could be nothing other than Resilusio. That is: capital intensive, unprofitable, a business that gobbled cash flow to start…then produced dazzling revenue growth and criminally high profits. Next, a series of retail leases for major cities all over the world—New York, Chicago, San Francisco, Tokyo, Seoul, London, Paris, and more. She skimmed the files and counted at least fifty. They must be for Resilusio arenas—what else? Places for people to plug in and experience the world, which could not, clearly, be an in-home experience. At least not yet. Purchase orders followed, factory scheduling, all the steps one might need to produce rigs and arenas and get people in them. She dug further and found something else.

Something extraordinary.

A neatly written list of twenty-four words. A private key to a cryptocurrency wallet, otherwise known as a seed phrase, which allowed anyone to re-create the wallet from any computer, no other information required. Here was the promise and peril of cryptocurrency. Fully transportable. Fully fungible. Fully anonymous.

She opened a wallet app and re-created the wallet.

Inside were five hundred million shares of a crypto token. REALCoin. Web searches revealed minimal information save this nugget:

REALCoin is a non-fungible governance token built on the Ethereum blockchain.

REALCoin's business owns the source code and all development plans of the Resilusio metaverse.

One billion coins were in circulation, which meant that this wallet owned 50 percent of the business. Smart contracts governed the token. For example, a simple majority—51 percent—caused any resolutions to pass: ownership, sales, projects, anything. Any owner could submit a proposal. And with smart contracts, the "governor" was technology, with all voting done automatically, using the blockchain. She examined the trading profile. The current value of REAL was $0.000001 per token, the same as its debut. The tokens in this wallet were worth $500. Zero trading. Seemed to exist just to exist, at least for now. If she was craftier, braver—stupider?—she might transfer those tokens out to a new wallet, one controlled only by her. They might be important evidence. Depending on what, exactly, she'd just stumbled on, they might be necessary to keep her alive.

But...no. Stealing "shares," even anonymous crypto tokens, seemed queasily close to her father's crimes. Even if it was solely to safeguard her life, her actual sanity, whatever, she couldn't do it.

She transferred the documents to a storage service on the dark web, in a file accessible only with two-factor biometric identification. That was it. Done. Time to go home. Or "home."

Yes, that was it.

But it wasn't.

When something is wrong, your animal brain will sense it first. Pay attention. By the time your cerebral cortex weighs in, you're toast.

Her father's voice in her ear, as clear as if he were sitting at her shoulder. The man who had all the right moves, always. *Dad, I don't need my animal brain for this one.* The documents had a major problem. They were...basically paper. Electronic paper, but paper nonetheless. Paper had fatal flaws, what the oenophiles might call provenance. Anyone could forge them. And they came from an unnamed, unavailable source. Olivia? Someone else? She could not authenticate them. She had no proof of the data within. The author of these documents was anonymous. Who could prove they were real? They might be a planning exercise. A prank. Scam. Mistake. Of course, Kayla didn't believe that.

And yet.

Paper was worth the paper it was printed on.

She needed those tokens.

If they meant nothing, so be it. But that was unlikely. They meant something. This could easily be the funding conduit for Resilusio. Laundering money through a "corporate" structure on a crypto blockchain bypassed all US reporting requirements and laws to onshore the funds. It was an ingenious and elegant way to move money. Borderline untouchable. And maybe someday she could use that structure to tease out an immutable link tying Resilusio to GR, or even to Monahan, because the blockchain was forever. It was pseudonymous, not anonymous.

She transferred the tokens to a wallet she owned and created (which changed the seed phrase to something only she knew), then she smashed the flash key, erased and restarted the computer, pulled out the hard drive, paid a cabbie to run the whole thing over (twice), tossed the mangled chunks in a dumpster, and left. She did not sleep that night. Back in her apartment, she passed the hours staring at the ceiling, ignoring her phone and overflowing email and everything else. Should she go to work like nothing happened? Should she call the cops? Quit and disappear? So. Many. Options.

All terrible.

❧

The next day, she opened a safe-deposit box and left a piece of paper with the seed phrase to her new wallet inside. Her bank used a keyless hand-scan system, so she didn't have to worry about hiding a key. Then she went to work, barely noticing the beautiful fall weather, all crispy rustling leaves and thin, bright air, intense sun, and the mildest possible nip. Brimming with fearful energy, she fidgeted at her desk, red-eyed, with chills, a sore throat, a headache. Her body was rejecting this place. No surprise there. Monahan was out again today, probably supervising the illicit production, compilation, and analysis of piles of deeply personal, illegal, and invasive data on people across the globe, then scheming to get it into Resilusio. To manipulate users. Social media had pioneered the use of personal data, preferences, and user actions to target, influence, manipulate. But garbage data...exactly what you eat, drink, medicate...toothpaste, shoe size, shampoo...was so obviously powerful. It was breathtakingly specific and incredibly predictive.

A goldmine.

But. Enough. She had work to do. Namely, calling brokers to sell them some gently used data centers. She didn't have a plausible excuse not to, only the unshakable feeling something bad would come of it. That animal brain, again. She thought of her father, sighed and picked up the phone.

"Don't touch that dial," a very familiar voice called out from behind her.

She turned.

Sameer.

Somehow his sudden appearance didn't surprise her. She had dreamed it, held that inevitability somewhere inside. He would come for her.

"Sameer," she whispered. Her insides jumped.

He wrapped his arms around her and breathed her in, bringing with him a warm calm. But then, with a jolt, her thoughts turned dark, jumping to horrible, wildly implausible conclusions. Something terrible must have happened. Yes, something terrible.

No. She ignored those feelings. It was him. He was here. And only good things could happen now.

She pulled back and studied him. He was different. How? She searched his face. His eyes were brighter and well rested yet somehow older and wiser. His body was leaner.

"Why—why are you…?" She swallowed. "How did you come here?" She clung to him. He tightened his grip on her.

"How did you know…?" She bit back the last words…*that I needed you.*

He held her face in two hands and gazed at her. It was unmistakable. Her chest fluttered. He was, still, mad for her.

One of Monahan's two sour assistants frowned and glanced over at them. They had names, but Kayla always thought of them as Gargoyle One and Two. Gargoyle One narrowed her eyes at Sameer before typing furiously, which sent spiders scurrying over Kayla's spine. Sameer's back straightened, and he cleared his throat. Maybe he sensed the odd tension.

"Your father called me."

"My father?" She frowned. "He called you? Why?"

He paused, as if choosing his words carefully. "He's worried about you."

Kayla shrugged, conscious of the dangers of speaking here. She glanced around. Surely the walls had ears. Probably the desks, phones, bathrooms too. "They've been running me hard. Crazy hours."

He laughed and pointed under her desk, to the rolled-up sleeping bag and deflated pillow, accessorized with discarded food wrappers. "I gathered." He backed up, his hands not leaving her hips, pulling her toward him, his voice low. "Let's go to lunch. I want to talk to you." He cleared his throat. "It's important."

CHAPTER FIFTEEN

HER MIND RACED like a bird trapped in a room. Then she remembered her calm. The feeling of seeing him. She refused to imagine anything bad. And whatever it was, they weren't discussing it here. She jutted her chin at Monahan's scowling assistants. "Let me tell them."

As she approached, Gargoyle Two whispered into her headset, eyeing her for a moment before deciding to mute her call.

"Out to lunch," Kayla said, words that she never, ever, said before. "Call me if you need me." She left her phone at her desk. Her hands shook as she took it out and pretended to forget it. Sameer observed all and said nothing. On the street, she scanned, the paranoia rising in her chest, searching for anyone taking an unnatural interest in them. Eyes were on her, sure, but were they standard GR security, or something more sinister? A careful three-hundred-and-sixty-degree scrutiny of her surroundings revealed no spy candidates, at least in her amateur analysis. This calmed her down not at all.

"What's going on, K?" Sameer asked quietly. "You're definitely not yourself."

"Not here," she whispered. "Let's get away first."

He nodded and pulled out his phone to order a car.

"No." She said it too sharply.

Sameer humored her. "Let me hail a cab. Don't worry. I'll pay cash too."

At the taxi stand on Eleventh Avenue, the yellow vehicles lined up, waiting for passengers. She refused to take the first one and scurried into the third one before the drivers in the front cars honked in protest. Sameer slid in next to her, taking all the clumsy Jason Bourne moves in stride. As they waited for the taxi to pull away, she examined their surroundings again. But this was Manhattan. The view changed every eight seconds. To the left, a man dressed in a sharp suit, with a gleaming, oversized watch and a Louis Vuitton briefcase at his feet, tapped impatiently into his phone. Farther up, another man in a rumpled suit, a Timex-ish watch, with a battered briefcase at his feet, tapped impatiently into his phone. A street vendor sat on a fat red vat of kerosene, puffing on a cigarette. They briefly made eye contact before two tourists walked up to buy hot dogs. And on and on. Cold comfort. She shook her head and ducked her face. A trio of police cars, sirens blazing, sped down the avenue past them. The sound made her wince.

Sameer directed the driver. "The Carlyle," he said, glancing at her for confirmation. Excellent choice. They never went to the Carlyle, and it was far from GR headquarters. Touristy. Well, that was harsh. The Carlyle was a famous hotel, a glorious New York landmark with an equally famous bar, Bemelmans. Bemelmans had a compact early-twentieth-century interior design with banquettes pushed squarely against the walls. Kayla had seen enough spy movies. They needed compact, to preserve lines of sight, including the door. Especially the door. They needed small. They needed loud. It was perfect.

She opened her mouth to speak. Sameer squeezed her hand and lifted a finger to her lips. "When we get there."

They crawled in crosstown traffic, Kayla glancing out of the cab to check for a tail, a few times directing the driver down deserted side streets. Inside Bemelmans, men in Brioni and Gucci mingled with women in Chanel and Louboutins and sore-thumb tourists in the usual Gap and New Balance. Murals by the bar's namesake, Ludwig Bemelmans, covered the walls, all charmingly New York: whimsical scenes of Central Park, with balloon vendors, picnicking rabbits, ice-skating elephants. Usually very cute, but not today. Today they were jarring, watchful, sinister. Kayla and Sameer took a corner booth against the wall with a direct line to the exit. But if it came to that, truthfully, they were hamburger.

Nonetheless.

They sat and ordered. Stiff drinks, unusual choices for both of them. Martinis. Bemelmans had a reputation for excellent martinis, but still. Kayla did not drink during the day, because she was a lightweight, and Sameer didn't drink anything but five-hundred-dollar-and-up Bordeaux and White Burgundy and the occasional unicorn Napa Cab.

Nonetheless.

"Turn that off." She glanced at Sameer's phone like it might detonate a bomb. "Just in case." He blinked and complied.

The martinis arrived. Oddly, calmly, they sipped. "Okay now," he said, grimacing at the bite and sliding the glass away, "tell me."

And so she did. About Resilusio and the concert and the mind fuck of the entire experience, about Olivia Chen, her videos, her flash key, her insanity. About the tracked garbage, the profiling. Sameer had the most questions, unsurprisingly, about Resilusio. But as she described it, a pang of desire jabbed her. A need to go back. To that fake video-game world. An odd fluttering, full-body craving to haul herself into a cab—screw the evasive maneuvers—and plug herself in. She ignored the feeling and finished the story.

After all of it, Sameer took her left hand in both of his. "You don't owe this creep anything. Fuck your lost bet." He kissed her ring finger. "Come with me to London."

"I can't, Sameer. That won't solve this—" She pulled her hand away.

He held it tight and cut her off. "Listen to me. I've been in London all this time, with nothing but time. To think. About us. Come back with me, Kayla. Play poker. Do the Euro tournament circuit. Amsterdam, Ireland, France, Monte Carlo. I know the money's good. You can make it on your own. Fly back as often as you need. We'll pull every string. When your father gets out, he can join us in London. He'll be with us. Forever."

She stared at him. "What? How?"

He shook his head. "You're the woman I love. I want to support you. Be with you. No one else comes close." He squeezed her hand. "And never will."

Everything I wanted.

My dream come true.

And yet. The Mean Voice interrupted.

Sure. He'll fix all your problems. Since you can't fix them yourself.

You can't make it on your own, it sneered. *You failed.*

But the voice didn't sock her in the gut like it once did. Somehow. She searched for regret. For shame. Found nothing. Maybe this would be the push she needed to jump into a new, beautiful life. She missed Sameer. And oh, how she loved him. It radiated from her body.

That was enough.

Sameer pulled out a small velvet box. "I asked your dad for your ring size. If I got it wrong, don't worry. We'll resize it."

Was this a hallucination? She opened the box. A glimmering Asscher-cut diamond, exactly the ring she would choose. Inside, an inscription.

All In.

Forever.

"Say yes," he whispered. "And we'll get out of here. I have a jet ready to take us home." He caressed her fingers. "Home. To London."

She took the ring out and gave it to him. He slipped it on her finger. Of course, it was the most amazing diamond, sparking white fire in every direction. What girl wouldn't want this diamond on her finger?

Don't overthink it. A very reasonable voice.

She exhaled and curled her hand around his. "Yes, please."

They traveled to Teterboro, the nearest private airport to NYC. An hour later they sat in a jet fully outfitted in blond and white leather, studded with rivets.

"Custom made for someone else, clearly." Sameer laughed, nodding at the decor. "A rock star, perhaps."

"What? The Anithis don't do white leather?" she teased.

He took her chin in his hands and kissed her. "As you'll soon learn, Mrs.-Anithi-to-be, we do all-black everything," he said. "Because we mean business."

She prepared a resignation letter on the ride over and emailed it to Monahan. No response yet, but she wouldn't expect one. In fact, she would prefer if he never responded. That way she could pretend she never met him and wouldn't *ever* meet him. Out the window, the ground crew prepared the plane. The pilots and flight attendants stowed bags and climbed aboard. This flight was for two passengers only.

Yes, please.

"Ready, sir?" The ground crew chief, a shorter Indian man with a British accent, popped his head into the cabin. She stared at him for a moment longer than necessary. His face was familiar.

Somehow.

Where have I—

"Absolutely." Sameer squeezed her hand, and the moment, the connection, dissolved into thin air.

They settled in. The jet's engine roared to life. It taxied and turned, pulling to a stop at the edge of the runway. A few minutes later, it moved, gathering speed.

Faster.

Faster.

As they took the tiniest amount of air—a few feet, maybe—the cabin shook, hard and jarring.

Was it supposed to shake this much? Kayla had never been on a private jet before. Her family never had money like the Anithis. She glanced over at Sameer. His face confirmed it.

Something's wrong.

The engine roared like a trapped, desperate animal. An alarm blared inside the cabin. Masks fell from the ceiling. She stared at the dangling yellow orbs in disbelief. It was too loud to speak, but she tried anyway. She opened her mouth.

The plane slammed to the ground with a violence that sent them both flying across the cabin. No seat belts required when flying private, unfortunately. Out the window, flames licked the windows. Lights flickered. Metal fell from the ceiling, right above her, fast and sharp. With the force of a guillotine, it sliced through her torso like a knife through thin paper. It barely missed her chest. Barely missed stabbing her in the heart. Blood bubbled out of her. She gasped for air, received only smoke.

The next minutes pulsed like stop-motion animation. The plane came to a stop. The door burst open. People swarmed in. A man reached for her. More violent shaking knocked him off his feet down to the plush carpeting.

From behind, implacable hands clamped on her and *pulled.*

"Sameer!" she screamed.

His terrified eyes locked on her. Disaster was imminent. And yet, somehow, still, he mouthed those three beautiful words.

I love you.

CHAPTER SIXTEEN

A PHONE, RINGING.

Old landline. Shrill ring.

Her eyelids cranked open, halting and grudging, like some ancient garage door. Slow and then wide. Bug-out wide. Because her surroundings were crazy. Wrong.

A bed. A—a *hospital* bed. She looked down. A hospital gown. All around her was *hospital*, and something terrible had happened—what was it? A phone rang, loud and jarring, the sound emanating from behind a curtain to her left.

She stared. The phone stopped.

Where am I?

She scanned the room. Clues. *There are always clues.* This was another element of the Kayvan Masouvi Tao of Poker. Okay. She blinked. Analyzed. No balloons, no flowers. No *Get Well Soon* banner. For a moment the thought crossed her mind...was she actually here? Was this...Resilusio?

"Resilusio." Her voice emerged weak and croaky, someone else's voice. "Exit."

Nothing happened.

Both hands on the sides of her head. The motion to pull the helmet off. An impromptu, emergency, get-me-out-of-here move.

Nothing. What the fuck? She was actually here.

She examined her body. Scrapes, cuts, some covered, some not. A wound on her left torso. That didn't hurt, but the bandage had a sunken look, like a puncture wound. It would usher in agony when the painkillers wore off. And her blood coursed with painkillers, no doubt about that. Her thoughts slumped like damp cotton wool.

She glanced at the foot of the bed.

A chart.

She lunged for it and loosened a memory.

Rabbits. Picnicking.

Bemelmans. Sameer.

"Sameer," she breathed. "Fire."

There was Sameer. And there was fire. Where was he?

Her fingers pressed hard, unyielding metal. She looked down. Oh. The folder.

The phone. Rang again. She should…get it? A deep breath, which made her cry out in pain.

Two feet on the floor.

Her arm was blessedly free of an IV. No tubes or wires attached anywhere, in fact. Standing and moving proved relatively easy. One step to a curtain. The ringing. Louder. From behind the curtain. Yes. That made sense. Same as before. She shook her head. To clear the fog.

It did exactly nothing.

She pulled back the curtain. Another bed, empty. But… someone was just here. Mussed sheets. The sunken imprint of a body. Flowers. A balloon. And in the corner, a phone.

Ringing.

She hobbled there.

Five steps away. Four.

Three.

Two. *Stop.* The room swam, and her breath came scarce. What a new misery, to fight for oxygen. She gulped air.

One. Her fingers closed on the phone. She picked it up. Only then, finally, did she wonder why she was answering a random phone in an unfamiliar room.

"Kayla Masouvi" came the voice. It jarred her ear, a genderless, nonhuman voice. A nonbinary AI. Creepy as hell, even given the circumstances. She almost didn't reply. She almost replaced the receiver.

But she didn't. "He-ello?" Her voice, again so wrong, so foreign. She winced.

"Listen carefully, Kayla. You need to get dressed. Now."

She opened her mouth, and this time nothing came out but a stuttering hiss of air. Rendered speechless, for real. The voice carried on.

"Take leap of faith." A pause. "Trust me. You need to run."

"What?" She found her words. "I need—I need to—to *what*?"

"Run."

"Who is this?"

"Kayla" came the empty, electronic voice, followed by a metallic hiss. The computer voice was...annoyed? Exasperated? "Someone is coming to kill you, okay? So get dressed. Make a left as you exit the room. Find the janitor's closet. There's a phone behind the bleach. You have forty-five seconds." The line clicked.

Sameer is dead. The words popped into her head, all on their own.

What?

No. She denied the words. Put her hands to her temples and physically pushed them away.

Not true not true not true.

Lies. Those words were lies. But the part about an assassin chasing her...That was probably true. Had this same assassin chased Olivia Chen? Cornered her, murdered her? She gave it very good odds.

Get moving. Go.

She was lucky. Even in her state, terrible and compromised, she had excellent reflexes, reaction times, and just plain old speed. She had the high school track and field team and the treadmills in the GR gym to thank for that. She had a shot at getting this thing to happen. This getting-the-fuck-out-of-here thing.

She straightened, fingers scrambling, sliding over injuries just carefully enough. A flash image zapped her brain.

Sameer, his face full of love. Did she dream it?

A ring...

Her hand flew to her finger, closed around a large rock. She looked down. On her finger, there was a ring. A large diamond, smudged but beautiful. She dry heaved. Once. Then turned the ring stone-side down. Touching the ring loosened another memory.

A private jet.

Sameer.

A flight. A takeoff. *We were in a jet, Sameer and I, and—and...*

And Sameer is dead.

And—and...I am supposed to be dead.

Too.

Her mouth, dry and sour. She swallowed thickly. It did not help. She moved in one direction, and the room moved, too.

But, unfortunately, not in the same direction. In fact, it rotated. Wide, slow, miserable arcs that were somehow more nausea-inducing than a rapid, jagged carnival ride. She needed water. She swallowed again. No time. She had…seconds left. Twenty?

Let's assume. One Mississippi. Two Mississippi.

Of course, her own clothes were gone. But her erstwhile roommate had three shirts and two pairs of pants in a sterile, pressed-wood closet. She tugged on a T-shirt and wide-legged trousers two sizes two big.

Three Mississippi.

Four Mississippi.

She laced sneakers that flopped on her feet like elephant ears…

Five Mississippi. Six Mississippi.

She pulled a belt tight to keep the pants on…

Seven Mississippi. Eight Mississippi. Nine Mississippi.

A hat. Yes. Plan. *Think*. A hat…

Ten Mississippi. Eleven Mississippi.

Out the door. To the left, a janitor's closet. She lurched and slid there in someone else's outfit and eased the door shut. The phone, an older, battered flip phone, nestled between two open bottles of bleach, along with a hospital ID badge with someone else's picture, someone else's name. *Karen Garabedian*. Great, she was a Karen now. She clipped it to her hip and turned on the phone.

There was a text waiting, but before she could open it, came the sound of—

Footsteps. Maybe. She was in a part of the hospital with a cacophony of loud, random sounds. Alerts and pagers blared. This doctor. That doctor. This code. That floor. Construction somewhere. Drilling. The loudest HVAC on planet earth. She shoved the phone in her pocket and listened closely, slowing her breathing to a crawl, centering her hearing to cancel the outside noise.

Unmistakable. Footsteps approaching. Men's dress shoes. Not a rubber shuffle or a soft sneaker slide. Not the clomp of women's heels or the flat slap of boots. These shoes had a brisk, confident click, accompanied by the rustle of paper. They moved into her former room, where less than three minutes prior, she was lying in bed, a drugged, injured sitting duck. An easy target. Inexplicably, her thoughts wandered.

Sameer.

Oh God…

No. The sheer force of will took over. *No despair. No remembering. Not now.*

Not yet.

The footsteps stopped. A voice, presumably attached to the footsteps, muttered something. The footsteps turned and moved toward her. Fingers tapped glass. A phone.

But.

Wait.

Coming from the other direction were more footsteps. Softer, quieter. A nurse, maybe, wearing…Crocs? Clothing rustled. Something metal tapped something else. Something plastic? An ID badge?

"Excuse me. Nurse?"

Kayla bit down hard on her lip to smash the inadvertent gasp. A man's voice, right outside the door. Maybe one foot away. Calm, authoritative.

With a British accent.

The same voice, with the same accent. The ground crew chief

clearing them for takeoff right before the plane blew them to smithereens. And he had reminded her of someone…

She had it now. The hot dog vendor. When she'd left the building with Sameer, her eyes had met his.

A million years ago.

The Crocs stopped. "Yes, Doctor?" A woman's voice, with a slight tinge of impatience.

Something slid away. A phone, maybe. He cleared his throat. "The woman, the patient just here." Paper rustled. Pretending to consult her chart, no doubt, admiring all the injuries he had inflicted on her.

You put the bomb in the wrong place, asshole.

I'm alive.

Anger erupted inside her and clamped her spine. This man had hunted her, was hunting her. This man had killed Sameer and maybe an entire flight crew and probably Olivia Chen. And surely…Rick Monahan had hired him.

Sameer is dead because of the Garbage Man.

Sameer is dead because of you, the Mean Voice accused. *This is all your fault.*

Rage. White fireworks before her eyes. Only her self-control kept her from bursting out of the closet and biting scratching tearing *ripping* at this man.

Listen to me, Kayla. Revenge later. Now, we live.

It was Sameer's voice now. The voice of reason. Coolheaded. Strong-willed. Confident. The voice that would lead her to success. Thank God for his voice. She needed it so. And he was right. The assassin was not her target. She exhaled.

Yes, breathe. Use your anger. Don't let it use you.

"Let me check." Nurse Crocs tapped into something. An iPad?

"Well," she said, "she hasn't been discharged yet. Did you have an appointment? Trauma team stitched her up eight hours ago."

"No, nothing as formal as that. I'm just a friend of the family, and they asked me to look in on her."

A pause. "Oh, how nice. Well, maybe the attending scheduled her for a procedure and it didn't make it onto her chart. Ask at the nurses' station. She didn't just walk out of here. Not with those injuries."

Well, that was accurate.

"Of course. Thank you. I'll follow up."

Nurse Crocs retreated. Dr. Assassin didn't move. He just... stood there, until finally he stepped forward, directly in front of the janitor's closet.

So close. So horribly close.

"Where are you, Kayla?" he muttered. She closed her eyes and held her body still, slowed her breathing. A few moments later, mercifully, thankfully, the footsteps moved away.

Or not. Because a second later, the door crashed open.

CHAPTER SEVENTEEN

"FOUND YOU," HE singsonged.

"Fuck you," she replied, and with brainpower she probably shouldn't have at this moment, she clued in to why that bottle of bleach was open and sitting in plain sight.

She was supposed to fling it in the monster's eyes. And that is exactly what she did.

He screamed.

Yeah, I'm sure it hurts, asshole.

For a second satisfaction flowed through her body in waves. She longed to savor him writhing in pain, but she smartened up and ran, because he probably had elite-assassin-level weapons on him. She raced down the slippery hall. The hot dog vendor doctor followed, staggering and yelping. She made it down two flights of stairs and into a patient room, mercifully unoccupied, before her drugged, shredded, cramped, compromised muscles seized up. She dug into her arm to keep from crying in pain. When it subsided, she turned to the phone.

There was a text.

Are you there?

Yes, she typed back.

The next words appeared all at once.

Back service stairs. Other end. Twelfth floor. Handicapped bathroom. Right side. Hide there.

She typed.

Now?

Again words materialized.

Now.

She jammed the phone into her pants, nudged the door open a crack, and glanced into the hallway.

Empty.

She made it to the service stairs. Up three flights to the twelfth floor and she encountered no one. She slipped into the bathroom and eased the lock in place. The phone tremored.

Type yes when you read this.

Yes, she typed. *Who are you?*

The loading dock on 2. There's a linen truck. Be on it.

One second later:

I'm Vapor, by the way. We met in Paris.

The girl in the club. Vapor.

She took a deep breath and cracked open the door. The hall was deserted. She hop-walked the entire way, biting back the pain. Under the bandage her torso had the wet, cool tingle of active bleeding. Something had broken, torn, yanked wide while she ran for her life. Well, running was over for now. She physically could not.

Back inside the stairwell, she made it one flight. Each step sent a hot sting up her body. Her vision crowded with silver fireworks, bursting wide open before her eyes. And now, the stairwell had considerable traffic. It took all of her willpower to screw her face neutral as she passed the first few people. She hissed out a few hyperventilating breaths until she slapped on her poker face and logic took over. This was her skill set. *Self-control. Ignore the pain.* And above all, *no panic.* Her assassin might appear at any time. Heck, maybe the hot dog vendor had a partner—a fake orderly would probably do the trick. But so be it. If it came to life or death here in the stairwell, she was toast. So, hopefully, dying on a flight of dirty hospital steps was not what fate had in store. She calmed, descended. Somehow the pain ebbed. More people materialized. Hospital personnel on their way down for a coffee break. A janitor trotted up, hauling toilet paper. The chief of endocrinology (her title helpfully embroidered on her jacket) jabbered into a phone about college applications.

The pain on her side disappeared. Probably shock. She made it to the second floor and texted her new best friend.

Here.

Words materialized.

Two rights, one left. Careful at the loading dock. You will stick out.

A pause.

Find Omar.

Easy enough. Slowly, casually, she did as directed, two rights and a left. The loading dock appeared, a grimy, diesel-smelling, grease-shimmering dream, swarming with activity and noise. Workers from a linen service loaded containers of soiled laundry into the body of a large truck parked near several others. If all went well, she'd be leaving with the dirty laundry, and this appeared to be the better option, as workers loaded two other cargo holds with bright red drums of medical waste.

She shook her head to clear it. To plan. There were at least ten people here. An office yawned open to her right. Desks with notepads and pens. Should she walk around and scrutinize name tags? No. An idea came to her, a pretty stupid idea. A risky idea, but less stupid and risky than squinting at name tags or standing aimlessly. She stepped into the office and swiped a notepad and pen, turning over a page in the pad and scribbling exactly nothing as she walked. With purpose.

Starting at the far end of the dock, she pretended to write, and she didn't move from each loading bay until she eyeballed the ID badges. At the medical waste truck, where she narrowly avoided a collision with two workers hauling overflowing sharps containers, a compact, dark-haired man with a mustache emerged from behind the engine. She scribbled. He came closer. She glanced casually at his name tag.

Omar.

Procurement.

Omar from procurement would save her life, God and fate willing. He walked up to her and smiled; she lowered her eyes to her notebook. *Yes.*

"Were you able to check the manifests, uh, Karen?"

She nodded. "Done."

He jutted his chin at the linen truck. "Great. The laundry's all loaded up. Go ahead and clear them."

She scribbled away. "Will do."

"Follow me." He said it so rapidly and imperceptibly, like a ventriloquist, that she almost missed it. When the words registered, she swallowed and trailed behind him.

The linen guys finished loading and eyed Omar expectantly.

"You're good." He waved them on. "We'll double-check the units and close the cargo bay. Go ahead."

Omar and Kayla pretended to chitchat, phony smiles on their faces, until the linen guys disappeared.

"Get in," Omar hissed, "to the back, behind the farthest cart. Stay there. Don't get out. Don't move. Someone will come for you."

"Got it." She took a deep breath and met Omar's eyes. "Thank you."

He nodded. "They're good people. You'll be safe."

Who?

He snapped his head, a warning. "Go."

Live now, question later. She dragged her battered body into the cargo bay, pawing her way through scuffed bags of dirty laundry and rickety carts. In the back, she eased herself down, wincing in silence, pulling her knees close, making herself as small as possible. The doors slammed shut. The lock clanged and clicked into place. A thick darkness enveloped her, muddy brown and purple, punctuated by grudging little slits of light. She took a deep breath chock-full of diesel fuel, heavy-duty detergent, air freshener, and of course, dirty laundry. The truck rumbled to life, jangling her already twisted nerves and yanking her poorly clotted injury into a searing damp.

She leaned back, gritted her teeth, and did not cry.

CHAPTER EIGHTEEN

NO SHOCK ABSORBERS on this truck, or so it seemed. The cargo bay rattled violently with no reprieve. Kayla, the laundry, and the carts slid in every direction. The driver slammed the brakes, took turns on a knife edge, dug into potholes, and generally drove like an asshole. She protected her injury, babying it with an intensity that left every other body part (head, arms, legs) victim.

Finally, after endless misery, the truck stopped. The driver cut the engine. Doors opened and slammed shut. As instructed, she waited and waited. One hour, then two, restless, terrified, in pain. She longed to text Vapor, but she stopped herself, remembering Omar's instructions.

Finally, someone yanked the cabin doors wide open. She froze, then deliberately loosened her muscles. If this person wasn't a friend, she would have to hope it was just the linen crew and make a run for it. To where, exactly? That would be the next problem.

Silence for a few moments, save the sound of her thumping heart. Footsteps in the cargo bay, hands pushing aside bales of laundry, aiming deliberately toward her. The stranger threw the last bag aside and revealed himself: a nondescript Asian man, medium build and medium height, in a Yung's Cleaners uniform.

He stopped, eyes sliding over her, and stretched his hand.

She took it, and he hoisted her up gently, with only the faintest frown at her injury, wet with blood that had smeared onto the floor and walls.

She trailed after him outside the truck and into the waning afternoon light, thick and gray with the unromantic aspects of fall in NYC. Dreary days when a sharp breath or a frigid wind betrayed the winter to come: an icy slap off the Hudson, a demon whistle of chill through the skyscrapers, cold fingers that crept up her skirt. She blinked in the gloom, crossing her arms and shivering. Yesterday was a movie-perfect New York fall. Bright sun. Mild weather. But today the world had changed. She was behind a Chinese laundry, in some godforsaken armpit of the city, without a coat, and without Sameer, the one person who had made sense of the world.

She gritted her teeth and moved the feelings aside except for one. The stark and cold determination that she'd be dead before she'd let Monahan get away with what he did.

Pay attention to your surroundings. Take note. Absorb the details. Doors, streets, fences.

Faces.

This is important, Kayla. Pay attention.

Sameer's voice again, guiding her.

Okay. She scanned her surroundings. Factories and industrial buildings. Ahead, smoke and noises bellowed out of a warehouse, YUNG'S CLEANERS in faded red letters on the side. To her left, the reassuring skyline of Manhattan, Midtown about even with where she stood. That meant that, most likely, she was in Queens or maybe Brooklyn. She scanned for street names, street numbers, something, but there was nothing to see. She was somewhere in Queens or Brooklyn with warehouses.

Probably.

She stumbled behind her new friend, so distracted that he stopped and she nearly rammed into him, almost toppled over. He didn't notice, because he was searching for something on the back of an adjacent factory that glowered, abandoned and dark. Eventually, he found it: a door labeled "15." Okay, then. Door number fifteen.

Which was, apparently, unlocked. He pushed it open and stepped aside, gesturing for her to go in. "To back." He smiled a row of gray and broken teeth.

She nodded and walked in. The door slammed shut, and this time, locked.

Dying daytime streamed in from high, half-broken windows. Detergent and rust and wet metal hung in the damp air. The outlines of monsters greeted her. Old industrial-grade washing machines, fifteen feet across, creaking and groaning, even though they appeared abandoned and unused for years. Dryers large enough to fit a baseball team lined the opposite side. Ironing stations. Giant presses. Brackish puddles spread across the floor. She hurried down. The windows allowed just enough of the rapidly fading light to reach the back. There, she saw the outlines of a door, cracked open. She bolted for it, not mindful of her injury, which screeched with pain. But she didn't care. This place gave her the most horrible creeps.

She nearly leapt outside, even though, of course, out might be worse than in. Another nondescript Asian guy loitered there, smoking and regarding her like a dog who'd pooped on his shoe. He stubbed out his cigarette and grunted, gesturing for her to follow to his truck.

Here we go again. He nodded and made for the back, opening an empty cargo bay and stepping aside. She got in and the door rolled shut, leaving nothing but another stingy little sliver of light across the bottom. A large lock banged and clicked. She swallowed her terror as nightmare scenarios raced through her head. If this man wanted to drive her directly into the Hudson, she could do nothing but drown. But mercifully, an hour later, the truck stopped. The driver hauled the door open, and the air brought the odd and cloying smell of rotting fruit.

Kayla stepped out of the truck or, more accurately, stumbled in pain out of the truck. Immediately, the source of the smell revealed itself: forty-foot-high piles of orange peels. They were inside a juice factory. Giant vats hulked over a sticky concrete floor, equipment hissed and belched, pulp machines vibrated. Conveyor belts and metal pipes snaked away into nowhere. Rotten-orange smells jammed up her nose, and sharp pinpoints of acute pain zipped out of her ruined side. Her guide took off, and she followed along until they stopped at a spot that made no sense to her but apparently did to her new friend. There was light, but not much. He searched the factory floor, scanning the broken, tar-slapped concrete. For something. For what? When he found it, Kayla's throat closed hard.

A manhole. Well, okay, a *sewer access hole*. Which sounded worse.

He rocked the cover back and forth until eventually it came loose, then wormed his fingers under the bottom and lifted it.

He's not going to...

I'm not supposed to...

He removed the grate with a sickening scrape and stepped aside, gesturing. She stared, frozen in place. He pointed down the sewer again and then at her, a pantomime that didn't change the situation.

"There?" she whispered, disbelieving this latest, horrifying plot twist. Wasn't it enough that some madman nearly blew her to smithereens, murdered her love, and sent an assassin to kill her, injured and nearly helpless in a hospital bed? Wasn't it enough that she'd agonized and nearly died of fear through two separate truck rides from hell? Now she had to go down into a *sewer*?

"Down." He pointed to the hole in the ground, and Kayla mustered the courage to peer inside. Rusty iron rungs, stairs leading into a murky brown fate.

He grunted impatiently. "Down," he repeated, his arms jerking back and forth like he would most definitely shove her if she didn't go on her own.

So. The sewer, one way or another.

Okay. Here goes nothing. Kayla would describe herself as about average on the claustrophobia scale. But voluntarily climbing into a sewer? That took, undoubtedly, some strong nerves. It might be rats and doom down there.

But it was pretty much rats and doom up here, too.

The man produced a flashlight and held it out to her. She took it, hooked it into her three-sizes-too-big blood-splattered belt, and climbed onto the rusty rungs. The entrance was only a few feet wide and a few feet long, and even though she was small (five foot two and a buck seven), her shoulders brushed the sides as she picked her way down, haltingly, one wobbly step at a time. Her shoes, too large and meant for other feet, barely gripped the rungs. She almost slipped off with each step. When she got to the bottom and jumped onto a concrete landing, she craned her neck up to the meager light. Her escort had not moved. He stood above, his face expressionless. A moment later, he scraped the cover back into place, and she was all alone.

For now.

Maybe.

CHAPTER NINETEEN

THE NEW YORK City sewers. Cold and dank, old pipes and rat feces. Kayla breathed slow and shallow to avoid a painful whiff of the nastiness. She shined the flashlight all around. Behind her, nothing. Some mechanicals and a wall. In front, a tunnel, tall enough for her to walk through, stretching so far into the hollow emptiness that it might travel several blocks. What exactly flowed through this very large pipe? For a second she had an idea, but she shuddered and shoved it away.

An inch of standing water filled the bottom, murky but thin enough to maybe, *maybe* be runoff. She glanced at her borrowed, floppy shoes and steeled herself. The repulsive seep soaked her feet as she forged ahead, picking her way through the ever-encroaching dimness. With each step, the world above dissolved, first leaving wan streaks of light, then nothing. She fired up the flashlight. The water level rose, immersing her feet in disgusting liquid to the ankles. Eventually, the path bent to the right, stretching into another inky black hole of emptiness.

Until she shined her flashlight down.

She sucked in a sharp gulp of rotting air. Farther down, maybe a few hundred yards away, there was a door.

She slipped and slid her way there, a pathetic, noisy scramble. Her approach was anything but stealthy, and she cringed at her gigantic, ungainly splashes. Eventually, mercifully, she reached the door, an industrial specimen made of battered steel. The handle, a short, beat-up bar, jutted out.

Now what? Was she supposed to knock? Try the handle? She ran the flashlight all around the opening. At the top, perched like a chubby little bird, sat a security camera. A blue light blinked. On and recording. She turned the door handle and pushed.

Locked.

She gazed up at the camera.

"I'm here," she croaked, unleashing a ghostly echo in the pipes.

Here... here... here...

Somehow that worked. A second later, the door clicked open. A long hallway. Wood paneling. Nice, *expensive* wood paneling. Gray and white slate tiled the floor, with a lighted strip interrupting the pattern, and a blue arrow, electronic and pulsing, directed someone (her?) ahead. Thick, continuous whooshing filled her ears. Industrial-grade climate control. Air purifiers, HVAC. Conical lamps beamed out blue-tinged light overhead.

She followed the arrow. The door shut behind her automatically. As she walked, she stared out at a modern, painfully bright office space. She glopped past in her soaked shoes, passing sliding glass doors, each one a different saturated color, with white desks trimmed to match. The first room she passed held three people, a man and two women, their backs to her. Complicated code—gibberish to her eyes—flew from their fingers across stacked monitors. They did not acknowledge her presence. She might as well be the wind.

On she walked, through an octopus warren of coders, each room containing between one and four programmers, soldier-straight in front of wide monitors projecting their mesmerizing glow, their backs to her, each absorbed by the work. Some typed, some screened odd, primitive-looking videos, some played games, but all with serious purpose. Grim faces. No fun. Small lamps shot out cold artificial warmth like tractor beams. One had an alcove with a Resilusio VR rig suspended from the ceiling, the complex, delicate astronaut gear jarringly out of place. Three people fiddled with the suit, consulting iPads as they removed panels and examined cables. She hobbled past, injured and waterlogged, apparently invisible. To where? She had no idea. Ahead. That was the extent of it.

Onward. More offices, these with the doors pulled shut and shadows behind. She passed a conference room carved out of the rock, the walls artfully chipped into swirls and waves. An oval table, executive chairs, and blue fluorescent panel lights gave it an odd modernity, like someone sticking a Picasso next to a cave painting. Potted plants ringed the room.

She passed a small fountain with running water and moss. Next, a tree, real and tall. Someone had blasted this office out of dead rock and then bombard it with greenery to give it life.

Eventually, she arrived at the end of the hall, which revealed a glass-covered peek into the structure underneath: chunks of rock and, in the middle, what looked like a…skeleton of an animal. She peered closer. Was that a—

"It's a real fossil" came a voice behind her. "An ancient fish. Around thirty million years old."

A woman emerged from the dimness of the office at the end. Her feet came into view first, then the rest of her. Shadows from the overhead lights slid across her face. Tall, with long, lean muscles, and—and…very familiar. She had the platinum-blond streaks with spiky, vivid purple that matched the girl she'd met in Paris. But the face.

Someone else's face, even matching the scar on one cheek.

"Kayla." She smiled encouragingly and stepped forward but then stopped awkwardly, as if unsure what to do. "It's so nice to meet you. I'm Vapor." The source of the electronic voice from the hospital. But this woman's real voice matched the clips Kayla watched at Bark and Byte.

She lifted a finger and pointed at her. "You're here. And you're missing. And you're Olivia Ch—"

Who the hell was this girl?

But that would have to wait. Kayla's body must have decided that danger—at least imminent danger—had passed, because it chose this moment to methodically, step by step, shut down.

First her muscles weakened, jellied wholesale. She staggered, flayed her arms out for support. Her hands brushed over a table, missed the grip, then closed over the back of a chair. Yes. Definitely. That would do.

And yet it wasn't enough.

She slipped. Something—someone?—caught her gently as TV static invaded her vision. She turned her head. A face. Close to hers. Oh yes. The girl. Olivia. Vapor? The same person? Well, the same but…not. Not the woman in Paris, whose face was entirely different. And not the woman in the videos, though that was closer. This third person…seemed tougher. More weathered. More weary. Kayla frowned. She was about to lose consciousness, this she knew, but wow those eyes, so wide, so—so unnerving, a pale shifting gray like stormy ocean water. Behind them stirred something that made Kayla recoil. Something cold. Something violent. Kayla's lips blubbered unintelligible words.

"You'll be fine," the girl murmured gently, and turned to someone who must have just entered the room. Kayla's face involuntarily buried itself into her neck. Trying to hide. Forests and wildflowers and freedom invaded her nose. And something else.

Blood.

"Tell the Director," Olivia said to the person. "Tell him we got her."

She stared back into the girl's intense, inscrutable eyes. "But you were different," she said plaintively. "You weren't you."

"Just a skin," she whispered. "Just a skin."

A shiver ran down Kayla's spine. An inky slap of paint, the black of unconsciousness, covered her eyes.

Hours or moments later—no idea—a searing pain in her side shoved her awake, a throbbing so intense she opened her eyes to the sound of her own whimpers and clotted sobs. Why? Why was she crying? The answer eluded her, produced a complete blank. Her heart hurt. Her soul hurt worse. Something terrible had happened.

An explosion. A *bomb*.

Sameer was dead.

Her thoughts careened. The despair came quickly, enveloping her like poisonous gas.

I should be dead too.

She missed him, longed for him. A physical ache. To see him again, apologize a hundred times, beg his forgiveness. Only now, too late, did she see. Really see. He was the only person in her life who had never abandoned her, who had held on, come back, believed in her. Something tangible in her deep blue-red insides, the places where the blood pools in dark caverns that never see the light, gathered and hardened for good at that moment. The only good thing in her life was dead because of her.

She could never deny this.

But the guilt would have to wait, for now because…pain. Real. *Bad.* Wowza. An invisible assailant stabbed her with metal barbecue skewers. That was, exactly, the feeling. She yowled.

"Sorry," muttered a woman from behind her. "I don't have any good painkillers." The owner of the voice appeared a moment later. A doctor (maybe?), white coat and all, tapping rapid-fire into a phone. Her borrowed clothes were gone, replaced by a hospital gown. Kayla lifted her arm to the odd and unpleasant surprise of an intravenous drip taped down inside her elbow. It snaked up to a bag of clear liquid plopping placidly a few feet above.

"Antibiotics." The doctor nodded at the bag. "To prevent infection."

Kayla pressed her fingers against her forehead, overwhelmed. Whatever pathetic drugs they gave her had fogged her brain. She tried to sit. Almost got there until the barbecue skewers went at it again. She slumped, winced, and straightened, gritting her teeth so hard they creaked. The doctor observed all this, disappeared, and came back with a syringe.

Vapor's voice came from behind. "No can do. I need her brain right now."

"Don't bother. Won't work anyway," Kayla mumbled and… yawned. Exhaustion flopped over her like a dirty blanket. Her body ached. She was supremely *out of it.*

Vapor stepped into Kayla's line of vision, half her face in

shadow. The woman from Paris again, mixed with the woman from the videos, Olivia Chen. "True enough."

So weird. The doctor, or whatever she was, exchanged glances with Vapor, then left the room, coming back with pills and water. Probably Tylenol, Kayla thought miserably.

Still, she downed them while Vapor surveyed her, frowning. Her hair was more purple in this light.

"You're more banged up than I thought."

"Thanks." She glanced around the room. Blue walls. A cot. Shelving and cabinets. A hospital bed, and her on it. She sat up. The room swayed. She needed to get out of here.

And go where?

And do what?

That made panic surge, because there was just despair. Nowhere to go and no plan, either.

The voice in her brain interjected.

Yet.

She laughed inside her head, for a moment.

Don't laugh. Say it with me. Yet.

That voice was pure Dad again. The Tao of Poker (Life Edition). Manifesting your destiny. It's not that it *won't* happen. It's just that it hasn't happened *yet*. So, onward, and—

The girl who was both Olivia Chen and the girl from Paris wiggled fingers in front of Kayla's eyes. She said something. Her mouth…Yes, it had moved. Words. Her hands exerted gentle pressure on Kayla's shoulders. "Hey. Stay with us."

Kayla closed her eyes, summoned her stamina, and nodded. "I'm here." She exhaled and got to her elbows. No rest for the wicked. "Tell me. Tell me what this is." She straightened, willing the pain away. "Tell me—" She almost said the words in her head, but she didn't. She swallowed them. Not because she thought better of it. Because the hate swelled within her. Subsumed her. Closed her throat. Vapor met her eyes and nodded, and she didn't have to say another word, most especially not the words in her head.

Tell me how to get to Rick Monahan.

I need to make him pay.

CHAPTER TWENTY

A FEW MOMENTS later, two large security men materialized with a wheelchair. On it lay a fresh set of clothes—jeans, shirt, and shoes.

Kayla stared at the chair, then at Vapor, who had an amused look on her face. "I'm fine," she said. "I can walk. He didn't blow my legs off."

Vapor cocked her head to the side, and the purple streaks did a boy band flip kind of thing, landing at an artfully mussed angle. "Preserve your energy," she finally said. "You'll need it."

In a bathroom, Kayla changed into the borrowed clothes, which fit well enough. Then she slid into the chair and sank in, her tired body all but collapsing.

Vapor stood beside her. "We'll take care of you. I promise." Her face was a picture of stillness, calm and flat, very much like an avatar.

"What is this place?"

"One of several secure facilities of our organization."

"Which is?"

She smiled and patted Kayla's hand. "The people saving the world."

Okay then. The two large men wheeled her to Vapor's workstation, where the electronic blue lights washed out her purple hair, and she flew long fingers over her keyboard and produced news reports. Kayla was missing, hunted, wanted. She gave Kayla a moment to absorb, then glanced back. "So you know what you're up against. He'll do anything to get his hands on you."

Kayla tore her eyes from the news reports and studied her rescuer. "What about you? How did you escape from him?"

"These people saved me. This organization. Monahan tried to kill me too."

Kayla gazed at her. "So, who are these people? And where am I?"

Vapor ignored the questions. "What have you figured out about Resilusio?"

Kayla blinked. Did she know Kayla moved the tokens? From the wallet that Olivia Chen gave Francine for safekeeping? "Monahan profiles people based on their garbage, then uses that information to get them addicted to Resilusio."

Vapor glanced away. "Did you know that GR barcodes your trash? That they catalog and sort everything you throw away? That AI-powered predictive technologies decide who it came from? A person? A name?" Vapor laughed ruefully. "They can trace every single item you've ever thrown away back to you. If he wanted to, Monahan could deliver your groceries, stock your medicine cabinet, call out every addiction or bad habit, predict when your period starts, recite your hopes and dreams. Think about it. Pretty terrible."

"It's not something I want to think about."

Vapor nodded slowly. She had more to say. "And that's only the start." The gray eyes widened. Mesmerizing, but not because they were beautiful, exactly. More because they were curious and engrossing.

"Go on. Please."

"Can you handle the rest of it?"

The oddest memory came into her brain. She had taken a few sessions with the GR life coach, who saw "patients" out of a decorator-curated, whimsical and soothing office on the Fun Floor. A place to "let down your guard" while simultaneously getting "in touch with your inner child." Her advice, summarized:

1. Unclench.
2. Relax it all.
3. Repeat your mantra. *Whatever comes, comes.*

Kayla couldn't believe it, but she was relying on that advice right now. The time for denial, for ignoring, for pretending… Those days were over. Probably forever. She swallowed and met Olivia's eyes, clenched her teeth, then, of course, unclenched. Relaxed every muscle deliberately.

Whatever comes, comes.

"Show me."

Thank God her ability to express or feel emotions was about zero right now, because the truth was so much worse than she ever expected.

One programmer opened an app on his expansive screen. Camera feeds. Many, many camera feeds. Fuck. That was her apartment. Her furniture.

Her own body, moving through the space. Oblivious, of course, to the fact that every square inch of this place was on tape.

"The towers are a giant experiment. To monitor the user experience and assess the aftereffects of Resilusio. Sleep, eating, changes in mood…everything." Vapor glanced at her.

Kayla did not move. She was grateful to be so numb.

Vapor went on. "In Resilusio, nothing is random. And the world is always learning and honing and perfecting your profile. It starts with your trash, and then it learns from your behavior in the world. At every fork: guess, learn, guess, learn, until it knows you better than you know yourself."

"Believe your eyes." Kayla echoed the Host, remembering her tour through Resilusio.

"Precisely. And highly addictive. The most magnificent of dopamine hits. People get in and stay in, no matter what that cost."

But Kayla hadn't experienced that, exactly. More like a mild craving. She thought for a moment. "How does that work?"

"Some theories. Nothing definitive. That's where you come in. Why he hired you. Resilusio was too good. *Is* too good. Too addictive. Monahan wants cigarettes, not crystal meth."

Sure. A manageable addiction.

"As with any drug, a small percentage of people somehow resist addiction. People whose brains process differently. Monahan needs to study those people to solve his problem."

Oh damn. Now the pieces fell into place. "The hiring exams." One of the most curious features of GR recruitment: psychological tests, personality tests, math tests. A full day filled with odd, ridiculous questions.

Have you ever been on a diet?

Have you ever smoked a cigarette, even once?

Are you allergic to anything?

Maybe far less ridiculous than advertised.

"You scored in the top one-hundredth of one percent on the addiction resistance tests. And he had a job opening recently vacated." She smirked. "A job working for him. So he decided to study you himself."

CHAPTER TWENTY-ONE

WHY DID HE pick her?

Here was the answer. She was a lab animal. A test subject for this sadistic creep, on camera since the moment she moved into the GR tower. Her stomach twisted so hard it might break skin. Vapor had followed her, tracked her too. Had she watched this feed, this view into her most private moments?

Vapor caught Kayla staring at her. "I'm sorry," she said, reading Kayla's mind. "I really am."

Though it was almost beside the point to care for her privacy at the moment, she did. "I hope I don't drool when I sleep." she deflected.

Vapor didn't laugh or smile. She looked very sad, actually. "It wasn't like that."

Kayla stared at her, said nothing.

She shook her head. "You should see the rest."

Someone pulled up yet another feed. A psych experiment. Video cameras recording research subjects in a medical facility, living in bare apartments, spending most of their time plugged into Resilusio. He split the screen to reveal more surveillance. Researchers in offices and therapy sessions, conducting procedures.

"This is a research study. Testing addiction to Resilusio." She nodded at the screen. "Day one." Day one and nothing alarming. The test subjects were normal people hooked up to a very abnormal Skynet-about-to-take-over-the-world-AI. As normal as a bonkers psych experiment might ever be. Living, basically. Eating, sleeping, showering, using the bathroom, plugging in. They waved at the cameras, aware of the surveillance. Stupidly, unreasonably, outrage bubbled up inside her. *How nice to know when you're being watched.*

"Now," Vapor said, as her colleague clicked a few video files, "day fourteen. Same subjects."

Day fourteen bore little resemblance to day one. The subjects behaved like heroin addicts: bug-eyed, jittery, staggering, sleep-deprived, running and crawling into the rigs with such a desperate longing that Kayla averted her eyes. Some of them had injuries. Most of them had ripped, dirty clothes, the men with untended beards, the women with matted, wild hair.

"On day one, subjects spend an average of seven hours a day in Resilusio. This is what experimental protocols dictate. On day fourteen, twenty-three-point-two hours. And that's only because researchers forcibly pulled them out to eat, to sleep…use the bathroom.

"Then came phase two," she continued. "Researchers ordered the subjects *not* to plug into Resilusio, using either a carrot approach or a stick approach. They paid one group a thousand dollars a day to comply. None of them collected a penny. They found Resilusio that irresistible. They punished another group with electrical shocks if they tried to plug in. The researchers told them that after ten shocks, the system would electrocute them. And that was not just for show."

"Electrocute them? Murder your own test subjects? And the cops don't show up to shut you down?"

"That's a whole 'nother story. How they get their subjects." She paused.

Maybe, again, she had something more to say. But the moment passed. "The patients tried to break into the system, tamper with it, dismantle the security, smash it…everything." A tragedy unfolded over a dozen cameras. Crazed addicts who would do anything for a high. All ended in a murder or suicide, hard to tell which, each subject writhing in agony, electrocuted by the rigs. Kayla stared at the screen in horror.

The feed ended, and they sat in silence for a moment. Kayla finally spoke. "No. No." She shook her head. "It's only a game."

"There's more in the test facility. Operating rooms. Mutilated bodies with brains missing."

Could an experience truly be as addictive as a drug? Heroin altered the neural pathways in the brain, murdering some, birthing others. It was a chemical, inserted directly into the body. A chemical that did what chemicals do. It changed the body's *chemical* reactions.

Could a video game do that?

Kayla thought for a moment, her mind on the tokens. "What do you want from me, then?"

Vapor scrutinized her. The overhead lights, blue and cold, flickered inside her eyes, like life inside a statue. Kayla refused to look away. "Come," she said, "you must be starving. We'll eat. I'll…show you everything. What Resilusio can do. So you can decide for yourself whether you want to join us."

Kayla swallowed all of her replies as they erupted inside her. *Who is "us"? I don't want to stay here! I have work to do. To prove*

Monahan killed Sameer. Tried to kill me. Before he finds me. And kills me, for real.

Which he would do inevitably. Tears filled her eyes.

I have so little time and no idea where to start. I only know that it is not here.

But she could say none of this because the same large helpers materialized out of nowhere, ready to push her…somewhere, and Kayla's battered body and mind had little fuel to protest. She nodded her assent, and they trailed Vapor down the sleek glass-paneled halls that revealed the stone behind like a museum display. They wheeled Kayla to a door that opened with a scan of Vapor's Apple Watch which displayed neither the date nor the time. Behind was a food hall that resembled a scaled-down version of the one at GR—one long table, plush booths in multiple shapes, some of them enclosed to resemble extra-large gourds. The seating area fanned three food stations and a salad bar.

"We can't leave, some of us for days, so we have a good spread here," Vapor said, "though not as good as our former employer."

The smell of food sent hungry ripples down the sides of Kayla's mouth. Her throat tightened in anticipation. But then she rebuked herself. There would be no eating. No food. No sustenance or pleasure or anything until she made things right. Until she fixed…all of this. But that plan had problems, because—

You can never make this right. You can never fix this mess.

She reminded herself: Sameer was gone. It still did not feel real. Her mind did that thing that minds do, refusing the truth, refusing to engage with it. But fate hadn't granted her the luxury of such denial, such misplaced self-preservation. So she forced herself to recite the facts.

Forty-eight hours ago, Sameer was alive. That was a fact.

But today, he's gone.

He's dead.

No. No.

Yes. That madman blew him to smithereens, and it's your *fault.*

So many voices, all in her head. Her eyes squeezed shut, so tightly that she thought her eyeballs might catapult back into her brain, so tightly that she saw stars, great lumpen masses of blackish gas. The truth would come only alongside pain. She came up for air to Vapor gazing at her with compassion. Did she say something? Kayla rubbed her head. That was good. She could just pretend her head hurt, instead of the truth, which was that her brain was in a cage match with itself.

"You're in shock," Vapor said softly. "Your mind is fighting all of this. To protect you." She bit her bottom lip, and Kayla got the oddest sensation that Vapor was biting back an urge to touch her. "It's normal."

Her pity burned like hot metal. "I'm—I'm okay." Kayla swallowed and clenched her muscles, forcing control. "I'll be fine." She looked around. There were some people at the tables, eating. There was a buffet-style line forming, a few people waiting. She changed the subject. "How many people work down here?"

A pause. "Not that many."

"And they all come to work through the sewer?"

"No." Vapor said it slowly, eyes on her. "I can't share too much yet, Kayla. I'm sorry. When you join us, we'll share everything with you."

Those same words again. *Join us.*

She nodded, shrugged, stared at the food, steeled herself against hunger. "I suppose if Monahan tortures me for hours,

I might break and tell him all about your operation under the juice factory."

Vapor ignored her. "You must be hungry—"

"No," Kayla said quickly, too quickly. "I'm not. I'm not hungry."

How crazy was it to vow—and believe—that she wouldn't eat until Monahan paid for Sameer? Her mind, currently crazy, accepted this as the right plan, even as basic logic pled in the background that starving was clearly, obviously, not the solution.

Good luck with that.

Back to Vapor, who had that look again. "You're injured, Kayla," she said. "You have to eat." She scanned the food tables. "Tell you what. Carrots and water. Warm tap water. Especially appetizing down here. We've got both. That way you can punish yourself. Live like a prisoner in a Russian gulag."

Her storm-cloud eyes zeroed in on something behind the buffet. A smile spread across her face. "We even have a moldy apple and stale bread in the compost heap, if you want to go wild."

CHAPTER TWENTY-TWO

BRACKISH WATER, STALE bread, moldy fruit. This appeased the Mean Voice. The Mean Voice was of the opinion that she didn't deserve even that. But at least this food would not taste good. Would not be pleasure. Would not even be proper sustenance. It would merely keep her alive. To fight another day.

Yes. Perfect.

Vapor conferred with the cooks and returned with the meal. Dark water swimming with floating particulates accompanying bread so stale that Kayla's injured jaw struggled to produce a texture capable of a swallow. And the apple. Ha. It had about eighteen bruises, a chunk ripped out (bitten by a rat?), and a close relationship with fungus. Kayla cut out the mold and wolfed down the rest. Swallowing hurt, badly, but for now abject hunger won the day.

She bit, chewed, gulped. No conversation. No talking. Just eating. Vapor sat with her, observing, her phone—again no time, no date—on the table. "Maybe tomorrow you'll eat an actual meal," she said.

"Phones work down here?" Kayla gestured at the device with the bruised end of her apple. A mealy chunk took to the air and landed with a defeated plop on the sleek metal table.

"Yes," she said. "But it's all monitored. Our team members

come and go. Some are in residence. There are living quarters here. But we don't encourage long stretches. It can cause mental problems. Humans require sunlight. We have several facilities. Only some are clandestine, like this one. Most of the others are just offices, like any other office."

"How do you keep this a secret?"

She laughed. "Lawyers. And it's more 'secure' than secret, if that makes sense."

It did. Kayla took a final bite of her apple, chewed, winced, and got to her feet. "Thank you for your hospitality. And for saving my life. And the uh"—she stared at the remnants of her gulag meal—"the food. But I've got to go."

Vapor gazed up at her for a second.

Then burst into laughter.

"Kayla. Seriously. Sit down."

Kayla did exactly that, tensing as the movement—any movement—set her injury to agony. Injured. Hunted. No money, phone, or car. No nothing. "Why did you save me?"

Vapor's face turned serious. "Kayla, when I worked for Monahan, he didn't hire me to do strategic projects. He hired me to create Resilusio. I was the lead programmer."

Kayla took more than a few seconds to process this new information. "You created this disaster?" she finally said.

"I did." Vapor nodded. "And now I'm going to make it right. And I hope you decide to join me. Join us."

Kayla swallowed. "Why would I do that?"

Vapor's jaw worked. Clenched. "Because this is the most important fight in the history of humanity. We need to get this right. Resilusio is in wrong hands. In the worst place possible."

Kayla thought back to the videos of Vapor—Olivia—going

crazy and being carted away by orderlies, but swallowed the questions, because they would lead to the information that Kayla had met with Francine Chen. "You didn't live in GR housing."

"I didn't want to be watched."

"You didn't get your cost cuts."

Vapor laughed. "Monahan didn't care. My only real job was Resilusio. She paused. "My creation almost destroyed me. And Monahan would have let it happen. He was content to let me go crazy and then murder me when it was convenient for him." She leaned forward. "And it almost happened. But these people got me out. Took me to safety. When I got better, I knew I'd spend my life making this right."

"You must have been so afraid." *Scared enough to leave papers and the seed phrase to REAL with your sister.* "Does ... your family know you're alive?"

Vapor's laugh faded from her face. Her hand clenched. But she shook it off and spoke. "Of course not. Too dangerous. He'll kill anyone in his way."

Murdering the person who made the magic happen seemed on brand for Monahan. So that she couldn't take her talents elsewhere. But something tugged at Kayla. Despite it all, she didn't get it. This was still just a game.

Murder, for a game?

Vapor seemed to read her mind. "It is so much more a game, Kayla. Much more powerful. We need to get there first."

And "we" are...who?

She stood up abruptly. "Let me show you. Believe me, you'll understand the power of this technology. The promise. The danger." Vapor signaled abruptly to Kayla's large, hairy, male nursemaids. "Come with me."

Not that she had a choice. The men helped her get into the wheelchair. They passed dorm-like living quarters: bunk beds, bathrooms and showers, common rooms, a movie room. A gym. All functional. All nice. Finally they reached their destination. Two wide, blank double doors, painted a corporate gray. Key-carded.

Vapor passed her watch over the lock. The doors unlocked. She spread a hand out. "Behold our Resilusio VR Arena."

And so it was. A mini version of the one tucked away inside General Recycling, by way of someone's unfinished basement. An earlier model, maybe. The rigs hung from the ceiling in a mass of clipped, twisted, and tangled wires, worn out from use—older, less sleek, less ergonomic. No helmets. This VR Arena had four of them, in a space that must be about a thousand square feet, squeaking and burping like old cars amid the loud underground HVAC. No host. No quiet, calming hum. No undulating floor.

And no machines that seemed alive. At least so far.

"After everything you've seen. Those experiments. The dead people." Kayla walked around the space, in search of…well, she didn't know. "You still have this." The suits had taped-on wires, patched-up cables. These rigs had none of the sleek, sci-fi *Tron* vibes of the GR arena. Instead, they were akin to an old car repaired a few too many times. And still it made her queasy, repelled her, even though she didn't buy into the video-game-as-heroin theory. She pointed to the ground. "The arena at GR has a floor that moves. Motion sensitive. It's like it talks to you, in a…mind-meld machine language."

Vapor rolled her eyes and massaged—yes, massaged—the rig. "That's because his actual product sucks. Compensation for half-built garbage. Ours needs none of that."

"But *you* built that one, right? That was all your vision, Vapor?"

"So I did. But with a very fortuitous twist of fate, I had my biggest revelation here, under the oranges." She ran her hands over the patched, bumpy material of the nearest suit, with something suspiciously close to the Host's affectionate, starry-eyed reverence.

"No spying on your garbage. No AI stealing your soul." She gazed around the room, almost shaking with pleasure. "We have painstakingly crafted this magical technology into something amazing. Something that can eliminate so much suffering in the world." She sighed, her eyes dreamy. Kayla looked away with sudden irritation. She'd had more than her fill of culty nonsense.

Vapor snapped her face back to Kayla like she had read the thoughts in Kayla's head. "Someday the world will experience Resilusio as intended. As it should be. It will cure mental illness. Eliminate greed. Selfishness. All those behaviors that cause suffering. This creation will bring peace and happiness to the world. And to make that happen, we need to understand it, cultivate it, protect it."

Images flashed in her head from her night at the Depeche Mode concert. At the punk rock club. Dancing with abandon. Exploring a different version of herself, or maybe a version buried deep and desperate inside her. No real-world repercussions. Her chest rippled, remembering the intense pleasure that had burned there, for just a moment.

Nice, but world-changing? Maybe. She didn't have the gene. The lady said as much. Maybe that was the problem. Maybe she could never understand.

Vapor's fingers trailed off the end of a suit. "You're right, of course. This is my baby. Years of my life working on this, perfecting it." She paused. "Because of the way your mind works, it might not be as intense, but you will see it. Feel it. It won't own you, but you'll understand."

And that was the real problem. She didn't *want* to understand. She wanted nothing to do with this contraption. The most hideous nausea of déjà vu gripped Kayla. She'd been in this horrible place before, trapped in someone else's dream. She turned away. "I don't think I can do it."

Vapor regarded her with those glassy eyes. "Please. We can help each other. Let me show you. If you hate it, or even if you love it, we'll take you to the surface. You will never hear from us—from me—again." For a brief second, she placed a gentle hand on Kayla's arm. The touch, so foreign, somehow comforted her. And alarmed her. For them both, it seemed. Because as quickly as Vapor touched her, she pulled away and mumbled. "Anywhere you want to go."

CHAPTER TWENTY-THREE

ANYWHERE YOU WANT *to go.* Ha. That was an amusing concept, in a gallows humor sort of way. She "wanted" to go exactly nowhere. Nowhere on earth at least. That probably made her the perfect candidate for Resilusio. Theoretically.

She ignored all the ways this could go wrong while she prepped for the plug-in. Vapor handed her the iridescent bodysuit. This time, she held it close, stretching and peering. "What's in these things, anyway?"

"Motion detecting technology. We've developed our own. It's...pretty extraordinary. We start with heart rate, sweat, breathing. That's the base model. Monahan's version uses these inputs to heighten the addiction. But we use it for a different purpose." She exhaled and glanced around. "Make no mistake, Kayla. This is a cause worth fighting for, even worth dying for."

"How comforting."

A staffer helped them don the full suits and dotted their entire bodies with the adhesive haptic sensors. When it came time to put the gloves on, the left glove snagged on her ring. Her ring from Sameer, the only thing she had left of him. The staffer tugged unsuccessfully for a few moments.

"I'm not taking it off," she said.

The staffer and Vapor exchanged glances. Vapor shrugged,

the woman tugged harder, and the glove eventually got on her hand. Vapor adjusted Kayla's VR goggles herself. They had a different shape and design than the one in GR. They covered more of the forehead, pressed against the temples and wrapped around, making a buzzing contact to something new—sensors attached to her scalp.

"You ready?" Vapor slid the thin, tight goggles on. At the touch of a button, the lenses lifted, revealing her eyes. No helmets made this version seem far less immersive. That was comforting, to a certain extent.

Kayla gave the arena one last look: bare room, bare bulbs, bare-bones electronics and rigs held together with spit, glue, and prayers. She shrugged, pulled her goggles over her eyes, and leaned into the welcoming arms of Resilusio.

⁂

This time there was no black, no earth spinning beneath her feet, no Ms. Resilusio to guide her to the most addictive experiences possible.

She opened her eyes. Or were they already open? An uneasy tremor rippled through her insides. This session had barely started, and already she had the deeply uncomfortable feeling of losing the most basic control of her very own body.

She steeled her spine and examined her surroundings. A clearing in a forest. Trees on all sides. Warm summer air. The sun shone down, thick golden streaks that zoomed through dappled branches in every direction. A deep breath revealed the smell of flowers, tree bark, piles of leaves slowly warming in the sun. It soothed her body, her senses, and she need that. She ran her fingers over her face as a breeze tickled her cheek. Her fingers identified skin, and the marvel of that never ceased to impress. Her hands were in gloves.

They were touching technical fabric, and that was all.

She gazed down. She wore fitted pants. Knee breeches, actually, silk stockings, and leather shoes, pliable and squared, with stacked heels. On her upper body was a flowing linen shirt with frills. Her fingers found her head. Ah, her hair. Tied behind with a ribbon. A jeweled amulet hung around her neck, depicting a headless body carrying its own head up a hill, *Saint Denis* etched on the back. She touched her chest. No bra. Now, that was truly a dream, a world where such torture devices were unnecessary. So, Resilusio had turned her into a nineteenth-century...boy? She fingered the shirt, running her hands over intricate embroidery. A nobleman's son, or maybe a girl who just didn't like dresses.

From behind came the sound of a horse. A snort. A whinny. Metal bridles and bits clanging softly. She whirled. Indeed, a horse nickered and idled, tied up to a tree, waiting for a rider. Was he there before? No way. How could she have missed a *horse*? Now the pants (breeches?) made sense. Very tough to horseback ride in a dress.

She approached him, whispering softly, "Hello there." Well, if Vapor got this from her garbage, that was extraordinary. The living creatures that Kayla loved the most were animals. She grew up with an assortment of dogs, two very grumpy cats who were highly stingy with their affection, and a menagerie of birds and aquatic species. Her mother was the architect of all this. They didn't have horses—too complicated—but they did at one point have a lazy little Shetland pony named Nougat who Kayla loved like crazy. Nougat had boarded at a friend's farm, and Kayla had visited once a week until he died of old age.

"You look nothing like Nougat," she murmured, rubbing the horse's nose, "but you'll do."

Behind this horse was another one. Another rider. Kayla whirled. Vapor appeared across the clearing, dressed in the same 19th century flavors.

"Are we riding?" Kayla hollered over. She glanced again at her horse and examined him critically this time. He wasn't a "pony ride" pony. He was an animal that required skill to manage. Vapor didn't seem to hear. Kayla approached her, "I'm rusty, and I wasn't all that great to begin with."

Vapor shook her head and walked away, all around the clearing. Searching. Like something was missing from this picture, which could easily have been a picture. Kayla gazed past the trees. Unmistakably, a river gushed in the near distance.

The banks of the River Dordogne, 1785.

The thought slipped into her head just as if she had asked two questions and someone had whispered the answers in her ear.

Where am I?

When am I?

Crazy. Insane. A trick of the game. Kayla shook it off.

Vapor either gave up the search or found whatever it was. "We can ride after." She took a long leather case off her horse. The case was sleek and brown, at least three feet long and thin. No zipper.

Hadn't been invented yet. 1892, Whitcomb L. Judson. A flop, at first.

The knowledge surfaced in her thoughts. Impressive. Resilusio dug up the relevant obscure bits from a user's brain, though she couldn't remember learning about zippers. Ever.

But, anyway. "After what?" She gestured at the leather case. "What's in there?"

Vapor stepped a yard or two away from the animal and dropped the case on the forest floor, unfolded the leather to produce two gleaming swords, both encased in shiny, metal-laced scabbards. "Now, these"—she stood and handed the first one to Kayla—"are classic examples of spadroons." She examined the sword in Kayla's hands. "They got most of the details right. Splendid." She pulled her own sword and scabbard out of the bag, unsheathing the weapon with a dangerous-sounding swoosh.

Kayla turned hers over. The blade was thin and long—no more than an inch and a half wide and maybe half an inch thick. The grip on the brass hilt had the exact look and feel of elephant ivory. It was neither especially heavy nor especially light, substantial, probably designed just for her. Kayla balanced it in her hands. Maybe a pound, but she imagined that hoisting even a pound of metal over time would prove excruciating.

But maybe not here, right? Not in a magical world where the rules of life on earth didn't exist. "We're going to have a sword fight? A—a *duel*?" Kayla asked, amused for a second, before remembering that amusement was on the list of emotions she did not allow anymore. No amusement, joy, laughter. Never again. She cleared her throat. "That's the magic of your Resilusio? Nineteenth-century sword fights?"

"Eighteenth century, actually," Olivia replied. "And just wait a minute. You'll see."

Kayla ran her finger over the intricately carved hilt. "It's a beautiful weapon."

"That, Kayla, is a five-ball spadroon."

"Five ball?"

"Yup. The five ball refers to the knuckle guard." Olivia pointed to the hilt, where five spheres jutted out of the metal.

"When this blade was developed, somewhere around the early 18th century, it was a major innovation in military swordsmanship and weaponry." She took her spadroon and stepped back into the clearing, took a few practice thrusts.

Show off, Kayla thought. Vapor danced. Heck, she almost levitated, extraordinarily light on her feet, moving her body with confidence and elegance. To Kayla's unpracticed eye, she had beautiful sparring form, assuming that was even the correct terminology. If she wanted to convince Kayla this wasn't her first rodeo—er, swordfight—she succeeded.

"It's a light cut-and-thrust blade," Vapor called out, dropping her arm and walking back. "Which means it's useful for slicing *and* stabbing, if you catch my drift. Double-edged, of course. Sword makers of that era called it 'the master of all weapons.'" The blade flashed as she flitted it from side to side. "So, should we try them out?"

Kayla stared at her. "I don't know how to fence. Or duel. Or whatever this is."

Vapor half turned, shrugged a shoulder. "Are you sure about that? Let's go into the clearing and try."

"Why would I want to—" Kayla trudged after her.

"Give it a try." Vapor whirled around, fixed those reptile eyes on Kayla. "The rules of the game are simple. First player to score fifteen touches wins. We're allotted nine minutes total, divided into three bouts, but for now we'll do one bout. Three minutes." She paused. "I promise you enlightenment at the end."

Curiosity prickled her skin. Vapor created questions in her mind, uncomfortable questions, but with answers that might find her a way to Monahan. To get justice for Sameer. "I accept."

CHAPTER TWENTY-FOUR

"DOES MONAHAN KNOW we're in Resilusio? Will he find us?"

Vapor shook her head. "No. This version is something we've developed. And that's why we're here, all of us, under a juice factory." She nodded gravely. "For what you're about to see."

Vapor took her place at the end of the clearing. "We shall fence. However, for the match to begin, we need a referee, who was supposed to be here already." On cue, a referee stepped out of the woods and into the clearing. This referee wasn't wearing stripes. No whistle around his neck. He wore a suit. He nodded at each of them solemnly, then waited.

Vapor regarded him and, when satisfied, turned back to Kayla. "First things first. You raise your blade to your chin and drop it."

Kayla followed Vapor's actions.

"You then assume the *en garde* position. I'm sure you'll agree that we should follow the saber fencing rules, given the weapons we're using. But"—she spread her arms out wide—"we make the rules here. That's the beauty of it. So if you want to do anything differently—"

Kayla raised an eyebrow. "Saber it is."

And now the most severe oddness clamped on to her body. It *moved*—on its own, with no direction from her. Her physical body, the one encased in a Resilusio rig. Triceps and biceps, quadriceps and hamstrings—muscles that functioned as, more or less, 100 percent voluntary. Her feet arranged themselves at a ninety-degree angle from one another. Her right foot took one step forward, the knee bent gently. Her weight, on its own, shifted. *Centered*, so that her upper body hovered exactly balanced over her lower torso. The movement had none of the forced feeling that might occur when another person adjusted posture or grip. Nothing like what a coach might do. Instead, she moved the muscles, and her consciousness just now caught up to that fact.

Instinctively, she accepted that this "floating" stance was crucial in a swordfight. That balance when under attack and when advancing would make all the difference between point and poke. The game might have knocked loose this factual knowledge from somewhere inside her actual brain. Sure, okay. But where her body existed in space right now defined the perfect sparring stance. The stance that would power all of her moves. And this instinctive sensation was utterly, completely new. The knowledge rippled from deep within her bones, radiating out to her limbs, tendons, and skin. She had it now. Muscle memory. Practiced. Expert. Instinctive. It came from someone else.

Or something else. Game mechanicals, she thought. A machine, moving my body.

Just a very good machine.

Next, her upper body adjusted. Her torso rotated at a forty-five-degree angle. Her right arm lifted, pointing forward, gripping the spadroon, and the elbow gently tucked in, stopping one palm length away from her body. Her left arm rose, levitated like a saint in a Renaissance fresco, floating on air, to stop in perfect balance with her front arm. A perfect balance that requires years of fencing training and practice. A harmonious, well-prepared state. Her shoulder, elbow, wrist, knee, and toe all aligned vertically. She could float like a butterfly all over this pretend forest.

And that was it.

Vapor grinned, unsurprised, watching it all. She stood in position herself. "I see you're ready," she said, flitting her eyes to the ref. "Let's go."

"*Pret*!" the ref yelled, and instinct took over. *"Allez!"*

She had a strategy.

Well, her body. Her body had a strategy. A strategy to win.

Someone else's instinct gripped her, hard. She extended the sword fully, smooth and natural. Her right foot stepped one pace forward, then her left foot. Her right foot lunged forward, her weapon arm still fully extended. The move was a success. Vapor retreated. She did it again, and this pressed Vapor back into a stumble.

A double advance lunge to take Right of Way.

Was that an actual thought? In her head?

Right of Way: When both fencers hit each other simultaneously, the fencer who started the attack gets the point. The fencer with the RoW has the "right" to score a point.

Okay, and what about that? She was thinking a—a *dictionary definition*? The information was not intrusive exactly, more like a helpful whisper in her ear. Strategy she needed to have a chance. She had never fenced, never held an épée, a saber, anything. Never learned the meaning of Right of Way in fencing, much less how to apply it.

Something had wormed its way into her head now, not just her body.

Kayla's throat seized. She choked. Gulped air. She could not pretend this process was game mechanicals, the rig moving her body. Nope. An alien life form had invaded her brain. But an instant later, sharp metal whizzed very close to her face, and that thought was neither here nor there as she fought for her metaverse life against a very skilled opponent.

Right of Way.

She'd relinquished the Right of Way to a smooth series of moves. First Vapor successfully parried her attack.

Parry: a defensive action where the fencer blocks her opponent's lunge. When parrying, only the blade moves. The arm should remain straight.

Next she executed a riposte.

Riposte: a counterattack by the fencer who has blocked her opponent with a parry.

In Resilusio, Kayla was a skilled fencer. These definitions, and more, were already in her brain, already known and processed. Her opponent's riposte had been unsuccessful. Kayla advanced again, seizing the Right of Way.

And on it went. Kayla observed her body, almost from the outside of her virtual body while still inhabiting it. She had opinions on Vapor's moves, a running tabulation of her responses, her thrusts and parries, her gaining and losing of ground, each element running through an analysis in her brain. These thoughts were not her own—or were they?

Sure they were. She reminded herself that Resilusio was just a game, a game that apparently, no matter what, got in your head with its weird AI ways. She relaxed. Observed. Let the conclusions come to her.

First suspicion.

Kayla had advanced with little resistance. Her opponent had retreated far too easily. She was swift and practiced, and no way was she giving ground without a plan.

Vapor had a strategy.

Kayla feigned, twisted, bought herself time for her mind to figure it out. Her opponent was setting up…something. Vapor nudged and slid, positioning Kayla just so, backing up, giving ground, but leading Kayla to an odd, cramped position. Kayla's mind analyzed several moves ahead, and her opponent's plan unfolded.

Fencing was an elegant battle of mostly physics on a defined space. One might call it physical chess. Angles. Pulleys. Levers. Arms. Legs. Swords. Positions. And a board, upon which the fencers must plant their feet. Take all the laws of Einstein. Add a move from chess. A queen sacrifice. To present as almost defeated in order to set up greater power.

And that was it.

If Vapor suddenly reversed course and attacked, she would pin Kayla. Kayla's only parry could come from a muscle-limited, ineffective angle. A bent arm.

As simple as that. All of this…for a bent arm.

A bent arm meant far less power. Her opponent purposefully adjusted her posture to leave deliberate openings, to subtly but inexplicably dictate where Kayla would attack *her*.

Well, it worked. This time.

Touché.

Point Vapor.

Twenty seconds later, Kayla had her own plan. A riposte that landed her a point. And that was the actual thought in her head: both to execute a riposte and the steps to do so. Resilusio Kayla was a skilled player and held her own. But her opponent was better. And each time she scored, Kayla could rifle through both players' moves and lay out, step by step, how she had screwed up. A necessary talent of elite players.

After three minutes that stretched out like an Einsteinian experiment in space-time, it was over. They both gulped air.

"Good game." Vapor bowed, sword down.

Kayla walked up to her and searched her face. "That was in my head. All of it. All of this." She gestured around her.

Vapor smiled triumphantly. "Amazing, isn't it? That's what I wanted to show you. That's what it's all about." She stepped back, still gulping air. "Welcome to the real Resilusio."

CHAPTER TWENTY-FIVE

THE "REAL" RESILUSIO. Artificial intelligence that moved your physical body and infiltrated your real mind.

Back in the offline world, under the juice factory, they returned to the food court. Kayla peppered Vapor with a thousand questions about *this* Resilusio. Vapor's eyes leapt with passion as she shared her vision.

"We've built much of the technology. And yet…we have a long way to go. But this is our purpose. The meaning of our lives. Not to get people addicted. Not to rob them. No." She shook her head. "What we could do for the world…the suffering we could erase. The applications are truly endless. We can help the injured walk, the blind see. You don't have to be a slave to whatever shitty hand the lottery of life dealt you. We can fix so much of what is terrible and unfair in the world." She paused. "Dreams can come true."

It was so seductive. A wondrous concept—to control your destiny. "Dreams can come true," Kayla echoed. Maybe for some people. She had a few dreams still, but none that AI could conjure into reality.

Vapor exhaled. "Kayla, Long before GR, you knew this feeling. Being a…character in someone else's play, with only the illusion of control."

She ignored that way-too-personal insight. "How did it… get into my head?"

"What did you experience?" Vapor leaned forward, searching Kayla's face. "Walk me through it."

"I've never fenced before. Never once. But I knew fencing strategy. Advanced fencing strategy. My body moving—maybe I can get that. It's a game. My body under the control of the game. But my mind?"

"That's the magic."

"How?"

"We use the subconscious. We feed it the information you need. Evolution has programmed humans to absorb and assess information from the world around them. We give you that information, not presented to your conscious mind, but to the cognitive layer beneath. The skill set of a very experienced fencer for you and an Olympic-caliber fencer for me."

Kayla stared. "And that's why you won. Because you programmed yourself to be just that much better."

"Exactly."

Kayla frowned. "But how?"

Vapor smiled. "Monahan has magic tricks. We have actual magic."

Kayla waited. A beat passed. Nothing. "That's it. Wow. That's it. You don't know. Like you said, Resilusio works in mysterious ways, right? This is one of them. You have no idea what it does, how it does it, whether it has side effects, or anything."

"We've observed zero side effects," she replied carefully.

"You have no clue how this crazy mind-control technology works."

"I prefer to think of it as an upgrade. An integration with

your mind. First, you moved as an expert. Now you think as an expert."

"This is not just an upgrade to some game. You're messing with people's *brains*."

Vapor went on. "You're missing the point. We can bring such happiness to the world. Open doors for so many and just...bring humans closer together. Once people see what we have, they will join us. We can undo the misery that passes for life on earth today. We can change it all. Create blissful, peaceful harmony."

She leaned forward, hand on Kayla's arm. "Would you join us?"

Kayla didn't move. "Explain something about the GR Resilusio. Or yours."

Vapor. "Sure."

"Is it all rigged?"

Vapor laughed. "In ours? No. In Monahan's? Always."

"So if I play a...poker game, for example? In Monahan's? With a real person."

"The algo chooses the winner. With one exception."

"Which is?"

"The house always wins."

Kayla's eyes widened. "Monahan."

"He was hard-coded in. To always win."

"Was?"

Vapor nodded. "Right before I left, I messed with the algo. I made his outcomes random. It will take years to fix, when they figure it out." She paused, considered. "If they figure it out. He doesn't go to casinos, from what I hear."

"What about your 'Director'? Is he hard-coded in, like Monahan?"

Vapor blinked. "Absolutely not."

"So who is he?"

Vapor met her eyes. "He's a visionary. A seer. He gives us strength when we need it. A natural leader." She paused. "I consider him to be a true mentor."

Kayla spread her arms out, which hurt. She winced, having forgotten about her injury. "He's funding this revolution."

Vapor bowed her head. "The Director has been extraordinarily generous with all of himself. Time. Leadership. Money."

Kayla examined a world that reminded her so much of General Recycling. Clean, sleek, expensive. Someone had a lot of time, leadership, and money for all of this. She pushed back from the table, which was easy, thanks to the wheelchair. "I want to meet him."

A slow smile spread across Vapor's face. "I was wondering when you'd ask."

"I'm asking now."

"He's dying to meet you." She got up and signaled to the minders, who materialized out of the corners and crevices of the seating area. "Come."

They wheeled through endless corridors and several security doors that opened only with a swipe of Vapor's Apple Watch. Inside the final door was a series of rooms, in front of which was a large desk helmed by two men in headsets, fanned by more sour-looking security.

"Is he ready for us?" Vapor asked.

They nodded and pointed to a room at the end of a hall, where they entered the most uninspiring of places ever in the history of uninspiring places: a bland conference room, complete with a standard-issue videoconference setup.

Inside this quintessential example of the American corporate experience, staring serenely out of a video feed, with a backdrop that looked to be the middle of a lush green forest but which truly might just be a filter, was General Recycling's cofounder and current head of the Genesis Foundation, Evan Schechter.

CHAPTER TWENTY-SIX

THE DIRECTOR.

Of course. Dr. Minieri had called him just that when Kayla had visited the bacterial production floor, what seemed like a million years ago. Evan Schechter, the Director, because *"Who does he think he is, Steven Spielberg?"*

"Evan Schechter?" Kayla gaped.

After leaving GR, Schechter disappeared from the public eye, sparking many rumors:

He's studying to be a Shaolin monk in China.

He's climbing Everest. No, wait—he summitted Everest. No, wait—the Seven Sisters.

He joined a caravan. Of Bedouins.

He joined a cult.

The business press had largely forgotten about him, because if there's one thing the business press hates, it's a recluse with nothing to sell. In the end no one was sure he was actually alive but for the missives, video clips, and foundation announcements that he beamed out periodically. Kayla had watched some of these. He ended each video reminding viewers of the foundation's mission:

We will heal the planet.

Kayla studied the vaguely pixelated man on the screen. The face matched the pictures in Dr. Minieri's office, albeit older.

Thinning sandy-blond hair, now long and tied behind his neck. Beard, glasses, tanned skin. His beatific smile revealed a set of perfect white teeth, much like Monahan's. Must go to the same dentist.

"Please. Call me Evan, and welcome to the Genesis Foundation, Kayla."

He wore a white tunic that flowed with every movement, beaded leather necklaces and an earring in his left ear. He didn't have a shaved head, crazy eyes, a massive sunburn, or look like much of a mountain climber, so she supposed none of those rumors were true. Nope. Evan Schechter ran a clandestine organization creating AI-based mind control to help humanity (maybe), competing with his former best friend who was using more or less the same technology to addict humanity to a game. No, wait, an *experience*.

She glanced around. Not much to see in this standard-issue expensive corporate conference room. "You're the director of all this?"

He considered her first, the question next. "I am."

"I take it you and your former business partner had a falling-out?"

A pause. "We had competing visions for the business. He didn't respect the bugs"—his lips twisted in disgust—"and the bugs are everything."

"So you went head-to-head with him in mind-control AI? See who could turn the world into zombies the fastest?"

He blinked. "We plan to save the world, Kayla. Make it a better place. Heal the suffering. The sick. As for my former business partner, you and I both know that is not his goal."

"I guess we don't have to worry about this operation running out of money."

He laughed. "You don't."

She paused. "Why do you want me to join you?"

He raised an eyebrow. "Why do you think?"

"You tell me."

He leaned into the frame, and now he looked large. Sinister. Terrifying. He fixed his eyes on her. They were intense and dark and metaphorically pinned her down. "He didn't kill you, did he? That means you have something he wants. He needs you alive, right? You follow that logic?"

"Sure."

"Okay, so hypothetically, you might have, say, some cryptocurrency that owns half of Resilusio. If you or anyone else has it in their possession, that's a problem. He can't develop Resilusio without those tokens. You come out of the woodwork and sue him, he'll have to doxx himself or lose control of his baby. After some standard lawsuit discovery, everything comes out, all development and rollouts grind to a halt. So he needs those tokens. For now, until he gets them, he's stalled. That's perfect. Gives us time. We're developing a virus that will delay him for a few more years. Which is more than enough."

She stared at him, dead-on. "I'm not staying. I have to get out of here."

He nodded. "Yes. You want revenge, I can imagine. But it will have to wait, and as it turns out, it is rather unnecessary." He stopped himself. "You'll have to stay here for some time."

"As the Director mentioned, we're developing a virus," Vapor interjected. "The experimental facility. The place in the videos. It's called Escondido. If we can get in, we can destroy Monahan's

Resilusio. I know what I created. I can access it from Escondido. And all the innocent souls trapped inside? We'll free them." She exhaled, and her face got dreamy. "His Hiroshima moment starts here."

That reminded Kayla. The facility. Something about it didn't make sense. "The research subjects—none of their families have spoken up? Not even the families of the dead?"

No one said a word. Kayla finally went on. "Were they kidnapped? Are they missing"—she turned to Vapor—"like you?"

Vapor shook her head. "The research subjects are inmates. All given a chance to cut long sentences short."

"How evil." Something rippled in Kayla's mind, something that bothered her, even alarmed her, but she refused to acknowledge it. "And no one says a thing?"

Vapor went on: "Originally he recruited from the domestic penal population. But the mortality rate was too high, so the researchers expanded their recruiting." She paused. "Internationally."

"He's *importing* research subjects?" Bleak thoughts took turns cycling through her head. "From other countries' prisons?"

"Overcrowded prisons in developing nations. They pay the families when they die, or let the wardens select inmates with few outside connections. It's not the first choice, but it's necessary."

"So you see, Kayla." Schechter interrupted her thoughts. "We have a plan, and that means that you and your tokens will stay safe and sound with us. For now. After, we will get you back to your old life, or…whatever life you want."

Gears turned in her head. She scarcely heard him.

Inmates. Now the queasy twinge materialized. Her father was an inmate, and if Kayla was Monahan, kidnapping Kayvan

Masouvi and holding him out as bait is exactly what she would do. It was just too useful, too perfect.

She stared at the pixelated face, so close to the screen. His eyes held the sorry truth.

Already done.

She said it anyway. “My father is an inmate. At Rikers.”

Vapor and Schechter exchanged slight glances.

She went on. “Was an inmate at Rikers.” It was a statement, not a question.

The room was silent except for the hum of the HVAC and the low buzz of electronics. “They have him, right? In that horrible place?”

“We haven’t checked that,” Vapor said.

“Let’s check it now. Rikers has a website. You can look up information on any inmate. If the prison transferred him, it should be there.”

No one made a move.

“Let’s look it up. Let’s see if they moved him to that facility. What did you call it?” She glanced at Vapor. “Escondido?”

For a moment, neither Vapor nor Schechter responded. Then Vapor finally spoke. “The website will list him on a temporary work detail. A farm upstate or something.”

“But that will be…a lie?” Kayla choked out the words, scarcely believing them.

“Yes,” she replied, “because he’s at Escondido.”

CHAPTER TWENTY-SEVEN

THE SCUMBAG HAD her father. And time was running out.

She had to get into his Nazi experimental facility. And soon, before her father ended up just like Sameer. Dead.

Fuuuuuuck.

All she did was get people killed.

She closed her eyes. Self-control took over, and there were no tears. Only cold planning. "How long?" Her eyes snapped open. "How long until—"

Vapor held out a hand and shook her head. *No, no.* "That's a suicide mission. Wait for us to make a mess of the place. That way you might actually get in and get out. If Monahan catches you, you're de—"

"How long?" Kayla cut her off. "How long before the subjects go crazy?" But she knew. Day one. Day fourteen.

Vapor glanced at Schechter again. He gave her an almost imperceptible nod.

Something worked in the woman's jaw as she spoke. "Two weeks, right? You saw."

"Where?"

No one answered her.

"Where is it?" She glanced from Schechter, looking decidedly uncomfortable onscreen, to Vapor, who had nothing to say, either.

She pushed back from the conference table, stepped out of the wheelchair, and tried her feet. Vapor put a hand out but didn't stop her.

Her feet worked fine. One step in front of another. She *was* fine.

Time to get away from this place. "I have to go," she said.

"*Kayla, wait,*" a vaguely familiar voice called out from behind Schechter, tinny but recognizable.

Kayla turned. There, sitting next to Schechter, holding his hand, was Dr. Minieri. Not that this was surprising. When Kayla visited the bugs all those long days ago, she absolutely believed that Minieri was not a fan of Rick Monahan. She and Evan Schechter were close. Very close, it seemed.

Minieri squeezed Schechter's hand and smiled at Kayla, all welcoming and encouraging. "Hello, Kayla. I'm so glad you're safe."

Kayla raised an eyebrow. "You're like, what, a spy for the 'bug resistance'?"

Minieri's face broke out in laughter. "I never thought of it that way, but yes…that's not a bad characterization. Collecting vital information. Saving the world."

"That's nice for you. I'm glad you're not in cahoots with that murdering scumbag. But nonetheless, I have to go."

Vapor glanced from the video to Kayla and placed a gentle hand on her arm. "You're injured. You don't stand a chance."

"Let us do it," Minieri added. "We'll get him out."

"When?" Her voice rose in panic. She stared from Vapor to

Schechter to Minieri. "You're on your own timeline. Who knows when that will be?"

Schechter spoke up. "We'll move up the timeline, okay? As fast as possible."

Kayla narrowed her eyes and thought about this. "That's not good enough." She turned to the door. "Thank you. For saving me. For everything. But I have to go now."

And then her two large minders appeared from the woodwork.

Vapor stepped forward. "Can you please sit back down in the chair?"

Kayla pressed her eyes shut. "You're going to keep me prisoner here?"

No one said a thing.

"Please sit, Kayla." Minieri sighed, like one might with a wayward teenager. "It's for your own good."

"Listen. You want the tokens, right? Why don't I just give them to you now? Spare you the time?"

Vapor shook her head vehemently. "It's too dangerous, Kay—"

Schechter interrupted. "Where's the seed phrase?" Kayla appreciated his lack of pretense, at least.

Vapor turned to the screen, her eyes widening in horror, or so it seemed. "He'll torture her, kill he—"

Well, maybe it was genuine. Kayla ignored it anyway. "A safe-deposit box in a bank."

Schechter leaned forward. "Where?"

"Brooklyn."

He and Minieri exchanged glances. "If it's real, Kayla."

"You can check when I get it out. Then you let me free and give me the GPS coordinates of the facility where Monahan's holding my father. Agreed?" What she was going to do with said coordinates, she didn't know.

Yet.

She smiled at the memory of her father.

Okay, yes. *Yet.* She did know the following: that she needed to get away from these mind-control crazies, and she needed to know where she was going next, in order to go after a different, possibly, probably more evil mind-control crazy, though that was based on limited information.

It was a start.

You'll find a way. That was Sameer.

You're so fucked. That was not Sameer. That was the Mean Voice.

Go to hell, Mean Voice. She almost said it out loud.

And maybe she did. When she came back to the present, Schechter regarded her with his flat, analytical eyes. Those eyes missed very little, those wanna-be-Jesus-pretending-to-be-a-burnout eyes.

He knew she was planning something, but it didn't matter. He trusted his team to get what he wanted out of her. "I would shake your hand, but it's over a video." He held a palm up to the screen. "We have a deal, Kayla."

CHAPTER TWENTY-EIGHT

SHE POSED ON a blank white background, and a few hours later someone pressed a fake NY driver's license into her hand. Fresh clothes (jeans, a hoodie, a hat) made her feel like a new woman. She slipped her engagement ring into a pocket, and that made her feel empty and confused. She ignored the feeling. A blindfold covered her eyes, and strong hands led her out to a thick afternoon sun that pressed warmth into her body.

"Let me take that off." Vapor's long fingers slid the fabric back to reveal a city street in Brooklyn or Queens. Not that it mattered where they were, now. A town car idled nearby, reminding Kayla queasily of the ride to the Borgata and the poker game with Monahan. The exact time and place where she'd met this fate.

Vapor pointed to the car. "Hop in."

They climbed into the back. Vapor signaled the driver, and they were on their way. Kayla checked the time on the dash. Five P.M. The branch closed at seven. She ignored the thoughts of what might happen and where they might take her if they didn't make it in time. Now that she was out from under the oranges, she could breathe, as if a hand clenched on her throat had loosened. That place, these people, gave her the massive creeps. She might actually have a meltdown or a breakdown if they tried to take her back.

And then where would she be? Exactly SOL.

As much to distract from dark thoughts as actual interest, she turned to Vapor. "How did you do it?"

Vapor slid her eyes to Kayla. "Do what?"

"Build all that technology."

Vapor said nothing.

"I mean, I assume you're the magic behind Resilusio. The vision."

A pause. "I did a lot of the heavy lifting. But nothing like that comes into being without the work of hundreds."

"But you came up with it."

Vapor said nothing for a moment. "You know, what you're doing is very brave."

That made Kayla think about her father, which made her sad. "Bravery is a decision," she finally said. "This isn't one." She glanced at Vapor. "Were you close to your parents?"

A sad little smile passed across her face. "I was really young when they died."

"I'm sorry."

"Thanks." Vapor exhaled. "They were revolutionaries. Radicals. They founded a leftist militant organization. To overthrow the US government. All that hopeless stuff. Protests. Marches. Violence. Bombs."

"Wow."

She nodded, her eyes flitting across something. Maybe a memory. "They died in a shootout with police." She glanced at Kayla. "I've seen people try to change the world while poor. Doesn't work. Cash is the oxygen of revolution."

Kayla bit her lip.

Vapor paused for a minute, like she forgot—then remembered—that she just told Kayla about her parents' violent end. "Yeah, they took out two cops with them."

"How horrible."

Vapor shrugged. "That's the *other* problem with most revolutionaries. Ninety-nine percent of them are just anarchists. They don't have plans or a clue about what they'll do if they're actually successful. They have more passion than sense. The Genesis Foundation is exactly the opposite. We have management. Direction. We work professionally. We've been patient. Waited. That's not a feature of most people dying to change the world." She caught her breath. "And now the time has almost come. I'm going to do it right. Not screw it up like my parents."

They passed a few beats in silence until Vapor spoke again. "What about your parents? You were close?"

"Yeah," she replied honestly, surprising herself. "We were. Until my father messed up. Bad. My mother had cancer. It went into remission. The Feds charged him with insider trading and conspiracy. My mom's cancer came back. She died." She turned her face away, toward the window. Her mother's remission. That was a happy time for their family. They had hope. Hope and a terribly naïve belief that everything would be okay. Her mom loved the beach. Her father claimed he intended to use his ill-gotten gains for a beach house. Now Kayla could barely glance at a puddle in the pavement without a panicky grip of despair clamping her stomach. But, of course, even that story was Kayvan Masouvi spin. The real story? He loved money. Well, maybe that was too specific. He loved winning.

Vapor nodded knowingly. "You never got the chance to figure out for yourself who you were. Too busy being angry and grieving and worrying."

"Maybe." A memory distracted her. What was it he always said? Oh, right.

"Inside every great company is a great crime, my girl."

At the time, it seemed like a convenient mindset for the guy insider trading his way to a ten-year bid at Club Fed. Today, in contrast, the words were more or less pure truth.

"Did you ever find out? What you wanted to do with your life?"

Kayla snapped back to the present. "I thought my dream was poker. Maybe it still is. Hard to tell now."

Vapor squeezed a shoulder up. Down. Unconvinced. "Maybe that dream was just…negative space. Maybe it was just a stand-in for rejecting what the world expected of you."

Silence dripped by. Despite everything, the words hit her hard, along with her own doubts, buried so far underneath her pain and desperation that she had lost them long ago.

Vapor seemed to think for a moment. "Do you know our motto?"

"Our?"

"The Genesis Foundation."

Kayla thought for a moment. *"We will heal the world."*

Vapor considered this. "What do you think it means?"

A pause. "Poverty, wars, climate change, disease."

"No." Vapor smiled. "Those are noble goals. But not ours. Ours is healing the brain. Healing the soul. Murderers, rapists, child molesters…a thing of the past. We can heal the mind of such evil intentions. Evil thoughts."

"By taking away free will?"

She shook her head. "You can explore your desires. Safely. You can pursue your dreams. Safely. You can achieve humanity's core desire: to be accepted. To find purpose. Safely." She leaned back. "A drastic change in the human experience will bring about a drastic change in the human condition. No more war. No more conflict."

"What about wars over land? Lots of those. Hard to fix with a computer program."

Vapor shook her head. "There's plenty of land in Resilusio."

Before Kayla could properly articulate her thoughts on this madness, Vapor snapped her head in Kayla's direction. "It's not crazy. I promise."

Kayla took a deep breath. "Sounds like a religion," she finally said. "Evan Schechter's the prophet. And the messiah."

"When I joined Monahan's operation, I was desperate to be the opposite of my parents. Make myself rich. Really rich." Vapor clenched and unclenched her right hand. "I was wrong. I hated who I was. And I saw no way out." She stopped, the color in her cheeks high, her eyes pale and sapped. "I woke up one day and…I chose a new destiny."

Kayla stared out the window. "You don't know how it works. Maybe it makes users crazy desperate addicts, just like the GR version."

"We will figure it out." Vapor's voice held an icy edge. "It doesn't."

They reached their destination an hour later, in silence. Night had fallen. Vapor's eyes darted, analyzing. Deciding. She jammed her hands into her ratty jacket, pulled something out with her left hand. Kayla caught a glimpse of metal.

But then she stopped, shook her head, and pointed to an envelope in the seat pocket in front of her. Escondido's location. Had to be. "I'll be here, waiting."

Kayla eyed the envelope as anger and impatience flooded her.

We have so little time.

I need to know where he is.

Where is he? Where is he? Where IS HE?

She exhaled a raggedy breath as Vapor eventually fished a cigarette out of her pocket. She lit it, inhaled, opened the window, and exhaled. "I'm hoping I can trust you."

"Nervous?" Kayla jutted her chin at the cigarette. "I wouldn't peg you for a smoker."

"We all have bad habits we can't fully shake, right?" Vapor gazed at her meaningfully.

Kayla recoiled at this comment, which reeked of *knowing*. The betrayal of her privacy and autonomy that Vapor's own creation had encouraged, required, created.

Stop. She must not think of that. It would make her crazy.

She focused on the fact that Vapor had saved her life in the hospital, with the doctor assassin chasing her. He would have snatched her. She'd be dead by now.

"Thanks again for saving me."

They stared at each other for a second, and Kayla sensed a tiny lean forward from Vapor. "You have the Director to thank for that. We have supporters everywhere. Believers who'll do anything for our vision." Vapor took another drag on her cigarette and turned to blow the smoke out the window. "Anyways, don't thank me just yet. You may not like this deal, after all."

Fair enough. Kayla turned away and closed her eyes. There he was again. Sameer.

You can still win, he whispered in her ear. *Don't lose faith.*

Only for you, Sameer, she replied. *Only for you, I allow myself hope.*

CHAPTER TWENTY-NINE

FIRST CAME THE gauntlet of ATMs, with their smooth, blank, vaguely threatening faces. Then the actual bank. Empty, harshly lit and uninviting, as most banks were these days. Ropes cordoned access to the lone open teller. An older man stood in front, counting out bills and coins deliberately from a large red pouch. Kayla stepped inside to the scrutiny of a bored security guard.

"Can I help you, ma'am?"

For a second Kayla imagined herself in her hospital roommate's clothes, ill-fitting and out of place. She panicked. That would not do.

But she looked down at her body. Jeans. Sneakers. All roughly her size. The surge in her chest subsided. She smiled at the security guard. "I need to get into my safe-deposit box." She worked hard to look calm, act calm, to be the most nonchalant safe-deposit-box customer ever.

He pointed at some scratchy-looking corporate chairs. "Wait there. Someone will come."

A minute later a harried Asian woman dressed in a blue suit and fake pearls hurried over. "You need the safe-deposit boxes?" Her name tag identified her as the branch manager.

"Yes." Kayla willed herself to stand in a controlled fashion and not leap like she was on fire. They hurried down back stairs that led to the vault. Descending nearly gave Kayla a panic attack. All thanks to her time under the oranges. She breathed in and out, deep with a full exhale, one foot in front of the other. They were not far underground. No worse than the subway. And this helped.

Her body calmed.

At the bottom, another security guard stood in front of two sets of double doors that required her escort to slide in an old-school key card. Behind the doors sat the bank's vault, cranked open, very imposing and secure. The branch manager turned to her. "Are you ready?"

Kayla nodded. Her face and a pin were required to enter the room with the boxes. Her hand and eye would open a lockbox that held the renter's key.

She should be all set. Again, she willed herself calm. Even though the circumstances were crazy, this activity was normal and no big deal.

You got this, Sameer whispered.

But even his voice barely helped. She breathed too fast. Caught herself. Swallowed. The branch manager eyed her curiously. Her side ached. Dull and diffuse, then thick and throbbing.

Get in. Get out. She focused. The first doors opened without a hitch.

She stepped inside with the branch manager. She entered her hand and presented her eye for the biometrics of the lockbox. It slid open, revealing the renter's key.

Two minutes later she was in a private room, opening her safe-deposit box. Her fingers closed around the paper with the seed phrase.

And that was when the lights went out.

She officially panicked. She was underground, behind two locked doors. Underground: her new phobia. And in the dark. Even better.

Starbursts erupted everywhere in her vision. Her knees jellied. It was only through force of will that she sank to the floor rather than collapsed.

Someone screamed. Long and deep. She clamped her hand over her mouth. The scream continued.

No, not her.

She stuffed the paper with the seed phrase in her pocket. Then she slipped open the door to the private room and eased her way out.

A thin beam of light illuminated the double doors. She ran for them and gently pressed the button to unlock them from the inside. They clicked open. She pushed through, because she was a sitting duck by the safe-deposit boxes. The next set of doors was already ajar. In the scrawny elbow of light from above, at the top of the stairs, a profile came into view.

Her pursuer. The doctor ground crew hot dog vendor.

The assassin. He would find her, interrogate her, torture her, murder her. In that order.

Someone grabbed her arm. She nearly screamed. By some amazing luck, she swallowed the sound whole.

"Miss." Keys and badges jangled. It was the security guard. "Come with me."

She stared longingly at the light from the stairs, knowing full well that it was a mistake to go that way. Fortunately, her new best friend had a plan. He led her to a blank white door. An emergency exit. It required a key card, which calmed her and gave her hope. Her assassin did not, most likely, have a key card, and they had not cut the power to remove that security feature, if that was even possible. He opened the door to reveal a long, red-lit corridor, ghostly and demonic.

"Only goes out," he said, reading her thoughts. His name tag read ATIQ N. He was gangly and young, his dark skin covered with tattoos. He took her hand. They ran, and Kayla thought that if she never, ever set foot in another tunnel again, it would be too soon.

At the end of the line, he pushed opened the door to reveal a row of very nice Brooklyn town houses, a tidy and well-maintained street that started half a block from the bank branch, all leafy, bumpy sidewalks, planters, and white shutters. He motioned her out. "Off with ya," he said. "Get as far away from here as you can."

"You're not coming?" Kayla said, her voice rising. She paused. "There's someone in there who's very dangerous. He'll kill anyone in his way." Guilt slapped her. Here she was, maybe getting more people murdered. God.

"I have to go back," he said. "I'm security."

Right. Of course he was. She decided then and there she would never breeze by security guards again, because one just saved her life. "Thank you, Atiq."

"Anytime." He gently pushed her out and pulled the door shut. The night stilled, and the empty street yawned ahead of her in either direction.

She stared plaintively from one side to another, begging for a sign of what to do. Left? Right? Across?

But there was nothing.

CHAPTER THIRTY

SHE TURNED IN a slow circle and debated. She could not walk back and find Vapor. Too risky. She could never, in fact, go back there. Maybe Vapor would circle the block and look for her. She'd have to wait and hide.

A few houses down, where the street darkened, she spied a cluster of construction equipment: dumpsters, trucks, pallets, a few workers straggling out onto the sidewalk, ducking under garlands of temporary lights strung up across a crumbling facade. A home renovation. They must be finishing for the night.

The door was open.

She waited until they had almost disappeared, then ran inside, where she found ghostly shapes and construction materials covered with wood planks, drapes, and a healthy layer of dust. Equipment sat in corners, powering down for the night. She walked all the way to the back, where battered French doors—original, not yet replaced revealed glimpses of a garden behind. She examined the handle, not wanting to turn it and set off an alarm. There was no visible lock on the warped, creaky wood. She sank down behind the drapes, her back pressed to the paned glass, made herself small, and waited. Ten, fifteen, twenty minutes. The remaining workers left, laughing and talking, pulling the door behind them.

The house grew creaky, city-quiet. Kayla exhaled.

Too soon. Work boots scraped pavement. Someone yelled in Spanish, joined by another voice. Another yell accompanied the sound of blows on human flesh. A weapon. Gasps of pain. Scrapes that might be bodies slumping down. Then came more heavy footsteps. From the street, a scream erupted. It hit Kayla like a two-by-four to the face. The front door screeched open. Someone walked in. Many someones. Many footsteps. Thick clomps.

They would be upon her soon.

The garden.

She shoved aside the drapes and hauled herself upright, yanking the handle. The door barely budged, and her stomach lurched. She tried it again. No luck. The crappy door barely moved.

She squinted in the dark. The crappy door had a lock.

Not just any lock. A good lock.

Wait, that meant it should *unlock*. Somehow. And it was at that moment that Kayla truly understood how normal brain functions short-circuit in times of stress. This door had an internal lock. Common in garden doors. All she had to do was lift the handle and push.

But it wouldn't be that easy. She scrambled at it, her fingers suddenly clumsy and wholly incapable. Finally, one hard turn and one yank later, the doors opened. She lurched out amid excruciating noises: brutal hands trashing the entire house. Furniture crashing to the floor. Someone yelling orders in a foreign language.

The hot dog vendor.

"Not today, motherfucker," she whispered. She gulped air and shoved the doors closed, breathing in smoke, her own fear, sawdust and drywall and paint and the sharp animal smell of danger. The backyard offered little in the way of escape. Two slatted wooden walls. The third made of crumbling brick. Scraggly shrubs, indifferent planters, heavily abused slate pavers, and grass. The rigidly demarcated rectangular plot had literally nowhere to hide. She scanned the walls, convinced somewhere there'd be a hole, a foothold, a hand beckoning her out, to freedom, away from this misbegotten place. Her desperate eyes darted everywhere.

What am I supposed to do? Scale a brick wall? Crouch under a shrub?

And indeed, the best of the bad choices was to hide behind a five-foot-tall hedge, a few steps ahead.

Halfway there, someone appeared at the top of one wall. She almost screamed but stopped herself. This creature hid in the shadows, appearing and disappearing, almost a trick of the lighting. A hallucination? Magical thinking? She stepped forward. It shifted.

No. *Real.*

A man, a real man, all black, his head and face covered with a balaclava, the eyes smeared out with thick greasepaint like the work of some demented, nihilistic painter and all but invisible behind tinted glasses. A ninja or video-game character. Kayla blinked and opened her mouth. He put a finger to his lips and one in the air.

Wait.

She blinked again. He was gone.

Not real. A hallucination. An apparition.

Thump.

There was a rope. A real rope. That convinced her. He was not here to kill her. At least, probably not. He hopped down into the garden, wildly silent, and gestured to Kayla first, the rope second. She got it, of course.

Grab on to the rope.

Kayla wrapped two hands around a thick black technical twine, feet on the slats, one in an increasingly long line of decisions-that-were-not-much-of-a-decision. Behind her, heavy feet slammed closer and closer, breaking, knocking things down. Fast and efficient, her rescuer shoved her up and over. Kayla landed with a cracking thump in the neighbor's backyard. In a comic-book flash, he was at her side, hustling her over another fence. They crouched under bushes in a backyard, where the occupants were very much home.

Lights shone out through the French doors. The occupants had drawn their curtains, but shapes moved behind, along with voices and dinner noises and sudden whiffs of dinner scents—clanks and sizzles, onions and meat. Her rescuer muttered something unintelligible into a tiny black headpiece that snaked nearly invisible against his cheek.

He whispered close to her ear, "Can you run?"

Not really, but she had limited options: run or die.

She nodded.

"Straight line. When you get out, one right, two lefts. At the end of the block is a van. Verizon Cable. Lights off." He listened for a second. "Cops are coming."

"Right, left, left," she repeated in a whisper, ignoring the part about the cops.

He nodded reassuringly and swiveled his arm around to show her an iPhone strapped on with a blueprint, presumably of this house. He traced her path to the door with a gloved hand. A straight shot veering slightly right.

She was thankful to be in Brooklyn with its narrow, predictable town houses.

He handed her a balaclava and she slipped it over her head.

He whispered close to her ear. "Watch."

She nodded and he crept out from the bushes, so stealthy and inconspicuous that detecting his presence would require actually knowing he was there, like parsing through an optical illusion. At the doors, he crouched underneath, inserting long thin pieces of metal into the spaces between them and into the lock, the house probably chosen exactly for this purpose. Less than thirty seconds later, with just the barest of scraping sounds, he'd wrapped a gloved hand around the handle. One twist, and it would open. He turned to Kayla, his face a question.

Ready?

At her nod, he pulled. The alarm screeched on cue. She ran-stumbled inside, past a modern, gleaming kitchen, into a living room, where two kids and a man ate popcorn in front of a television beaming out a reality TV show.

Well, they *were* eating popcorn and watching reality TV, until a girl in a ski mask shot through their home. Now they were up, terrified, staring at her, open-mouthed. As she barreled past, the man pushed the kids back, behind him. Parental instinct. On the left, Mom hurried down the stairs, tying an apron. At the sight of Kayla, she froze and gripped the banister, the apron ties forgotten and dangling.

The front door. Three feet away. Locked, right? She turned the dead bolt and yanked the handle with all her strength. Not locked, actually. She twisted the dead bolt back and pulled again, successful this time. The house sat at the top of a long, curving set of stairs. With a cry of hope, she lurched down, tripping, caught herself, turned left.

Wait. No. She was supposed to turn right.

She spun, scurried in the correct direction. Sirens approached, their long angry wails piercing the thin air, mingling with the alarm still blaring from the house. Lights flashed in the distance ahead of her. She ran toward them, because those were her instructions from her ninja rescuer. Right, left, left.

Jesus, where was that left?

The sirens. Louder and louder, brighter and brighter. The sidewalk broke into an intersection. Finally. She took the left hard, tripped on mangled pavement. Her injury screamed and she gulped curse words. A vehicle screeched around the corner toward her, headlights too bright to identify. The balaclava. A problem on, a problem off. She weighed her options for a split second and pulled it off. If that was the hot dog vendor, the balaclava would not fool him.

The sirens. Louder now. But the oncoming vehicle was the most pressing problem.

Nowhere to hide. Not enough time.

It slammed its brakes next to her.

A van. Verizon Cable. Yes. The cable guy. As promised.

The door flew open. "Get in." The voice belonged to her rescuer.

But.

She froze. An odd, not uncommon reaction to stress and trauma. Her legs and arms refused to move. But ninja didn't miss a beat. He leapt to the sidewalk, snatched her rigid body, vaulted her into the van, and jumped in behind her. The vehicle raced down the street as a grasping medley of other hands pulled her into darkness. To safety.

For now.

CHAPTER THIRTY-ONE

SHE CAUGHT HER breath and gradually identified her surroundings. Three people in here, other than her rescuer, all dressed like members of an elite military unit. Two were checking geolocation software and surveillance tapes on small tablets strapped to their arms, muttering unintelligibly into earpieces. The driver, apparently trained by NASCAR, burned rubber, squealed the tires, and took every turn tight enough to nearly flatten the passengers with torque.

But it worked. Ten minutes later, they were safely away. Tension melted. Shoulders calmed. Tablets darkened. At least one person fell…asleep? Her rescuer peeled off his helmet and revealed himself, dipping his face into the streetlights streaming by.

"*Miles*?" Of all the shocks of the night, this was the most extreme. Her colleague at GR was now a ninja in all black scaling walls in Brooklyn? Just in time to save her ass from a hot dog vendor assassin?

He nodded and smiled and mouthed something. Well, maybe. His lips moved, but whatever he said didn't register. Her ears were semi-functional at the moment.

He leaned over her shoulder and repeated, "Are you bleeding? Injured?"

No. Not sure. Yes. She stared at him dumbly.

He patted her hand reassuringly. "Good. Just relax."

Eventually, she understood the words and nodded.

They sat in silence for a while—Kayla, Miles, and three Navy SEALs or commandos or whatever they were. Nobody else removed their masks. The driver, of indeterminable gender, turned from the road and nodded in Kayla's direction.

"We have to delouse her."

Miles nodded grimly. "Well, pull over, then."

They parked behind a deserted gas station. Miles opened the door, waited for her. Kayla sat, frozen.

"Tracking devices," he said, holding a hand out. "We have to get them off you."

She stood up. Followed him. Disappearing into shadow form again, he led her out of the light and handed her a bag. "Change into these clothes. I'll take everything you're wearing."

She blinked. He expected her to strip right here? Behind a gas station? In the bitter cold? That might actually be enough to make her lose it. Really lose it. She had not yet cried for Sameer. Not yet cried for her new, miserable, fugitive-hunted-like-a-desperate-animal life. Nothing and none of it had made her cry. But here, right now, because she had to change clothes behind the ExxonMobil, she just might.

God, it was hopeless. All of this. She should give up. She'd never find her father in time. Hot dog guy would find her first. That was his job. He was probably good at it. She didn't stand an ice cube's chance in hell.

You should give up.

For once the Mean Voice was not just mean but also logical. Kayla turned slowly. Cars sped by, spewing thick flashes of lights.

Go walk in front of the highway. End it all.

The urge was sudden, potent, so, so real, and her face must have shown it. Her face must have shown it all, because Miles's hand was on hers and he was squeezing it, and he was pulling her close, speaking low enough to thwart any listening ears.

"Maybe you want to give up," he said. "Don't."

She stiffened at the words. Because they were true. Because the entire world had blurred to blobs and bright myopic Van Gogh lights.

"You have so much to live for, Kayla," he said. "I've been where you are."

Unlikely, she thought.

"I'm fine," she said. *Snap out of it.* The picture came into focus. Her body screeched out of fight-or-flight mode. All these emotions. The terrible feelings. They were real, yes.

But they will not help you, Sameer's voice whispered, *and you have your father to save.*

"I'll give you privacy," Miles said, and angled his body away from her. He opened a bag, thick canvas and metal-lined. One gloved hand reached to her. "Give me your clothes. Don't drop them."

The clothes he gave her fit suspiciously well, as if whoever picked them had all her sizes. Jeans, T-shirt, shoes, socks, even a bra and underwear. She tugged them on, retrieved the paper with the seed phrase and shoved it into her pocket, then slipped her ring on. Immediately, her body calmed. The ring. Her last connection to Sameer.

I'll make you proud, my love. "I'm ready."

Finally he looked at her. "Good."

Back in the truck, someone ran a scanner over the bag. It yelped mournfully, and the van's occupants grunted in annoyance.

"Sleep, Kayla," Miles said. "We have a long ride."

She pushed the seat back and closed her eyes.

She woke to his hand on her shoulder, solid and soft. It made her flinch. Reality settled on her, and she almost fell down the hole. The black hole of despair and suicidal thoughts. She clenched her teeth so hard, they creaked. Her right hand flew to her left ring finger. She squeezed her engagement ring as if it would teleport strength into her body and repeated the words in her head.

I will save my father.

I will make Monahan pay.

I am not afraid to die.

The van slowed to a stop at a block in TriBeCa. They were back in the city.

"We're headed to my place," Miles informed her gently. He had changed clothes. No longer a cat burglar. Now he was… himself again, in trendy jeans, an ironic T-shirt, and a battered burnt-orange baseball cap. UT Austin. Backward.

Kayla frowned. "I thought you lived in Harlem."

He nodded. "Someone lives in Harlem."

She looked away. "Got it."

He went on. "You'll decompress. You need a break. Then we'll discuss next steps. I'll share everything with you. You can make your own decisions."

Your own decisions. That made her laugh.

He leaned into her. "Be my girlfriend for our walk to the building? People stare less at couples."

She took his hand and forced a saccharine smile. "Would you like me to kiss you, too?"

❧

The cable van stopped at a gleaming high-rise, directly on the West Side Highway, a perfect vertical tower of steel, firmly pruned planters, clusters of carefully chosen flowers. They walked through a leafy courtyard with grass and benches into an oversized glass lobby of marble and polished wood. Kayla had never visited his apartment (or rather, his "apartment"), and even though she lived an elevator's ride away from their desks, he hadn't visited hers, either. He hadn't even tried. Not once. It occurred to Kayla now that Miles had never tried to hit on her. Just to be her friend.

And pretend to rock out at phony Depeche Mode concerts with her.

The doorman smiled at them. "Welcome home, Sir. Miss."

Past the concierge desk, Kayla dropped Miles's hand. Human touch repelled her.

The elevator was high-speed, crazy high-speed, just like the one in the GR building, her old home. Kayla's ears popped as her stomach lurched at the memory.

That was never home, she thought. *That was a rat cage in a laboratory.*

They walked into a postage-stamp-sized apartment with a dazzling view to the south and west, above the green puffs of trees and the jagged stair-steps of building rooflines. The Hudson lapped across the middle, an inky black paintbrush. Behind that sat New Jersey, low and comparatively pastoral, stretching into faraway worlds and thick mounds of mountains that hung like snapshot backgrounds. The interior of Miles's apartment was cozy and inviting and not particularly *guy*. Homey yellow rugs, an overstuffed couch, and a rustic wood coffee table. Framed snaps dotted each surface. Kayla walked around, peered at them. His family. Golf. Miles and his family playing golf. Pictures of travel to exotic places. Most of these had mementos clustered nearby. Miles, face weathered, flashing a thumbs-up atop Machu Picchu with a group of friends, an Incan carving propped nearby. Miles and a very pretty girl hugging and grinning in the middle of an insane Tokyo intersection, accessorized by a Kikkoman soy sauce key chain. Memories. Nice ones. It was normal and calming. Kayla's muscles unclenched bit by bit. Her flight or fight instinct, on full alert every waking moment since the explosion, dulled. She glanced at the bathroom.

"Can I take a shower?" Now that an actual shower was more or less in front of her, she longed to jump in, twist the water to take-your-skin-off hot, and just stand there cooking. As she contemplated it, the craving cranked up. Damn, she might sell a body part for a shower right about now. Miles disappeared into a closet and returned with fluffy, fresh towels in a tasteful taupe. Kayla glanced at the label. Sferra, a luxury brand. Not cheap.

"I'll ruin your beautiful towels," she told him. "I'm bleeding." Well, that wasn't entirely true. Her wound might have knitted, or it might be ready to ooze out various staining bodily fluids. Either way, the towels were in peril.

"I'll get new ones." He shook the pile. "When you get out, we'll talk about everything. I'm glad you're safe."

The bathroom had a deep marble soaking tub. *People have drowned in bathtubs,* she thought. *I could, too.*

Miles read her mind. "Are you sure you'll be okay in here?"

You can't kill yourself, another voice snapped, exasperated. *You have work to do. Someone needs to suffer.* Okay. That was definitely not Sameer.

You've got this, Kay Kay. You can still win. We *can still win.*

Ah, there he was. She touched his ring. It was the closest she could get to touching him.

"I'm okay." She shut the door, locked it, set the water to blistering, and stepped in.

She would take a shower. Nothing else. Yes, she would.

She would be fine.

CHAPTER THIRTY-TWO

FOOD. TANTALIZING. FRESH. Not the smell of stale takeout—congealed fats and lukewarm meat. The smell of cooking. Real cooking. And the sounds! A wooden spoon scraping cast iron. Confident chopping against a nice substantial cutting board. So this Miles had actual cooking skills, something Kayla did not possess. Her stomach somersaulted with hunger. An actual meal without a vague threat of death. It would be a treat.

It would be a miracle.

She dressed and opened the door, took a deep breath. Olive oil. Tomatoes. Garlic.

Comfort.

The living room table perched on a corner next to one of the million-dollar views. Glass and polished wood. Miles had set it for both of them, with nice silverware. Nice plates. A bottle of red wine with a fine aged label. A grand cru, maybe even. Two glasses were currently breathing. She pictured herself inhaling all that oaky goodness. Then pushed away the thought, the anticipation of pleasure.

No. Nothing. Nothing good.

Well, you did just take a very relaxing shower, you selfish bitch.

The guilt poured in. The Mean Voice was right. It was wrong to enjoy anything. Anything at all.

Miles popped his head out of the kitchen, holding a pan, frowning at something sizzling inside. He lifted a crispy oblong item and flipped it.

"I make a mean chicken parm." He grinned at her gently. The kitchen towel flung over his shoulder slipped. He caught it just in time. "And—finally—I have a captive audience to show off my culinary skills. God has answered my prayers."

You cook? She stared at him, bewildered, though for all she knew, he'd been cooking all this time. *Actual food?*

He paused. "I know this is a lot to take in, Kayla. Let's eat. Then we can talk."

She turned her head. Exhaled all the magical scents. They were life, food, nourishment, thriving, existing. She wasn't interested. "I'm not hungry."

Miles slid the cutlets onto a plate, turned off the stove, and came over. "Seems to me your two goals are in conflict."

She twitched. "Which are?"

"Avenging Sameer." He held out one hand, palm up, holding a spatula. "Versus punishing yourself for Sameer's death. Abusing yourself." He held up the other hand. He dropped them both. His voice lowered. "Finding a way to kill yourself."

She ignored his words. "Thank you for rescuing me, whoever you are."

He slid another chicken breast onto the pile. "I suggest tackling one problem at a time. Let's get the Garbage Man first. Then you can hate yourself. In that order. It's the logical progression, wouldn't you say?"

Out the window, a boat emerged onto the Hudson. A little tugboat, pushing mightily against a strong current, cutting the gray-green water. A moment later an identical one appeared in the other direction, hauling a boat quadruple its size.

"And there's another consideration," he said, handing her a bowl filled with salad. "How will you stab Rick Monahan in the eye if you're weak from malnutrition?"

She gazed at the view, at the wine, at the food. She breathed in her longing for all of it, and then she plopped herself on a cushioned dining room chair, at the table. Miles had carved a tiny chip in her icy heart.

But it wasn't enough.

She turned away from the food. "Tell me." Then she closed her eyes for a second, because she had been here before. The day before. So many people trying to get their hands on this technology. To stop it. Control it. Or something. Murderers. Megalomaniacs. Craven negotiators. And she was just a sad little hopeless pawn in the middle. "Tell me everything you know. I'll do the same."

He blinked some disappointment in her direction. "Okay. I work for the US government. Infiltrating GR is my assignment, and so far I've made progress."

He buttered a piece of bread and handed it to her. "Eat."

She took the bread, stared at it, then deposited it on her plate. "Please," she asked, "Do you know what Escondido is? A research facility where Monahan's doing human experiments. Nazi stuff. My father is there. The Genesis people promised to get me the location…" She cut herself off and swallowed. At least she didn't tell him about the tokens.

He gave the bread a pointed glance, then her. Shrugged.

Jesus. This guy. Craven negotiators, all of them. She took a bite, awakening a ferocious hunger, which she ignored. "Happy?"

"Yes." He thought for a second. "And yes. We know what it is." He took his own bite. Chewed. "Where it is."

She leaned forward. "If you work for the government, why haven't you raided it? Shut it down?"

Another bite. He tilted his head to the side. "I'll give you one guess."

The world shrank a little. "You don't have proof."

"Not yet." He stared into his wineglass. Sipped. "We've never been inside. We can't even get a confirmation of what's down there. If *anything's* down there. We lost good people trying."

Lost good people. She shuddered and thought for a moment. "How do we get proof?"

He nodded. "We have some ideas. But for now, we have a more pressing problem. Resilusio comes out of beta trials soon. Couple of weeks. The product goes live. Soon we'll never be able to stop it. And then it will all be over."

CHAPTER THIRTY-THREE

She didn't understand.

Kayla walked to the window. Stared at the dark black ink of the Hudson. "You're talking about the retail locations, right? The arenas?"

"That's part of it." He put his hands together. "Fifty locations. Fun Saturday-night activity. How would we shut that down? It's just a video game. There's no proof that it's addictive. That it's anything other than entertainment." He sipped his wine. "What do you know about open-source software?"

Open-source software. Computer software released with its full code free and available to all. Nonprofit foundations backed these projects, and they compiled and released versions of the software based on changes—bug fixes, improvements, and generational edits—submitted by the project's dedicated developer community. The Linux operating system and the Apache web server were prominent examples, governed by the Linux Foundation and the Apache Software Foundation, respectively.

Another example could be the Resilusio metaverse, governed by the anonymous entity in Vapor's files. Kayla now owned 50 percent, via her anonymous wallet holding REAL tokens. Monahan wanted to gift Resilusio to the world? Why? "No."

"Open-source software is—"

"No, no." She took a deep breath and sat back down at the table. "I meant...why open source?"

"No clue. All we know now is that he's releasing the source code." Miles eyed her barely touched food, maybe scheming for a way to get her eating. "At least, some of it."

"He's not trying to make money." Kayla followed the logical bouncing ball. "This isn't about money."

And that was a problem. Without money flowing in and out of a corporation, even the most skilled forensic accountant would struggle to track the business. But she could follow the tokens. Monahan needed voting control—51 percent—to release Resilusio as open-source software in an untraceable and anonymous path.

"I agree. Millions of developers around the world will create products. Certainly some won't require rigs. Even if we shut him down in the US, it won't matter. It will be everywhere, and maybe the users won't even know it's Resilusio." He thought for a moment. "What do you have that he wants so badly?"

"Let me ask you this," she said, deflecting. "How did you know to find me? The bank?"

"You're all over the news," he said. Inwardly, she winced, remembering the headlines on Vapor's computer.

"And?"

"The entire surveillance infrastructure is on high alert for you. And, of course, Olivia Chen. Imagine our surprise when both of you show up, together, rolling into Manhattan on the BQE with Monahan's goons right on your tail. I sprang into action. Well"—he shrugged and took a sip—"the head of our group sprang me into action, I guess. I'm just a lackey who takes orders."

"Lucky me."

"Why were you at the bank, Kayla?" He leaned forward, his eyes on her, warm and discerning.

"Maybe I'll tell you," she responded. "Maybe you can guess."

He looked like he was about to say something. He hesitated, almost spoke. She held her hand out. "I was in the hospital. After. Monahan sent one of his goons after me. Someone saved me. In the nick of time. It turned out to be Schechter."

Miles nodded like none of this was a surprise to him. "Schechter. The Genesis Foundation. We're familiar. You have something Monahan wants, which made Schechter want you, too."

She laughed. "Correct. Genesis had a secret location. Well, several, I guess. That was where they took me. They showed me their own version of Resilusio. Their product…gets into your head. It can dump knowledge into your brain that was never there, move your body using your mind."

"The one we tried at work…It got inside my head—it really did." His face darkened.

She paused for a moment, wondering how much of their time together consisted of Miles playing a role. Pretending. Not that it mattered. "I know," she finally said, "but this…It's like someone opened your head and stuck controllers into your brain directly. They want to use the technology to save the world. That's what they say, at least."

"Damn," he said softly, "that is not good."

"Right? But Monahan has my father. At Escondido. I don't know when he got there…how long until he's permanently brain damaged. And Schechter offered to give me the location in exchange for something in my safe deposit box."

"Uh, oh, wow." He fumbled for words. His eyes held hers,

with compassion and questions. "That must be some safe-deposit box," he said carefully.

She ignored him. "You said you need proof to raid Escondido. You need someone to go in."

"Kayla. No. You are a ci-vi-li-an." He dragged each syllable of the word out. "Tomorrow I will escort you to a safe house."

She ignored him. "You help me. I'll help you."

"He'll be expecting you. And even if he wasn't..."

She shook her head. "No way his PowerPoint jockey little assistant has the resources and guts to sneak into his insane asylum. He expects me to come to him, up the elevator, swipe my key card, try to bargain."

"Because you have something. Something that will keep you alive."

She said nothing.

"You don't trust me yet. I understand."

"I don't trust anybody." *And you also lied to me, for months...*

He turned his palms up. "Well, I did save your life."

"Completely out of the goodness of your heart."

"I'm taking you to a safe house. Tomorrow."

That made her laugh. "Keep telling yourself that. I'm going with or without you."

"How do you plan to find it? The Nevada desert is a pretty big place, Kayla."

"The Nevada desert, huh? Thanks for pointing me in the right direction."

He stared at her. Stalemate.

Kayla broke the gaze first. "Please help me." She squeezed her hands together to keep them from trembling and took a deep breath. "Please."

His face reddened, slowly but surely. A stress reaction, and one he was permitting her to see. All that training…he could hide it if he wanted to. He just didn't. He lowered his head into his hands. "I'm taking you to a safe house," he repeated.

Silence fell on both of them like a dark cloud.

Finally something worked in his jaw. The high color drained from his face. Spy Miles returned. "Maybe. Okay? Maybe. I won't promise. I will see what I can do. But"—he straightened—"before I go to bat for this, we need some ground rules."

"Which are?"

"We go in together. I'm in charge. You listen to me and do what I say and you don't question a thing."

"Fine."

"Second, you eat your dinner. For real."

And for the first time since Frederick Douglass Monahan blew her life to smithereens, Kayla smiled.

CHAPTER THIRTY-FOUR

SHE HAD TO hold up her end of the bargain.

She had to eat.

The table squeaked under the load of chicken, salad, and bread. The food had cooled a little. Fat had congealed. Sizzle had sputtered. No matter. She took a deep breath this time. The tantalizing smells wafted up, nearly sending her into delirium. Miles filled her plate and slid it in front of her. She stared for a second and then took a bite. Her entire body relaxed. Nourishment. Unwelcome but necessary.

Fine. She would eat just enough.

Miles waited until she finished chewing. "Tell me something." He leaned back, swirled his wine, gazed into its depths. "What did the Genesis people tell you about their cult?"

She chewed on an extra crusty (amazing!) piece of bread. "You think it's a cult?"

"Have you seen the pictures of Evan Schechter on the website? Or anywhere else? It's like stills from some super-cheesy yoga retreat for rich people."

She shuddered. "I had the same feeling when I met him."

His eyebrows shot up. "He was down there?"

She stuffed a floret of broccoli in her mouth. Now that she

was eating, her self-control flew out the window. "Via video feed."

He leaned back, thinking. "Then you definitely had something he wanted. Ever since Monahan screwed over the bugs in favor of spying on people's garbage, Schechter's been on a mission to destroy him."

"I heard something about their rift from Minieri. She was with him." She chewed. "Also on video."

He paused. "We know Dr. Minieri well."

"Oh?"

"She likes to think of herself as a French Resistance spy infiltrating Nazis in occupied France."

Yup, that tracked. "Seems like she's Schechter's eyes and ears inside GR."

He nodded. "Microbiologists are a weird lot."

"Respect the bugs, right? Monahan didn't respect the bugs, so Schechter left."

"It was more than that. There was a power struggle at the board level. Schechter was never a CEO type. He wasn't as business-minded as Monahan. More into the technology. So Monahan got all the support. It was his idea to monetize the trash. He positioned it as anonymous data collection. And maybe it was at one point. But then everything changed."

"Your group has been following this for a while."

"The Genesis Foundation informed the FBI that Monahan was profiling people. Individuals. Using their trash. Spying on them. FBI turned it over to us, because spying is our department. *We* are the spies. Anyone fronting our game like that will get attention."

Who is "we"? "But you did nothing."

"We had nothing"—he regarded her with admiration—"until now."

"Genesis has footage of the experiments."

"What?" The surprise might be genuine. Or excellent acting. Kayla questioned everything right about now.

"Based on what they showed me, the exact evidence you need. It's pretty awful."

"They have proof? Of the experiments?"

"Yes." She thought for a minute. "Actually, you should join forces. After I get my father out, that is."

"Hmm. We're sort of lone wolves. In my group, at least."

"Your group being...?" She opened her palms and waited.

"Mason Capital."

"Mason Capital?"

He swirled his wine for, like, the tenth time. Stared at it, frowning. "Mason Capital's an asset management firm," he said, "with several assets. One is money, and that's how we fund our operations. Tax dollars only cover so much, and they leave a paper trail. The other assets are people." He paused for a second. "Like me."

She raised an eyebrow. "Jason Bourne–type stuff?"

He laughed. "Mason Capital isn't Treadstone 71, and I don't do black ops." Treadstone was the name of the shadowy, murderous organization that trained and created Jason Bourne. "But we have autonomy. No CIA, no NSA, no State Department, no DOD."

"So you're a financial analyst and a spy on the side?"

He rose and gathered a few plates. They clanked against each other. "Me personally? I'm just an asset managed by Mason Capital, a preeminent asset management firm."

She helped him carry dishes to the kitchen, then leaned against the counter, crossing her arms. "Miles. Is that even your name?"

"One of them," he answered simply. "I've had it a long time. It's sort of mine now."

He balanced the plates atop others in the sink. "Mason recruited me right out of college and sent me to a training program. There were fifty of us. Four years of hell on earth to get a PhD in how to murder and spy by way of a Turkish prison camp. Brutal. Maybe too brutal. Only twenty finished. The experience messed us all up. All different and all damaged."

"Wow."

"Yeah. I was lucky. I came out more or less mentally intact. Mason Capital sent me to business school. So I could get executive jobs. Infiltrate a company. Ultimately they assigned me to GR. Monahan gave you the job I wanted, so we had to go another route."

"Did you know what was going to happen? What he was going to do?"

Miles's eyes flitted to her hand and the ring. "No. We got intel late. That Monahan was going to kidnap you. I got to Teterboro just as his guy was dragging you away. We fought. Over you, as it were." He paused, gathering his thoughts. "Meanwhile, the cops came. Paramedics. Firefighters. Monahan's guys disappeared, and the cops arrested me. Holding you. By the time Mason bailed me out, which was a rather perilous proposition, you vanished."

Miles stared at her, unblinking, waiting for her to share.

Not happening. She slid her eyes away, and they landed, unfortunately, on the food. And she was still ravenous. The creeping guilt at allowing herself any nourishment, simmering in the background, sprang forward.

You gave in and fed the hunger. You're a horrible person.

She cleared her throat. "So Mason's a front?"

He laughed. "We have a real business. Not many covert ops can say that. Most are just fronts."

"You actually manage someone's money?"

"A lot of someones. Several billions under management."

Hiding in the spotlight. "So whose money do you manage?"

"Government money. We fund all of our own operations out of our fees. Our two and twenty." This was the classic fee structure of a hedge fund: 2 percent of fees under management and 20 percent of returns. Miles went on. "Everything aboveboard. We never miss a filing. We show up at conferences, ask good questions. No stealth. You can find us on your Bloomberg terminal." Bloomberg was a closed-circuit real-time financial market data application. Virtually every single trader and analyst had Bloomberg, either a terminal or an app. More serious traders had multiple terminals.

Kayla leaned back. So much information. Too much. She pressed her fingers against her eyelids. "So we're stuck with each other. For now, of course."

"We are." He stared at the view first, his wine next. Kayla processed his explanation, her eyes running over his shoulders. Another poker trick. Look for shifts in posture. Changes. And, indeed, tension laced his upper body, and an odd twinge of discomfort hung in the air.

She surprised herself by speaking up. "So then…tell me a story," she finally said. "A story about Miles."

CHAPTER THIRTY-FIVE

"I NEED A category."

"Your origin story. Your real one." She had asked, and received, so little about his past before now. Grew up in Utah. Skied a lot. Plays golf — maybe? What else? She hadn't really inquired, and that embarrassed her. Was she so self-involved that she hadn't even probed enough to get his (fake) cover story?

Apparently. "Every superhero has one. You know, like how Batman got to be Batman?"

"I know what an origin story is." He laughed and got up. "One sec." A sleek black whiskey bunker sat at the opposite side of the room, displaying at least a dozen bottles out of a glass-lined front panel. Miles took out glasses and a mostly full bottle, placing them on the table.

"Bourbon," he said.

They had spent all their time together at work. Never once had they left the building together. Never once had they gone to a bar, a restaurant, or a movie. She had never once shared a drink with Miles, her work husband, her friend.

She made a face. "Only a little."

He poured, as requested, a little for her, more for him. Kayla actually loved the *smell* of bourbon. Vanilla. Caramel. Butterscotch. She hated the taste. Did Miles somehow know that already?

He picked up his glass. "Can I ask you a question first?"

"Sure."

"It's about poker." He took a small sip of the bourbon and rolled it around in his mouth.

"Okay." She stilled. Poker was now synonymous with tragedy. She doubted seriously she'd ever walk into a casino again. Kayla took a sip of the bourbon. Very good. Didn't send a nasty pulse down the back of her throat, unlike most hard liquor, which made her gag. She pulled the bottle toward her and glanced at the label. Parker's Heritage. Hmm. Tasted better than any booze she'd ever had. "Good stuff."

"Very good stuff," he replied, not taking his eyes off her. "The best."

She thought for a moment. "What do you want to know?"

"Who taught you? How did you get into it?"

She thought for a moment. "My dad taught me. He was…" She sighed, deep and raggedy, as emotions tidal waved her body. "He was the *best* poker coach." Her voice caught. "I learned in the kitchen." The image shimmered in her memory. The old, used card deck, the yellow linoleum and brown refrigerator of their dingy rental, her mom's incessant disapproval. "My parents didn't have much money when I was little, and my dad was always working, But he always made time for poker. I think he saw it as a life skill. Reading people. Sizing up situations. And he was right."

"Most parents sign their kids up for soccer or ballet."

She laughed. "Well, mine taught me to play cards. When I got old enough, we started going to the casinos together. The moment I first stepped inside one, I knew it was for me. Each time I pushed through those revolving doors, I felt all my worries and troubles slide away. It made me calm."

Miles said nothing.

"I…know that's a crazy thing to say about a casino," she said slowly, "but it did. And it felt like home. I felt like myself, where I saw the person I wanted to be everywhere else."

"You liked that version of you the best."

She nodded. "Exactly. Anyway, my dad…he was … great at poker. Could read people in a heartbeat. Had a videographic memory, if you can believe it. His memories were literally videos—he could rattle off the cards you played six hours ago. But…he would get tired, he would drink, he would tilt, do weird stuff. And lose. A lot. I figured maybe if I learned from his mistakes, I could do well"—she shook her head from side to side—"with some luck now and then."

She exhaled. "So I went through all the motions of doing 'real jobs,' to make my mom happy, but my heart was never in it." Tears filled her eyes, which she observed with surprise. Tears. Crying. Finally. She could scarcely believe it, having truly expected to never cry again. "Now I wish I'd never picked up a deck of cards. I wish that I'd never seen the inside of a—of a—" Her voice broke. She gathered herself and went on. "Of a casino."

"Hey." He touched her shoulder. "You've got to stop blaming yourself. None of this happened because of poker."

She moved. His hand slid off. "You're wrong. It *is* because of poker. I'm working for Monahan because I lost a poker game. That's how he got me." She stopped crying. Now she just had the sear in the back of her throat from unshed tears. "We bet.

On me. And he knew exactly where to hit." The words from the recruiting dinner zapped through her head.

I always remember that I'm not as smart as I think I am.

A harsh laugh erupted from her throat. "He picked up on all my tells. And he...owned me." This was not exactly true, but it felt like the truth.

"Come here." He pulled her into a hug. Kayla was not much of a hugger. But now, after everything...she was the worst hugger *ever*. Stiff and unyielding. She had to force herself to lift her arms, approximate a hug back.

"Everything I ever thought about myself was a lie." His shoulder muffled her voice. "And so now...on top of everything else... it's like I don't exist anymore. Or worse. Maybe that girl never actually existed." She pulled away, squeezed her eyes shut. "It makes me want to kill myself."

"Please don't do that." He tightened his grip on her.

"I want to. Didn't say I would."

A pause. "Well, that's a start."

"So." She pulled away completely now. "Don't think you can get out of answering my question." Miles handed her a tissue. She blew her snotty nose and wiped her clammy wet cheeks. "And I want the truth."

"Okay," he said slowly. "Well, my family are prominent members of the Church of Jesus Christ of Latter-Day Saints. You know them as Mormons. Descended from the original followers of Brigham Young. For generations, we have been absolutely, unquestioningly devoted to the church. True believers. I am...my parents' only son. And not from lack of trying. I have five sisters."

"Wow."

"Yeah." He moved with some discomfort. "Wow. From a

young age, I was encouraged—strongly encouraged—to pour myself into everything LDS. Nothing less than full indoctrination. And I wanted to make my parents happy"—he gestured at Kayla, acknowledging their common motivation—"so I threw myself into scripture studies, volunteer work...everything. The church elders said I had a prophet's understanding of the Book of Mormon. No one was more pious. More devout. I was the number-one true believer." A muscle clenched in his jaw. "And I never questioned it. Never thought about it or asked if it was for me. I just did as I was told."

"So what happened?"

"LDS kids go on missions. Mostly the boys, but some girls too. They travel to various countries around the world and proselytize."

"Right. Yes."

Miles sipped his drink. His eyes turned glassy. "So I got my call to serve. My ability to learn languages impressed the Mission Center, which meant I had my pick of posts. My parents had already lined up several young women, also from prominent Mormon families. Future wives. Everything...was all set."

Miles stopped speaking, and Kayla said nothing. A painful, heavy silence hung between them.

Finally Miles continued. "The night before my flight, something cracked. In me. In my, I don't know, *head*. I had a... panic attack. My face got so cold, I thought it might freeze off. I thought I was going to die. I chalked it up to nerves, took a sleeping pill, knocked myself out completely. But when I woke up, I knew. I *knew*."

"Knew what?"

"That it was over. I was done. I wasn't the person who did all those remarkable things. I was just the person pretending to be him. And I couldn't pretend any longer."

"Brave decision."

Miles laughed. "Didn't feel that way at the time. It felt like a mental illness. Like a nuclear bomb went off. It devastated my family. Devastated the church. Everyone spent so much time and energy trying to get me back into the fold. None of it worked. For a while I wanted to kill myself, really wanted to kill myself, so I understand. I completely get it. I actually might have gone through with it…if suicide wasn't such a sin and everything." He paused. "I'm babbling. The point is, I let the darkness in. But one day…it left. And I didn't feel bad anymore. I felt free, but more than that, I felt like me. Not an impostor. Me. Like I finally had the right to know myself. To like myself." He stopped, thought for a second. "I learned that you can't run from who you are. So…I expect a short life with eternal glory."

Achilles. The recruiting dinner. Kayla laughed. Actually laughed. Miles did too. Then he gazed at her for a second. Just a second. He slid his eyes away, the only sound the faintest of city noises from the ground far below.

"You never told me any of this," she said softly.

"I wanted to," he replied.

She leaned forward and broke the spell. "Well, then. Along those lines. I believe it's my destiny to get into Escondido, and it's yours to get me there."

He blinked and cleared his throat. "I can get you on a subject collection bus." Pain crossed his face for a brief second. Or did she imagine it? "Out of Pennington. It's a women's prison in Pennsylvania. In three days."

"Three days." A miracle. Her father had a shot.

"Yup."

"How do I get in?"

"You commit a crime," he replied gravely, "and as far as the world's concerned, that will be the truth. Something happens to me, something goes wrong, and you're probably stuck. In prison. Are you ready for that?"

Kayla ignored this bleak outcome. Why think about it? She had no choice. "Just don't make me a child molester, please. Or a rapist."

"Okay, then." He held her eyes, searching them. "How about a murderer?"

CHAPTER THIRTY-SIX

"I CAN'T TAKE your bed."

He handed her a brand-new toothbrush, still in its package. "You can and you will. The housekeeper just came today. Fresh sheets. I left some sweats, too."

She ignored him, gazed at the couch. "That looks comfortable." Cream suede. Very nice.

Miles rolled his eyes. "Look, tough girl, I need to protect you. All that training, right? Remember? Let's take advantage of it." He walked into the room and lowered the drapes on the two wide windows, even though, of course, they had no line of sight into other apartments. He surveyed the space. "Lock the door. Don't open it for anyone but me. I'll be out here."

"On the couch."

"Exactly. Take another shower. Get some sleep. Things will be dicey on both fronts. But before that"—he opened a closet and rummaged, coming back with a basket of first aid supplies: gauze, bandages, disinfectant, and two prescription bottles—"your dressing needs to be changed." He nodded at her side. "And the wound restitched. I'll do it for you. Also antibiotics." He handed her a bottle filled with little blue pills. "One a day until you go."

She stared at him in horror, imagining exactly what "restitching" entailed. "How bad will it hurt?"

"Not at all." He fished out an injection bottle. "Because I have the good stuff."

Miles attended to her with surprisingly adept medical skills, stitching her wound with slow, painstaking detail and minimal pain.

"Did they teach surgery at your spy training program?" she asked, after it was mostly over.

"Of course," he replied, glancing up from her torso. "If you're surrounded by the enemy and need medical attention, you have to take care of yourself." He finished sewing and moved back, examining his work. "Usually, the alternative is bleeding out and dying."

ᔕ

She slept long and thick, with no dreams. And when she woke, she shot up, wide-eyed, two words blaring in her ears: *TEN DAYS.*

Ten days—and that was being generous—until that monster destroyed her father's brain. Or killed him in the name of "science." Or both. She breathed in, breathed out the panic. *Escondido Escondido Escondido*. She visualized it all, ran through the steps as she imagined them. Racing down those creepy quasi-hospital halls. Freeing him from his room. Finding Miles. Getting out. It calmed her. Sort of.

"Kayla?" Miles's voice traveled through the wood of the door, muffled but wide-awake. "It's just me. Everything's all right. Come out whenever. Breakfast is in the kitchen. I'll be back soo—"

She opened the door to a spill of white light. The bright apartment sparkled in the morning sun. Miles stood in front of her, dressed for…work.

"Hey," he said, his eyes planted on his polished shoes like he'd caught Kayla in her underwear instead of the shapeless NYU sweats he had given her.

"Hey."

He exhaled. "Uh, how did you sleep?"

"Fine."

"Good. You needed it." He handed her a very basic flip phone. "Only answer me. I'm programmed in."

She peered at the pixelated green screen of the circa-1996 contraption, pressing the menu button and scrolling to the address book. Indeed, it had one entry. "M." She snapped it shut. "Where are you going?" she asked, though she knew.

"Got to keep up appearances," he said seriously. His phone pinged. He checked it, his smile fading. "Kayla, don't leave the apartment. For any reason. And don't answer the door."

"Yes, sir."

The air crackled between them. Flavors of tension, not all bad. Achy uncertainty and a restless energy that she both feared and welcomed.

"One other thing." He held his phone up. "I have to take a retinal scan of both your eyes, to match it to your new identity. They want it today." He pressed his lower lip against his teeth. "After that, there's no going back."

She glanced at her surroundings, a guy's version of her own apartment.

I should be in my own business casual, skipping off to work. I should be out to boozy lunches, first dates, manicures, Christmas in St. Bart's. Or I should be in London, in a perfect, gorgeous flat in Knightsbridge, planning both a wedding and all my stops on the European Poker Tour.

For the first time since Rick Monahan murdered Sameer and sent her on the run, she let herself long for her life back. *A* life back. When would that be? She clenched her shoulders so hard they creaked and answered her own question.

Never. That girl was gone forever. Thus followed, so was her life.

She nodded once. Unsure. A second time. Firm. Took a deep breath, pulled her hair back with restless hands, and opened her eyes wide. "Do it."

Later, with Miles gone, she took her engagement ring off her finger. She put it in an envelope, along with the paper with the seed phrase, and sealed it. She wrote a note on the outside:

Save this for me
—K

She slipped it into the bottom drawer of a sleek blond wood nightstand in Miles's bedroom. Where she was going was no place for diamonds.

CHAPTER THIRTY-SEVEN

EIGHT HOURS LATER, Miles returned with a duffel bag and three overstuffed manila folders, chock-full of information on Kayla's new identity. Fatima Ubaldi. A twenty-five year old murderer from Tallahassee, Florida. So how did Fatima end up at Pennington?

The story started, as it often does, with the boyfriend.

Committed gangbanger Miguel Cervezas, aka Mikey Beers. Mikey and Fatima fell in love over the internet. Very romantic. Mikey convinced Fatima to come to New York City sight unseen. The South Bronx projects, to be specific. Fatima hopped on the Greyhound directly into the waiting arms of Mr. Beers. But paradise had its troubles. They argued all the time, over money, over Mikey's shady dealings, over his "side pieces" (Fatima's words, courtesy of her confession). Soon, she was selling drugs and robbing bodegas alongside her career criminal boyfriend. But when she got pregnant, she hatched a scheme: one last robbery, and then the Greyhound, without beer boy.

A plan, but not much of one.

During the robbery, the owner produced a gun and shot Mikey twice. Fatima shot the owner in the chest, Mikey shot him in the head. Security cameras recorded every move. Mikey almost bled out atop a spilled pile of Froot Loops and scored a life sentence, being a habitual offender. Fatima got fifteen-plus, miscarried, and fried her life. And now she was on her way to Escondido, to have her brain fried to match.

Kayla plowed through the dossier, committing it to memory, quizzing herself, internalizing the story as her own. What a remarkable work of fiction. Searing and tragic. The folders held not just words and narratives but also maps and pictures. So many. So detailed. One series documented Fatima's apartment with Mikey—broken windows, a disgusting refrigerator, filth, peeling paint, and probably lead poisoning and asbestos for fun. Another series was her family life. Parents, siblings, weddings, graduations.

"The level of detail," she murmured.

"She's a real person, isn't she?" Miles had changed into sweats and brought wine.

A new problem occurred to her. "Wait. I can't look like me, can I? I'm too recognizable."

"Not to mention facial recognition, you know, just as a concept," Miles replied, disappearing and coming back with a contact lens case and a few close-up shots of a nose. A nose that was not her nose.

He held up the lens case. "For the retinal scans. You put them in, you can get a week, and then you must remove and clean them or they'll hurt like a mother and eventually snap out on their own. They match Fatima's record, and more importantly, will not match *your* retinal scans." He then handed her the picture. "Our sculptors make the nose from a proprietary modeling clay. Highly adhesive. Once set, you can get two weeks out of it before it goes bad. I myself got three weeks once."

"Three weeks with an ugly nose, huh?" She examined the

picture. It was larger than hers, crooked. Maybe broken, once. "What was that like for you?"

"It was a chin, actually, and it was excruciating," he said. "Though not excruciating as what the target did to me when it fell off."

He met her eyes for a moment, like he had something to say.

Don't go. This is a terrible idea.

Or, the worst possible words. The best possible words.

Let me protect you. Please. Let me protect you.

She hated herself for speculating what she might do if that came out of his mouth. Would it sway her?

No. *No*. No matter what, she was going in. To save her father. To avenge Sameer. She was going in, and that was that.

The moment passed, and Miles turned away. Fled, or so it seemed, to the kitchen and dinner. Eventually, tantalizing smells and sounds wafted out, chopping and slicing and sizzling and garlic and butter. She got up and admired his skills. Something on the stove. Something else roasting in the oven.

"A chicken," he said, chopping onions. "I figured you'd be engrossed in learning your new identity, so I planned to do the cooking."

She shook her head. Food. Eating. Still a betrayal, when it came down to it.

"We had a deal." He slid the knife away and blinked through the onion tears.

"That was last night."

He opened the oven and stabbed a digital thermometer into the bird. It beeped. He peered at the display, furrowing his very nice brow. She furiously shoved that thought away. Another betrayal of Sameer. Now, and maybe always.

"Food will be scarce for the near future," he said. "Prison first, and that's the easy part. In Escondido you'll have to eat as little as possible. Drink as little as possible. Might be drugged." He pulled the bird out. "Suit yourself, but your best shot at saving your father is to eat now."

She turned on her heel, sat back down to Fatima. Miles arrived in several trips with the food. She forced down bites, her brain screaming against each one. Her own body betraying her in every direction. Longing to starve itself into oblivion one second. The next, to cram enough food in her body to make her sick. And above all, a longing for her would-be protector here to…protect her. No matter. Logic and duty would prevail. Kayla pushed her head down into the files, chewing slowly. Miles sipped and gazed off into the distance, a gloomy look on his face.

"Don't do it, Kayla," he blurted, searching among the twinkling stair-steps of metal and glass for something. "We'll find another way."

She'd sensed this was coming. "Lose the second thoughts. Won't help."

"I'm responsible for you."

"Not officially."

He said nothing.

"My father's in there, Miles." She touched a finger to his hand, which might be, possibly, slightly, trembling. "And, anyway, you're coming to save us."

Something worked in his jaw. "I can't go in with you. I'll be there to extract you. It might not be such a smashing success."

"You're a covert operative. Like a paratrooper, right? You parachute in, forever surrounded by the enemy. You're used to it."

"This is different." He said nothing else.

Kayla had no idea how to respond.

He shook off his feelings, whatever they were, and continued exactly as if he'd said nothing at all. "Tomorrow night the FBI will come to collect you. They won't know anything. Three days later you'll be on a flight to Escondido. Pennington houses over eight hundred inmates. No one will notice you're there. No one will notice you're gone. The psychologists who run the facility are very excited for prisoners like you. You're just the type they've specially requested."

A full convulsion pulsed through her. "And what type is that?"

His jaw set. "Women. Relatively sane women. Apparently they're done with the crazies and the sociopaths. They mess up their bell curves. The protocol is non-crazies now, or as close as possible."

"That's nice to hear." Her voice echoed small and faraway in her ears.

The wall clock read nine. "Anyway, it's getting late. I hate to get all drill sergeant on you, but you should spend the rest of the night memorizing the details of your life. Mother's name, maiden name, grandma, dad, address, etc. You never know who might lob twenty questions at you. Be ready."

The minutiae of Fatima's life. High school: Nomar L. Dutton Memorial, nicknamed No Duh. Family: father Kamel and brothers Kasim and Ali. Hometown: Havana, FL 32333. She recited it all to herself dozens of times. Then Miles took over.

"First job?" Miles quizzed.

"A yogurt shop called Sunshine Swirls. Started in high school, junior year."

"After high school?"

"Broward Community College."

"Your major?"

That was a tough one, deep in the files. "Well, before I threw my life away on Mikey Beers, I wanted to be an accountant. I like numbers."

After four relentless hours, she internalized Fatima, let the character's tragic life dissolve into her consciousness. Miles yawned and went into his bedroom to change. Kayla was on the couch. He came out with an annoyingly charming smile.

"Bedtime," he said, and pointed to the couch. "I need my beauty sleep. And so do you."

"Sure." She gathered her pile of paper and trudged into the bedroom.

"Don't forget to lock the door," he called out behind her, "and don't open the door—"

"—for anyone but you," she finished. "I know."

"Good night."

"Good night."

Safely locked in, she took a moment to practice with the contact lenses. They gave her normal vision—that was a plus. They didn't hurt. She washed up and headed for bed, the living room lights already dark, the room quiet. In bed, she closed her eyes, summoned some supposedly soothing images. Sitting on a beach, napping. In the woods, smelling the trees.

And none of it worked. Insomnia wrapped her in bony clutches and refused to let go. The worst part of insomnia? It was unbelievably boring. She sat up, stretched, flopped down. No. She needed water. She got up.

But when she opened the door, Miles was not asleep. He sat on the couch, with the covers bunched around him, staring listlessly at his phone, rubbing his eyes like an overtired baby.

His shirt was off, and the silhouette of his back and shoulders in the dim light had an unassuming, mesmerizing poetry to it. And something else. A tattoo on his shoulder. A four-leaf clover. Even in the dark, it was green. Irish pride? Or just for luck? She stared for a moment, long enough to recognize that the tattoo was a *five*-leaf clover. Five. Before she could look closer, he sensed her presence and turned to face her, phone tossed aside, alert and ready for anything. One foot on the floor.

"Is there something wrong? Are you oka—"

Her muscles worked faster than her brain. She stepped forward and pressed herself to his body and her lips to his.

And then he gently tugged her to him, and all of Sameer came flooding into her brain like the chemical spill at the end of an electrical synapse, and she sprang back like he was on fire.

You can't be alone forever. Sameer.

Your ashes are barely cold, asshole. That one was hers. *Anyway, yes, I can.*

You are so pathetic and stupid and fucking needy. Mean Voice.

"No," she said.

Miles, to his credit, got it right away. "Go back to bed," he said gently, his voice hoarse. "I'll bring you some water. Then I'll leave and lock your door." Gentle pressure on her arm. "Go."

He was right. He cared. He saw her wounds and saw past her wounds. He brought her water and locked her door. Seconds later, or so it seemed, sleep came.

CHAPTER THIRTY-EIGHT

SHE WOKE TO the inevitable, horrifying words: *NINE DAYS.*

Nine days until that monster turned her father's brain to mush.

The ticking clock gave her all the energy to absorb her training. Miles drilled her visual and spatial recall with blueprints of the facility. Escondido was almost entirely underground, with six-plus stories of offices, experimental rooms, equipment, and life support. Five passenger elevators and three massive freight elevators. As isolated as being on the moon. He quizzed her dozens of times, and the repetition seared the layout into her brain. She had one spy gadget to operate: a pinhole camera disguised inside a button, which she found very cool and James Bond until she googled "button cameras" and found suspiciously similar ones available for less than $100, two-day shipping included. The more accurate conclusion was that nothing was safe from video these days.

Miles planned to pass her the camera inside Escondido in order to bypass the expected multiple strip searches. They practiced handoffs—brushing past each other while Miles slipped her the button. The camera attached to clothing with a tiny four-prong hook, but Kayla first had to remove the real button on her uniform. She practiced slipping it into place on her lapel and said a silent prayer that the actual buttons matched the plasticky white of the camera button.

After she mastered a passable concealed handoff, Miles went over the rest. “I’ll be in the facility before you. I won’t look like me. Be ready when I find you.”

She raised an eyebrow. “Your job?”

“Facilities.”

“You’re going in as a janitor?”

“Maintenance. Weakest background check. Also other advantages. You’ll see.”

She frowned. “How are you getting in, anyway?”

“We hacked into the HR system last year to prep for going in. The first two operatives went in as patients, and it didn’t work, so…”

Kayla shifted her eyes away at the uncomfortable implications.

Miles went on. “Anyway, we needed another approach. Getting inside isn’t the problem. It’s getting out. It’s on lockdown. They monitor everything. Leaving for the surface is a long process and very secure. We haven’t cracked it. Yet.”

Yet. Just like the famous Kayvan Masouvi *Yet.* Miles and her father might get along. Her dad, Six Sigma Positive Mindset Black Belt. Or something. *Kay Kay, it’s not that it won’t happen. It’s just that it hasn’t happened* yet*!*

She swallowed the lump in her throat. “And now? How are we getting out?”

“I have a plan. But that’s not for you to worry about.” He made a goofy face at her. “Stay in your lane, Masouvi.”

Despite herself, she smiled. “Sure. Consider the Q and A closed.”

"I will tell you one thing," he said. "We're not leaving through the front door."

⁂

They took a break for food. Miles made them sandwiches. "Try to stall any visits to Resilusio until I find you," he said between bites. "Obviously, Fatima gives us cover, but still." The researchers pulled blood daily. If she didn't show the correct hormone changes, eventually they'd investigate. "I'll be there."

"You promise?" Her voice wavered as reality hit her hard, and sheer terror rapidly encroached. Until Miles appeared, she was on her own, clicking through a devastating and treacherous checklist: surviving Pennington, making it onto the flight, arriving at Escondido with brain and limbs and cover intact.

Yesterday she had been full of energy, courage, determination.

But that was yesterday.

"I promise. Unless I'm dead in a ditch, I'll be there." Miles gave her a reassuring smile, then bit his bottom lip. "We need to talk about drugs."

Being drugged, to be specific. "The drugs may be in your food, your water, or they may give them to you outright. Be prepared for anything."

What a magnificent setup. Starved and dehydrated to prepare for escaping an underground, heavily guarded Nazi-experiment bunker with her father, a sixty-something guy in decent shape, but still a sixty-something guy who'd been rotting in prison lately. Quite a recipe for success. No matter. She studied, ate, slept. Miles woke her at 12:30 A.M.

EIGHT DAYS

"It's time," he whispered, a gentle touch on her shoulder.

She clutched the prison jumpsuit he handed her and nearly fainted in the bathroom putting in Fatima's eyes. Anxiety hit her like a bucket of ice water to the face. Her legs nearly jellied out from under her as she walked out.

"Easy there," he said, supporting her shoulder. "You okay to do this?"

For a brief, terrifying moment, she could not speak. The fear owned her. A panic attack radiated out of her body in seismic waves. She gasped and choked and nearly lost consciousness. What a nasty surprise. Numbness had been her constant companion for the last few days, the feeling of being deep underwater. Everything muffled. Difficult and uncomfortable, and yet it suited her, unlike this full-body pandemonium. The desire to live. The will to live, poking its head out of her shame and guilt and self-loathing. She refused this truth at the surface of her consciousness. But deep down, inside, it lurked. She wanted to live. To have, once again, a life, even though said life had no real shape anymore.

The prosthetic nose took thirty minutes, the edges smooth and foreign like wax melted into her skin. He cut five inches off her hair, too. Now it was barely chin length and falling in her face. Miles took pictures of her. Prison jumpsuit, white wall, someone else's nose. She didn't recognize the person.

"Perfect," he said. "So perfect." He scanned her face with facial recognition software, set it to "Fatima Ubaldi," then emailed it somewhere.

Soon, too soon, the time had come. Miles drove her to a parking lot, a desolate empty place somewhere in Jersey City, in the shadow of a dark, abandoned factory with a clear view of the back of the Statue of Liberty.

Even Lady Liberty turns her back on me, Kayla thought sourly. From this angle, with the moonlight sliding across the stone, it was her actual rear end brightly illuminated. That was just about right.

Miles and Kayla sat in silence until an unmarked van arrived and stopped next to them. A woman in a shapeless suit emerged, made no eye contact, and spoke not a word. She escorted Kayla to the van and shackled her in place. And they were actual shackles. Arms and legs. As the woman grasped the handle of the door to pull it shut, Miles held out a hand to stop her. She glanced at him in annoyance but stepped aside.

He climbed in and whispered in Kayla's ear, "Don't lose faith. I'll see you soo—" He gulped down the last word and pulled back awkwardly to meet her eyes. His wide baby blues gleamed like a cat's in the moonlight, bursting with little reflected spills of the sallow industrial streetlamps. "I'm...I'm sorry you have to be alone."

She nodded, looked away, bit back tears. God, tears? Again?

You are such a sad, loser little—

But Miles's face distracted her from her self-abuse. He was... in pain? Clenching his jaw, trembling like a man pulling a shard of glass out of a limb. She blinked, doubted. Did she imagine it? His eyes caught the light again. Glassy now. Maybe tears. He ducked his head goodbye and perhaps, perhaps...wiped one away.

CHAPTER THIRTY-NINE

THE PENNINGTON WOMEN'S Correctional Facility at two in the morning on a whistling icy night was horror-movie perfect. The stuff of nightmares. Floodlights battered the perimeter. A harsh white tractor beam shot out as the van approached, trained in a dead-on clutch. At the first security checkpoint, the agents flashed IDs. A horn blared. A guard pushed a button and a heavy, creaking gate jerked open.

They proceeded under the relentless spotlight. It did not skip or lose them, even for a moment. At the interior checkpoint, Kayla exited the van to a smaller, still-blinding beam that pinned her like an ant under a magnifying glass.

The building itself, after all that light, was curiously dark, a hulking seven stories that seemed to secrete misery. The agents led her in, and the small group buzzed through endless gates and doors—one plate glass, another laced with metal, a third double-paned, a fourth triple-paned. There was a line. There was a wait. But it made sense. One might even call it inspired. Of course they transported prisoners at night. Less chance of escape. Fewer cars on the road. Keep them hidden and out of sight of the nice, non-incarcerated public. Her mind wandered to the imminent horrors of Escondido. When she tuned back in, the FBI agents, her last link to the real world, had vanished.

A female corrections officer took her into a room and observed her with a yawn, glued to her phone as Kayla changed into her prison blues, which were, in fact, beige. No squat search, thankfully, actually not much of a search at all. Arriving in the company of the FBI apparently counted as good enough. The guard threw over a toothbrush and a towel, and another walked her to a cell, unlocking the door with a massive set of keys to reveal a space of maybe one hundred square feet, holding only a bunk bed, a sink, and a toilet. Her new cellmate wheezed in the bottom bunk, a small, trembling lump under mangy blankets. Kayla climbed to the top, curled fetal, and slid into a miserable sleep.

SEVEN DAYS

She woke to the voice of a very loud, very hoarse woman yelling bloody murder. Her eyes snapped open, fear gushing through her body like a floodwater let loose. She launched a jumbled prayer to any sentient being possibly listening.

"ROLL CALL! GET UP, LADIES! WAKE THE FUCK UP!"

The source of that voice, a metal-jangling guard, stomped back and forth in the hallway, yelling continuously. Kayla rose, forced her brain into alertness. In daylight, the walls sported a horrible, torturous, split-pea-baby-poop green, a color so odd and terrible that the Bureau of Prisons might have specifically chosen it to cause the most psychic pain. In the bunk underneath her, scratchy bedding rustled aside. A head popped up, child-sized and blond. A delicate, pale arm emerged next. Then a pert, pixie face. *Cute as a button,* Kayla thought, though she had never once uttered that phrase. It fit until Ms. Button smiled. That was not so cute. She had terrible teeth: crooked, yellow, and discolored. Meth teeth. Kayla covered a wince with a cough.

"Whassup?" Button yawned awake.

Another scream from the guard.

Button blinked. "You the new girl? Dumped you here in the middle of the night, right?"

Kayla nodded. "Ass-crack of dawn."

She laughed. "Yeah. They like that. Keep the nice God-fearing populace from seein' us, ya know? Society's bad seeds gotta stay under da dirt."

This she had already figured out. "Makes sense."

Button hopped off the bed, stretched, and motioned for Kayla to join her. "Get down. Pasternak'll have a shit fit if you're not standing here, all 'Aye aye, sir!'" She threw a mock salute.

Kayla scrambled to her feet a second before a very large, redheaded woman, one of the biggest, heftiest females she had ever, ever seen, strolled by, slapping her keys like she was auditioning for Officer Krupke in *West Side Story*. Her name tag read, as advertised, PASTERNAK.

The redheaded giant stopped cold at their cell and rolled her eyes at Button, her mouth set in a pinched sneer. "Already getting the new girl in trouble, huh, Rizzo?" Her eyes slid from Button to Kayla, appraising her like she was day-old McDonald's.

"Not at all, ma'am," Button (Rizzo) replied without missing a beat. "I'm just helping her learn all the rules, so she can be a model prisoner at this fine institution. Just like I am, ma'am. Pay my debt to society and all that."

Pasternak snorted and moved on.

Rizzo turned to Kayla, giggling like a demented teenager, and stuck her hand out, a jerky movement that made Kayla jump. "Jennifer Rizzo. Everyone calls me Rizzo."

"Kay—Fatima. Fatima Ubaldi." Rizzo blinked at Kayla like

she was insane, and Kayla mentally smacked herself in the head. Fucking up from the get-go. That did not bode well.

"What you in for, uh, Fatima? What they gotchu on?" So far Rizzo was a basic white girl in nearly every category, but she talked with a ghetto-street inflection that Kayla found curious and engrossing, because it jarred with her appearance.

"Uh—murder. Armed robbery. But I didn't do it."

She laughed. "Murder? Me too. I did it, though. Killed my pimp."

Kayla started. "Jesus, and you still ended up here?"

She shrugged and rolled her eyes. "It's called a white girl with a shit lawyer."

Hours into her incarceration, Kayla observed that prison wasn't just an adjustment to a different life. That FBI van had transported her, like an astronaut, to a different planet. Rizzo took Kayla under her wing, and that helped. The others respected her. She pointed out the inmates to avoid and the ones to cultivate, though the latter information would be of limited use.

Pennington housed eight hundred women who had thrown away their lives in one way or another. Kayla presumptuously expected them to be terrible—thuggish, crazy, evil. However, in this brief introduction, many were the opposite. Nice, funny, and cool. But maybe that was just courtesy because Rizzo took a shine to her. Kayla ate meals with Rizzo's posse, a motley crew if there ever was one. The first member was a sixty-something very butch lesbian named Chummy. Second, a thirty-year-old chola (a Latina gangbanger, Rizzo helpfully explained) named Salcido. Finally, two very tall white twins, Chloe and Carrie, with wild hair dyed rainbow colors. They claimed to have been Playboy bunnies before the cops nabbed them for hers-and-hers first-degree felonies. They were a few credits away from earning their beauty school certifications through the correctional education program and ran a salon out of the machine shop.

Each day, the women ate their hog slop in silence, everyone chewing slowly, the whole experience entirely uneventful until Kayla's second—and second-to-last—lunch. Chummy, who so far had only displayed a perpetually baked expression, suddenly perked to life. Her eyes widened with unpleasant surprise. "Well, lookie, lookie, another new girl."

The twins perked up from their food. Salcido ignored Chummy completely. Rizzo followed Chummy's gaze, chewing a dry morsel of bread for an extraordinarily long amount of time before speaking. "She gonna have to pay top dollar to the twins' beauty salon to keep up that Easter egg shit."

Kayla turned nonchalantly, the move timed to coincide with tossing a wadded-up napkin into the trash, and nearly choked on her turkey sandwich.

Olivia. Vapor. Hair now baby blue and light pink and bleached underneath that. Her skin was darker, like she'd fallen face first into a bottle of spray tan. But it was her. The same boy eyes, boy hands, lanky body. Only the smile was different. There was no smile.

Until she turned.

And stared right at Kayla.

And smiled, in a vague, unfocused way, with no recognition.

Kayla froze and shrank down, swearing inside her head. This one moment might just have blown her cover. And everything else. Or was she here to help? The Genesis Foundation had its own agenda, of course. But they wouldn't screw her over just for fun…would they?

Well, they probably would. After all, Kayla was supposed to trade her seed phrase for Escondido's location. That had gone sideways. And it was not like they were looking out for her or cared about her. In fact, Vapor was probably here to blackmail her again, because they still didn't have the tokens.

"Anyone know her?" Kayla asked, weaving disinterest through her voice, slowly sitting up.

No one did. She risked another glance. Vapor shuffled to a table, her back to their group. Kayla touched the nose, grateful for the armor of her disguise. Maybe, maybe, she'd gotten lucky. It would be about freaking time.

CHAPTER FORTY

FIVE DAYS

HER TRIP WAS tonight, late, according to Miles. So far she'd evaded death, dismemberment, criminal activity, and Vapor. She said a prayer that Vapor wouldn't be anywhere nearby. She racked her brain for a way to warn Miles. But the only computers were in the prison's library, and her block didn't get library time until the day after she left. Pennington seemed full of contraband cell phones, but she had no commissary credits—the currency of the incarcerated—to borrow or buy one. She was on her own. Kayla said a final helpless prayer that all of this wasn't a trap. God, what if Monahan had an unspeakable, sadistic plan for her, all ready to go? Or maybe even a horrific mundane one, like dumping her in Resilusio all day, every day, until her mind broke?

Eight in the morning and a stroke of luck. Rizzo contracted the stomach flu and threw up all over their cell. Guards carted her to the infirmary and parked Kayla in the rec room for the entire day while the cell got a hose down and disinfection. The rec room was a shabby brown-carpeted box with the same pea-green walls as the rest of the place, a few sad ping-pong tables missing balls and paddles, two unidentifiable, battered exercise machines, an ancient television, and various other contraptions of indeterminate origin. Someone brought her a tray for breakfast, and she sighed with relief.

A tray for lunch and she got positively giddy.

Less than ten hours to go, and Kayla, maybe, slightly, relaxed.

Until.

"Ubaldi. Let's *go*." Pasternak. Large, scowling, and red all over.

Dinnertime. Kayla had hoped they would forget about her in the rec room until departure time, but sending her back to her cell was even better. She would hide under the covers and count the minutes. But Pasternak led her somewhere else. The cafeteria.

She stopped short. "I'm not hungry."

Pasternak rolled her eyes. "We have to feed you. State law. I know. Too bad, right?" She poked her thumb toward the dining hall. "Get in there."

One last meal. What were the odds?

Kayla's mother had died of a very rare cancer. A nasty brain tumor called a glioblastoma. Diagnosis rate of 0.59 to 5 cases per 100,000 people. Kayla herself was a one-in-ten-thousand scorer on Monahan's addiction resistance test. The acceptance rates of the schools she attended were in the single digits. She had won and lost tournament-life hands in poker where the odds were in the hundreds of thousands to one. Her whole life had been a series of rare events, one after another, one on top of another. Odds meant nothing to her. So when she rounded the corner to the mess hall, took her tray, accepted her slop from the inmate servers, and collided directly with Vapor…well, it figured.

"Oh. Sorr—" Vapor pitched her stewed gray carrots on Kayla, freezing when their eyes met.

"You," she whispered and sighed with something suspiciously close to relief. "You're here."

"I'm here," Kayla echoed.

"When do you…leave?" Vapor's face was neutral, conversational.

Kayla considered. "Soon. Very."

She nodded knowingly. "Just in time." She said the words one by one.

"Listen," Kayla said, "if you think I'm going to a bank to get you the seed phrase, well, I'd rather die, and furthermore—"

"Not at all." Vapor interrupted. "It's…something else." She cast her eyes around the room. No glances in their direction. No eyes suddenly slipping away from a conversation to land on them. "Sit with me," she finally said under her breath.

Kayla followed to a deserted cluster of Formica cafeteria tables and sat down across from her. "Well?"

Vapor stared at her food, took a deep breath, seemed to think. "Going into Escondido is a suicide mission. Rick'll be waiting, with a whole army. Not that he needs it. You'll be trapped." She picked up a piece of bread, slapped some turkey on it with trembling hands, topped it with another piece, and spoke with the sandwich over her lips, scanning all the while. "You don't stand a chance."

Kayla shoved some stewed prunes into her mouth and chewed slowly, wiping and covering her face, too. "That's what you came here to tell me?"

A pause. Vapor said nothing.

"Thanks, but I already figured." Not true. She had hoped, wildly, that somehow she had a chance. To get in, get her father, get out. "And I don't care," she finished defiantly.

Vapor swallowed and picked up a juice box, stabbed it with the attached straw, and sipped from it. "If you're sure." She raised her eyebrows over the top of the juice box.

"I am."

"Then I have something for you," she said. "Something that will help."

Kayla leaned forward. "Will you blow my cover?"

Vapor shook her head and touched Kayla's hand with hers, a cold and smooth slip. "No. Come to my cell after dinner." After dinner, the inmates had a half hour of free time before lockdown. "We'll talk then."

At T-minus around four hours, Kayla found herself at Vapor's cell. The woman glanced up from a book and motioned her in. Her roommate was nowhere to be found, if she ever existed.

Kayla searched her eyes. "How did you know I was here?"

Vapor unbuttoned her shirt, and Kayla stared, dumbstruck, given how completely out of context that was. "We have access to the Escondido intakes." She reached inside her bra and produced a thin metal and plastic disc, the shape of a SIM card with an additional tiny prong. She gazed at it with reverence. And fear. "Take this."

Kayla's hand reached out to close on it and almost missed, because as Vapor leaned forward to button her shirt, part of her shoulder emerged in the sallow light.

And it had a five-leaf-clover tattoo.

Kayla stifled a gasp. Her hand trembled and she almost dropped the tiny electronic object. "Uh, what is it?" She had to fight to listen to Vapor's response, because the question she actually wanted to ask was *Why do you have the same five-leaf-*

clover tattoo as Miles? Kayla shook her head and listened. At the moment, a random matching tattoo didn't matter.

"It's an admin key. You use it to locate anyone who's plugged into Resilusio." She closed Kayla's hand, still trembling, with hers. "You can use it to find your father. Escondido's a big, confusing place."

"Okay," Kayla said, turning the key over in her hands, willing her attention where it needed to be right now. "Why are you doing this?"

Vapor looked away, and her face contorted as if in a painful memory. But she shook off her thoughts and stared at the admin key.

Kayla sucked in a breath. "Your virus is on this."

Vapor nodded. Then she leaned forward. "Kayla, as soon as you get in, hide. There's no way he won't see you coming, even with all this." She waved her hand at Kayla-as-Fatima. "Get into Resilusio. Plug in the admin key and launch the virus. It's disguised as an executable. Denali.exe. Open it. You'll have fifteen, thirty minutes max before all hell breaks loose. Then everything will go on lockdown, and you won't find your father. So don't waste any time. Get him and get out of there." Pain and worry laced her voice. And another emotion. Doubt.

But there was no time for that right now. "Will they search me? Where should I hide this?"

Vapor opened her mouth and lifted her tongue. "Under here. They don't generally do cavity searches. Ruins the vibe."

"Where do I plug it in?"

She pointed to her left inner wrist. "There's a port on the glove."

Kayla turned over the tiny metal key. How would she actually speak with this thing under her tongue? She'd just have to hope talking wasn't a big part of the Escondido experience. She closed her hand and smiled a sad little smile. "We'd have made a good team, you know, in some alternate universe."

Vapor's eyes planted on the ceiling. She shrugged and blinked out a tear. "I don't want you to die. You may not think I care, but I do." She looked away. "I care very much."

Kayla stared. "You don't know me."

Vapor chuckled. "That's the thing, Kay Kay," she said, using her father's old nickname for her, "I do."

Kayla froze. "You spied on me."

"Yes," she replied. "Not for fun. Because I had to. But the human brain is a funny thing. When you watch someone, you get to know them, and if you like what you see…that's how you fall in love. Not that I am, you know, in love, I just…" She swallowed. "I guess that's my weakness. I convince myself I can control my feelings. Get out of being human. Eyes on the prize, focus on the goal, everything for the future…but in the end I can't. I'm just as stupid and sentimental as anyone. Probably worse."

Kayla laughed. "Well, my weakness is thinking I'm so smart, but actually not *being* so smart."

Vapor broke into a warm smile. "I care about you. And I hope you'll be okay."

Pasternak bellowed down the hall, ending their conversation. "ONE MINUTE LADIES!"

They had such little time. Kayla took Vapor's hand. "I hope we meet again," she said, and meant it. She glanced at her closed hand, which held the admin key. "I'll take good care of this."

Vapor straightened and hugged her. "You'll be the one that

cracks the code wide open. I know it." Her voice faltered, and terror clenched Kayla's chest, unpleasant and unexpected. Stars erupted from the corners of her vision, and panic snatched the oxygen out of her lungs. She was about to go to a lunatic asylum. Many feet underground. Run by a sociopathic murderer. And she'd probably die.

She did not want to die.

Vapor seemed to sense the bout of terror and hugged Kayla close until she stilled. "You can do it. Believe."

Kayla hesitated. She had something else to ask. Now or never. She pulled back. "That tattoo you have," she blurted out.

Vapor looked up at her sharply. "What about it?"

"I know someone else with the same one." She studied Vapor. "Five-leaf clover. Distinctive."

"BACK TO YOUR CELLS, LADIES! NOW!"

Vapor leaned into her. "Ask that someone else about it. Ask them about Project Trifolia."

"Project Trifolia," Kayla repeated.

"Yes." Vapor took her hand and squeezed it. "Now go."

"Thank you." *Inhale. Steady. Exhale. Slow. In. Out.* Her breathing evened. "See you when I get back." She ducked her head and walked away.

CHAPTER FORTY-ONE

BACK IN HER cell, it seemed as if she were in a Resilusio Experience with a capital *E*. A world not real, not touchable, that would disappear in a sudden, random moment and slip out of her memory like the fringes of a bad dream, leaving only a lingering unease, to be shaken off once her head left the pillow. She had to remind herself repeatedly.

This was not Resilusio.

This was reality.

Thick fog gathered outside Kayla's window, enveloping the landscape like a dirty, forgotten blanket, obscuring the open area where inmates received their state-mandated one hour of daily exercise. Said exercise seemed to consist of sitting in huddled groups in the corners of the battered and warped concrete yard, planning a variety of unapproved, unadvisable, and illegal activities. A group of inmates was out there right now, brownish clumps and flashes of movement and metal in the creepy Hollywood fog, drifting in and out of thick gray.

"Beautiful, isn't it?" Rizzo came to life from the bottom bunk. Kayla jumped. Turned. Rizzo flashed her palms.

"Didn't mean to make ya jump. Sorry."

Kayla shook her head. She must release this tension. It would be of no help. She needed to be calm but alert, ready for anything but relaxed. She unclenched her shoulders and arms slowly and deliberately. "No worries. I'm just out of it. Are you feeling better?" One last glance out the window. Exercise time was over. The fog lifted. Now the women were ghostly outlines, shuffling into place, shackled to one another for the walk back inside. Snatches of conversation reached Kayla, ricocheting across the walls.

"That *puta—*"

"Gotchu—"

"Better be—"

She walked back to her bed but stopped short of getting in. The scratchy, worn, state-issued blankets and pillows repelled her implacably. As if the inmate-run laundry service had doused them with skunk spray. She closed her eyes. She'd be leaving soon. To worse.

"Sucks at first." Rizzo smiled kindly, watching her the entire time. "But you get used to it."

Her roommate still looked a little green. "I hope you're feeling better."

"I am," she said, and flopped back down on her bed, patting the spot next to her. Her blankets were prison-issued, but underneath, her sheets and pillow were a little girl's dream, unicorns galloping through a pink space leaving trails of glittery dust in their wake. The pillowcase had a giant unicorn head. The design put a smile on Kayla's face.

"My daughter's." Rizzo nodded at the sheets. "Makes me feel, you know, like she's here." She ran her hands over the unicorn's face. "I tell my mama not to wash them. They got her smell."

Kayla sat at the foot of Rizzo's bunk. "You must miss her."

"I...do," she finally said, "but I don't let that take over. Some girls here, they're so consumed by anger. So bitter. Too busy cursing the system and feeling sorry for themselves, they don't got nothing left inside." She shook her head. "Even the ones that're gettin' out. I mean…what are they gonna do with themselves when that happens? When all they've spent their time here doin' is bitching? Moaning?"

Gloom had given way to night. The prison lights sputtered on. The warden must be in energy-saving mode. It was long past the need for some illumination. Kayla turned to Rizzo. "How much time you got left?"

"'Bout a year." She bobbed her head from side to side. "Well, okay. Twelve months, eighteen days, and some odd hours until I am eligible for parole, and let me tell you, I'm gonna get it."

"I'm sure you will," Kayla said, and meant it. "And I think that your daughter is hella lucky to have you for a mom."

Rizzo groaned. "Tell that to my mama, who thought she was done with diapers and runny noses and sippy cups, you know?" She laughed for a moment, and then her face got serious. "I let her down." She shook her head quickly. "But I'm gonna make it up to her. I got plans."

"What is it you wanna do?" Kayla fluttered her hands. "I mean, when you get sprung. Like, for work."

Rizzo smiled shyly. "You really wanna know? I mean, I'm probably boring you to death with my lame story. Just like every one of these losers' stories—"

Kayla shook her head. "No, I want to know." And she did. Hungry for a human connection maybe, before she plunged, literally, to her death.

Rizzo reached under the mattress, rummaging around, and came out with a sketchbook. "Well, ever since I was little, there *was* something I loved. And I actually did it for a while, before I got hooked on heroin and lost my daughter and started working for a pimp that I then had to kill."

"Rizzo! Don't keep me in suspense." Kayla actually smiled, a still-abnormal movement, and shockingly, the smile pulsed through her body as a small tingle.

Warmth.

Connection.

Rizzo scrunched up her face for a moment. "Well, okay. But you gotta keep it between us. I don't want Chummy or the twins to make fun of me."

"Your secret is safe with me," Kayla intoned solemnly, "and I'm gonna grab that notebook outta your hands anyway if you don't show me."

Rizzo took a deep breath. "Cabinets," she announced. "Before I got all mixed up, I was a furniture maker. Apprenticed to a real artisan. Thackeray and Sons. They make nice stuff, expensive stuff. Thousands of dollars, and, uh…they liked me. Said I had talent. They said I should come up with my own designs. They would make some, and if people bought them, they'd back me someday." She opened the notebook. Detailed, hand-drawn designs of cabinets in every shape and size filled the pages. Rizzo held it out to Kayla. "Here."

Kayla examined the pages. Of course, she knew absolutely nothing about cabinets or cabinetmaking, or joints, or furniture. Each design had sketches from different angles, swatches, finishes, fixture ideas, and wood specifications. She flipped through. It popped into her head that if she sat in Schechter's Resilusio with this notebook, an extensive history of cabinetmaking plus a near-expert level of carpentry and interior design would be hers, like it or not, jammed right into her brain. It was funny but chilling. She shuddered.

Rizzo smiled shyly and shrugged a shoulder. "So what do you think?"

Of course, she had no idea. "You seem like you know your shit," Kayla finally said, hoping she came across as encouraging and positive. "Your designs are super cool."

"That's one of my favorites." Rizzo pointed down. Kayla had landed on a page depicting a cabinet that stored and displayed items like fine china and linens. It had rounded glass panels on top, shelving below, and four graduated long drawers on the bottom. Seemed to be a replica of an antique piece. Something made for a very grand house hundreds of years ago.

Rizzo went on: "It's inspired by a George Hepplewhite design." At Kayla's blank face, she laughed. "He was a famous English cabinetmaker in the eighteenth century. Like probably one of the most famous ever. Anyway, none of his actual pieces still exist today, but he's still well-known because after he died his wife published a book with all his designs, and everyone used it and oh, what was the point of that?" Rizzo frowned. "Oh, yeah, so his style became famous. They still use his design book for, like, replicas and stuff like that. His work is elegant, slender, well-balanced but still ornamental. The word I would use is 'intricate.' Never boring. Always cool. And I love it."

Kayla stared at her, too shocked to actually hide any of her shock. "Wow."

Rizzo smiled proudly. "Didn't expect that, did you? Your prison bunkmate discussing some old-timey furniture maker dude."

"No, I have to be honest. I didn't."

Rizzo pointed at the sketchbook. "Well, I live to surprise and delight. Anyway, this is a two-piece cherry breakfront cabinet. A mid-nineteenth-century piece designed in the Hepplewhite style. Double doors, arced glass panels opening to polished shelving. Below, long drawers. Bracket feet hold the whole thing up, which was one of Hepplewhite's hallmarks, that big-heavy-furniture-floating-on-air kinda thing. He used cherrywood. That's a great choice, but expensive these days. Those needle-like things"—she pointed to the top of the structure, which sported thin metal spires—"they're called finials. Don't see them too much anymore." She traced the ornamentation with her fingers. "It's sort of my unique touch."

Kayla admired the design, and an overwhelming wave of sadness crashed into her. "Maybe one day, when I'm rich and famous, I'll commission you to make this for me. You're very talented."

"Aw, thank you." Rizzo smiled shyly and blushed a little.

An additional set of prison lights slapped on, a cold green fluorescence that gave human skin a patina that was alternately sallow, shadowy, and heavily bruised. Their eyes met, startled. Rizzo instinctively scanned the bed for any additional contraband. Kayla closed Rizzo's notebook and handed it to her. Footsteps shuffled and keys clanged down the hallway.

Someone was coming.

CHAPTER FORTY-TWO

RIZZO SLID THE notebook under her mattress just in time for the chain gang to materialize, a steady stream of jangling, rustling, wildly unfortunate humanity. This was the final exercise group, herded by sour guards who probably drew the short straws for the night shift. Two by two, the women shuffled unceremoniously back into their cells. More than a few of them nodded at Rizzo, then passed their eyes over Kayla with a practiced, automatic blankness. They didn't know her from a hole in the wall, and the rules dictated no emotion, not even simple curiosity, without information first.

Rizzo waited until they had moved out of earshot. "So, what about you?"

Kayla's stomach sent a ripple upward and outward. She nervously recited the most pertinent Fatima facts in her head. "Me?"

"Yeah. You. What's your story, Fatima?"

Kayla blinked. A hard knot of panic twisted in her chest, though she had practiced this exact scenario with Miles and already recited her story to Chummy and the twins and to Rizzo herself. And yet. And yet. She absolutely, fully, blanked. She had opened a connection to her real self and hid Fatima. Her inability to find her now was an unwelcome surprise.

But Rizzo, blessedly, sort of, maybe, missed all of that and placed her hand on Kayla's, mistaking her reaction for reticence, or sadness, instead of what it was, a mad scramble for her cover identity. "I don't mean how'd you get in here or anything, you told me about Mikey and the bodega and the robbery and all that." She smiled encouragingly. "I mean just you. What's your story? What do you dream about doing?"

Kayla flayed about for a moment. "Well, I went to school for accounting, but I really dreamed about...uh...acting." This was the first wildly improbable profession that jumped into her mind. "And, uh, it was going well. I had someone who loved me and believed in me and encouraged me...and somehow I, uh, fucked it all up." She put her head in her hands and squeezed her temples. "He relied on me. Trusted me. And I let him down. Something bad happened to him, and it was all my fault. I don't mean Mikey—"

"Phew." Rizzo exhaled, then threw her hands up. "Oh. I didn't mean the story. It's just I was hoping you didn't still have feelings for that guy. Seriously, it's the downfall of a lotta girls here. They stick to creeps and scumbags. Don't think they deserve better."

"Is that what happened to you?" Kayla eagerly changed the subject back to Rizzo.

Rizzo considered. "No. Nah. I was...you know, going through a tough time. My sister's boyfriend offered me some dope. I was at a low. A real low. So I said okay. And that was that."

"Sucks."

Rizzo nodded. "I didn't grow up around drugs or nothing. Did nothin' more than chug a few Mickeys and smoke a few blunts."

"I want to kill him for you," Kayla said, and kind of meant it.

Rizzo shrugged. "Nah, it was random. I missed the bus to my

job. So I walked to my sister's. She said she'd give me a ride. Her guy was there. She wasn't home yet. And he was in the middle of smoking. I don't think she even knew he did that. He offered me some, and that was it." She snapped her fingers. "I got hooked."

"He should be the one in prison."

Rizzo laughed. "Well, he is in prison actually, but not before he stole five grand from my sister, trashed her place, then identity thefted her just to make it fun."

"Damn."

"Yeah, right? I mean, in the end it isn't his fault. It's just all random, you know? All because I missed a bus. I used to blame myself. Like it was my destiny or something to get addicted to dope and become a hooker. Like I was nothing more than street trash who would OD in an alley somewhere. But I stopped that. It's all just random. Just random-ass decisions, one after another, everything, all day, any day."

They sat in silence for a moment, both thinking.

"But enough about me and my lame deep thoughts." She turned to Kayla. "We were talking about you. About Hollywood."

"Oh, right." Kayla paused, gathered her story. "Like I said, it was, ah, well, ah, before Mikey. That was why I left Florida." She was making this up as she went along. "Not because I was in love with that scumbag but mostly because I couldn't face what I'd done."

Rizzo nodded knowingly. "You were running away from yourself. From your pain and suffering, you know? I seen it. My family. Myself. But you got to have dreams, too, Fatima."

Kayla shrugged. "If I ever get out of here, make it big, hire you as my personal furniture designer…" She trailed off, and they both giggled. Kayla turned serious again. "If I ever get out,

I'm on a mission. To make things right. I owe him. That's my only real dream." She shook her head. "You know, it's funny, I used to think I was in control. Of everything. Of my destiny. But now.... That life is over. That woman's dead." Kayla congratulated herself on getting herself right, finally.

"Don't be so hard on yourself," Rizzo said. "You just have to give life a chance. Sometimes it seems like you don't got a shot. Sometimes it seems you got it all. But it's neither." She met Kayla's eyes. "The answer is on a big huge blinking neon sign like, I don't know, in Times Square or sumpthin'." She spread her arms wide at the ceiling. "'There Is No Answer, Motherfuckers!'"

Kayla burst into laughter. "That's a good billboard."

Rizzo fluttered her hands. "So what I'm saying is, don't give up your dreams. Maybe you just need new ones. Maybe I'll see you on a billboard in Times Square someday. The star of the show." She squeezed Kayla's shoulder. "It don't make sense, and it's not supposed to, but that's kinda cool. Because maybe it gets good again, any minute now."

Sure, Kayla thought darkly, *but probably not in this life.*

CHAPTER FORTY-THREE

SHE MUST HAVE fallen asleep. She woke to the cell door squealing open, jarring her to consciousness. Made sense. Of course they didn't oil them.

"What the fuck?" Rizzo murmured.

A flashlight in the dark, aimed right in her eyes. Pasternak's rough voice shook her awake.

"Get up, princess," she growled. Her bad breath activated Kayla's gag reflex. She sat up straight, shock coursing through her in disorienting waves.

"What—what is it?"

Pasternak emitted a noise, somewhere between a grunt and a laugh. "You've got a carriage waiting for you, Cinderella."

Kayla slid her feet over the side of the bed and found the rungs. She shrugged into her prison-issued jacket. The admin key poked from under her tongue. Still there. Good. She had a shot at getting out of here with it. A shot. If Pasternak didn't search her so carefully.

Sure enough, Pasternak, lazy cow, did nothing, not even a pat down, just led her through the three separate sets of double doors to the outside world, where she shackled Kayla to five other inmates while a darkened van idled nearby. Bodies shifted in the passenger and driver seats. She squinted, but the poorly lit yard conspired with the roving searchlights. Shapes. Shadows. That was it.

The six women shuffled into the van one by one. Kayla kept her face down except to steal a glance at her captors. The driver slumped in his chair, bored and yawning, scrolling through his phone, and a chaperone faced the cabin, a gun prominently displayed on his hip. Dressed military, not Bureau of Prisons.

The doors slammed shut, and the van rolled away. Hours later, in the deepening pitch-black of the earliest A.M., it pulled up to a dark set of low-slung buildings. No lights, no shape, no movement. But when they herded the inmates through a set of double doors, Kayla recognized her surroundings. An airport, tiny and tucked away, nothing but one suspiciously mangy airstrip. A small plane idled on the tarmac. Judging by the number of windows, it seated a dozen. Waiting guards unchained the women from one another and prodded them into the cabin, where they handcuffed them into their seats. The last time Kayla sat in a private plane, she was jetting to a dream-come-true future. What a difference a few days made. Tonight she was on the airline to hell.

FOUR DAYS

Kayla woke to the sun beating a hot laser beam into her head. Morning. Out the window, the stark, barren landscape below indicated they might be close to Escondido, deeply nowhere in the Nevada desert. Eventually, amid exactly zero hint of civilization, not a building, a road, or anything human-made, the plane descended. As they got closer to the ground, a runway materialized and, hidden behind a parched hill, a collection of dusty old buildings.

Another "airport."

After a rough landing, shackled together once again, the women shuffled out into the oppressive heat, which hit like a hard shove. It took Kayla exactly five seconds to become viciously uncomfortable, scorched for breath and squinting in the relentless sun. A small bus waited on the tarmac, a battered, idling bump on the landscape.

After about an hour on the road, one inmate asked for water.

"When we get there," a guard gruffly informed her. That shut everyone up. There was no food, that was a given, but not even water? Kayla, for her part, desired neither food nor water. Her fear had repressed most human urges.

A few hours later, the bus slowed, right before the first few pangs of hunger and thirst broke through Kayla's terror. Their destination was a decrepit, windswept building, one small story. A convenience store, perhaps, or a gas station, once upon a time. Blacked-out windows. Boarded-up doors. It blended into the surroundings, an irrelevant, possibly abandoned structure in the middle of exactly nowhere. But, of course, in there were the elevators down to Escondido, where truly depraved researchers tested the world's newest, most-addictive entertainment experience on unsuspecting subjects. Soon she'd be deep in the earth, buried in the Nevada desert like an unfortunate mob informant.

They herded the women out of the van and inside the shabby brown structure. Inside something extraordinary awaited: a shining, gleaming, spotlessly clean and bare room, where administrators in white coats consulted clipboards, greeting them and checking off names. Behind them stood five watchful security guards, two women and three men, all large and muscled. The guards' uniforms reminded Kayla of fast-food workers—collared shirts, khakis, and matching sneakers. The one exception to the Burger King getup was the multiple weapons per person. They were all packing serious heat.

Two large elevators occupied the back of the room, the kind found in hospitals or warehouses. Security cameras peeped from every corner. While the other "patients" examined the odd surroundings, fidgeted restlessly, and inquired about food, water, the bathroom, Kayla kept her eyes focused on the door, straining for the last few glimpses of the world outside, as dull and desolate and soul flattening as it might be. She was well aware these fleeting moments might be her last glimpse of the sky and the earth.

Forever.

CHAPTER FORTY-FOUR

DOWN, DOWN, DOWN. The longest elevator ride of Kayla's life. Five minutes? Ten? They were not just underground. They were on a slow boat to the center of the earth. When the elevator finally stopped, her teeth creaked from clenching and her vision swirled and tipped from inadvertently holding her breath. The guards hovered tight on the women, watching, waiting, alert. She forced a cough and poked the admin key with the tip of her tongue, to reassure herself it was still there.

The door opened onto a bustling medical facility. Clean, sleek, and technical. A room that would fit nicely at any top hospital system in the world. Men and women in white lab coats breezed by, frowning over documents, scribbling on charts and notebooks, talking in low tones. They had no name tags or key cards. No identification of any kind. Neon green neoprene cases enclosed their phones. Signal interceptors for outside communication, probably, and signal enhancers for internal. The guards nudged the women forward, and before long one of the White Coats approached, a gray-haired, bespectacled specimen with the unmistakable air of the Man in Charge.

He appraised the women like cattle at an auction—ugly cattle at that, given his expression. "These are the new volunteers?"

One of the guards nodded. "Yes, sir."

He frowned. “What took you so long? We’re on a tight timeline here.”

“There was a delay at the airstrip.” She cleared her throat. “Sir.”

“Hmmmph.” He grunted. “Well, go find ops and get them settled.”

“Sir.”

He surveyed the new recruits doubtfully, frowned even wider, and moved on.

The guards split them up. Now unshackled, one female guard took Kayla’s group, which headed toward a hallway that was, unlike the central hub of activity, dimly lit and completely empty. “Welcome to your new home, ladies,” she chirped back at them with a tight smile. “Let’s get you settled in.”

She strode down and the women dutifully followed, Kayla scanning left and right to memorize escape routes and match reality to the blueprints she’d pored over. Two prisoners walked ahead of her, five behind. A string of guards brought up the rear.

They took a left and arrived at a security door made of thick, shiny, unbroken steel. The malevolence that emanated from this door hovered in the air, like the metal itself announcing that it had absolutely nothing good behind it. The guard stepped in front of a retinal scanner with a piercing blue light. She lifted her eyelid and pressed herself forward. The light danced across her face, paused at her eye, roved back.

The door beeped open.

Another hall. This one with a dim, hazy end so far away, Kayla squinted and still didn’t see it. The guard directed the women, one by one, to the metal doors that appeared every few feet. Each door had a security camera, a retinal scanner, and a screen that glowed with a yellow identification number. No names, of course. Soon enough it was Kayla's turn. One retinal scan—Kayla held her breath—and the door slid open.

Kayla knew better than to ask questions. She walked in, and the door whispered shut behind her, pressing firmly against the wall. Kayla surveyed her surroundings. A tiny studio apartment, about three hundred square feet. An open kitchen to the right, basic but clean and newish, a bed and a dresser in the corner. A desk and dining table with a basket of fruit on the kitchen island. The bathroom held generic toiletries. SHAMPOO. CONDITIONER. LOTION. Blank bars of soap. Another door in the bedroom—highly unsettling—but locked. Probably the rig, for when she got too addicted to leave her living quarters. Kayla wandered, opening drawers, peering behind curtains, and pulling back the covers on the bed. The psychologists had furnished this place like a corporate apartment. The refrigerator had food, all of it fresh—milk and eggs, fruit and portioned cuts of meat in vacuum-pack containers. Snacks in the cupboards, drinks, all nonalcoholic. Uniforms in the closet, marked with the same identification number, in Kayla's case, 3-2460. There were slippers, just like in prison. Every room had cameras, some obvious, some surely hidden. Back in the kitchen area, woozy and famished, she pulled out a few food items and stared. Yogurt. Crackers. Apple juice. Drugged? Tainted? She had hoped to eat nothing, but… hunger. Hunger drove a metal knot into her stomach. Painful. Implacable.

No. Not yet.

Now what?

I'm here. Really here. Like a bad dream come alive, the truth doused her in a new level of terror—armed guards, cameras, and security procedures that left few, pathetic options. She probably wasn't getting out alive. If by some miracle she did, her likely destination was into the poison arms of Rick Monahan, en route to a location useful for disposing bodies.

Oh fuck oh fuck oh fuck. Her breath came out fast and hot, dangerously close to hyperventilation. To madness.

The doorbell chimed. Saved by the bell. She had no control over the door, so it was more like an FYI. The visitor was a cafeteria worker, here to bring a meal. He deposited it and left. She squeezed away the panic and washed herself in fake calm.

Self-control. Self-control. Self-control. Focus.

Her tongue slid over the admin key. She had to find a more secure place. She glanced up and around, zeroing in on an idea. Every room had eyes. But every surveillance operation must have blind spots.

She clutched her stomach and feigned nausea, running to the bathroom, opening the toilet seat and pretending to dry heave. She grunted and yowled and spit the key into her hand. Yes, they may have cameras everywhere, but her earlier examination strongly suggested none under the toilet. While face down in the lapping white bowl, she clutched her injury and yelped in pain. She sat back, peeled off the bandage at the corner, and pretended to examine it for bleeding. As she pressed the adhesive to her skin, she slipped the admin key in.

Miles, this surgical tape had better hold.

Kayla made her way back to the living room and collapsed on the couch, her eyes fixed on the door, aching for Miles, irrationally hoping for him to appear. Expecting to see him at this exact moment would be, she acknowledged, magical thinking. And yet. He needed to pop out now. They had very little time.

Sleep hit her, and she woke to another door chime. The metal shivered open to reveal a White Coat—a man with messy dark brown hair, glasses, and bad posture. He glanced at her and did not smile as he scribbled notes on his tablet. A rumpled man of "science." He held his body differently, his eyes differently, his face differently, and yet it was him. Miles. She reflected, fleetingly, that both Miles and the hot dog vendor doctor ground crew assassin had a talent for disguises. And even, actually, Vapor, a real-life video game avatar who apparently did a pretty convincing cosplay as Olivia, a nerdy Asian girl.

"Patient 3-2460?"

"Yes." She hid her joy. The Garbage Man was watching.

Miles nodded, clicking on an iPad. Polite, professional, non-threatening. "I'm here to take you to your first session."

"I'm ready."

"Splendid. Has anyone told you the nature of the study?"

"Uh, no."

"Well, you're in for a treat." Miles said this with a bouncy, creepy enthusiasm that almost made her laugh out loud, despite everything. "You'll be one of the first to experience a magical world, a virtual reality unlike any other. It's called Resilusio, and it will blow you away. Now, if you'll follow me."

"I'm ready." Kayla nodded and marshalled her energy.

Here we go.

CHAPTER FORTY-FIVE

THIS MAN HAD one telltale bit of Miles that shone through the disguise: the million-watt grin that reached the faux deep brown eyes. He flashed it at her, but so quickly she wondered if she imagined it.

"You came," Kayla said under her breath. "I was so scared."

"I told you I would," he replied to his iPad. "You should trust me."

"I thought you were going to be a janitor or something."

"Change of plans," he said under his breath, "for now. The previous owner of this device is resting comfortably in an exam room."

"How did you find me?"

He flashed her the iPad for a brief second. There she was, a pulsating pink dot, moving down a map of the facility. She patted her clothes.

"Yup, in there somewhere. I have a clean set." He led her down a dark corridor, then pulled a tiny flashlight out of his pocket. He used a key card to open a supply closet. They both went inside, and he pulled a set of clothes out from under his lab coat. She changed quickly, wadding up the tracked set under a bucket of bleach. She stared at the bucket for a second, remembering the hospital, and throwing bleach in the hot dog vendor doctor's face. God, so much bleach in her life these days. Miles touched her arm gently. "Bite the top button from your uniform. Don't pull—it might rip."

Kayla got to work as Miles went on. "I got you assigned to the most addicted group. The hopeless cases. Cohort three. Desperate zombies dying for a dopamine hit. Some plug in directly from their living quarters, since all they do is eat, sleep, and live Resilusio. Others still use the arena. That's where you're going. If we capture this cohort on film, it will mean everything. I'll be trying to access the records, too. That might take time."

"Were you able to find my father?" Kayla finished with the button and handed it to him.

Miles hesitated. "He's there. Cohort three. He's either in the arena or living quarters. We'll try the arena first." He produced the camera and clamped it in place on Kayla's uniform. The button didn't quite fit, but it wasn't noticeable at a glance. He frowned and adjusted it. "Take a step."

She did. He examined his work. Picked off a thread. Finally satisfied, he squeezed her hand. "Let's go. I'll drop you off and pick you up, okay? Wait for me."

She opened her mouth to tell him about the admin key.

He shook his head. "Don't talk."

They exited the supply closet and back into the light, Miles leading her as if she were a subject, Kayla with her eyes to the ground, until he stopped at an unmarked door.

"Here we are." He moved forward for a retinal scan. The security panel beeped green, and the door slid open. A guard appeared. Miles nodded at him and slipped away. Kayla stepped into another sterile space—a desk, computers, and three White Coats.

The guard addressed her as he frowned into an iPad. "Subject 3-2460?"

"Yes."

"One second and I'll scan you in." He indicated the door to his left, labeled WAITING ROOM.

"Thank you."

He appraised her, hesitating for one brief agonizing second, before leading her to the door. "If you don't mind me asking, 3-2460, how long have you been in cohort three?"

"Well," Kayla said, "I just moved up. I guess I impressed somebody. We get the good stuff eighteen hours a day, right?"

"Yes," he said, searching her face. Finally, after another excruciating wait, he gestured at the door. "Very well. Go ahead."

The scanner roamed over her eye. She held her breath. The door beeped and opened.

Inside was nothing more or less than a waiting room for an insane asylum. Or, more accurately, an insane asylum waiting room as conjured up by a horror writer. Stephen King, perhaps. A large space, several thousand square feet, with chairs and tables bolted to the ground. One look at the people in this room, and it was obvious why. As expected, they were indistinguishable from heroin addicts: unkempt, rail-thin, sores, scratch marks and cuts. Some shook like they were in the advanced stages of Parkinson's; others cursed and mumbled to themselves, crawling on the ground and weeping, clearly in the throes of mental anguish. They picked at their skin, paced the room, and argued with each other. Periodically, a door slid open, and Kayla glimpsed a vast arena with users floating through. Infants in utero. Blind astronauts in space. Kayla walked a few shuffling laps, conscious of the button camera, determined to capture it all. No face matched her father's, which gave her both relief and a chill. That meant he was in the arena or plugging in from his apartment. Every few minutes, a White Coat called a number and that subject would race over to hustle through the check-in, fidgeting through vital signs and interview questions before hurling himself or herself into the arena.

"Subject 3-6458!" a bored White Coat called out, her eyes roving over the space.

No one responded. She rolled her eyes and yelled again, "Subject 3-6458!"

A tall, gangly man with an injured leg bolted to life and plopped himself in front of her.

The anguish in this room tore at Kayla's battered psyche. Monahan should pay for this manufactured addiction and misery for the rest of his life. Anger seeped through her.

And then despair.

Good luck, the Mean Voice whispered. *You'll die here. Under the dirt, where there's no daylight. Only suffering.*

She shrank to a corner and slid down. This was what Resilusio did to people. The final stage, the forever legacy. It destroyed brains. With a bit of luck, it would destroy humanity. Seeing it on a surveillance tape was one thing. Seeing it in front of her face was another. She had to find her father. Find him and get him out of here, before he became this tragedy, if he wasn't already. And what about her? Could she end up like these people? Yes, she was resistant, but how resistant? And how much did that count for? Of course, Monahan sought this exact answer, and of course, Kayla had no interest in finding out.

"Subject 3-2460!" the researcher announced.

"Here!" Kayla rose to her feet. The time had come.

CHAPTER FORTY-SIX

A WHITE COAT led her into the arena, and a guilty, welcome relief washed over her as she left the insane asylum waiting room, even though, of course, that was just the frying pan.

This was the fire.

In the locker room, she changed into the smooth synthetic bodysuit required in the arena experience, fussing with it and transferring the admin key back under her tongue. She stashed her clothes neatly in the locker, careful to fold over the button camera, and waited in line for the White Coats to apply sensors and adjust haptics. The subjects' perpetual convulsions made the process slow and stuttering, earning several reprimands. But once plugged in, their bodies calmed. Relaxed. The change sent a shiver down Kayla's side. Sure seemed like a hit of heroin. She searched for her father.

Nothing.

At her assigned rig, she climbed into the suit. She pulled on her gloves, squinting in the dim light to locate the port for the admin key. Left glove.

Nothing.

Was it the right glove? Did she remember it wrong? She held up her hand.

Nope.

The researcher made final adjustments to her helmet. Kayla pretended to fuss with her clothes to buy herself some time, and hey, maybe Vapor meant the left *foot*.

Negative.

The White Coat stared at her expectantly. In maybe thirty seconds, she'd get suspicious. Why would a desperate addict dither and hesitate? The first splashes of panic spilled over her carefully constructed mental controls. Soon, accessing the key under her tongue would be impossible, even if she located the port.

With the White Coat watching her every move, Kayla adjusted the helmet. As she did, her fingers passed over a small, rough indentation. The port for the admin key. To the left of her chin.

She had to do it now.

Kayla feigned a coughing fit, the biggest coughing fit of her life, actually, and retrieved the key. She slipped on her helmet. The White Coat walked away. She jammed the key in.

The journey began with a black screen. No hurtling through space. No oil spill. No gently rotating earth below her feet. For ten long seconds, nothing happened. Kayla spidered her gloved fingers over the key. Should she pull it out and plug it back in? Did she need to reboot or something, like a computer? She almost yanked it out a split second before Ms. Resilusio finally chirped.

"Administrator protocol," she trilled. "Welcome." The sound of the electronic voice sent miserable little stabs down Kayla's spine, reminding her of the last time she'd had a conversation with Ms. Resilusio. How things changed. Now, she would call the shots, not some Armageddon-inducing AI. She scanned the view in front of her. Where was the virus? There was nothing to launch. No Denali.exe, or any kind of icon at all. She ran her hands over the screen, searching for a hidden menu, a hidden button. Nothing.

She shook her head and focused on her most important task. "Resilusio, take me to Kayvan Masouvi."

A silence. More darkness. And then a beep.

"Locating."

A cursor appeared, an old 80s'-style white square, pixelated and pulsing, like the metaverse had time traveled to the used Apple Macintosh her dad would fire up in his study when she was a kid. Code spilled across the screen as the machine crunched its algorithms. No Superman air travel this time. Not for a Game Master. For the wizards behind the curtain, Resilusio offered no clever design, no addicting experience, nothing to suck her in.

The screen morphed to inky popcorn blackness. And the next image before her eyes was her father. He sat on a striped lounge chair with a wide umbrella on an expansive whitewashed hewn-wood balcony, his feet up. Under a shiny, laminated sun, the ocean roared nearby and the balmy air held perfect warmth. Not too humid, not too hot. Steps led from the balcony directly to the beach and water, blue and frothy, tantalizingly close. Kayla breathed in the Resilusio experience. The program had replicated the smell of the Atlantic Ocean exactly, exactly right.

She scanned her surroundings. A two-story house, painted white with toasty brown shingles, small and compact. Nothing fancy, except…no other houses for miles and miles. Utterly secluded. Her father had a cigar in his hand, smoke wafting lazily away, a hat over his face. A bottle of Macallan whiskey, his favorite, sat on a sturdy wicker table in front of him, one finger poured into a sparkly crystal glass. Baccarat, if she knew her father.

A beach house. Of course.

It had always been about a fucking beach house.

"Daddy?" Kayla whispered.

He did not stir. She touched his arm. Kayvan slid the hat away and sat up.

"Kayla? Is that you?" He blinked languidly, his bright blue eyes dull and slow. "You look different." He frowned and brought a hand to his forehead, rubbed it in confusion. "Something's wrong."

Kayla took his hand. Warmth. Home. Love. Family. Despite everything, it all flowed through her. She missed him so very much. But his hand did not curl around hers. It didn't move.

It was the limp hand of a person in a coma.

He tried again. "Who are you?"

She took a deep breath. "It's me. No time to explain. I have to find you. In real life. Where are you?"

He stared at her.

She spoke slowly, like he had a brain injury. "In real life?"

Something passed over his face, gone the moment it arrived. He closed his eyes and sighed at the tickle of the fake breeze, then opened them to gaze at the fake sun and the fake ocean. He'd been at Escondido this whole time, of course. No one told him about the plane. About Sameer. Her status as a missing person / fugitive / hunted animal.

But she had no time for that now.

"Daddy." She stepped forward and gripped his shoulders, leaned down. "I need you to focus. I need you to tell me where you are."

"But I like it here," he said, his brow furrowing. "It makes me happy, and I haven't been happy in so long, in so, so long…"

Her greatest fear coming to life. She prayed she was wrong. That she wasn't too late. That he wasn't an addict. Mentally destroyed. Brain mush. "Daddy, this is fake. An illusion. You know you're in an experiment, right? An *experiment.* An experiment that kills people."

"My life is worth nothing," he said with a dreamy expression. Her words bounced off him. "At least I feel good."

"Don't say that." Kayla shook him. Dug in her fingers. *Wake the fuck up!* "You'll win the appeal. You'll get out."

He exhaled and frowned, pushing his hat aside. When his eyes met hers, they were stern. "They promised me a shorter sentence, Kay Kay. For a few weeks here. Seemed like a no-brainer. So don't worry. It's taken care of." He stood abruptly. Shook her off.

Her hands flopped onto the cushion.

"You're wr-wrong," she stuttered after him. "It's a death trap."

He stepped back to her, eyes hard and empty. "Sure. Maybe it's all a scam. Maybe I'll never be a free man. Maybe I'll die in jail. That's my problem now, not yours. So get out of here. That's an order directly from your daddy." He made his way across the porch and started down the steps to the beach.

Her brain reeled from the sudden change in his demeanor. "You're right," she called out. "You're not a free man. We haven't won." She took a deep breath. *"Yet."*

He froze. She hurried over.

"You made me believe I could accomplish anything. Turn around any situation, with a lot of ingenuity, hard work, and a bit of luck."

A pause. "What are you saying, Kay Kay?"

"You raised me to think for myself," she replied firmly. "So, with all due respect, Daddy. I'm not leaving without you. No. Fucking. Way."

And you know what? She was an admin.

A Game Master. A veritable god in this world.

A Game Master who didn't need anyone's help to find…well, anyone.

She said two words. "Subject location", and finally, something worked.

Cohort four arena flashed in the corner.

"Don't move," Kayla whispered, squeezing his limp hand.

CHAPTER FORTY-SEVEN

KAYLA PULLED OFF the helmet to sharp, suspicious attention from a White Coat monitoring her session.

"I'm really sick," she blabbered. "I might have to throw up."

The man stared at her for a second, then waved his hand. "Very well."

She scrambled to secure the admin key under her tongue, and when she changed in the lockers, she pretended to examine her wound again, slipping the key back under the bandage, the adhesive in very poor shape. She had to worm the key under a scab and a stitch. At this rate, it would end up buried inside her. In the bedlam waiting room, the same guard that brought her there emerged to escort her back to her living quarters, with Miles nowhere to be found. She stalled, dithered, but she had no choice. She had to leave with this guy. As before, the man appraised her frankly, but this time he seemed to be actually checking her out. So gross. She ignored him.

Cohort four, cohort four. Miles didn't mention a cohort four. She had to find her father, and now. Once they locked her away again, it might be over. She glanced at her escort. Tall but not particularly muscular. The guards in the arena areas did not have visible weapons, but that didn't matter. Escaping him in this hospital of horrors, where every inch was on camera, had nosebleed odds.

Out the door, down a dim hall. She had one idea. One. And she ran with it, or more accurately, stopped in her tracks and doubled over. "Oh-*oooooh.* My stomach." She groaned and lowered herself to the ground. "It hurts. Bad."

He glanced up and down the hallway, then crouched down to stare at her, eye to eye. "Can you walk? I'll take you to the infirmary."

She peered up at him and undid a button on her shirt. This revealed skin and concealed the lapel camera. He glanced down, not bothering to hide his pleasure. She shook her head. "Actually, I was hoping to lie down. You know, take a break? Then I'll be fine." She held his eyes meaningfully.

He pulled back and scrutinized her face. Kayla bit her lower lip and pointed at the closest door. "If I…If I could just lie down in there, I'm sure I'd feel a lot better."

He checked the hallway. Then his iPad, clicking it off. "Come on," he finally said. "You really should lie down. I mean, you're collapsing."

Kayla took the hint and fell sideways against him, swaying and weakening her knees. He caught her and opened the door. The lights stuttered on to reveal a bland psychology session room with couches and chairs. The vibe was inviting and non-threatening and cozy, which was hilarious and ridiculous in a gallows-humor sort of way. She scanned every surface for a heavy object to bring down on this man's head.

"You were looking at me," he said, distracting her from her search. He pushed her against the wall, alarmingly far away from any weapons. "Because you're hot for me." He dove into her shirt. She pushed him away and undid the buttons herself, since one of them was not a button. She tossed it aside. He felt her back for the bra clasp, yanking it off. Then, horribly, he bit her left nipple. Hard.

Kayla swallowed a wave of revulsion. "Oh yes, yes, *yes*, I did," she replied. "I'm so glad you noticed." She moved them both farther into the room, toward a coffee table with a vase that held fresh flowers. Mercifully, wonderfully, it was in front of a couch.

She would get this man there.

Yes, yes, *yes*, indeed.

She straightened and pulled him off her chest, working hard not to recoil at the drool on her breasts. He panted, his eyes cloudy with desire.

"Don't forget, I'm sick." She glanced at the vase. Heavy, maybe. She would have to grab it with both hands, hit him sideways. A terrible plan, but she had no other.

"Like I said, I need to lie down." She wiggled away and pulled him to the couch, naked from the waist up save her bandage, swallowing bile. "You need to examine me."

"Oh, I'll examine you all right, you little slut. You've been a bad, bad patient." He came at her just as Kayla had hoped. She lowered herself onto the couch, her eyes on the vase. The vase was in arm's reach. But she waited. Hit him now and he would thwart her. No, she needed him mostly naked and ready for sex and distracted. She committed to the task and blotted out the repulsiveness. *Hurry.* She unbuttoned his pants, and he went for hers. She stopped him.

"No." She pulled his hand back and straightened. "I've been a very bad patient. And I would do anything to apologize." She tugged at his pants.

"Yes," he groaned, hopelessly, blessedly distracted.

"Anything to get better," she replied, never more grateful than this moment for her poker training.

He leaned back. So trusting for one so evil. She pulled his pants down halfway. Stopping just above his knees. *Good luck getting up.*

She averted her eyes from his penis and the thick hair between his legs.

"Suck it, baby. Suck it," he moaned.

"Ooh, it is so big," she cooed, her voice alien to her ears. She glanced at the vase.

It was now or never.

She bent over and bit his penis as hard as she could. He wailed like an animal and, for one crucial second, went limp. She leapt away from him. He jerked upright, but he had limited range of motion, given where his pants were. In the end, he couldn't catch himself. He fell to his left, hitting his shoulder on the end of the coffee table with a satisfying thump. Kayla grabbed the vase with both hands, which was much heavier than she expected, and slammed it down on his vile head. A noise like splintering wood reverberated through the room.

Maybe he screamed. She wasn't paying attention. Kayla lifted the vase and hit him again. But he recovered from the blow, faster than she expected. He whipped around and walloped her across the face. The pain was outrageous, and her prosthetic nose went flying, accompanied by the horrible sound of skin ripping along with it. The vase flew out of her hand. It smacked the table and shattered. She lost her balance. By the time she was steady, he had yanked his pants to his waist.

He stared at her like she was an alien. "What the fuck…?" he muttered, wiping the blood and water off his face. "Who the fuck are you?" She touched her nose, barely noticing the ripped skin, and for a second they simply sized each other up, calculating and planning.

He attacked first, clamping his hands around her neck, knocking her flat onto the hard floor. She struggled upright and made it a few feet toward the broken glass. He slammed her down and climbed on top of her. The remnants of the vase crunched under her back. His arms pushed hers down.

"You little bitch!" he screamed. "I'm going to kill you! Fucking kill you!" His face contorted into something inhuman, like a fun-house mirror, abnormal and crazed. Blood spurted from him, smearing their writhing bodies and dripping into his eyes. He blinked and took one hand off her, swatting to wipe the blood away.

That was her opening.

She closed her fingers around one shard of glass. Not a big one. Maybe not big enough, but beggars couldn't be choosers.

She rammed it into his throat, and Jesus this shard was small but mighty, or maybe she'd nailed the jugular just right, because out of his throat gushed *red*, streaming and shooting like a burst pipe. Kayla pulled herself out from under him, gulped air, and raced for the door.

CHAPTER FORTY-EIGHT

AND STOPPED HERSELF as reality sank in.

She was naked from the waist up, covered in blood, some her own, some his. This place had cameras everywhere. She had no idea where to go.

Her escape would be short-lived.

She glanced back at the guard. Eyes open, body stilling, blood pooling.

Dead.

I just murdered someone. Killing was a messy proposition. Mentally, none of it registered. Not yet, at least.

She grabbed his shirt, intending to switch it with hers, but something nagged at her, breaking the fight-or-flight, nothing-but-survival response. Her shirt. It had something she needed. The camera.

She turned on her heel, grabbed her shirt, buttoned it, then pulled the guard's on top. She found her prosthetic nose and jammed it on, which probably should have hurt, but she was too distracted to notice. It barely stuck to her raw, red skin. So much for spy adhesive. Her appearance would not pass much of a basic muster, but it was her only choice.

Something else. The cohort four arena. She needed the location. The dead man's face opened his iPad and she located it, a floor below. Elevator, make a left, walk down a long corridor. She stared at the directions, memorized them, and screwed on a professional face as her eyes fell on the shattered pieces of the vase. Her mind worked clearly now, and thank God for it, because these shards might be useful. Better than nothing. She gathered three of the sharpest and most portable, shoved them into her pocket, and fled.

❧

In the empty corridor, the fluorescent lights flickered overhead in a sinister Morse code. Her feet longed to flee. Her head forced a walk. All the corridors were under surveillance. No running. So she walked, though it killed her. She slowed down when she reached the next corner, glancing around the bend. Clear. She found the elevator, pressed down, and set the iPad to never sleep, because she didn't have access to the owner's face anymore.

The elevator opened. A White Coat stood inside, a youngish man, tapping on his own iPad. She nodded hello, willing him to overlook her blood-spattered, research-subject pants and the ill-fitting rest of her. He nodded back and returned to his iPad. She glanced over. He was playing a game. No wonder he didn't notice her.

Her father was on floor four. Cohort four, of course. The man pressed five. She would get off first. She counted the seconds, and of course this was the slowest elevator in the world. Fortunately, her ride-share companion had his Minecraft or whatever. When the door opened, Kayla walked out. He called out after her.

"Excuse me?"

Kayla turned, natural, smiling, holding the door. "Yes?" *Poker, I love you.*

"I thought we finished the cohort four experiments for the day." He frowned, thinking. "Did I get that wrong?"

She held her smile. "Uh, no. You're fine. Somebody messed up an exam. Needs a redo." She rolled her eyes as the elevator dinged its disapproval.

"Phew. Thanks." He lowered his eyes and resumed his game.

"Sure."

The door closed, and Kayla exhaled slowly, her vision rippling at this horrible new twist. If the researchers had completed cohort four testing, that meant her father had left the arena. That meant he was back in his room. And those were impossible to penetrate. She did not have the correct eyeballs.

Maybe the goon's iPad had an entry code. She searched as she walked. Then she searched for Miles. She scrolled through White Coat pictures—no names—and no Miles. Maintenance also came up empty.

She did not have a plan.

She found directions to her father's room. Patient 4-3271. Left, right, right, she recited in her head. She took the left. Walked. Slowed at the corner, peered casually, walked.

Almost there.

Finally, they appeared: the horrid numbered screens of the living quarters. She stopped at Patient 4-3271. Still no plan to get in, but finding it gave her a jolt of hope.

She'd figure it out.

The screen came to life, flashing the subject number and INFIRMARY in bright blue letters. Maybe a shot. Whipping around her stolen tablet, she located her new destination and headed there.

Kayla walked into the infirmary, tapping on the iPad. The

infirmary had one main room with two smaller exam and treatment rooms branching off, both doors tightly closed. A guard sat at a reception table, tapping impatiently into his own device. She glanced at the screen.

A game.

"Hello." Kayla aimed a calm smile at the man. "I'm here to pick up patient 4-3271."

The guard barely glanced over, which, given Kayla's dubious appearance, was certainly a plus. "I didn't get a notification. No transport without a notification clearance."

"Ah." She had to think quickly here.

He finished tapping and regarded Kayla with the beginnings of suspicion. "Let me scan your code," he eventually said. There were no names here, of course, just…technology. He held out his hand, eyes steeled on Kayla.

Kayla felt for the glass in her pocket and wrapped her hand around it. Eyed the guard's neck, looking for the vein. There it was—the place she'd sink this shard.

"Sure thing," Kayla said. "Let me, uh, just finish something." She rummaged around in her pocket and stepped forward, preparing to stab him. *Don't think too hard about it. Here comes another messy proposition.* "Oh, actually, one thi—"

Her words disappeared in the ear-piercing howl of a madman who burst out of an exam room brandishing an office chair. He let loose a mighty roar as he lifted the chair high and brought it crashing down on the guard's head with a sickening crunch. Once. Twice. Kayla jumped back just in time, and her fake nose went flying, this time to disappear for good. The crazy guy got in two devastating direct hits, and the guard barely made a noise, just gurgled and crumpled to the floor.

Kayla recognized the man. Her father.

"Daddy?"

"You shouldn't be here," he scolded. "I told you not to come." He squinted at her. "What happened to your face?"

"Well, I ignored you. Let's get the hell out of here." She took his hand and made for the door. But then she froze. They had nowhere to go. No plan. They needed to find Miles. But how?

Her stolen iPad buzzed, flashing a blank profile. Miles?

Here goes nothing.

It was him. "Stay there. I'm coming for you."

How did he know to call her on the guard's tablet? "Am I…" She swallowed the word…*blown?*

"I retraced the path you took back…" he trailed off.

That meant he found the guy. So…probably. If not now, then soon. The infirmary guard whimpered on the floor. "Come fast."

She ended the call to Kayvan's incredulous stare. "You thought I came alone?" She searched the iPad for any security alerts. "Of course I brought backup."

"Your backup better be ready to save you no matter what. Or he'll have me to deal with." He touched his nose. "Kayla, your face?"

The guard stirred. "Don't worry about it now, Daddy!" she snapped, gesturing at the guard. They would have to hit him again. "Lock the door." But neither of them could figure out how to do that, or if it was even possible. They would have to wait here for Miles like sitting ducks.

She scanned her father suspiciously. "How come you look so normal? So alert? You're not addicted to Resilusio?"

He laughed. "Hell no, my girl. You know I don't like video games, and did you see the other subjects? Homeless. Like *drug addicts*. I made up my mind. Not me." He patted her hand. "That was a performance, my love. Acting."

He was resistant, just like her. She'd probably inherited it from him. "Why didn't you say something when I found you?"

"They sometimes monitor the sessions. But I was on my way to you. Infirmary computers list every patient location. I had a plan—to brain this *goh sar*, get on his computer, and find you." That word was, literally, *shithead* in Farsi.

"Wow." Kayla considered this for a moment, duly impressed. "You actually had…a plan." Though given she had the face and name of Fatima Ubaldi, it might not have worked too well.

"*Harf-e dahaneto befahmi*," He raised his eyebrows at her. *Watch your mouth*. "Anyway, your timing was great." He leaned down and slapped electrical tape over the man's mouth. "Go find something to tie him up with."

As Kayla scoured the exam rooms, Miles burst through the door. She rushed back out just as Kayvan hauled the chair up to hit him, too.

"Wait!" Miles said, holding his hands out.

"Thank God." She raced into his arms. He pulled back, fingering her blood-splattered clothing with concern. She examined him, too. No longer a researcher. Now, as originally planned, Miles was in maintenance, wearing a jumpsuit and a tool belt with jangling keys. And his own real hair.

Miles glanced from Kayla to her father. "Is everyone okay?"

"Who are you?" Kayvan asked, lowering the chair and squinting at Miles.

"The cavalry," Kayla breathed, thrilled to see him. "Let's get out of here."

CHAPTER FORTY-NINE

"WE STILL HAVE to tie him up." Kayla nodded at the guard, moaning underneath the electrical tape.

No rope anywhere, of course. Fortunately, the beds in the infirmary had strong restraints, a feature that was both nausea-inducing and logical. They strapped him into one, but not before her father swapped outfits with the man. Now, officially, they were two guards and a janitor. It would have to do.

"We have to go. *Now.*" Miles scanned her face, his eyes sliding over her nose, and said nothing.

"Some asshole smacked it off," she said.

"I'm glad he's dead," he replied.

They slipped out and walked at a normal pace toward the elevator until Miles buzzed them into a janitor's closet. He pushed to the back, where there was a grate, and fished in his tool belt for a screwdriver. He removed the screws and the metal covering. Inside was a long passageway. Dimly lit but large enough to climb through. "I'm in maintenance." He grinned at her.

"Now it makes sense."

"The beauty of underground," he said. "Extra-large crawl spaces to avoid cave-ins." He turned to Kayvan. "Can you do it?"

"Don't worry about me." Kayvan waved him off. "I'm going last, or I'm not going. And don't stop for me."

Miles shined a flashlight down the passageway, which revealed an endless tunnel. "I have to bring up the rear to close the grate. Kayla first. One of my colleagues is at the end."

Kayla's chest levitated. She allowed herself a flutter of hope and relief. The Cable Guys (Girls) were in the building. She glanced at Miles in his maintenance getup. It was the Janitor and the Cable Guys versus the Garbage Man.

She climbed in first and moved ahead to make room. "Should I go?" she whispered to Miles.

"One second." The sound of scraping echoed from the distance, bouncing off the thin steel walls. Kayla cringed. What was that? No time to care. A moment later Miles whispered back, "Go."

Kayla didn't need any encouragement to get moving through the narrow, terrifying space as fast as her scurrying self would take her. The metal was altogether too smooth, leaving her to splay out a maddening, unhelpful scramble each time she tried to accelerate. So she army crawled, losing precious energy, sliding and catching herself repeatedly.

After ten long, excruciating minutes, the crawl space darkened considerably. This section had no lights, and that was both ominous and encouraging. No lights meant they were getting away from the places with people. Then again, no lights meant a dead zone. If they got stuck here or something happened, they were fully, completely dead.

But. Sweet relief. A few minutes later, up ahead, was a single bright white beacon aimed down the shaft, illuminating the last of their way. A homing beacon. Closer, she made out a grate. Here the crawl space got bigger again, and standing behind the grate, encouraging her on, was a Cable Guy.

Miles saw him, too. "Almost there, Kayla!"

"We got this!" she replied, giddy.

But the joy was short lived when the entire pipe creaked to an all-encompassing hum. It shook and trembled.

Was that a precursor to splitting apart?

"Kayla, hu-hu-rry!" That was Kayvan.

And yet, a human being traveling through a narrow, slippery crawl space had but one speed. A crawl. That was the fact of it. The shaking deepened. Heightened, if that made sense. At first the floor shook. Then the ceiling, the walls…everything convulsed like the epicenter of an earthquake. Then came a roar. Louder and louder. The light at the end of the tunnel extinguished, literally, plunging them back into full darkness, and the tremors culminated into a bang so loud and violent Kayla was convinced, for a moment, that the space must have caved in and they must be dead.

Miles called out. "Everyone okay?"

Kayvan spoke next. "Kay Kay, are you there?"

"I'm here." She squinted at the approximate location of the light, where the Cable Guy used to be.

Nothing.

Miles urged her on. "Keep moving!"

The pipe rumbled again, followed by the second-most-unfortunate development after an actual cave-in. Voices. Everywhere. Behind them, in front, from every side, echoing away. Gunfire. A bullet screamed into metal, somewhere above her. People were shooting. At them? Kayla crawled forward, willing herself to remain calm, fighting the instinct to scramble. To bolt. They had no way back. There was no speeding up. There was this path, this speed, this direction.

And that was it.

A few seconds later, the voices receded, replaced by a sickening, bloodcurdling whine descending from all over, but loudest ahead.

"Oh, fuck," Kayla whispered. Were they sawing through the pipes to get to them?

"Keep moving, Kay Kay!" her father called.

She had stopped, an involuntary reaction to the noise. She shook herself straight and got back to it.

I will not die in this tunnel.

To chop her in half, they'd have to catch a break.

With every scurry forward, her fear surged. Stabbed her. Knocked her unruly with confusion. She clenched and unclenched her muscles. *Self-control.* No matter. Whatever happened, Miles would get them out. She was sure of it.

Finally, somehow, she made it to the grate, to find the entire opening…blown away.

At the edge, she peered out. Boilers, generators, water mains. Some kind of mechanical room, mostly dark, with only emergency track lights bathing the ghostly monsters in a dim blue.

"Come on out," came a voice from the darkness. "Don't be afraid."

She froze.

That voice.

That voice lived rent-free in her nightmares. In her hauntings.

"No no no no *no*!" The words tumbled out of her, each one a gash of bitter despair.

"Kayla, what is it?" Miles's voice, from so very far away.

"Who's there?" Her father's too.

"The way I see it," the voice said, flipping on the lights, "you don't have much choice. Unless you fancy slowly starving to death dozens of stories underground, or having these security idiots saw you in half or shoot you. They're pretty pathetic, but you *are* in a tunnel." The voice chuckled. "It's quite the fish-in-a-barrel sort of situation."

The voice stated the obvious. There was no way but forward, into the welcoming, welcoming arms of the fake hot dog vendor / airport ground crew / doctor.

The man chasing her.

"Do you have a name?" she called out.

A chuckle. "You can call me Houdini."

CHAPTER FIFTY

ONE BY ONE, they crawled out. Kayla, Kayvan, Miles.

The man who called himself Houdini stood in front of the door that led out to God-knows-where. Short, nondescript, entirely forgettable Houdini. He wore all black, like a spy-movie assassin: a leather jacket, black gloves, a gun at his hip, and a disgusting sneer on a raw and peeling face. Kayla studied the patches of red mess. Oh yes. The bleach.

Might as well be a million years ago.

Flanking him were two very large, heavily muscled men in combat gear holding semiautomatic rifles with fingers on the triggers. On the floor, slumped to the side, was a Cable Guy. The man who would rescue them, spirit them out of here. And he was dead, recently dead actually, blood gurgling out of multiple gunshot wounds. His head, his arm, his legs.

It didn't shock her, at least not like it should. This just about figured. They weren't getting out of this place. It was a pipe dream. Ha. A *pipe dream*. Exactly. And "Houdini." Sure. That computed. You could probably saw him in half and he'd still pop right back up and come chasing after you. She laughed. At least she had laughter still. That was a plus.

They were a hundred (two hundred?) feet underground. Surrounded by stone. A thousand hostile enemy combatants swarmed the place. Better equipped. Better armed. Better fed. Less injured.

The enemy tightly controlled egress. Ingress.

The enemy had impeccable surveillance.

And the surface—should they make it there by some miracle—held nothing but desolation for miles and miles.

It was hopeless.

And as she stood in front of the hot dog vendor doctor assassin, the mysterious man she now knew as Houdini, she stole a glance at Miles. No surprise on his face. He had known. The whole time, he had known that this was probably, likely, almost definitely…a suicide mission.

He had only done this, all of it, for her. Because he refused to let her go alone.

All I do is get people killed. Had she had any tears, the most bitter of all would have fallen at this moment. But no. No tears. She would go down fighting. She would make her father proud. And Miles. And Sameer.

They deserved nothing less.

"Backups with semiautomatics, huh? Can't bring us in on your own?" She squared on Houdini. "You're less impressive than I imagined."

He laughed, low, miserable, and threatening. A comic-book-villain laugh. "The big guns are for him." He jutted his chin at Miles. "Someone trained him very well."

"Suleiman." Miles nodded. "Always a pleasure."

Kayla stared, slowly, from Miles to Houdini (Suleiman?) and back to Miles. "You know this guy?"

Neither man said anything.

Houdini examined Miles with interest. With respect. "I'm

sorry you're involved," he said, "but you don't have to be. You can go." He touched his own shoulder. "We are still brothers."

She turned to Houdini. "Don't tell me. You have a tattoo of a five-leaf clover there." She jutted her chin at his right shoulder. The same place where Miles had a tattoo. The same place where Vapor had a tattoo. Miles, who was not Irish. Olivia—Vapor—who was not Irish. *We lost good people,* Miles said, without elaborating more. Could he have been referring to Vapor? Was she working for Mason Capital, at least at some point? And now this guy…

…who was not Irish.

"We were in a training program together," Miles said to Kayla. "But that doesn't matter now." Then he addressed Houdini. "No thanks."

He was right. It didn't matter. Houdini had the big guns, literally. That was what mattered.

The assassin's eyes flitted from Kayla to Kayvan and back to Kayla. He laughed. "Always the hero, right? Especially when there's a pretty girl involved and her father to impress." His smile faded. "Very well. Suit yourself." He addressed Kayla. "Someday, Kayla, ask *Miles* here about Project Trifolia. He'll tell you all about the hell on earth we endured in the name of patriotism. And how they destroyed us from the inside out." Then he frowned at her. "What happened to your face?"

She glared at him. He broke out in a scornful grin and turned to Miles. "Let me guess. That was your disguise for her? A clay nose? To *thwart* the facial recognition?" He said "thwart" like it was a filthy word.

She regarded him with disdain. "What happened to *your* face, Mr. Houdini? Rumor has it some cleaning supplies attacked you."

His smile faded as he ignored her. One of his thugs zip-tied their hands behind their backs, then searched them. They confiscated all the tablets. Mercifully, they did not remove her bandages. They did not find the admin key. But they found the button camera. Thug One crunched it unceremoniously under a heavy boot. That hurt, really hurt. Now they were officially screwed. Kayla resisted a mighty urge to find Miles's eyes, to mingle her despair with his. Nobody said a word. Houdini walked up to Kayvan, and Kayla balled her fist and dreamed of smashing him in the face.

"Dad, it's nice to meet you." He cocked his head to the side. "You've got quite a daughter here."

Kayvan had an expression full of such disgust that he might actually spit in Houdini's eye, and for one sick second Kayla braced for it and the subsequent pistol whipping. But Kayvan merely hauled up to Houdini, face-to-face. Defiant. "I know. She's spectacular."

Houdini stepped back. "Kayla." He turned to her. "You love your father?"

If someone had told her six months ago that some master-of-disguises lunatic assassin would ask her this vaguely patronizing question today, she'd have bet her life against it.

Really and truly.

She aimed steely eyes at him. "I'm here collecting him, aren't I?"

He nodded and seemed to think.

And then, without the slightest change of expression on his face, he shot her father.

In the leg.

More or less point-blank.

CHAPTER FIFTY-ONE

HER FATHER CRIED out and collapsed, clutching his pant leg, while blood darkened a large, raggedy hole. Kayla ran to him, babbling *oh my God oh no* on repeat, the words tumbling out of her.

"Daddy?"

He gasped in response as pain contorted his face. She glanced down. Blood everywhere. She wrapped her zip-tied hand around his and bit back a cry. "Squeeze my hand."

"Suleiman, you asshole," Miles spat, ignoring the gun pressing into his neck.

"We have to…get him…to a doctor." Kayla barely choked out the words. Miles, his eyes wide with compassion and helplessness, said nothing and everything. *Even if we could go back… it's hopeless.*

She wailed. *Oh God.* This was happening.

She glanced at Houdini, hoping, irrationally and stupidly, that he would—could—help them. But his patronizing smile erupted a white-hot rage from within her.

"You!" she screeched and lunged at him. Thug Two clamped implacable arms around her and held her still with one arm as she struggled. "You fucking monster!" she screamed. "Why did you do that? WHY?" Her voice was animal, guttural. Barely human. She collapsed to the ground.

"Why?" she croaked.

He walked up to her. Touched a cool finger to her cheek. "Where are the tokens, Kayla?"

She calmed down. Caught her breath. Flying off the handle would fix nothing. She glanced back at the man holding her still.

"Get off me."

Thug Two released her after a glance from Houdini. She stepped forward, eye-to-eye with the assassin. Swallowed. "You shot him for some tokens?" She was back under control. Her voice was even. Measured.

He shrugged. "Not exactly. I mean, yes, it brings circumstances to a head. But no, I was just bored." He zeroed in on her, and it was like his insides unfurled, revealing dark pools of evil. "We were waiting…and waiting…" He trailed off and rolled his eyes. "This entire job's been like that. I had to wait *ages* for you and that boyfriend of yours to appear. And I didn't even get to see him die."

Breathe. Breathe. Breathe. Keep calm. You can still win. I believe in you.

Sameer.

Kayla did as Sameer instructed and kept calm by making mental notes of what she would do to Houdini if she ever had the chance.

"So, Kayla," Houdini said, "the tokens."

Her father yowled from the floor, staggering to his elbows, white and pasty with pain. "Whatever it is, Kayla, don't tell him!" he gasped. "Don't tell him anyth—" Thug One walloped him across the face. Blood sprang from his mouth. The brutal creep raised his arm to wallop him again.

"Wait! Wait!" Kayla cried out. Thug One paused in his assault, looked to Houdini, and dropped his arm. "Wait," she breathed and thought for a moment. "I'll get you the tokens."

Houdini barely flicked an eye, his red skin glistening in the fluorescent lights. "I'm listening."

"The seed phrase to the wallet is in a safe-deposit box. At a bank in Brooklyn." She gazed at Houdini with pure hate, her eyes traveling over his burned face. Jesus but did she want to do unspeakable torture to this monster. She breathed out.

The bastard smiled. "The box you emptied a few nights ago?" He nodded at Thug Two, who aimed his weapon at Kayvan's lone uninjured leg.

"Wait! Wait!" She caught her breath. "Yes. I emptied that one. And I just took it to another branch." She lifted her arms and dared not glance at Miles. She'd left the seed phrase, and her ring, at his apartment, in a drawer. Had he found them? "Mill Basin," she finished lamely, naming a Brookyln neighborhood she'd never visited.

The bastard smiled. "You'll take us there?"

"Yes."

At a glance from Houdini, Thug One tied off Kayvan's injury, clipped their zip ties, and led the way. Miles hoisted her father up, draping Kayvan's arm around his shoulders. Kayvan was ambulatory, at least, even if every step reflected agony.

The three of them trudged, limped, and staggered on, alternately defeated, defiant, desperate, and in Kayla's case, briefly suicidal, retracing their steps fully, passing the living quarters, the rigs, the waiting rooms. Patients and White Coats stopped and gawked at them, the White Coats far more startled than the patients, who undoubtedly lived this kind of stuff daily in prison. They stopped at the main elevator, which would take them aboveground. Houdini pressed the button.

Kayla turned to him. "Let them go." She gestured at Miles and her father. "It's me you want, right? Just let them go, and I'll do whatever it takes."

He laughed, his burned skin expanding and contracting on its own grotesque rhythm. "I'll consider—"

The rest of his words, whatever they were, dissolved into a sudden, earthshaking clap. The sound of rolling thunder from inside a cloud. It came from above. It came from the entrance. An alarm blared. Emergency lights flashed. Kayla figured it out immediately. The loud bangs in the crawl space. That wasn't security trying to stop them from breaking out.

It was someone breaking *in*.

Houdini gripped Kayla above the elbow so hard she cried out, her voice lost among the sounds, and Thugs One and Two jammed guns in the backs of her father and Miles.

And then.

Chaos.

Dozens of security guards materialized out of nowhere, yelling into earpieces and running in every direction. Terrified White Coats bolted for the emergency exits at the end of the hallways. The patients tried the same approach, but security corralled them, by force and weapon, slapped zip ties on them, and herded them into conference rooms.

Houdini communicated wordlessly with his thugs, and within seconds they shoved Kayla, Kayvan, and Miles deliberately through the crowd, away from the elevators, guns pressing into their necks. An unnecessary detail, because for the moment, Houdini was their best hope to get the hell out of here. Was he steering them to an unmarked exit? Possibly one that wasn't even on Escondido's official blueprints? They had no choice but to follow. The explosions might literally bury everyone in here alive.

Houdini raced them past walls of guards, who parted immediately for him, springing away as if scared for their lives.

But they made it only a few steps.

The next few moments unfolded like a movie before Kayla's eyes. Miles and her father exchanged glances. Miles gave her father an imperceptible nod.

And then the two of them launched themselves completely at the Thugs and Houdini. "Kayla," her father bellowed, jumping with his one good leg onto Thug Two. *"Run!"*

Miles, being Miles, tackled Thug One and Houdini. All five men fell to the ground, struggling over the weapons. Thug Two aimed his gun at Kayvan and shot.

Kayla did not look. She squeezed her eyes shut and ran for the nearest exit. Houdini would not kill her. He would not shoot her in the back. He would have to catch her, climb over the pile of fighting men, and tackle her to the ground.

The emergency alarm had unlocked the door. She pushed into a dark stairwell, dimly lit. Steps leading down into the darkness, steps leading up into the darkness. Up? Down? Up, definitely. She took the stairs two at a time. One flight, two flights, three flights, four. Here the stairs finally ended at a door labeled GROUND FLOOR. She rammed her shoulder against it…

…and emerged into a room identical to the one she'd left, the central office of a busy medical center. But this edition swarmed with men and women in advanced tactical gear. Dozens and dozens. Seemed like an elite military unit, not unlike Miles's posse. But this squad had something unique.

American flags on their uniforms.

Yes. Finally. The might of the U.S. military had come to save them. They herded White Coats and security guards into one set of conference rooms, zip-tying them, and the patients into another.

She flagged one down. “Please. They shot my father. He needs help.”

The man aimed his gun at her. “You need to go into the conference room, ma’am. With the others.”

“Look,” she babbled, panicky, “I’m not a, uh, researcher. Or a patient. My name is Kayla Masouvi. I snuck in here to save my father. He was a patient. And they shot him and he’s dying and I need…I need…”

He stared at her. “What did you say your name was?”

“Kayla. Kayla Masouvi.”

He muttered into a headset and glanced back at her for a second. “What floor?”

Kayla did some mental math. “Minus four,” she replied.

“We haven’t cleared that—” He listened on his headset, then flitted his eyes back to Kayla. “Is Ballard with you?”

Miles. “Yes,” she breathed.

A dozen soldiers appeared out of nowhere. One stepped forward. “Show us the way, miss.”

“Thank God.” Kayla nearly cried the words. She led them to the emergency exit and down the flights of stairs. She explained where her father and Miles had fallen. They took note and then positioned her at the back. A second later, they organized into an unspoken formation and executed a countdown.

The forward group slammed the door open.

Their leader bellowed, “Everyone! Hands up! NOW!”

The White Coats and the prisoners complied. The security guards did not.

They opened fire, and true pandemonium fully erupted. Bullets whizzed by. With order torn to shreds, people screamed and stampeded.

A soldier shoved her to the ground. "Stay down," he hissed. "Flat. Do not get up unless instructed."

She nodded fitfully. The team overturned a few desks and took positions behind them, communicating wordlessly. Someone moved her behind one. In seconds, they spread out over the space, creating a perimeter. That was great. She was sure they'd beat the crap out of the rent-a-cops. That wasn't her concern.

Miles.

Her father.

Part of the roof caved in, flattening soldiers, White Coats, and patients, and making her search impossible. She scrambled to her knees and peered over the desk, conscious of the continuous gunfire. The soldier protecting her had disappeared.

But then she saw Miles and Kayvan, and her heart leapt.

Thug One was herding them away at gunpoint, to the exit, while Thug Two fired at the soldiers. Houdini was missing. The soldiers fired back. One shot sent Thug One down, momentarily freeing her father and Miles.

But Kayla knew what was about to happen before it happened.

Clear line of sight.

Wide, slow-moving target.

One man dressed as a security guard. Another dressed as maintenance. And a third man in tactical gear, firing.

Oh, the cruelty of automatic weapons. In the space of 1.5 seconds, two shots hit her father. One hit Miles.

They collapsed and disappeared.

"NO!" she screamed, and throwing all caution away like used Kleenex, she ducked, scurried, and ran. But the gunfire was too much. If she died too, that would help no one. So she got on her hands and knees and crawled. By the time she made it to them, Thug One was dead. In the distance, Thug Two dragged Miles out an exit and disappeared.

But her father was on the floor. Alive. Barely.

"Daddy!" She nearly fell on him, wrapping her arms around him.

He was not long for this world. There was no sugarcoating it. He lay in a literal pool of blood. Multiple gunshot wounds littered his body, leaking out life. She held him.

"Kay Kay," he gurgled. "Be careful. Stay down."

She laughed despite her tears. Here he was, at the end, still being a parent. "Daddy, stay strong. These are American soldiers. They'll help us. They'll get you to a doctor. You'll be okay. You'll make it. I'll get us that beach house, don't worry. You just have to hold on."

She peeked around a pile of desks and chairs. Still gunfire. She couldn't move or call for help. Not yet.

She squeezed his limp hand. Picked a gunshot wound. Pressed on it.

He shook his head and pushed her arm away, propping himself up on his one remaining good arm. "Kay Kay, don't you… move…Wait for the Americans…Anything else…too dangerous." He coughed up blood, then cleared his throat. "That's an order from your father."

She shook her head and squeezed her eyes. Closed. Open. Closed. Open. She clamped down on the tears. "But I've got to get help. We don't have much time." She gasped out the words. So futile. So hopeless. "I can't stop the bleeding…" Her voice faded.

He smiled and raised an eyebrow painfully. And then they said it together.

"Yet."

They both knew. This was the truth.

And a lie.

His hand clenched and unclenched. He let out a groan. "While we wait for the rescuers to get here and save us, let me hold your hand. And dream." Kayla screamed in her head. All of this…all of this he did so that she wouldn't get up. So she wouldn't move. So she wouldn't put herself in any danger. "What did I always say"—he gasped, swallowed, then went on—"when you were little?"

Kayla blinked back tears. "How did I get so lucky to get you?"

As he nodded, his face suddenly turned blue. A dark, horrible blue. "God must have smiled on me…"

His voice trailed off.

"The day they were passing out daughters," Kayla finished for him in between sobs.

The gunfire continued. On and on and on. It seemed like it would never stop.

Kayla lay there, prostate, on her stomach, clutching Kayvan's hand as its warmth dissipated and his fingers stiffened. She cradled it. His hand grew heavy. Her head grew heavy. She lay on his chest and sobbed.

CHAPTER FIFTY-TWO

A SICKENING YAWN of metal opened above her, accompanied by an ear-assaulting screech. The rest of the roof was in the slow, horrible process of caving in. Concrete cracked and crumbled, sending chunks flying. The inevitable was happening. She would have to leave her father.

Now.

She kissed his cold cheek. "Goodbye, Daddy." She scrambled to her feet to run…where? She spun around. The stairs. She made it five steps before a crash of mangled building materials knocked her back to the floor, separating her, probably forever, from her father's body. The entire contents of the exam rooms above, including rigs, beds, sinks, and chairs, rained down. At least two White Coats disappeared underneath the rubble. Kayla coughed and sputtered out smoke. Gasped for air. Inhaled more smoke. Smoke everywhere. Filling the room, filling her lungs. The air purifiers kicked on. A loud whirring followed by a self-contained windstorm.

One crisis averted.

Ding. The elevator opened. More soldiers. They dispatched the last of the security guards and cleared out a space in the middle of the room at lightning speed. Their commander stepped forward, giving orders. A silence fell over the entire place. The alarm, somehow, shut off. As did the wind.

Hope we don't suffocate first, Kayla thought.

The soldiers herded zip-tied White Coats and patients into the elevators, organized and carted away electronics, moved furniture to triage the gaping hole in the roof. Kayla uncurled her body and stood. She had to get out of here, too.

Gloved hands clamped on her and covered her mouth.

Houdini. *Fuuuuck.* He was here. And he was alive. He muttered rapidly into an earpiece and pushed her ahead, pressing his gun into her side the whole time. She elbowed him in the ribs hard and whirled around. Sneered at the gun and then at him.

"Get that thing away from me." He wasn't killing her. Then he'd never get the seed phrase. His only leverage—her father—was gone. Debris or cave-ins had probably blocked all exits, secret or not. Houdini had no options but the welcoming arms of the good old US of A.

"I've still got your boyfriend," he hissed.

"Miles?" She nearly spat at him with disgust. "Prove it. And he's not my boyfriend."

For the third time, the elevator opened, and this time suits and worker bees swarmed in. Business casual, clipboards, boxes, and at the front, speaking into a headset and directing movements, a petite sixty-something woman with a blond bob and a commanding presence. This was the second wave, the team that would secure the computers, the patient logs, the equipment, the records, the data. Already several White Coats sat at desks, writing out lists of passwords, submitting to retinal scans and handprints.

Houdini tightened his grip on Kayla, turned her around, and

shoved her down to the ground. Well, almost. She stumbled over debris. Something stabbed her. She landed chin first. Up close, the mangled rubble creaked and sizzled with electricity. It might, actually, electrocute them.

"Drop the gun."

She turned slowly. Two soldiers materialized and pointed assault rifles at Houdini. He analyzed the entire situation in a glance and handed his weapon over. They zip-tied him and led him away, and that was it. Exit Houdini, for now. Maybe she'd be lucky. Maybe she'd never, ever see him again.

But he was Houdini, so she didn't give that the best odds.

As Kayla stood, she and the woman in charge caught sight of each other. She stopped her conversations abruptly and waved off questions, walking over with single-minded intention. Kayla inched away from the bare electricity and waited, smoke-addled and defeated.

"Hello, Kayla." She stuck her hand out. Kayla stared at it. Oh yes. She should…shake it. Very firm handshake, soft hand. An iron fist in a velvet glove sort of thing. "You're the reason we're here. You should be very proud." She had a lilting accent Kayla couldn't place. Somewhere in Europe, maybe.

I'm the reason you're here? Kayla regarded her carefully. One likely answer surfaced. The button camera. It had a real-time feed.

"You got the video. From my, uh"—Kayla rubbed her fuzzy, addled head—"button."

"Someone in maintenance installed a receiver," the woman said, her eyes warm but serious. She cocked her head towards the elevator. "In there."

Miles. The guy in maintenance. He did it. "Is he safe?"

The woman patted Kayla's arm. "We'll find him. He's very well—"

"Trained. I know." So Miles was out there, maybe safe, maybe not.

They sized each other up for a moment. Something about this woman made the little hairs on Kayla's arm stand at attention. "Who are you?" she finally asked.

"We're the good guys," the woman replied. "Would you like a business card?" She rummaged in a pocket and held one out. Vered Albright, chief investment officer, Mason Capital. The card listed a phone number. And an email.

"Miles works for you?" she asked.

"He does," Albright replied. The woman in charge, indeed, of Miles's super-spook investment manager employer. The leader of the pack (of good guys). A day late and way short. Her father was dead. Sameer was dead. Suleiman might have kidnapped Miles. Many "research subjects" had gone to their deaths, raving mad and in horrible psychic pain. Kayla longed to fall apart. Right here, right now.

But that was existential agony for another time.

She looked around, at the rubble, at the soldiers, at the firepower, at the mess of it all. "Can you stop it now? Shut Resilusio down?"

Albright stared as if she had just requested an abduction by aliens. "We are Mason Capital, Kayla. Our job is to gather evidence. We go where our skills can help"—she paused—"but that's it. What we find, we turn over. What they do with it is…a process."

"They".

"A process".

Kayla laid the logic out in her brain, piece by piece, because her brain was a mess, and she needed to do this slowly. "Do you have the connections? Between Monahan and all of this?"

Albright gestured around her, unconcerned. "It's here," she said. "We'll find it."

There went those red flags again, flapping everywhere in the breeze. Kayla would bet her life that absolutely nothing here linked to Monahan. Any connection would have to come from GR. If they didn't already have it, they were probably out of luck. The twinges and questions solidified. Something in this woman's reaction…was wrong. Unworried. Unbothered. And deflecting, deflecting, deflecting. Kayla's heart sank as the truth came into focus. Still, she tried. Because Jesus. She had to try.

"What about the source code?" she asked. "Can you destroy it? With a virus or something? Otherwise, it can come back. It will come back."

The woman seemed to think for a moment. "We're not Russian hackers," she said. "This is the US government, Kayla. We don't develop viruses. We follow the law. The only way we do things."

Okay. Confirmed then. They didn't have Vapor's virus, or their own version either.

They'd raided Escondido. Shut it down.

They'd saved some innocent lives and ended some not-so-innocent ones.

Maybe they stopped the world from getting hooked on Resilusio. For now.

But, most importantly, they'd accomplished the actual goals of this operation.

They scored a treasure trove of information on Resilusio technology.

They'd disrupted the experiments. Pulled all the data to cripple Resilusio's development.

They'd gotten their stuff. Sure. But this stuff was anthrax. A superbug. Instead of destroying it, they'd seized it. Preserved it. *Safeguarded* it.

For research purposes only, of course.

There would be no Feds. No indictments. The way they stopped Monahan was anything but legal. And stopping him wasn't even the goal. The plan.

"We're not Russian hackers." Yup. Exactly. Not *Russian*. The button camera provided crucial information. How to attack the facility successfully. Where the structural weaknesses might lie. They'd needed specs, locations, layouts, better, more detailed than what they had already. Up to date and confirmed by a first-person account, because whatever they'd relied on before… had gone down in flames.

Until she infiltrated Escondido with the button camera, they didn't have the information necessary to green light the attack.

That was the bottleneck. Not a warrant or the "Feds".

Information.

"Napoleon once said that war was ninety percent information." One of her favorite quotes, ever.

Napoleon…smart guy.

CHAPTER FIFTY-THREE

DESPAIR WRAPPED COLD, poisonous arms around her. It was hopeless. And over. Miles might be dead, might be Monahan's hostage. As for Mason Capital? They just wanted Monahan's stuff.

"*...spying is* our *department. Anyone fronting our game like that will get our attention."* Miles had said it to her. Straight-up, he had said it. She just hadn't known what to listen for, what to look for.

Give up give up give up, the Mean Voice whispered. *It's hopeless.*

But another voice countered. Sameer's voice.

No. No giving up.

The elevator dinged, and she reentered nightmare reality. More people came out—a motley crew of soldiers and government workers.

Kayla shoved Albright's business card into her pocket. "I have to go."

Albright touched Kayla's shoulder. "We'll find him."

Kayla nodded. Yes, that she sort of believed. They didn't abandon their own. Ever. "I have to go," she repeated. And she did.

"I understand," the woman said, her eyes never leaving Kayla's face. She called over one of her underlings. The man got to work scribbling something on his iPad. "He wants you alive, Kayla."

No need to clarify who "he" was.

She shrugged and glanced at the underling's phone. It was nine P.M., and two days had passed. "I came here for my father." She was just numb enough to say this without dissolving into a blubbering idiot.

"Of course you did." Albright would let Kayla leave, hoping she would lead them to her leverage on Monahan. Her small, pathetic leverage on Monahan. Someone whispered in Albright's ear. The woman spoke up. "One thing, Kayla?"

"Yes?"

"You may not know this, but a … unique corporate structure controls Resilusio." Albright paused, waiting for Kayla to confirm, which would be halfway to revealing the truth. "Something related to cryptocurrency. Something that makes anonymous control possible."

Kayla said nothing, keeping her face entirely blank. "I don't understand."

Albright went on. "Your former boss used cryptocurrency to denote ownership. A token. Called REAL." Another pause. Another impassive face from Kayla. Albright shrugged and finished her speech. "We're not convinced Monahan has control. Some of those tokens…may have…gone rogue."

Kayla spoke now. "Interesting."

Albright smiled pleasantly. "You wouldn't know about…any of that?"

Kayla laughed. "I wouldn't know a crypto wallet if it hit me in the face, but I'm flattered you think I'm so smart."

"Hmmph." Her smile faded. She gave up. Someone handed Kayla a phone. "For when we locate Miles."

She took the tracking device—er, phone. She'd figure out what to do with it later.

Albright cleared her throat. "Ah, do you want to say goodbye?"

Kayla spun around. The soldiers had not yet tackled the area where Kayvan's body lay under an intractable pile of concrete, steel, and plastic.

It's just a body. A body. Organic material. It's not him.

He's dead.

Oh, God…She wanted to hold his hand. Kiss him. Tell him she loved him. That she was sorry. But he wasn't here anymore. Her father was gone. The luxury of grief wasn't in the cards right now. Someday she'd feel that pain. But not today.

One last glance at the pile. "Bury whatever's left next to my mom?"

Albright's only response was a tiny duck of her chin.

Kayla closed her eyes as someone fitted a blindfold over them. Firm hands prodded her forward. It was time to go. And boy was she ready. She had a long road of treachery ahead, assuming they didn't take her into the Nevada desert and make her disappear.

Bad things will happen. Never waste them. Learn. Reassess. Develop.

The Tao of one Kayvan Masouvi, may he rest in peace. She was no closer to Monahan. Miles was missing. Mason Capital had no plans to stop Resilusio. She thought about Vapor, who believed that humans were in charge of their destinies. Miles, who had the soul of an ancient Greek and believed that destiny did the choosing. And finally Rizzo. Rizzo, who believed that life was nothing more than a random assortment of decisions and events. Maybe they were all correct, in their own ways, but she picked Rizzo for this moment. Kayla had flipped tails about ten times in a row here. She was due for heads. As in, some random good luck.

Luck is common. There he was again. Her dad. *Using it the right way? Very rare.*

Time to give herself the best shot for the next time luck visited. She would gather her leverage, every bit of it, aim directly at the source, and pray for luck to appear.

Frederick Douglass Monahan. Titan of American business. Modern-day Horatio Alger story. Triumph of the spirit, Exhibit A. World-saver. Philanthropist. Mad scientist. Nazi experimenter. Murderer.

If you come at the king, you best not miss.

Whoever said that got it right. If she missed, so be it. She would go down fighting. That was all she could ask for.

No more running.

CHAPTER FIFTY-FOUR

STRONG ARMS LED her up the elevator and out the door of the gas-station illusion. Nighttime. She had never been so grateful for night and day, for the privilege of experiencing the rotation of the earth. The desert dark kissed Kayla's cheeks, cool and probing. Fresh air. Beyond amazing. In one deep breath, she inhaled dust, desolation, freedom.

In short, magic.

A man's voice muttered behind her, low and unintelligible. Two sets of feet. Someone prodded her forward, guiding her into halting steps. They led her to an SUV or van. She had to step up to get in.

Then a plane. That was easy enough to figure out. Then another SUV.

She did not sleep.

Sameer.

Her father.

Miles.

Rough skin pressed something into her hand—a small, thin envelope. She traced her fingers around the contents.

A key card. Probably for a hotel room.

The vehicle slowed and stopped. They moved her to a taxi.

The driver, an elderly Asian man with shaky hands, removed her blindfold. He took her to Times Square.

"Your destination," he said.

The envelope bore the return address of a large luxury hotel. Room 3-2460. Of course. Her Escondido ID number. Inside was a plastic key and a prepaid Visa. She got out of the taxi into a brilliant bright fall day, all brand-new green and crisp breeze. *New York,* she thought, *you're back to the movie magic.* In years past, she would stride around on a day like this, living the classic New York privileged single-girl life. A tailored Burberry trench, the belt tied in a jaunty knot at her hip. Louis Vuitton boots, the kind that make you avoid puddles and street grime at all cost. Her hair freshly blown out for three figures, her body relishing small hints of warmth down to her sleek leather gloves, on her way somewhere trendy. A dream, entirely in glossy snaps.

Well, that Kayla was dead.

As it was, she wore a blood-splattered mental-patient uniform, with a guard's stolen shirt on top. She was a long stretch from her most recent shower, she had nasty injuries, and there was no Louis Vuitton going on. Inside her room, or, more accurately, "her" room, was a large tote bag and a full wardrobe: tops, pants, shoes, underwear, bras. All exactly in her size, even the bras, which were hard to guess. 32C.

We know you.

If we need to, we'll find you.

She stared at the innocent tag for many minutes.

As if she needed a warning.

As if she cared.

In the bathroom, a contact lens case and a prepaid FedEx envelope to somewhere in Virginia. Below that a note, typed.

At your convenience.

She took out the contacts and then placed the spook phone on the hotel room desk. That would stay here. Something scraped her injury. She touched her side.

The admin key. Buried inside her all this time.

She refused to touch anything in the room, knowing that Albright and Mason would track her and watch her, phone or not, but why make it easy for them? Outside, she bought new clothes and took a criss-cross subway and taxi route to a scuzzy-looking electronics retailer, leaving with a refurbished iPhone several generations old and a similarly situated MacBook. At a random Starbucks, a random cab ride away, she visited the bathroom, removed the admin key, and slipped it into her pocket.

"We have another chance, Vapor," she murmured. "Another chance at our goal."

Maybe the second time would be the charm.

She got on her computer and sent one simple email:

> *From: Kayla.Masouvi@generalrecycling.com*
> *To: Frederick.Monahan@generalrecycling.com*
> *Subject: REAL*
>
> *We need to speak.*

Her fingers hovered over ENTER.

You can still win, came Sameer's voice. *I believe in you.*

Her breath caught. Each time she heard his voice in her head, it was a blessing, but each time she wondered if it would be the last.

She pressed the button.

The return email landed in her inbox forty-five seconds later:

From: Frederick.Monahan@generalrecycling.com
To: Kayla.Masouvi@generalrecycling.com
Subject: Re: REAL

Come to work. We'll talk.

The response hit her like a sledgehammer to the head. For the millionth time, panic, unpleasant and unexpected, slapped her like a poison tentacle. Could she do it? The mental image of stepping back into that mind-control temple of doom filled her with such revulsion that she doubted, truly doubted. Would her legs move? Would her arms push through the revolving doors? Or would her body, justifiably in self-preservation mode, simply refuse, stay frozen in place?

The answer jolted her. She rejected every pang of intimidation. She was walking in there. Legs straight. Head up. Like a boss, because she was in a special, unique, once-in-a-lifetime situation:

She had absolutely nothing to lose.

This would either fix her problems or be the end of her. She hit reply and typed her response quickly.

From: Kayla.Masouvi@generalrecycling.com
To: Frederick.Monahan@generalrecycling.com
Subject: Re: Re: REAL

Tomorrow. I'll be there.

She logged off and pulled out Vered Albright's card, fingering the raised lettering.

Albright picked up on the first ring. "Kayla."

She took a deep breath and made the ask: "I need your help."

The line crackled for a second. "Talk to me."

Kayla took a deep breath. "I need your team to write two smart contracts." These were blockchain computer programs that automatically executed according to defined, specified terms that happened on-chain. No human intervention. "Time sensitive."

"Understood."

She hesitated for a second. Plowed on. "And…there's something else."

Albright laughed. "This isn't Burger King, Kayla."

But then Kayla explained. Everything. Each piece of the puzzle, as she saw it, as she planned it.

Albright stopped laughing.

CHAPTER FIFTY-FIVE

ANY POKER PLAYER who desires success must master branch decision-making. For every alternative on the felt, our hero needs a plan. Nothing vague. A real, if-this-then-that plan. For instance, assume our hero likes her cards. Assume she then bets. She must respond to each alternative:

If villain (poker opponents are always the "villain") raises the hero's bet between $X and $Y, then *A*.

If villain raises hero's bet greater than $Y, then *B*.

If villain simply calls (matches hero's bet), then *C*.

If/then statements bedrock many a winning strategy. It seems easy, until one sits down at a poker table, trying to apply them on every hand, every villain, in real time, with complex branches veering off if two or more villains come along for the ride, while also keeping track of pot size, odds, and with only seconds to plan and react. Layered on top—the absolute requirement to hide it all. To give off zero tells.

To have a perfect poker face.

For this matchup, Kayla had to think long and hard about her decision tree.

She had a Plan A, a Plan B, a Plan C, and a Plan D. Fortunately, there was only one villain. That reduced the complexity.

Plan A probably had the best odds of success but also the

best odds of death, torture, dismemberment, etc. Plan B was plausible, but she doubted the Garbage Man would give her a chance at that one. It had terrible odds. That was why it was Plan B. Plan C had serious limitations but some plausibility. If it worked, she'd make it out alive. Plan D got the most appropriate initial. Plan D. *D* for "desperation."

The next morning, she ate breakfast at a deli. She glanced at the *New York Post*, which had, unpleasantly, coverage of the plane explosion.

New Leads in Death of Real Estate Scion

She read the article with faint interest. Monahan's spin team working overtime.

Ground crew chief tampered with aircraft before explosion, next to a grainy shot of Houdini doing just that.

Authorities could not locate the ground crew chief. No surprise. The victim's father had a raft of powerful enemies. And terrorism was forever a possibility.

Kayla stared at the picture, fully aware of where she was and what she was doing at that exact moment. Doomed without knowing it.

Bad things will happen.

I know, Daddy, she replied. *I won't waste them. I'll learn. Reassess. Develop.*

And make you proud.

She left from the back entrance of the deli and slipped into a cab. She directed it to a random subway stop, deserted and stark. When she got out, she scanned. A hot dog vendor stood on the street corner. She half expected to see Houdini's face.

He's gone. He's in a CIA dungeon somewhere. Or dead. He can't hurt you.

She kept repeating this to herself. And it was probably, likely, true. But without a body in front of her, free of breath, free of a pulse confirmed with her own two fingers, she was not convinced. She scanned again, but it was no more useful than it had been all those very many—but really not that many—days ago. Reviewed her Plans A, B, C, and D. *And don't forget H and P*, she thought grimly.

Hope and Pray.

Another subway ride. Another cab, which she directed to several blocks west of GR headquarters. She needed to get her bearings, gather her courage, quiet her mind. The first block toward her fate was typical far-west industrial Manhattan—the commuter buses, dusty-walled construction sites advertising yet another luxury condo building "coming soon," and gravelly, crumbling parking lots waiting patiently for their turn to become luxury condos, too. This street had a hill, and when she crested it, the full peak-cycle splendor of Hudson Yards came into view: the skyscraper stair-steps, the thin clear shard of the Needle, the all-glass observation deck, above which no executive other than Rick Monahan lived or worked—not even the guy who developed the place. Next to that, the Vessel, an eight-story open-air climbable sculpture shaped like a giant vase, from which several unfortunate souls had jumped to their deaths until someone wised up and installed guardrails.

As she got closer, the walk might as well have been inside Resilusio. It was that surreal. To the left bustled overpriced coffee roasters and cafés. To the right, the tight, perfect, delightful landscaping. Ahead, finally, was the building she lived and worked in for those long months. The last time she'd walked over this concrete, it had been in the opposite direction. Sameer had been by her side. They were striding away, out of this death trap, on their way to a bright future. Sameer, who now lived only inside her head.

Wait.

And there he was.

You don't have to do this, his voice whispered, *not for me.*

She froze.

He went on. *Disappear into the crowd. Live your life. Move on.*

If he were here, he'd say all of this. He would. And it was *all true*. She was against the ropes, a blow or two away from permanent midnight. Anyone who cared about her would say it.

Give up. Live to fight another day. Live to fight another way.

But he wasn't here. And she was. And though he was dead—and, of course, because of it—she must make him proud. Make a ghost proud of her. To seep that truth into her bones like milk on bread. He should know that his killer paid with his dignity. His dreams. Maybe even his life. Stopping wasn't possible. Wasn't ever possible.

You deserve the best I have to give, Sameer. And this is all I have to offer.

Crisp air nipped her cheeks. A few fall leaves rustled at her feet. Lights on the mall twinkled. It was sparkling, warm, inviting. That was the illusion. Happy late-stage capitalism, down to the big friendly garbage company inviting you to buy everything and then, please, throw all of it—yes, all of it—away.

The reality was a prison, and it didn't fool her. Maybe it never did, and that was why she landed here.

She hurried to the headquarters. Stopped at the base, gazed up.

I've arrived, motherfucker.

The spook phone buzzed. That would be Albright with Plan A.

She pushed through smooth revolving doors, into the lobby, where overly alert security guards prowled, scrutinized, assessed. She approached the check-in desk and gave them her name. A few minutes later, Kayla had a barcoded visitor's ID, which activated the dividers.

And yet they parted with no swipe.

Mind games. She smiled in her head. *Go for it, Rick.* She walked through, her poker face as intact as ever. *I'm officially a hard target.*

She stepped into the marble elevator and pressed the topmost button. It zoomed skyward.

Above everyone. Almost above the clouds.

It stopped at the twentieth floor.

A mail cart rumbled on, pushed by a slightly balding, fairly round, very schlumpy guy in a sweater and khakis, with glasses and…dandruff.

She stared. She *stared*. Then she thanked God, for the hundredth time, for her poker training.

The man cleared his throat. "I have a joke for you."

She glanced over at those Windex-blue eyes and lifted her shoulder. He was alive. He was here. "Go ahead."

"What do you call a guy who works in a mailroom?"

"I don't know. What?"

"A mail escort."

She laughed and took him in, trying not to sigh with happiness.

"Oh, I'm just getting started." His lips smiled. His eyes were serious on her. "Lots more where that came from."

She exhaled some relief. Some brief happiness. She had her partner in crime (fighting). Her pot odds just increased. A lot.

The mailroom guy rummaged in the cart and came up with something. The envelope she had left in his apartment, slit open. He handed it to her. The paper with the seed phrase was not inside. Her ring was. She slipped it on, and immediately, her energy changed. "Are we…?"

"We're all set." He locked eyes on her. The seed phrase was safe. They had their precious asset secured.

For now.

Their ears popped. The elevator arrived at the topmost floor. She stepped out and turned left, toward the Temple. Miles turned right. One last glance at him, for mental strength, and she charged ahead, shaking out the tension in her body. She passed by her desk. Each item just as she left it, though that was a lie. Someone had picked it apart, then replaced or reassembled, as appropriate.

She approached Monahan's two assistants. They were busy today, jabbing their computers, muttering into headsets. They did not look up. She waited.

Gargoyle One finally addressed her. "Yes?"

"I'm here to see Rick."

They were not surprised she was here. They were not surprised she was *alive*. They did not greet her by name, just stared with their blank-stone eyes.

"He's expecting me," she added.

Gargoyle One nodded, pulled her headset down, and stopped typing. "He told us you were coming." She glanced at her colleague, who did not confirm this. "But he's not here."

"He's not here?" Panic clawed her, cold and clammy fingers

of doom. But her voice—thank God, for the umpteenth time, for poker—was calm, even uninterested.

"Not exactly." Gargoyle Two piped up, her eyes narrowing. "You'll find him in Resilusio."

A trap? A stroke of luck? Both? Neither? Instinctively, Kayla focused on her wound. The administrator key was again nestled inside the bandage. That was an integral element of Plan B.

And that's where she was now. Plan B. The plan she liked the best but never thought she'd could execute. Never did she believe he'd meet her in Resilusio.

Here comes some luck.

Good? Bad?

Hard to read, the future is.

Lol.

Thanks, Yoda. I mean Dad.

Plan A. Simple but problematic. Kayla had to get Monahan to connect the wallet with the other half of the REAL currency to Kayla's wallet with her half. Mason Capital had programmed a smart contract with malicious code. The contract purported to transfer Kayla's tokens to Monahan's wallet. But it did the opposite. With all the tokens, Kayla's wallet would fully control Resilusio.

But Plan A required Monahan to connect the correct wallet, the one with the other half of the currency. It also required him to be clueless enough to miss the perils of that action. Theoretically, he might not believe she had any access to the kinds of programmers who could write malicious contracts. Theoretically, his guard might be down. A long shot, but worth preparing because if it worked, it would be perfect.

Kayla fingered the tiny plastic spray bottle in her pocket.

The look, feel, lettering of a perfume sample. That was Plan C—spy-concocted poison. Kayla only had to spray it in his evil face.

Plan C seemed to be off the table.

So for now, she would execute Plan B. Her favorite — and until this second, the one with the worst odds, because it had failed before. Attempting Plan B meant that Plan A was off the table, because if Plan B failed, she'd never get Monahan to connect the wallet with the other half of REAL.

Gargoyle One squinted at her screen and typed something, frowning. "Rick says that the mailroom guy should plug in, too." She raised those dead eyes to Kayla. "By the way, what happened to your nose?"

CHAPTER FIFTY-SIX

MILES MET HER in front of the Temple. His entire being radiated *mailroom guy*. Not that it mattered. Gargoyle One confiscated their phones. He took her hand. They walked together to the elevator.

"How much did you crave it?" Kayla glanced at him from the side, unsettled by the combination of the sort-of-real Miles mixed with the fake mailroom guy. She slid her eyes away.

The hybrid shook his head. "What?"

"After last time," Kayla said as the elevator dinged open. "Did you want to go back?"

"Yes," he answered, meeting her eyes. "But he'll have to work harder than that to get me hooked."

She stepped inside. "Just keep reminding yourself. It's designed to make you fall in love."

"Wait a minute," Miles said, holding up a hand. He yanked the padding out of his torso, pulled off the wig, and shook out his hair. "Ahhh, much better." He tossed them both to the floor. "Let's do this."

She touched his arm. "Take it seriously."

"I've been very well—"

"Trained. I know."

He found her hand and squeezed it. "I guess we'll find out how good."

The button for the amenity floor was already lit. When they got out, shivers raced down Kayla's arms. The concierge desks were empty, other than Sachin, who led them to their first Resilusio experience all those many lifetimes ago. He greeted them with the same wide smile.

"Welcome," he trilled. "Welcome to the amenity floor, Kayla and"—he consulted his iPad—"Miles is it?" He raised an eyebrow and glanced up for confirmation.

Miles said nothing.

He typed something into his iPad. "Right. You'd like some time together in your own special world." He grinned like a game show host introducing an all-expenses paid trip to Europe.

"No." Kayla stepped forward, abrupt enough to wipe the smile right off Sachin's face. "I'm here to find Rick Monahan. He's in there. Waiting. For me."

"Ah." Sachin typed something else. His eyes widened. He clicked his iPad off. "Well. Splendid. Let's get to it, then, shall we?"

It was a queasy trip down a dark memory lane. Down the hidden elevator to the odd floor. The desolate, movie-set space station. Handed off to the Host, who perched on the stool in the waiting room as if she'd never left. Then, finally, the door slid open to reveal the humming, beckoning creature known as Resilusio: five thousand square feet of living electronics.

Kayla stepped in, breathing in the hyper-oxygenated air, heavy with perfume, burn, and metal. This time she readily identified another smell: craving, bodily and chemical. This was probably her superpower, the innate "talent" Monahan sought.

Observing and identifying the process. The ability to step outside Resilusio's implacable chemistry. It ruined the high. She glanced at Miles. His eyes darkened with suspicion. Nothing like the first time, when they reflected the wonder of the magic before them.

Or maybe that was all an act.

The walls shimmered with every earthly shade of gray, punctuated by dim blue and red lights. The rigs, which today bounced and slid in a pantomime of giddy anticipation, twinkled like crazy. Probably an upgrade. And the floor…Before it had moved as if alive, trembling and humming and almost breathing. Now it was an insane Martian landscape—bumps and ridges, the surface thickening and thinning, undulating as fluid as mercury. As Miles touched it, a look passed over his face, like he was communing with an extraterrestrial being, his eyes a hair short of glazed. The floor swirled and puckered at his hand. He pulled back roughly.

"That's new," he said, grimacing.

Kayla thought back. To her time underground. Her duel with Vapor. Resilusio invading her brain like a marauding virus. Perhaps Monahan was not so far away from achieving that. Her eyes slid over the Host. Over Miles. Over the arena. He certainly had better bells and whistles.

Miles shook his head like he was shaking it straight. "Like I said, I trained for this."

"This?"

He held her eyes steady with his. They had turned the color of ice. "Torture," he said simply. "Pleasure bombing. Removing it, leaving an injury and excruciating pain. Real pain. Real injuries. False relief." He set his mouth grimly. "So don't worry about me.

Whatever happens, I'm coming in with you. And I'm coming out with you."

Here goes the H and P. No one could explain the "new" Resilusio, could they? It had to be experienced. Miles had no idea what wonders to expect.

"Who's going first?" The Host smiled her creepy, robot-lady smile.

Kayla. "I am."

She changed in the locker room, transferring the admin key, currently burrowed in her bandage, to under her tongue.

Step one of Plan B.

The Host stuck the sensors to her body, helped her into the space suit, smoothed it down, and strapped her into the harness. "Enjoy," she whispered.

Kayla slipped the admin key to her fingers. If Plan B worked, she would destroy this Resilusio. End it all. Then she would yank the helmet off, grab Miles, and…run?

Good luck with that.

But there was nothing else to do.

She closed her eyes. Centered her mind, as she had always taught herself, as she had learned to do all these years, from her first days catching cards to the nights working the felt for her rent, her tuition, when the bills would go unpaid if she didn't win enough.

When her eyes fluttered open, the view was familiar, above the world, floating, an astronaut in space, a fetus in the womb. The menu blinked in the upper-right-hand corner, and the earth rotated languidly below her feet.

"Hello, Kayla," said Ms. Resilusio. "What's our destination?"

Kayla ignored her question. Slipped in the admin key.

Step two of Plan B.

Nothing happened. No MS-DOS-like screen. No blank out.

Kayla tried a command. "Initiate admin protocol."

Ms. Resilusio was silent for a minute. Analyzing, maybe. Zipping through algorithms with abandon. When she spoke, her voice held a bone-chilling emotion.

Glee.

"Access denied."

Kayla's stomach fell to the floor, so rapidly and suddenly that she actually stumbled. She scrambled her fingers over the admin key. Pulled it out. Pushed it back in.

Nothing happened.

"Ms. Resilusio?"

"Yes, Kayla?"

"Admin protocol, please."

Ms. Resilusio chuckled like a demented doll. "Ah, here we are. Miles Ballard has entered the world."

The fake space to her right shimmered, like a hundred thousand falling stars descending to earth. They dissolved into Miles, blinking like he'd just stepped into a brightly lit room from the dark. They exchanged glances, and she mentally willed him to follow along. He nodded.

It was now or never. "Resilusio, admin protocol."

And then, blessedly, the blank screen. The cursor.

And this time, an icon. Denali.exe.

She practically leapt onto it. Step three of Plan B. The third and final step.

The view shimmered. The view stuttered. Screeched. Like an old vinyl record given a hard shove.

And then nothing.

Nothing.

She tried again.

Nothing.

She screamed obscenities in her head.

The file didn't work. Or maybe GR's Norton Antivirus or whatever stopped the download. Kayla closed her eyes. When she opened them, Miles gazed at her with an imperceptible nod. He got it.

They had lost.

The AI lady chose this moment to speak, with the gravity of an undertaker. "I don't recognize that command from your location."

Kayla blinked. Dry heaved. Plan A thwarted. Plan B thwarted. Plan C thwarted.

Plan D…Oh, who was she kidding? None of her ideas had worked.

Yet.

And there he was. Her father. Dead in the real world. But alive in her head. For a moment, she smiled. Kayvan Masouvi, Mr. Six-Sigma Positive Mindset.

You can still win. I know you can.

Sameer.

They were merging now. One voice, living inside her head. A voice of strength and a voice of hope. A new voice that might convince her to believe in herself.

Kayla shook her head and took a deep breath. "Ms. Resilusio?"

There was a very human exhale in her ears. "Yes, Kayla?"

Time to descend to the belly of the beast. All other options had been exhausted. "Take us to Frederick Monahan, wherever he may be."

CHAPTER FIFTY-SEVEN

Ms. Resilusio chirped her response. "Right away."

"Get ready." Kayla took Miles's hand.

They descended, travelers in personal rocket ships through space, rocket ships with a very smooth ride. Down, through the non-atmosphere of Resilusio, into the searing burn of ozone, which now had an actual smell.

Must be an upgrade.

They zipped through the clouds, whizzed across continents. They zoomed across China, then made a left turn, closer to India. Kayla squinted as a soaring snow-capped mountain came into view, stark and pointed to the sky as if intent on piercing the atmosphere.

"Everest," Miles said. "It's taking us to Tibet."

She glanced at him. "Denali."

His eyes said it all.

They descended further, passing dizzying peaks that jutted so close to their bodies that Kayla jumped and recoiled. A vast glacier unfolded below, locked immobile in unsettling motion, a flash-frozen river. Next came desolate moonlike landscapes with steep, tree-covered canyons, plunging deep into the earth.

Closer and closer. A meandering ribbon of water passed under with the speed of a brisk escalator. Finally, they dropped feet, through puffy, cotton-ball clouds into a remote green valley, next to a long, languid pile of rocks that might be a dried-up riverbed. More mountains, gray-robed and white-peaked, serrated a bright blue sky. And no roads, no paths, no civilization except one tent—dirty and perhaps once white, lashed into the valley floor and covering maybe a few hundred square feet, surrounded by meager, shabby camping supplies: piled-up sleeping bags, a rickety portable stove, a tank of kerosene. Nearby, two bored yaks chewed grass, tied to the one tree in sight.

Kayla and Miles exchanged glances. She pointed at the tent. He moved to go with her. She shook her head.

"Alone," she said.

He froze, regarding her meaningfully. "Only because this isn't real."

It took a few minutes to find the tent's entrance, two pieces of thick leather tied tightly with frayed twine. She undid them and stepped in.

Inside was smoky air, burning juniper leaves that emitted a vegetal, earthly musk. Textiles covered every available surface. Colorful tapestries adorned the walls, depicting Buddha and other deities in thick weaves with heavy embroidery. Tasseled fabric hung from the ceiling. On the far right, flickering candles blanketed a small shrine adorned with bronze statues. Kayla recognized Buddha in the middle, surrounded by what appeared to be his own personal supply of incense sticks, chalices, and flowers. Rugs covered the floor, everything in shades of red and gold, with carved wooden benches ringing the perimeter.

Rick Monahan sat on a small cushion, swathed in robes of more red and gold, his eyes closed, his head shaved. His lips moved, and his fingers trembled over a string of prayer beads, carved stone orbs on a string. Disgust rose like bile in her throat. Meditation brought peace and contentment, which were the last blessings in any world that this monster deserved. She dreamed of wrapping those prayer beads around his neck and strangling him with her bare hands. Even though they were in a fake world and any actions here were strictly imaginary. Even though she wasn't real, and neither was he, still she almost tried it.

But. She breathed. Centered and cooled her rage.

A few minutes later, his eyes snapped open, and he caught sight of her. He took a deep breath. Exhaled. "I come here when I need to think. Contemplate life."

She stared at him, said nothing.

He gestured at a well-worn embroidered cushion facing him. "Please, Kayla. Sit." His manner was welcoming, benign. Disarming. An impressive act. He gestured at a steaming mug on a nearby tray. "Tea? It's made with yak butter. An acquired taste, but actually quite delightful. Would you like to try some?"

"No."

He nodded. "The Tibetan nomads of this region regard the yak much as my ancestors must have once regarded the buffalo. A source of transportation, sustenance, warmth…" He gestured around the tent. "Local artisans made these textiles, all from yak wool." He sipped his tea pensively, savoring it.

She blinked at him, unwilling to play into the outrageous charade of a Zen, deeply connected version of the sociopathic murderer this man was. She sat in front of him, closer than she should, to menace his personal space, ever grateful for her God-given ability to get under a person's skin.

He lingered on a prayer bead and then slipped the strand away, into the folds of the voluminous fabric enveloping his body. "You know"—he gazed at her—"we haven't missed a beat since Escondido. The facility meant nothing." For a brief, non-Zen instant, his eyes hardened.

"You're on track, then," she replied. "To launch. Eventually."

A dreamy smile spread across his face. "Something like that." His eyes flitted back to her. "Those tiresome party crashers got nothing of consequence. They'll find that out soon enough, if they haven't already." He chuckled and shook his head. "The G-men are always a few steps behind. Don't you think?"

"I wouldn't know," she replied, her mind full of if/then statements, her next moves, contingency plans.

"Ah, but your boyfriend, the covert operative, might." He tapped his head. "How much does he share with you?"

"I don't have a boyfriend." Kayla turned her palms to the ceiling before dropping them to her lap.

"How charming." His voice hardened as a flash of the real man broke through again. The viper.

"You have something that belongs to me," he finally said. "I need it back."

"I have forty thousand pages of documents from Olivia Chen. They show the connection between your illegal data collection and this monster you've created." Kayla paused. "I've already sent them to a forensic accountant. The government doesn't have them. Yet."

"Is that where you found the private key to steal my tokens?"

"So you admit that all of this is you?"

He cocked his head to the side. "That depends. Were you hoping I'd connect a wallet filled with REAL tokens to a malicious contract?"

So Plan A was dead for good. "Someone's been filling your head with conspiracy theories."

"So we'll both say nothing, Kayla. Sound like a plan?"

"Maybe you could talk about how you murdered Sameer Anithi."

"I should probably tell you why you couldn't access your virus."

"No clue what you're talking about."

"Thank you, though, for initiating the connection. It got us a good idea of their location, so we can plug that leak."

Kayla moved not an inch. *Stillness,* she thought. *Self-control. He's lying. You can't get someone's location from a virus…Right?*

A warm breeze rustled outside. A yak brayed. Harnesses jingled. Then Monahan spoke. "Kayla, I'm dying."

She exhaled. "We're all dying, Rick."

"Well, my life expectancy is two to five years. If I'm lucky. That's why I've been working so feverishly on Resilusio, why I've pushed the team so hard. I cut corners. Many. I hope they aren't fatal to the world. To the vision."

"You're dying." Kayla thought about that for a second as more pieces of the puzzle came into focus.

"Amyotrophic lateral sclerosis. Better known as ALS. Today I can walk and talk. Move normally. But that will change. One day the ability to eat, breathe, smile, touch…all of it, gone. But not my brain. Once, that was the special hell of this disease, that it left cognition intact."

A random memory popped into Kayla's brain. Well…not so random. Marcella Minieri's office at GR. Her haphazard collage of pictures. Microbiologists on a charity run, Evan Schechter among them, all wearing T-shirts that depicted a microscope and the words TIME TO B. CEREUS ABOUT ALS.

There were clues.

He held out a hand and unfurled his fingers, gazing at them. "But now, maybe, that day will be…just the beginning. My birthday in a way. My rebirth. I'll take my brain with me. Out of my body. I'll be born into Resilusio, and maybe that means I'll live forever."

CHAPTER FIFTY-EIGHT

"WHAT?" KAYLA SPUTTERED, unable to help herself. "All this"—she gestured around her—"to integrate your brain into an AI world?"

And yet it made sense. Monahan had developed Resilusio for his mind to live as his body died. For not the first time, Kayla gazed at her shimmering surroundings, at the magic that money could buy. Billions of dollars could conjure anything into existence. Billions of dollars could move mountains. Why not make human-AI integration happen? The field was in its infancy now, mostly science fiction, but in a few years? With that kind of investment? She closed her eyes. Another memory pinged her brain. Vapor. The Genesis Foundation. That day, under the juice factory.

"Operating rooms with no camera feed. Mutilated bodies. Brains missing."

Human-AI integration was exactly his goal.

Whatever he said next would be monstrous. Utterly monstrous. She almost cringed in fear. "Escondido isn't your only research facility."

He paused. Exhaled. "There are others."

"In places where human life means little and humanity counts for even less." She spat out the words, the hate practically flying off her body.

He was contemplative for a moment. "Well, I won't lie to you," he said gravely, like he was speaking to a child. "Those places exist."

"Open source," she muttered. And now the *why*...why Monahan would release the source code and invite development from anyone in the world. Out of necessity. Time. The one luxury he didn't have. He needed the entire world working on the problem.

"A billion dollars to the first person who integrates a brain into Resilusio. And another billion to the person with that brain, you know, in his or her head." He took a purposeful breath and closed his eyes like he was about to zone out and fake meditate again. "I'm willing to bet many of my fellow ALS sufferers will jump on the opportunity. They're doomed anyway, right?"

Kayla wavered, dizzy and nauseated. "How many people will die for your dream?"

He blinked, the only acknowledgment of her words. "I have spent all my time in Resilusio meditating or taking instruction from Buddhist monks, never venturing into the cities, barely interacting with others. But that will change. I'll be an indelible part of Resilusio. All the world's secrets will be in my brain." He smiled beatifically. "Do you know what trepanning is?"

"What? Yes." Trepanning was one of the very first surgeries in recorded human history. Ancient practitioners drilled into a patient's skull, sometimes for legitimate injuries like head wounds or brain bleeds. However, they also drilled for other, more dubious therapies, such as to release evil spirits, alleviate headaches, or cure mental illness.

"Someday, humans will regard artificial intelligence in that same light. A primitive, brutal way to enter the mind. When there is a far more elegant path"—he gazed at his surroundings like one might a favorite child—"called Resilusio."

Despair. Inevitable, horrible despair. Her guts sank to her toes.

"But I need those shares, Kayla," he said, sliding his eyes to her. "Well, only some of them. One percent. With that one percent…I launch."

She shrugged. "You're a very resourceful guy. You'll find a workaround."

He frowned.

She leaned forward. "Say it."

He paused. Set his jaw, then relaxed it, as if remembering his faux-Buddhist principles. "It will burn the one thing I don't have. Time."

"Thank you for that. For saying it out loud. Now, do you have an offer?"

"My offer is this: join me."

"Excuse me?"

He nodded like it was the most obvious thing in the world. "I've been watching you for a very long time."

Kayla stared.

"Our tests identified you as resistant about…oh, ten years ago."

"Since high school?" Her throat dried and caught. She swallowed and went on, the words coming out as a scratchy whisper. "You've been perving on me since high school?"

"No." He frowned. "Nothing like that. I've been there to protect you. Watch over you. You're very important to me. I investigated every one of your boyfriends. Their families." He said it as seriously as a disappointed parent. "And the girlfriend."

Her pulse stuttered. *Self-control. Stillness.* "Sounds extremely boring."

He raised his eyebrows and squared at her. "Not at all. I enjoy a good exploratory phase."

"Fuck you." She wanted to rip his face off. That was not an exaggeration. "That information isn't from the trash."

"You feel that way now. But soon you won't. Soon you will savor being accepted and celebrated for exactly who you are."

She closed her eyes. *Daddy. Sameer. Help me. Give me strength.*

"Kayla, with your brain plugged into Resilusio, it will be perfection. You'll show the AI how to moderate its result. Train it. Bend it to your will. Together we'll create the most important technology the world has ever seen." He exhaled, considering something. "Then you can have anything you want. Date fifteen girls and guys. Whatever floats your boat."

Her eyes snapped open. "I'd rather die," she said.

His face fell into a picture of genuine sadness. "Suit yourself," he finally said. "But we are still at a stalemate."

Plan D.

She turned it over in her head. No doubt about it, Plan D… kind of sucked. Everyone would hate Plan D. Sameer, Vapor, Miles. Her father most of all. Still, it was his face she pictured.

Luck is common, Kayla. Using it the right way? Very rare.

She raised a glass to him in her head. *Here's to using luck properly, Daddy. Thanks for making me smart.*

It was now or never. "I'll make you a deal."

Monahan eyed her for a second. "Last time you made a deal with me, it didn't work out too well for you, Kayla."

Last time. The Borgata. Monahan beat her with quad aces, spiking his 4 percent shot, and Sameer had died. Her father had died. Monahan had destroyed her life. Now she was sitting here, in a phony yurt, in a phony meadow, across from a phony Buddhist monk, discussing trapping herself in this psychopath's phony universe. All that because of a 4 percent shot that had to, of course, hit.

But was Monahan really that lucky? Kayla reviewed the entire night. Walking into the private suite at the Borgata to find him sitting there...his presence a deliberate shock, designed to throw her off. The dealer, Angela, Kayla's favorite, her friend for all these years, who'd fidgeted uncomfortably and worked nervously, wearing a profoundly sad look on her face, all completely out of character. The game itself, which was supposed to have "whales in attendance" but had exactly one, the one sitting in front of her, who had cleaned her out without breaking a sweat.

It was all so obvious in the rearview mirror.

She played with Monahan even though heads-up poker was out of her element, even though Angela's demeanor was unsettling, alarming...a warning.

She made a deal, even though the deal was wrong, wrong, wrong...a betrayal of Sameer's love, a slap to his face.

She did all those things out of hubris. Out of pride. An arrogance that decreed she could outsmart a man with vast resources and a dead-set plan. Somewhere along the way, she had forgotten...ignored...or maybe even stopped believing her own self-proclaimed golden rule:

You are *never* as smart as you think you are.

Her bullshit radar had failed, miserably. She had, naively, expected honesty. Poker was not the most honest game. This was a fact. But her guard was down. Way down. Frederick Monahan would never cheat, right?

But he did.

"How much did you pay her?" Kayla's head swam, and her eyes would not focus.

"Enough," he said quietly. "She's quite a mechanic, it turns out."

The bitterness of betrayal, the ones she committed, the ones done to her, and most sickening and heartless of all, the one she had done to herself. She had betrayed her own integrity, her own character.

She was the architect of this doom.

But maybe, maybe there was a way out.

You can still win, whispered their voices in her head. *We believe in you.*

And then her own. *Here goes Plan D.*

"I was so glad when you joined GR, Kayla. I knew you'd be a spectacular addition."

She ignored him.

"So," she said, "our deal."

A pause. "Go on."

"We'll play poker again, for the one percent. For control of your world."

He sighed. "That part is acceptable, but how will we encode this deal?" He frowned at her. "Please don't try anything tiresome with a malicious contract."

"I need to get to my email."

"Resilusio," he said. "Kayla Masouvi's personal email."

It was at the very top. Unopened. The second smart contract, which did not have the malicious code. Just the following rules of execution:

Winner takes 1 percent.

Kayla clicked on it. "This is a smart contract. No malicious code. Your people can check it. When we both agree, we'll connect our wallets, put it on the blockchain. And begin."

Monahan thought for a moment. His eyes flitted. His brow furrowed. He was smarter than everyone. His assumption since probably forever. He had the game rigged. Brains plus resources… who could compete? Who had more?

Nobody and no one.

He met her eyes. "Three hands," he said. "We'll play them out."

Some luck. Some skill. And some timing. Just like life. She swept her arms around the tent. "You may not play fair. But Resilusio does, right?"

He nodded. Exhaled. "We have a deal."

CHAPTER FIFTY-NINE

THEY HAD A deal.

The smart contract was a simple piece of code. Monahan had one of his underlings review it. They both connected their wallets. Everyone agreed on what it was, what it would do:

Give one wallet sole ownership and control of Resilusio.

So, on to the game.

"Resilusio," Monahan commanded. "The Casino de Monte-Carlo." He turned to Kayla as their surroundings—the tent, the yaks, the mountains, all of it—disappeared into darkness to leave the three of them, floating, again, in space. They hovered above Europe for a second before descending. To the east of Spain, to the west of Italy, to the South of France, along the coast, dipping into a clear blue sky, dangling above an equally clear blue sea. Off the waterfront, they entered a large building with a green sloped roof, accented by pointed spires dotted amid steep cupolas, jutting balconies, and a round breathtaking rotunda with panoramic views of the Mediterranean. They zipped past wide gold doors, nodding bellmen, five-foot-high flower arrangements into a recessed alcove tucked behind a grand skylight with carved marble at every sight line. They alighted at a bronze statue of a man on horseback, dressed in the French Baroque style, his long hair flowing past his shoulders.

"Louis XIV." Monahan materialized next to her and shuffled in his monk robes to the bronze, gazing up at it.

She searched for Miles.

No Miles.

"He's nearby, don't worry," Monahan said.

Louis XIV's horse had his right knee extended, and it gleamed obscenely in the bright lobby lights, the patina completely worn off. "For hundreds of years, gamblers have rubbed this," he said, giving the appendage his own little swipe. He stepped aside, clearing the path for Kayla. "Best of luck to you."

She didn't move. "Chance doesn't know about horse knees."

He cocked his head to the side and gave her a funny look. "As you wish," he said. "To the casino."

Out the door. Across the street. They moved closer to a pale-yellow Belle Époque structure, with a grand staircase and stained glass windows spilling color into the surrounding streets. Manicured gardens and a long marble terrace ringed the building, shading strolling lovers. They passed through a portico. An entrance. Walls. And then into a breathtaking hall. A few dozen poker tables scattered over a rug that bore the coat of arms of the royal family of Monaco, the Grimaldis. Biblical scenes decorated the walls and two-ton chandeliers presided over it all, throwing sparkling light onto alabaster columns that curved and soared to the high ceiling.

They alighted at a table. Miles appeared, touched her arm. When she turned to him, his eyes roved over her.

"Kayla, you don't have to do this," he said. "Please. Please don't do this." The words were for show. Acting. Still, Kayla's heart leapt at the despair and longing in his voice. To a certain extent, it was real. She might soon be dead or worse, though

Miles probably planned to rescue her. Or at least try. All of that, she had to admit, meant something to her. She pushed it aside and focused on Sameer. Her father.

Everything she was about to do was for them.

Miles shook his head and read her mind. "I can't compete with a ghost." His voice wavered. "He's dead, Kayla. You aren't." He was getting into the part. Or maybe, possibly, this was all his real self.

"I have to do this, Miles." And she did. This was the truth. Their only shot. The plan must work. Or not. There was no waiting, no alternatives, no plan Es.

He held his hands up and backed away, refusing to look her in the eyes.

It was an excellent performance.

The table itself was as splendid as a prized antique. Beautiful new felt with shimmering markings, velvet trim, heavy, polished wood. A dealer sat in a gold-flecked pit.

Monahan appeared across from her, the red fabric of his habit spilling over the delicate chairs.

"Do Buddhist monks play poker?" she asked.

He observed himself. "You're right, of course." A moment later the man she expected arrived: a perfectly tailored Armani suit, Etro pocket square, Berluti shoes, gold cuff links in the shape of—what else?—garbage cans. He had hair again too, his real-life head of hair. He was the very picture. A billionaire with charm, brains, and good taste.

She might vomit.

"Your outfit?" he said, glancing at her clothes, which were nothing more than Resilusio stock: jeans, a T-shirt, sneakers.

She laughed. "This is how I play."

"Suit yourself."

"Let's get to it, then." She slid into an ornate velvet chair, almost bouncing on the tufted red cushion. A meticulously restored antique…illusion.

More real than real.

Believe your eyes.

The cards hit the air.

"Best out of three, Rick. Don't forget it."

"I'd ask you to reconsider," he said, glancing at his cards, "but the smart contract's already written. And that's the end."

CHAPTER SIXTY

AND SO IT was. The endgame.

First set of cards and her stomach twisted. The seven of hearts and the eight of hearts (in poker shorthand 7h8h). Not a trash hand, but not premium, either. It had potential. This hand could make a flush (five cards, all one suit), or a straight (5-6-7-8-9, for example). "Three hands against Rick Monahan?" She widened her eyes in mock fear, mostly to cover her disappointment in her holdings. "What was I thinking?" Monahan raised. She threw in a call, matching his bet.

He leaned forward, brushing his metaverse-perfect, real-life repulsive hand over hers. "That you want to live forever."

She sprang back.

They started with ten thousand chips and blind bets were five hundred / one thousand. Whoever had the most chips at the end of three hands…won.

The flop came out. Three cards that offered her nothing. All black, two queens and a ten. She had eight high and red cards. Monahan bet into her. A real bet. A bet that would hurt.

No. Continuing was suicide.

She folded.

The second hand. A suited ace. The ace of diamonds and the three of diamonds (Ad3d). This hand could also make a straight or a flush. The flush would be the "nut flush" (as it would have an ace), but the straight would be a weak straight (ace to five).

She was the first to act. She raised. It was a substantial raise, equivalent to four times the largest blind bet, the big blind. It was a bet that screamed confidence. The confidence that she had the best hand.

He glanced at his cards again, nodded, and matched her bet. "Let's go," he said.

The flop came out, and it wasn't to her liking. No ace. Not even a red card. Not even a three. Still, she was the raiser, pre-flop. That meant that she should usually bet. No reason to give up here. If she checked, moving the action to him, and he bet, she would have to fold. Calling with nothing made little sense. Re-raising would be risky. Neither option was great. Not here. Not tonight.

She bet.

Monahan raised her bet. Her heart sank, as she doubted, for a cold minute. Doubted so hard she almost called a halt to all of it, pulled off her helmet, and ran screaming from the arena. But logic bullet-pointed her brain.

She had a plan. It was a good plan.

She reviewed it all. Dug deep in the memories. The key points, the facts from the past that gave her the only actual shot at success she'd had since all of this started. A shot that was fifty-fifty. Which was a hell of a lot better than any other option. She had no reason to doubt it. But what if she were wrong?

The facts have not changed.

Sameer. She breathed the fear away.

If the facts have not changed, you *do not change.*

But what if the facts were not…facts? What if they were lies?

Another voice chimed in.

You've got this. Yes. Sure. You haven't won.

Yet.

Her father.

Her chest squeezed in despair. The power of positive thinking was of little use here.

Call it like you see it, kid. And let the chips fall where they may.

Who was that?

You know, you're actually pretty good at this thing. This going-toe-to-toe-with-a-homicidal-billionaire-sociopath thing.

Was that the…Mean Voice?

Something had replaced the Mean Voice.

If it doesn't work out, you should still be proud.

You did good.

Someone had replaced the Mean Voice.

Now, GO FOR IT.

Fuck yeah. It was her *own* voice.

She glanced at Monahan, so sure of himself. So sure of his superior information. So sure he had rigged the results, stacked the deck…literally. Greek mythology popped into her head. *Oedipus Rex.* Hubris. Was that his fatal flaw? What about hers? After all, she based this theory on nothing more or less than idle commentary from a disgruntled ex-employee. On one offhand comment from Vapor. A poker player would call this thin value, but it was not hubris. Not arrogance. It was making the best decision possible with imperfect information. For sure, she had a fatal flaw somewhere. She had her Achilles' heel.

But not this.

But not today.

Today, maybe, she had *this*.

I love you, Sameer.

I love you, Daddy.

Thank you for everything you taught me.

She swallowed and steeled her guts. And then she squared on Monahan.

You thought you could cheat death.

Control everything.

Bend people to your will.

She dumped the diamonds and got her final cards. And it was like déjà vu. Two black nines, clubs and spades (9c9s). Nine, nine.

He raised. She re-raised.

He glanced up at her. "Do you believe in fate?"

He was just talking, to get a read on her. Or more accurately, pretending to be trying to get a read. He thought he had this locked up.

She took a deep, casino-air breath. Pumped-in oxygen and perfume and cigarette smoke.

And all in her head.

"Sure," she replied. "For ninety-nine point nine percent of people, if the gods decree that you will kill your father and marry your mother, then that's what you'll do." Ah, Oedipus Rex.

Monahan seemed to think about this for a moment. More pretend.

He pushed all his chips in.

She went on. "But a tiny subset will fight fate. An even tinier subset will succeed."

"I agree."

"You're fighting your fate. Fighting ALS." She paused as compassion, unpleasant and unwelcome, pricked her.

But then she remembered. Her father. Sameer. And another memory.

Vapor. Under the juice factory.

"Explain something about the GR Resilusio."

Vapor. "Sure."

"Is it all rigged?"

Vapor laughed. "In ours? No. In Monahan's? Always."

Our fates await us, indeed.

Kayla: "So if I play a...poker game, for example?"

She called his all-in bet. They both turned over their cards.

Vapor: "The algo chooses the winner."

He laid his cards on the table, his face expressionless. "There are always exceptions. Outliers. I like to think of myself as one. Always have."

Vapor: "With one exception."

Monahan had, again, the aces.

Kayla: "Which is?"

The aces he'd cheated with, destroyed her life with, murdered Sameer with.

Vapor: "The house always wins."

Three cards. The flop. The beautiful red nines again. And an ace. Monahan leaned forward. "You're an outlier, too, Kayla. I think you've always known it."

Kayla's eyes widened. "Monahan."

Vapor nodded. "He was hard-coded in. To always win."

One card. The turn. A blank. The three of diamonds. Kayla cleared her throat. "Absolutely. I agree with you."

"Was?"

The river. A queen.

Vapor nodded. "Right before I left, I messed with the algo."

"You're not the only one who knows how to fight fate, Rick."

"I made his outcomes random."

A coin flip. Monahan's eyes widened. His mouth opened and closed in silent agony, finally gasping out something. Not a word. Just a choke.

Kayla shook her head and exhaled. "Today is just not your day." She pushed her cards forward to the imaginary dealer. "It seems"—her voice wavered; she calmed herself—"that today… *today* I win."

His eyes narrowed. He searched her face, processing, processing, processing, like the man-machine hybrid he might someday be. "I'm—"

"Hard-coded in," she finished. "The house always wins, right?"

A pause. "How, exactly?"

"Well, I gave you something. Something you never gave me." She leaned forward. "A fair shot."

He leaned forward himself, like he was about to bite her. "What did you do?" His eyes went dead.

"Ms. Resilusio," she commanded.

The host appeared.

"I'm the boss now."

Her eyes seemed to roll into the back of her head. She flickered, almost disappearing. She sighed, dramatically, and snapped her eyes open.

"Go ahead."

"Shut down. All systems."

A small red light flashed in the corner of her vision. Ms. Resilusio spoke: "Commencing emergency shutdown. Ten seconds. Please exit all experiences immediately."

Kayla turned back to Monahan. "I do love to snatch victory from the jaws of defeat. It's a feeling I've been chasing my entire life." She shrugged. "It's kind of like fighting fate."

The red light grew brighter and brighter.

Monahan gazed at her with the purest of hatred, flickering in and out, the image firm one second, transparent the next. "Kayla…" His voice whistled, like the wind. "We'll meet again. I prom—"

There was no preamble. No warning. It all just…ended.

Black.

Black-sick black.

She yanked the helmet off. "Miles? Where are y—"

She was in his arms, their eel-skin haptic suits sliding against each other. It was abnormal. It was sterile and clinical and very video-gamer and not romantic, and yet all of that meant nothing. Their spirits connected. Fit together. Sameer would have approved. He was a hopeless romantic, a deep believer in soul mates.

You can find love again, he whispered in her ear. *Go. Be happy.*

"You're here," she muffled into his shoulder.

"I am," he replied, "and it's over."

It was for the best that he didn't hear her response, buried somewhere deep in his chest.

"No. It's not."

Not today, my love, she whispered back to Sameer. *Not today.*

CHAPTER SIXTY-ONE

A FEW DAYS later, a man came to Miles's apartment, a man with the face of any man and no man, a face you could scrutinize for hours and never pick out of a lineup. As Mr. Forgettable walked through the door, the TV was on, flashing the international news on mute: beloved business titan Frederick Douglass Monahan had disappeared without a trace. Murder? Crime? Kidnapping? Plastic surgery gone awry? The speculation ran rampant.

"Quite the result," Mr. Forgettable said, sliding his eyes from the television. "Congratulations."

Was that sarcasm? Kayla shook her head. The Feds shuttered Escondido, granting early, compassionate release to most test subjects in exchange for silence. But there were other facilities, outside of U.S. jurisdiction, in unknown locations. Kayla, Resilusio's new owner, canceled the retail launch and the open source launch. So…maybe the world was safe. For now. Still, stopping Resilusio didn't stop Monahan. He would come back smarter and harder, and he wouldn't be playing any poker games for his virtual life next time.

Vapor had not yet come back to life. Olivia Chen was still a missing person. In contrast, the Genesis Foundation and its Director were hiding in plain sight, in the news for climate change projects, vaccination projects, clean water projects.

Schechter recently gave a speech professing a belief that AI was a "danger to humanity" and calling on tech leaders to create a "unified framework of ethics and control." Kayla wasn't holding her breath.

"What's next for you, Kayla?" Mr. Forgettable sat down on Miles's cream suede couch, sipped Pellegrino, and offered her…a job. With Mason Capital. The actual job offered was amusing in its setup. On paper, Kayla's job title was investment analyst, whatever that meant. In real life, she was now a spy.

Whatever that meant.

"You put in a good word for me?" Kayla asked Miles.

"The best," he replied.

She was up front about her requirements with Mr. Forgettable. "I have something I need to do first," she told them, expecting that to be the end of the conversation. "Monahan. I don't have a time frame. When I'll be available. If I'll ever be available." She was still a poker player. And she still loved odds. And they weren't in her favor now. Finding Rick Monahan—the real guy, not the apparition—had terrible, terrible odds. But as Yoda might never say:

Odds matter not. Trust you must, in the journey.

Yoda or an extremely cringey motivational speaker.

Miles, who was sitting next to her, had reached for her hand and squeezed it, and she hadn't minded and hadn't pulled away.

"We understand," Mr. Forgettable replied, earning her surprise, "and we share the same goal. He's a priority for us, actually."

"I might actually kill him." *We all have violence within us,* she thought. *I'll just have to find mine.*

"That would be acceptable."

And just like that, the odds of achieving her mission quintupled, at least.

He went on. "If you choose to join us, it's for life. There's no going back. You, and your body, will become the property of Mason Capital. We'll train you. Give you skills you never dreamed of. Skills you will need to accomplish your goal. But you don't quit us. Ever. When our colleagues age out of fieldwork, they transfer to analysis, handling, management...desk jobs. Discharges are extraordinary circumstances only. Think missing limbs or brain damage. You're with us until you drop dead, or thereabouts."

"So it's like joining the mafia? Omertà and all that."

"Exactly," he replied. "But with a pension and a 401K." He was a comedian, this one. "Oh, and we're the good guys."

"So I keep hearing," she replied.

"When can you join us?" he asked.

She exchanged glances with Miles. "Tomorrow?" Mason had dug out her father and buried him next to her mother, as she'd requested. A numbered account had paid off the Blah debt. She had no ties left. She was alone in the world. And she strongly suspected that was just how Mason Capital liked it. The darkness got to her every few hours. Would get to her for a long time. Like Miles had once advised, she let it in. Nothing would ever, could ever, be the same.

But it can get better. Miles whispered those words each of these last few nights, squeezing her hand, feeding her his home-cooked meals, wiping away her snotty tears.

So. Better, then.

Kayla and Miles flew to London on a military plane. That was an experience. Like traveling in a luggage compartment. Mason Capital housed them in an apartment on a smart block. Here they would wait for the start of the next training class. Kayla had requested a trip to London. She had matters to attend to.

A few days after a run through a nearby park, she walked into the apartment to the sharp smell of a chemical brew. Noises emanated from the bathroom. Humming. A metal implement hitting ceramic. Kayla searched for a sharp object when Miles poked his head out of the bathroom door.

"I'm in here."

He was mixing hair dye in two separate bowls. He held one up. "Have you ever been a blonde before?"

She shook her head and pointed to the other bowl. "You too?"

He nodded. "We'll be traveling. Mostly private, but just in case we show up on a satellite image somewhere." The compound. A training facility that didn't exist, for people who mostly didn't exist, some even miraculously reincarnated to work for a secretive investment fund at completely fake jobs. These dead and defunct would become the world's most dangerous and highly skilled covert operatives.

She went blond. He went dark brown. They switched. And it didn't look terrible. Kinda good, actually. She admired his work in the bathroom mirror. "Contact lenses? Fake noses?" Different hair was not enough, of course.

He laughed as he cleaned up the mess. "You know the drill." Vapor, Houdini, and Miles, all masters of disguise.

"Will I get a tattoo at the end? Maybe a five-leaf clover? In green?" She thought back to Pennington. About Olivia. Vapor.

"Ask them about Project Trifolia."

He stilled and said nothing.

She touched the spot on his shoulder. "Trifolium repens. The white clover. Typically presents with three leaves. Rarely, four. The odds of finding a four-leaf clover are about one in ten thousand. But a five-leaf clover, in the wild?" She stopped and examined him. He gave her nothing, of course. No information. "About one in a million…give or take."

He sat back.

"What is Project Trifolia, Miles?"

His eyes were wildly blue and translucent when he looked up at her. "We'll talk about it," he said. "Someday."

Fair enough. They gathered passports, destroyed documents, packed for the airport. One foot out the door and Miles stopped her.

"Before we go."

"Yes?"

"Stop for a second. Think. This is your last chance. No going back after we get on that plane."

She rolled her eyes. "You're always telling me this."

He went on. "You can be a poker pro. If that's still your dream, I'll help you make it happen." He took her hand. "You do this and, like the man said, there's no going back. Ever." Concern crisscrossed his face. Care. Tenderness. It was real.

Or maybe her perceptions were merely projections.

"You can make a different choice," he added.

She reflected, with some sadness, at the parallels in her life. Another man, another plane, another chance at her "dream," another fork in the road. Then she thought back to their conversation in his apartment, the night before she went to Escondido. "You really think so?"

He nodded. "I do."

She met his eyes and shook her head slowly. "You know. I know. It's not a choice. This destiny chose me."

He turned his face upward. Blinked. "I hope I don't lead you to doom."

"I like to think of it as a short life with eternal glory."

His laugh held no mirth.

She took both of his hands in hers. "If anything, you increased my odds of returning. Alive."

He thought for a moment. "If you let me, I can protect you."

"Save it for the damsels in distress." She mock punched him. "Hey, will you ever tell me your real name?"

"Sure. Maybe you'll kiss me, and maybe I'll tell you my real name."

But that made her sad. She would kiss no one while Sameer's killer roamed the earth, free and unpunished. "So never, then," she said, maybe meaning it.

He hugged her close. "Maybe someday," he whispered into her newly blond hair. "Your destiny will choose…me."

CHAPTER SIXTY-TWO

THE MEMORIAL WAS simple, elegant, understated, like the man himself. A walled city garden in the middle of a soaring cantilevered confection of glass and steel. A tiny oasis amid the splendid architectural wonder of the Anithi Group headquarters. White roses. A creamy marble bench. A fountain. The man himself was long gone. Body blown to smithereens, whatever left of him cremated, his ashes buried here. Somewhere. She scanned the tranquil space. Maybe under her feet? The bench? No.

The fountain.

She strode over and dipped her hands in the cool water. The security guards said nothing, their eyes a firm weight on her back. She ran her fingers over smooth marble until she found it. An inscription. A block on the side of the fountain, slipped in like a secret. She splashed some water aside.

Sameer Mirchandra Anithi
1996–2025
In Loving Memory

From the unreal, lead us to the real
From darkness, lead us to light
From death to immortality

"He's in there." A voice behind her head.

She froze. For fear, for guilt, for shame. The moment held itself in an Einsteinian curve of time and space, happening and not happening.

"Come." The voice softened. "Let me take a look at you."

She stood and faced the music: Kapil Anithi. Tall, patrician features, perfect posture, a very refined, older version of Sameer. A glimpse into the future man who would never be.

"You're alive." He hugged her and held her close before inspecting her face and body for injuries. "And all in one piece."

"I'm so sorry," she whispered. "I loved him so much."

"You did." He said it to the top of her head. "I knew that. So did he."

She pulled back. "Monahan killed him. It was because of me. And I won't stop until I find him."

Kapil frowned. "Most of the world believes your former boss is dead."

Kayla shook her head. "He's alive." And as long as he was alive, she would have no peace. As long as he was breathing, the world was not right.

Time to flip the script. Permanently.

Time to hunt *him*.

He thought for a second. "I have to remind you of what you already know. Which is that vengeance won't bring him back, Kayla."

"It's not vengeance. It's justice."

As he smiled, his eyes went cloudy. "Well, then. There it is. You were always the right girl for my boy." His voice broke. "But you deserve a life of your own. A chance at happiness."

Her eyes remained dry. There would be a time for true tears.

A Big Cry. Someday. "There's no life for me until it's done." She looked up at him. "Do I have your blessing? Your support?"

Kapil retrieved a perfectly folded snowy-white handkerchief from his pocket. "You're a character in a Greek tragedy, my girl." He handed it to her. "Whatever you need." She opened the handkerchief to find a scribbled number. London dialing code. A phone number.

Well, maybe, probably, a phone number.

She fingered the handkerchief, then slid it into her pocket.

He took her hand. "Your enemy is formidable, with unlimited resources." He glanced around. Kayla took in the view one last time. Marble, steel, precise landscaping, clear blue water, security guards, and probably a thousand hidden cameras. "I may not be exactly the same, but I'm close. And I have...other advantages."

She pulled a gold chain out from around her neck. On it hung her engagement ring. "Next to my heart." She fingered the diamond. "I won't let him down."

He spoke to the wind as he turned and disappeared. "I know."

CHAPTER SIXTY-THREE

THE TRAVEL WAS long and very elaborate in all its secrecy. Blindfolds and earplugs, long trips that might just be driving in circles, muffled voices and odd flashing lights and endless dark and always, always, Miles holding her hand.

They walked her into some kind of health care facility, so identified by the smell of disinfectant, the wheel of beds, and the *click-clack* of instruments. They let her use her eyes only long enough to observe a long needle coming at her. "I'll be here the entire time," Miles whispered. "Don't worry."

"Hey." She grinned at him. "Aren't you that guy from finance?"

"I was." He laughed. In the light, his eyes had a peculiar, washed-out clarity. "But now I work for the IRS."

"Right." She laughed, too. A welcome sensation, if strange. Air in her lungs. A smile given. A smile returned. "I'll make sure to pay my taxes."

She woke up to a bandage and a searing-hot pain at her clavicle and Miles reading a three-month-old *Wall Street Journal* next to her. Her hands flew up to her neck, mountainous with bandages and gauze.

"A microchip," Miles said, pulling his own shirt down to show her a tiny, faint scar, at precisely the same spot. "I have one too. Just like a dog, but better. You don't have to take yourself to a fire station or an animal shelter to get rescued."

Kayla probed the injury with her fingers. "Well, that's a relief."

"GPS and identifying information. They will always find you." He smiled and pointed above him, where a spy eye flickered in silent, buggy contemplation. "How's it feel to be the property of the United States government?"

For now? Freeing. Extraordinary. Full of possibilities. She never wanted a normal life. Maybe losing her old identity was just what she needed. Maybe by losing herself, she would find herself. Someday.

"Rest," he said, planting a kiss on her forehead, "Tomorrow your training begins."

Painkillers. Stimulants. More travel. Army guards deposited her at a place furnished like a college dorm room and locked her in. Miles came for her. They walked down a long hall. Not busy but not empty. A few people passed them. They stopped at a door with a retinal scanner. Miles inserted his face. The door slid open, whisper-silent. They walked into a bare room with a hospital bed and nothing more. The bed had straps.

A shiver jolted her spine.

"Kayla," Miles said, turning to her. "This is it. The most physically and mentally grueling months of your life. The trainers will test you in every way. Pound your weaknesses out of you. When Mason is done with you, Kayla Masouvi, you'll be ready for anything. And you'll be ready to be anyone."

Behind her, the door opened. A woman came in, smiling kindly, holding a silver box.

Miles turned to her. "This is your Matrix moment, Kayla.

Black needle. White needle. All of us who do this work…have this moment."

The woman opened the box. Inside, indeed, were two needles. One black and one white.

He gestured at the exit. "The black needle. You go, free and clear. Mason will keep tabs on you, but that's it. You'll fall asleep. Wake up and never hear from us again."

"My life back?"

"You'll start over. As a version of yourself."

She stared at the black needle. Oh, how irresistible that was. Her life back. Sure, she'd never start a car again without holding her breath, but maybe she'd have a semblance of normal, with the luxury of pretending all of this was a bad dream.

"Then we have the white needle. You'll wake up at the training compound, and everything will begin."

Her mind raced back. To the interview with Monahan. How her heart yearned for poker. Now poker lived in an alternate universe. In someone else's dreams. She was at peace with that. It was as it should be, as it was meant to be. Maybe those longings functioned as nothing more than a placeholder for her restless soul, for a yearning to live life on her terms. A rejection of a certain narrow path, rather than a true longing for playing cards around the clock.

Just as Vapor had said on their ride to the bank.

Smart girl, that Vapor.

Fate gave her a gift. A mission, a purpose, a real calling. This decision lived in a very different part of her brain—the automatic functions the body performed no matter what. Do you decide if your stomach digests food? If your kidneys function? Whether your brain allows your body to recognize the sensation of pain?

Those are not choices. And this was not either. It just *was*. Exactly was. Her fate. Just like it was her fate to pull air into her lungs every few seconds, or die.

She nodded at the nice lady with the needles. "The white one, please."

The woman prepared the needle. Kayla climbed onto the bed. Miles held his hand out. She placed hers inside.

"See you on the other side," he said, and squeezed.

The needle plunged into her arm. Her last image, before her eyes closed, was Sameer's face, in the moments before the explosion. When he said *I love you*. She never got the chance to say it back.

Now she would show him.

GLOSSARY

1. **Artificial Intelligence (AI)**

   The simulation of human intelligence processes by machines, especially computer systems. AI may involve, to varying degrees: learning, problem-solving, adapting, rationalizing, goal-setting, decision-making.

2. **Augmented Reality (AR)**

   An interactive experience where an application overlays visual, auditory, or other sensory information onto real-world sensory perception. The user experiences both reality and computer-generated content. Augmented reality applications always overlay the physical world, in contrast to virtual reality (VR) applications, which only sometimes do.

3. **Bloomberg Terminal**

   A computer software system provided by the financial data vendor Bloomberg LP. Bloomberg products can be configured as software applications or dedicated terminals. Both are colloquially referred to in the financial services industry as a "Bloomberg terminal." Regardless of the format, each method allows a user to access

Bloomberg Professional Services, a proprietary system that offers real-time monitoring and analysis of financial market data, including many highly specific markets in areas such as options or foreign exchange that are difficult or impossible to access publicly. Some versions of Bloomberg allow users to place trades via the company's electronic trading platform.

4. **Cryptocurrency**

A digital currency in which transactions are verified and records maintained using cryptography in a decentralized system called a blockchain. A hallmark of cryptocurrency, as opposed to "sovereign" currency, is the lack of control by a centralized (typically governmental) authority.

5. **Decentralized Autonomous Organization (DAO)**

An organization constructed by governance rules encoded and executed solely by a computer program. DAOs rely heavily on smart contracts (see definition) to accomplish governance. Members vote on proposals and results are tied to automatically executable outcomes. Voting power typically correlates to the total number of tokens held.

The DAO's founders must post the voting process, rules, and any relevant terms on the corresponding blockchain. The blockchain memorializes all votes and the associated wallets indefinitely.

6. **Digital Currency**

Any currency, money, or money-like asset managed, stored, or exchanged on digital computer systems, especially over the internet. Types of digital currencies include cryptocurrency, virtual currency, and central bank digital currency.

7. **Matrix (The)**

   A simulated reality created by intelligent machines to occupy human existence in order to use human bodies as an energy source. As described in the 1999 film of the same name, the Matrix represents nothing more or less than a mirror-image carbon copy of life on earth in the present day. No one has ever proven—or disproven—its existence.

8. **Metaverse**

   An immersive and multidimensional virtual world accessed through virtual reality (VR) and augmented reality (AR) programs and gear (visors, body armor, etc.). The metaverse mimics aspects of the physical world but can differ in myriad ways, including modifications to the laws of physics and space-time. As of 2023, people can "live" in the metaverse—working, shopping, interacting, gambling, learning, dancing—all from a single location in the physical world.

9. **Omnidirectional Treadmill**

   A mechanical construction that allows for multidirectional movement in a three-dimensional space. While a traditional treadmill allows users to move in one direction, the omnidirectional treadmill allows unlimited movement and mimics human motion in the free world.

Virtual reality (VR) and augmented reality (AR) programs make use of omnidirectional treadmills to create virtual movement in a digital world such as a metaverse.

10. **Open-Source Software**

    Software distributed with its source code "open" and available. Generally, anyone can access, modify, distribute, use, or enhance the source code of open-source software, for any purpose, at any time.

11. **Rig (Virtual Reality or VR Rig)**

    A mechanical device that creates a total immersion in virtual reality. Typically used to refer to full-body or near full-body designs.

12. **Smart Contract**

    Programs stored on a blockchain that run when the specific conditions encoded in the contract are met. For example, smart contracts automate the execution of an agreement so that all participants can be immediately certain of the outcome, without any intermediary's involvement and with minimal waiting time. Smart contracts can also regulate workflow, triggering actions or new conditions, such as a payment.

13. **Token**

    Technically, all cryptocurrency assets can also be described as tokens. But more casually, a "token" refers to a cryptocurrency asset that runs on top of another blockchain.

A token can be held, traded, or sold like any other cryptocurrency.

14. **Trepanning / Trepanation**

The oldest surgical procedure known to humanity, trepanning involved drilling a hole in a patient's skull in order to treat a variety of ailments, from brain bleeds, epilepsy and tumors to more dubious applications for psychiatric or religious reasons. Evidence of trepanned skulls date from the Paleolithic Era onward.

15. **Virtual Private Network (VPN)**

A protected network connection that masks the location and address of the device used. VPNs encrypt internet traffic and disguise online identity. This software prevents the tracking and collection of a user's activities and data.

16. **Virtual Reality (VR)**

A computer-generated environment that may or may not mimic "reality" but must immerse the user in its "world." The user experiences the VR world through a device—such as goggles, a headset, rig, or omnidirectional treadmill, in order to achieve the fullest experience possible.

17. **Wallet (Cryptocurrency)**

An application that functions to hold an asset such as cryptocurrency. A "crypto wallet" stores the passkeys used to demonstrate ownership of cryptocurrency transactions and provides the interface to access the currency.

Want more page-turning thrillers?

For updates about my new releases and exclusive promotions, sign up for my mailing list here: *www.tessapacelli.com*

ABOUT THE AUTHOR

Like one of my protagonists, I have an MBA from Harvard Business School and a background in finance. I will forever love finance – a complex, elegant discipline full of conflict, suspense, massive highs and lows. But something was missing from my life. Namely, I wanted to write, just like my childhood idols: Shirley Conran, V.C. Andrews, Judith Krantz, Jackie Collins, Belva Plain, Barbara Taylor Bradford. Their books got me through many hard times a kid. As a teen. Here were heroines who devoured life, never compromised, went through hell, refused to give up. As I got older, I started reading the great thriller writers. Ludlum, Clancy, Grisham, Koontz, Patterson.

It seems it all melded together, because today I write woman-centric thrillers. My protagonists have their feet on the ground and their eyes on the prize. They know just enough to be dangerous and run just fast enough to stay alive. For now.

www.tessapacelli.com
Join my mailing list for free stories, exclusive content and more. Link on website.
Follow me on Instagram @tessa.pacelli

www.ingramcontent.com/pod-product-compliance
Lightning Source LLC
Chambersburg PA
CBHW060554310726
48982CB00008B/1116/J

* 9 7 9 8 9 9 9 0 9 3 9 2 9 *